DAWN OF FATE & VALOR

AWAKENED FATES
BOOK TWO

LUCINDA DARK

REBECCA GREY

CONTENTS

ROZENTINE
ITURATH OCEAN
DRIAGE CASTLE
HOUSE OF BLOOD
SEVIRE MOUNTAIN RANGE
HOUSE OF CALADRIUS
SEVIRE CLIFFS
SUNFIRE PALACE
SANCTUS CITY
CARION CITY
HOUSE OF SUNFIRE
HOUSE OF STARFALL
HOUSE OF DAEMONIUM
VITAS ISLES
BARTOLI

PROLOGUE
SOLOMON

Somewhere in the near future…

EVERY CELL IN MY BODY BURNS. LIQUID FIRE PULSES through my veins, spreading farther and faster with every beat of my insidious heart. My vision pulses black, then red, then black again. Yet, no matter how far gone I am, I can only focus on one thing. *Her.*

Instinct alone has my body moving. I reach out, only feeling some small sense of relief when my fingers brush along Devonry's jaw then up toward her ear. Finer than silk, her hair caresses the back of my hand. Even over my hardened flesh, goosebumps appear. Touching her is as familiar to me as the act of breathing, though I can't recall any other time I've been allowed to explore her in such a way.

Touching her is a sin. It has always been forbidden. Even now, as I do so, I feel a twinge of shame. I know this is not allowed, but I can't stop myself. Not when my blood-thirst rides me so hard. I don't *want* to stop. Perhaps, then, I am only meant to be a sinner. For in this moment, I can think of nothing greater than taking her. I would give my life for this one singular moment where I am allowed to touch all of her tender flesh, to feel her against my naked skin, to breathe her in.

She's everything I'm not allowed to have. My Princess. My Queen. My Devonry. If we can never be then why do the gods plague me with this constant need for her? Why do my Awakened senses scream her name? Why do I want to claim her and ruin her for anyone else? Shame settles into my bones, an ancient ache that I can never quite rid myself of. In the end, I'm a weak man. Unable to keep myself from the intensity of my desires no matter the knowledge of her betrothal or commitment to her country.

With fangs protruding, my muscles aching from the stretch of my Awakened form, and my skin hardening, my mind races from one thought to the other. My imagination, always so vivid, comes up with a thousand different ways her blood might taste. All of them send a current of want straight to my cock.

Her petite frame feels impossibly small between my arms. Fragile even. The soft, feathery slide of her hair over her shoulder makes me so achingly aware of the scent that stems from her throat. Still, I try to touch her as if she's breakable. The rough pads of my scarred hands move over her unbroken pale skin, gingerly caressing it. Devonry shrinks away from the touch. Flecks of gold reflect in her gaze, glimmering like small gems in the ocean of her irises. Her eyes are wide as she watches me. In turn, I force myself to curl my fingers into my palms, the long sharp nails protruding from my fingertips digging into me.

With my back against the stone wall, all I see is her. The thick scent of soil further within the cave disappears until the pinpoint of my vision is centered only on the one in front of me. Hunger. Denial. Rage. Pain. I feel it all and it wraps its claws around me, stabbing deep and reminding me of the promise I made to her father. Even so, I cannot refute that this is what I've always wanted. Her. Just her.

A growl rumbles from the primal thing inside of me, the part of myself I try to keep caged but am so greatly failing at hiding now. The noise tumbles over my lips, every part of me that is human only a breath away from being gone. My chest heaves with the intensity of each inhale and exhale. Dangerous. I'm everything I've sworn to protect her from.

I want her. Gods above, I need her. Crave her. I fear that I'll take her whether or not she truly wants this.

I'm terrified that I will lose control. A tremble dances down my spine.

My cock hardens even more as her body brushes against mine. We're so close. I can smell the soft floral scent that always clings to her skin, and even in this low light, I can see a flush working over her cheeks. Her breaths are all but steady, bringing her chest almost against mine.

Only then do I realize I have her pressed against the stone, one hand wrapped around her waist to hold her to me. Never have I been so torn. Part of me wants to rejoice, another to fling myself away, but the part that controls me … that very vicious part … wants to sink my fangs into her —to taste her.

I reach for her face again, trailing my nail ever so gently against her flesh. I tip her chin up to me. "So soft," I say, though my voice doesn't sound much like I remember. "You're always soft, and you smell like the realm of the Gods. You smell like divinity itself."

No truer words have been spoken.

Despite the war inside myself, I'm desperate for her, I

move nearer still. I lean in until my nose brushes along the column of her throat. She sucks in a breath, impossibly still. The rush of her blood is brilliantly enticing in my ears. My fangs lengthen. There, just there, in the curve of her neck, I could sink my teeth into her skin and send us both into euphoria.

So close. We're so very close.

Instead, I breathe her in and groan. I am wildly aware that only the thinnest of cloth separates us. My chest is bare, making every small brush of our skin that much more noticeable. I hover over her trying and failing not to crush every part of me against every bit of her.

Devonry closes her eyes, long lashes curling against her cheeks. A shadow covers the slender curve of her nose and the perfect fullness of her parted lips. Dim light reveals the blush that kisses her skin. *Perfect, she's perfect.*

The rhythmic beat of her heart resounds in my ears, far faster than it should be. Her chest rises and falls against me.

"Are you frightened?" I ask, attempting to find any small piece of self-control.

Her lips are parted as if begging for mine to meet them, but her gaze is dampened with hesitance. She would be smart to fear me. It would be difficult—painful, even— but if she tells me to stop, then I will rip off my own arms to keep from touching her against her will.

"No." She shakes her head.

My attention travels over her, looking for some sign that I am not alone in this torment of desire, that she isn't lying to me right now. My nostrils flare when I scent her. The sweet tinge of arousal emanates from her body. Sweat slicks along her skin. The beast inside of me thrashes, and I grind my teeth together until my jaw cracks. Neverthe- less, my lips find her skin. My tongue swirls over the tendon in her neck before I press another kiss there, hips moving on their own accord.

The girl—woman—in front of me is nothing as I've tried to convince myself she was. Though a piece of me knows she was never exactly how I remember her. She *was* caged. Unaware of the world and content to simply be a rose rooted in a greenhouse. Now, she's everything. All that I need. All that the Rozentine Kingdom needs. My fucking Queen.

There is no denying that her body reacts to me much the same. Not when her heart races under my touch. I can hear the frantic way it beats in her chest as if it's beating in my own.

Devonry gasps. She's still for only a breath before her body arches toward mine. My teeth scrape at her, but never enough to break skin.

This. This is why I should hate her. This is why there should always be walls between us. Because now I've let her in, I've let myself yearn for her in ways I never should have and when she breaks my heart it will be my own Gods damned fault. So I kiss her as if this is the last time I'll ever be allowed to touch her.

"Solo." Her voice echoes off the stone walls and it's enough to get my attention.

I straighten. She shifts in the darkness. Her hands reach between us. She's going to push me away, she *should* push me away. Those long, slender fingers of hers pull gently at her stays. Fabric begins to give, showing daring amounts of pale flesh. I hold onto her hips, afraid that my next move might just hurt her.

She's … *oh gods. Devonry. Fuck.*

My body burns even hotter. My cock throbs between us, begging to be buried deep inside of her.

"Highness…" I try to speak, but the words are nothing

more than a hoarse moan. I should tell her to leave. I should be strong enough to pull myself away and create that much-needed space. But control is something I no longer have.

She shakes her head, sending a few loose strands of hair over her eyes. Gold lines her iris now, sparking brilliantly as if she is also struggling to keep her abilities contained. "No, don't call me that," she whispers.

My mouth opens as I struggle to find the words. In the end, all I can say is her name. And it tastes so bloody sweet on my tongue. "Devonry?"

Even when I was too young to know what desire was, I wanted Devonry. My soul luxuriated in her nearness, knowing not why, but that it craved her. Then as I grew older, that emotion—the need—grew stronger, angrier, harder to control. King Vernon had recognized the greed in me and he'd been smart to take me aside and confirm his worst fears. That his daughter—the future of the Kingdom—was my mate, and I … was not good enough. So I hardened myself, forced myself to hate the one person I could never do anything but love, truly.

She tips her head to the side, exposing the long expanse of her throat. "Take what you need."

I shudder. My claws retract and release while my hands grip her harder still, until I'm certain I'll shatter her. How far the two of us have fallen from what we once were…

"Solomon?" My name leaving her lips does something to me. Breaks me down until there are no barriers left to keep me sane.

"I should not want you as I do, Devonry," I whisper. The smell of her desire fills my nose once more.

"I—it's not your fault," she starts again, her hand finding the curve of my face. Her touch is tender, unlike anything this warrior's body has ever felt. Then her fingers begin to explore, walking up to my hairline and sinking into the strands.

Bloodlust turns into something else … not quite Blood Madness. I have no impulse to maim or kill. Only … only to feast, fuck, and fill myself on all things Devonry. This sense of bloodlust is more than I've ever felt, more than I thought my body might be capable of. What I would give to bury my face between her legs and taste all of the wetness gathering there. I might consider selling my soul if only to run my tongue against her until her body trembles and she's screaming my name up to the gods.

But the beast inside of me might be too great, my control too little. *What if I am too rough? What if I hurt her? Truly hurt her?*

I grimace at the idea and the throbbing agony building behind my fangs. Sweat gathers on my forehead and drips down my back at the effort it takes not to rip every ounce of her clothing to shreds.

The hand that plays in my hair, moves to the back of my head. Devonry arches against me until the front of her dress drifts farther down. More skin. More of her. What is she doing? *Why?*

"I could hurt you," I snarl.

Not even that scares her as she lifts her chin, defiant as ever.

"I don't care," she replies. "You need this, and…" she pauses, "I need *you.*"

Somehow her dress falls further still, until her full breasts are bare against me. Her small body trembles below me like some sort of frightened animal. But then she closes the last bit of space between us, pressing her lips against mine.

I can't move. I can't fucking breath.

"Please," she says against my mouth, her body warming.

I growl, the last of my restraint snatched away from me with one word. Devonry strips me of what little grip I have on my humanity. Forcing my tongue between her lips, I steal away the gasp that leaves her. I suck in her breath as if it's the only thing keeping me alive as my body burns on the edge of Blood Madness.

I grip her hips, needing her closer. Then I pull her weight onto me, suffocating any space between us. Her body rolls against mine, creating sparks in my vision. A small sound passes between us, and that too, I suck away.

With Devonry's hands in my hair, I've never before had someone's touch feel so sinfully wonderful. My tongue dances with hers, a wild back and forth. There's a demand in each of my touches met with an answer of her own. We spent years fighting each other; perhaps that was only practice for this.

There is a small nagging fear at the back of my mind as my arms encircle her that her small frame is no match to my hulking Awakened form. She whimpers against my lips when I tip her head allowing me greater access. My fingers itch to release the last of the ties holding her gown in place.

Gasping for breath, I pull away, hating every second I'm not kissing her. There is nothing greater than my need for her. Nothing to stop me. Not my honor, nor a sword, nor my sanity. My claws lengthen further as if to confirm that I am no longer in control. Fabric tears under my touch.

"Devonry." I try to take in some fresh air only breathing in her pungent arousal. "I'm sorry."

The points of my canines protrude further until they've reached their full length. I pull away, aware of the confusion tightening her perfect features. Her hair is mussed, lips swollen, and those wide gray eyes are rimmed with gold.

Confusion, yes. Fear … No. Gods, I wish she was scared. She *should* be scared.

I lower my face as she tilts her head, exposing her neck, and giving me access to the thick vein pulsing in my vision.

Devonry.

To her credit, she only flinches slightly when my fangs break her skin. The slightest gasp escapes her just as her blood hits my tongue. My entire body hardens. Her flesh is nearly bare against me, her dress gathering at her hips now.

I am lost.

And I never want to be found.

1

DEVONRY

The Bartoli Empire is a vast land scorched by the sun. With hills of sand that echo across long stretches, it doesn't take a genius to figure out the relation to their golden crest. Everything in Bartoli resembles the gold sands from which it rises.

Our ship rocks back and forth above the choppy waves, sending sprays of salty water into the air and over my face. I stare out at the horizon as the land we've been seeking for the last few weeks draws closer. Ahead, in the crow's nest, a man calls down alerting the rest of the crew that we're nearing the land.

It won't be long now.

Heavy footsteps echo across the wooden floorboards, creaking under the approacher's weight. Argyle turns and props his back against the railing as he turns his cheek and grins at me. I don't smile back. There's very little amusement to be found in my situation. Relief, perhaps. Exhaustion, most definitely. But amusement? Not so much.

"Well, now, Princess," he starts, "what do you think of your beloved's country at first glance?"

"He's not my beloved," I say. Maybe I'd hoped as much once, but now, I'll simply be grateful if the Crown Prince of Bartoli is diplomatic enough to understand the severity of his brother's crimes and if his understanding will be enough to lend me the aid of the Bartoli Empire. "It was an arranged marriage. I've never even met him."

I can only pray that my betrothed, Prince Enver, is nothing like his brother, Nasir. Even thinking about Nasir turns my stomach sour. It's all too easy to recall images of my father's blood on his sword, on the floor, on my hands... I swallow the bile that threatens to burn up my throat.

Argyle hums low in his throat, turning to stretch his lanky frame and place his forearms across the railing. He, too, stares over the vast ocean left to cross until we reach the docks. He's quiet for a time, allowing the two of us to relax into companionable silence. My insides tremble as I focus on the shoreline. Stone pillars jut up from the land built into the rocky mountains.

"How long will it take us to reach the Royal Palace, do you think?" I ask.

The depth of his dark skin glistens under the sun. Blue from the waters reflects in the oddity of his mismatched eyes, one cerulean, the other brown. Argyle hardly spares a glance at me as he answers. "Considering that the royal family of Bartoli are keen on ocean water, I'd say not long," he replies. "Half a day at most."

"They live that close to one of their port cities?" I'm shocked. While it can have the added safety of a quick getaway should they befall an invasion or even the benefit of obtaining fresh goods quickly, it is also a dangerous choice to have the royals so close to a city that would likely be the first under attack amid a war. It isn't something I would've considered before, at least not as seriously as I do now, but the fact is that I no longer have the luxury of pacifism. I cast it away the second I killed that slave trader back in Carion City.

"They're quite an arrogant bunch," Argyle says. "One thing you should be aware of, Princess—the Bartoli people are not nearly as reserved as those of Rozentine. They also think themselves invincible."

What does that mean? Before I can voice the question, a sharp call sounds behind us. "What are you doing here?"

Together, Argyle and I turn to greet Celine as she stomps forward, her skirts raised as she attempts to keep them from dragging over the dirty deck. Wind catches her long dark hair, tossing it about. Her cunning attention narrows, darkening her brown eyes. I glance down absently at my own attire. I never knew until recently how much easier it was to move in trousers. Perhaps I should offer her some. From the way her lips curve into a deeper frown as she takes in the pants I'm wearing, however, I doubt the offer would be accepted. Her eyes lift back to mine and her frown lightens in relief.

I don't know why, but she's been an easy companion to have around and far more forgiving than I'd expected of someone who suffered under my father's reign and at the hands of the slave trade he'd overseen. While I can't find it in me to be thankful for the reason for our meeting, I've never been so grateful for a new friend. A woman so loyal. A castaway noble, given to the House of Ravens whose clairvoyance guides us forward.

"Why, if it isn't our Highness' guard dog," Argyle quips.

That's all it takes. With a sigh, I watch as Celine's face flushes an angry red and the smile that had threatened to break through evaporates. She quickly alters her direction ever so slightly and marches right up to him, drawing out a finger to smash right against his chest.

"Don't think I don't know what you're about, Argyle," she snaps.

He grins. "Pray tell, lady, what am I about?"

Her eyes sharpen. "You're a horrible tormenter," she says, "and a bad influence on the Princess. If anyone is her guard dog, I dare say Lord Solomon would be it."

"Oh?" Argyle spreads his arms out and looks around. "Then where is he?"

Wouldn't we all like to know? As soon as the thought arises from me, however, the subject in question makes his appearance. Rising from the depths of the lower decks, the top of Solomon's dark hair appears to catch fire in the sunlight as he steps onto the upper deck. More sunlight shines from the buckles strapped over the flowing cut of his black shirt and hips, the hilts of several weapons bouncing gently against his body as he moves.

Red eyes the same color as rubies catch mine. That trembling from earlier turns into full-blown pulses. Tiny pinpricks—like invisible needles—stab into my flesh all over, arching across my limbs. Painful awareness that gives way to a pleasurable heat.

"See there." Celine crosses her arms over her chest and nods with a smirk. "My point has arrived."

"What point is that?" Solomon asks as he draws near.

I press my lips together as Argyle—with all of the glee of a child in a sweet shop—answers him. "Celine here was just pointing out that you're our cherished Princess' loyal guard dog, my friend."

Those ruby eyes of his clash with mine. Still, I don't say a word. Instead, I let the tension between us grow, feeling my stomach cramp and my core tighten as it does. Our conversations over the last few weeks have been brief but necessary. A fresh anger stirs in us both. The needs of so many others are a weight that can't be relieved. My kingdom needs me, and I … I need him, though I'm loath to admit it most days. Several beats of uncomfortable silence pass.

Thankfully, Argyle is the one to break it. "Looks like we'll be pulling into port shortly." He turns his gaze back out to the ocean and approaching land.

Solomon moves up to the lip of the edge next to him. "We'll need to secure transport to the Royal Palace," he says.

"Will they let us inside?" Celine asks. I glance in her direction to note the nervousness in her expression as she pushes a thumb up to her lips and parts them to bite down on her nail. "I mean, will they recognize the Princess as she is?"

Her attention returns to me and I look down, silently mirroring her worry. It's true—I no longer have the appearance of a Princess. My luxurious gowns have been replaced with commoner's clothes and even my once long blonde hair is shorter and the color duller. Argyle and Solomon both look back just as I raise my head once more.

"It was necessary while in Rozentine," Solo states. "But she's right—you'll have to at least wash the dye from your hair."

I nod. "That's easy enough. It's already fading at my roots anyway." I tilt my head down as if it's not already obvious enough that the blonde is seeping through at my scalp.

Celine sighs. "Thank the Gods," she says. "I've been hoping this wasn't a permanent change, your Highness."

"You've never seen me with my natural hair color, though," I reply. "Why would you worry about that?"

Her lips purse. "You're the heir of Rozentine," she

says. "Everyone knows that you resemble the Goddess Aerea."

"Her hair is redder than mine," I point out, fingering the shortened strands that linger around my face. Weeks ago, it'd been a solid pale white. Now, though, perhaps due to the dye mixture I'd attempted to wash out since, it's more of a murky strawberry.

Celine shrugs. "You're young," she replies. "Hair changes as you get older."

Yes, I think, but only to grow gray or white. Instead of saying as much, however, I simply turn back to the horizon. This is the land of Prince Enver—my fiancé. This is also the land of the traitor, Nasir. I don't know how to feel about it. In some ways, it's just as beautiful as Rozentine; in others, as I gaze upon the golden sands and the cliffs of the port ... all I see is a foreign empire.

Argyle and Celine disperse after a while, going below deck to pack up our minuscule supplies as they prepare to depart the ship that has been our transport and home for the last couple of weeks. They leave Solomon and me alone and I almost wish I could order them to come back. A part of me knows that I could, and they would follow the command, but I don't want to push the benefits of my waning power on them.

Right now, I'm not a princess with a throne. I have nothing to offer them. I am simply grateful for their continued allegiance and hope that when this all finally comes to an end, I will be able to reward them for that.

Hours have passed since I first saw the strip of land that is Bartoli and the morning has turned to afternoon. All the while, Solomon has remained at my side, silent but present. It's only now that the ship pulls into port, and sailors shout to each other, hurrying across the deck as they prepare to anchor. Captain Felix, a big brooding-looking man, stands at the helm, steering his massive vessel through the waters with expertise.

Solomon and I watch on in silence. I can feel a tingle of awareness where the heat of him brushes my side. When the ship has finally anchored to port, and it's time to disembark, the two of us meet our friends at the exit and take the panel of wood—expertly roped off for safety—down onto the docks. I stumble at the end, swaying slightly as I realize how accustomed I'd gotten to the constant movement of the ocean waves. There is no more automatic shift and sway beneath my feet, but instead, complete stillness. The feeling is now foreign. Solomon reaches out and captures my arm, hoisting me up as he ushers me out of the way of others as they, too, exit the ship.

"Sea legs finally caught up with you, aye?" Argyle asks with a smirk. "It'll take a moment to get used to land once more.'"

"I'm fine," I say, pulling away from Solomon as I speak. His hands on my skin make the tingles even worse. It's as if something within me is drawn to him, constantly seeking out his touch. I shake my head and hope to clear away the strange desire.

"Let's go," Solo says, frustration seeping into his voice. "I'd like to reach the Bartoli Palace before nightfall."

Argyle shoots him an incredulous look. "It's a half day's ride," he reminds him, "and half a day has already passed."

Solo arches his brow at his friend. "Then we don't have any time to lose then, do we?"

Argyle scowls. "We should seek an inn for the night and start off in the morning," he argues.

"No," Celine pipes up. "He's right. We need to get the Princess somewhere safe."

Argyle turns his irritated expression on her. "I understand you think you've become something of a general, lady," he says snidely, "but the men folk are talking now. Keep that pretty little mouth of yours closed."

My lips twitch as Celine's face scrunches up. I know Argyle doesn't mean as much. He's respectful of me and any woman I've seen him come into contact with over the last few weeks—well, respectful in his own way, I suppose. But he's never said something so … rude. My guess is he's likely doing it to draw a rise out of Celine simply because he, himself, is irritated and she's an easy target.

"You are the most frustrating, inconsiderate, p—"

Argyle's scowl morphs into a smile, a sign that I was right after all. "Careful there," he warns, cutting her off. "Ladies don't curse."

"I am not—ooh, you are the worst!" she half screams.

Turning my cheek, I hide my laughter with a cough.

"Enough. We have a spectator." Solomon's voice is quiet but serious.

Suddenly, all three of us are on alert. I lift my gaze and follow him to a man standing at the end of the docks. He doesn't even seem to be hiding his observance. He's dressed to stand out in a solid white and gold suit embroidered and marked with the crest of the Bartoli Royal Family. Shifting closer to Solomon, I stare down the docks as people filter past us and then this other man—their eyes seeking him out with nervous curiosity even after they've strode past.

When the man realizes he has our attention, he gives us a smile and waves.

"Should we get back on the boat?" Celine asks.

"No," I say.

Solomon's attention moves to me and I step in front of him. "We'll have to greet him. He's already seen us.

Getting back on the boat won't do anything. I came here for a reason and I intend to see it through." I don't necessarily have a choice. There is only one path and that is forward.

"I will go first," Solomon states, "to see what his purpose is."

"We're coming with you though," I say. His gaze flashes to me and before he can deny me, I continue. "Don't worry. We'll remain a few steps behind, but I need to be privy to the conversation."

His lips press together and his brows draw down low over his glittering red eyes. When his attention returns to the stranger, it's with suspicion. "Let's get this over with," he snaps, striding forward.

Celine, Argyle, and I follow a few paces back. Once we reach the end of the docks, Celine and Argyle stop and I continue forward until I'm between them and Solomon, allowing space as I promised, but close enough to keep the man's gaze as he shifts his attention to me and then back to Solomon.

"Lord Winett?"

Solomon frowns. "It depends on who is asking."

The man, whose suit is fit for a man of high station, bows slightly, wrapping an arm around his waist as he bends forward. Perhaps a servant to the crown, then? "I am Malcolm of the Bartoli Galeano Family," he introduces himself, answering my curiosity in the next breath. That name sparks a memory in me. Malcolm. Galeano—the cousin of Prince Enver and Nasir. "I am a close aid of the Bartoli Royal Family."

"And what are you doing here?" Solomon asks, his expression unchanging. I understand the need for his caution. I'd never had a chance to send the Bartolis notice of my arrival. How else would they know I'd be here? It's most certainly strange.

"We received a letter from Lord Frederic of Rozentine that Lord Winett and Her Royal Majesty, Princess Devonry, would be arriving here to meet with the Bartoli Royal Family concerning the matter of Prince Nasir's request."

Request? Rage pours through me. Nasir made no request. He made demands. He betrayed my friendship and trust. Nasir is a slaughterer. He is a criminal. As if sensing the trembling of my anger, Solomon puts a hand out as I press forward, holding me back and drawing Malcolm's curious gaze. It's clear he doesn't recognize me. I can't say I'm shocked, but still, his words are an insult that I won't let pass.

"You mean Prince Nasir's crimes?" I demand. "His assassination of King Vernon of Rozentine?"

Malcolm's expression twists for a brief moment before smoothing out once again. His earlier words—and the realization that Lord Frederic of the House of Caladrius, after helping us recover from our desperate fall from the Sevire Cliffs, had foreseen our issues and sent ahead a notice of arrival—fade from my mind.

"I'm not sure what the circumstances are," Malcolm replies. "Only that Prince Nasir has requested that the subject of the treaty between Rozentine and Bartoli be switched from his brother to himself and he will stand in as the Princess' betrothed."

"*Never.*" I bite out the word as I clench my hands into fists at my sides. "After what he's done, Nasir will never be King consort of Rozentine." And I will have the whole world know of his betrayal. That much, I can swear to the Gods.

Solomon's hands become even more firm as he cups

my side and drags me slightly behind him. Malcolm doesn't react as I expect him to. Me calling Nasir by his name rather than his title doesn't even seem to faze him. He simply raises his brow at the venom in my tone. He continues to stare at me for several more moments, yet no response comes my way. Instead, he returns his attention to Solomon.

"I have a carriage to take you to the palace," he continues as if I hadn't spoken at all. I'm practically shaking with my emotions and the only thing keeping me from launching myself around Solomon and taking Malcolm's neck in my hand is my guard's hand on my side.

Solomon grunts in reply.

Malcolm nods, seemingly used to men with little patience like Solomon. "If you have questions feel free to ask them."

"We've never met," Solo states. "How did you know who I was?"

Malcolm chuckles. "The Blood General is well known beyond the Rozentine borders," he answers. "Red eyes are a sign of the House of Blood. I knew who you were the second you stepped off the boat."

"That doesn't explain how you knew when we'd be arriving," Solo replies. "I'm sure Lord Frederic didn't give you a date in his letter." Solomon's words penetrate my mind with clarity. I stop pressing forward to look up at him. He's right; we hadn't even known when we'd be able to reach Carion City, much less when we'd be able to get passage to Bartoli.

"Someone has come down every day since the letter arrived to wait for your party," Malcolm replies.

"You expect me to believe that someone has stood vigil every day since you received Lord Frederic's letter, awaiting our arrival?" Solomon replies.

"Yes." Malcolm dips his head. "We were quite appalled when we heard that the Princess and Lord Solomon had fallen off a cliff. We were led to believe you'd perished until we received notice from Lord Frederic that your demise wasn't the case and, most blessed of all, that the Princess was alive as well."

Solomon hums in the back of his throat, his suspicion barely repressed. I reach down and grip his hand in a silent request to contain his fury, squeezing it once. Though his eyes never glance my way, he squeezes back before releasing me. "Fine," I say, stepping forward now and recapturing the aid's focus. "Suppose all of that is true, then what kind of welcome should we expect at the Bartoli Royal Palace?" I ask.

"And who, may I ask, young lady, do I have the pleasure of addressing?"

I sense Solomon's smirk rather than see it as he straightens at my back. I glare at Malcolm Galeano. "You are addressing her Royal Highness, Crown Princess Devonry of the House of Sunfire, Heir to the Rozentine Throne." Rarely given, my full title earns me a widening of his eyes and a quick perusal as he gapes at me in shock.

Malcolm's eyes flash up to Solomon's face, likely a silent inquiry as to whether or not my words are true. Whatever he sees in Solomon's expression must convince him because Malcolm's head turns down after a moment and he bends entirely at the waist.

"My apologies, Your Royal Highness," he says quickly. "Your portrait … I did not realize."

Of course not. The portraits that had been sent to Bartoli all depicted me as a luxurious noblewoman with golden white hair and dresses detailed in gems. Not the gutter rat before him with the reddish straggling strands soaked in seawater and body dirtied by days aboard a ship.

"You are forgiven," I reply tersely. "My disguise was necessary, so I understand your confusion."

"I will correct my behavior toward you immediately, Your Highness," Malcolm replies. "May I go attend to the carriage and bring it forth for you?"

"Yes," I snap. "Go."

Without another word, he nods and finishes his bow before standing, turning, and striding off.

"Harsh," Solomon comments lightly.

"I'm irritated," I reply.

"That's obvious."

I sigh. "We should be thankful to Frederic," I say. "Things should be faster with a carriage and the expectation of the Royal Family."

Solomon captures my hand as I move to walk away from him. My gaze finds his. "No matter what happens, Devonry," he says, "I will protect you. Have no fear of the Bartoli Royal Family."

"No," I say. "I don't fear them." In fact, there's very little I fear now. Everything I could lose is already gone. Everything save for ... *him.*

2
DEVONRY

The carriage bumps and sways as Solomon and I sit across from Malcolm Galeano. Somewhere behind us, in an adjoining carriage, Argyle and Celine are following. After being with them nearly every waking second of every day for the past few weeks, it feels odd not to have them so near now. I don't say as much, though, and I won't. Not in front of Malcolm. After everything I've been through, I'm not sure who is to be trusted and who isn't. Though, in my heart I hope that the Bartoli Empire is a safe haven, the memory of that bloody night—the night Nasir had slain my father—lingers, always, in the back of my mind.

"How much longer?" I ask as the carriage careens through a turn dusted in loose sand. My stomach drops, and my hand slaps out against the side of the carriage door as I swear the vehicle pops up on two wheels before slamming back down.

"Soon," Malcolm replies with an ever-present smooth smile. A sycophantic smile, one I recognize as seeking to appease and pander. He reminds me of the courtiers in the

Sunfire Palace, the ones who'd always smile at my face, yet the second they thought I wasn't looking would scowl. As if bowing to a woman was beneath them.

Solomon's gaze burns into the side of my face, but I don't return it.

"I expect to meet the King and my fiancé when we arrive. Has that been arranged?" I demand.

Malcolm closes his eyes when his smile stretches. It makes me uneasy. What is he hiding behind those eyes that he has to close them when he smiles wider? "All in due time, Your Highness," he says cordially.

I scowl. "What does that mean?"

"I'm sure he means that we'll be taken to our rooms to freshen up before we meet the King," Solomon says.

Malcolm's eyes reopen and he nods to Solomon. "Of course." Stinging eyes cut toward me, though Malcolm's head doesn't move as he keeps it turned in Solomon's direction. "His Majesty expects a certain level of … cleanliness when he's presented with his subjects as does the Crown Prince."

Shock at his blunt words slams into me and I stiffen. Before I can say a thing about how I'd be much cleaner if I hadn't spent the last few weeks fighting for my life to get away from *their* Prince's clutches as he assassinated my father and took over my Kingdom, Solomon leans forward and places a hand on the hilt of the sword at his hip.

"I'm sure you didn't mean anything untoward about my Princess, sir." His words are quiet and low, polite and respectful, but his tone is threatening. "We beg your understanding that we've been aboard a ship without many available amenities for the last few weeks."

My heart flutters in my chest. A note of possessive authority rings out in his statement. Though it couldn't be more than him defending his ward, it still stirs something I'd rather ignore within me.

Malcolm straightens and blinks in mock surprise as if he never even considered that his words would be taken inappropriately. "Oh, I understand completely, Lord Solomon," he says quickly. "I assure you, I meant no disrespect."

Doubtful. I level him with a look, letting him know with my expression that his words are something I highly disagree with. Nervousness overtakes him, though, as Solomon doesn't say anything, and instead, continues to stare at him. I know as well as anyone that Solo's blood-red gaze can be unnerving. If I hadn't spent years alongside him, I, too, might have been put off by them.

"Oh look!" Malcolm exclaims a moment later, turning his attention to the carriage's windows. "We're almost there. You can see the palace's rooftop from here."

I pull my gaze away and glance out the window, realizing that he's right. There, behind the next rise of a sandbank and then a rock formation, I spot the white stone tips of spires as they stab up toward the sky. Large bulbs of stone are twisted around them and tipped at the very top with fluttering flags that wave in the wind.

Solomon says something and Malcolm responds, but their words turn distant as I lean forward, pressing a hand to the glass. For so many years, I've wondered just what kind of place Bartoli was. What kind of country did the man I was contracted to marry rule? Now, I'm about to find out.

I can only hope that Prince Enver and the King can help me get back my throne. Even if it means that I have to marry the brother of my once friend, now turned enemy, I'll do whatever is necessary if it means I will save my people.

The Bartoli Royal Palace is glittering in gold. The white tile floors are smooth and create echoes with each step as Solomon, Celine, Argyle, and I are led through the massive dual-doored entrance lined with stone-faced guards. For a moment, I pause and look around wondering if things were to play out the way my father had arranged, would I have come to love a place such as this, which is so very different from my home?

The Sunfire Palace is a place etched in ancient history. Everything within it, though immaculately kept, is either several hundreds of years old or replicas of things lost in time. The Bartoli Palace, however, appears like a bright, shining new gem only recently discovered. Everything is white and gold. Everything is perfect. It feels ... colder than I've ever felt before despite the obvious heat of the desert-laden country it sits upon.

"This way," Malcolm states, making me jump as his voice reverberates across the smooth stone walls and floor seemingly much louder in this ample space.

Solomon takes his stance in front of me with Argyle at his side. Behind me, I can sense Celine's warmth as she trails a step or two back—the same any lady-in-waiting would. I wonder if she's had training. Despite our weeks together on the ship, there's still so much I have yet to learn about her and her past. Unfortunately, for both of us, now is certainly not the time to ask either.

The group of us trail Malcolm through wide, open hallways. Unlike home, the walls of these corridors are not littered with tapestries to keep out the cold, nor are they decorated in the art of Kings past. Instead, they remain bare. Empty. Almost desolate, lacking any kind of stimulation for the mind and soul. I cast my gaze down and keep moving.

After what feels like eons of walking, we come to a stop before wide gold doors etched with the emblem of the Bartoli Royal Family. Malcolm knocks and stands back. A moment passes and the door opens, a mousy-looking woman appearing in a neutral-toned sari. Her large brown eyes look up at Malcolm, widening slightly before her gaze moves past him to the rest of us.

"Y-yes, my Lord?" she asks, bowing her head.

"This is Her Highness, Princess Devonry, and her entourage," Malcolm announces, stepping to the side. "They shall be staying with us for a time. Please see to it that the Princess and her lady's maid are thoroughly washed and changed appropriately for tonight's banquet."

The woman opens the door wider, showing a large lounge-like room and open doorways beyond with long strips of sheer white fabric drifting down from each available alcove. "Of course, my Lord," she says before directing her attention to me and Celine. "My ladies?"

Solomon looks back as I step forward. Heat burns into my arm a moment later as he reaches out and snags it, stopping me from walking into the room. I look up at him in surprise, but he's not looking at me. Instead, his eyes are squarely narrowed on Malcolm.

"I am not leaving my Princess' side, Lord Malcolm," he says coolly.

"I was told that it is seen as inappropriate for men and women to bathe together in the Rozentine Kingdom," Malcolm replies. "We've arranged for a separate bathing chamber for you and your attendant."

"I will remain here," Solomon says, his grip on my arm tightening.

There has already been far too much he's seen—things

I had no control over. Now that we're among civilization and propriety, it wouldn't be proper. Perhaps it's best that I take a step back from him—and from the way my insides always seem to throb the second he puts his hands on me...

I'm torn as worry floods me with the idea of him leaving my side for longer than necessary.

"Solomon," I say, gently prying my arm from his grip. "I'm sure we're perfectly safe in the Bartoli Royal Palace."

The home of the man I'm promised to *should* be safe. I pray to the Gods that it is and that I'm not making a terrible mistake by forcing our party to come here.

Red eyes snap to my face and it takes everything within me not to react to the way his pupils dilate, the black swallowing up the red in nearly an instant. "I understand you may feel safe within these walls, Your Highness," he says. "But that does not negate that your recent troubles have all been caused by such carelessness."

I grit my teeth but force my face to remain impassive. "You're not coming into my bathing chamber, Solomon."

He arches a brow. "Of course not, Your Highness," he states. "I will remain out here until you are finished."

"And when would you expect to be able to leave me to bathe yourself?" I ask him. "I'm not the only one in need of cleansing. Or do you expect me to remain outside of your bathing chambers later?"

He blinks, but before he can answer, the two of us are rescued from what threatens to be a rather heated battle of wills and wits by none other than Argyle. "I'll stay behind and guard the chamber, Lord Solomon," Argyle says. "Perhaps if you bathe fast enough, we can switch places and you'll be here when she finishes."

Though I don't look forward to Argyle standing outside of my bathing chamber either, it's a far better option than Solomon. I nod. "That's a splendid idea," I say. "Shall we then?" I pull away from Solomon entirely and turn to Celine.

Her attention bounces from Solomon and Argyle to me before she nods and steps forward. I'm lucky she seems to sense my wants, as now that a suitable resolution to our problem has been found, I want to hurry up and get through these doors and into a bath before Solomon can think of a reason why he should remain behind.

The doors close and a rumbling growl sounds from the other side. My lips twitch, but I turn away from both the sound of his frustration and my feeling of having won our little sparring match.

The servant from before leads Celine and me into an adjoining room where a large milky-white pool awaits. Steam drifts from the top of the water's surface as red rose petals float past. Never in all my days have I so looked forward to the feeling of being clean.

Despite my initial intention to quickly wash and wait for Solomon outside, the second I step into the heated water, the muscles in my body all freeze and then immediately loosen. With a groan, I sink deeper below the surface and allow the servant—whose name I learn is Amelda—and Celine to work their magic as they help me wash the grime of weeks on the run and even more weeks upon the ocean waters from my body. The dirt that felt as if it'd made its home upon my skin sluices off.

Surprisingly, the Bartoli seem to have similar ingredients to Rozentine and Amelda brings forth a concoction to remove the last remaining vestiges of the dye I'd used to color my hair. As the leftover color leaves the strands, however, I pause and lift the locks toward my face for inspection.

Though a golden hue remains, the strawberry red

remains behind. "Celine?" I lift my hair for her to see. "Is the dye still not coming all the way off?"

Celine frowns and moves forward through the water. She dips her head and stares at my hair. "No, Your Highness," she says. "It appears to be gone."

I hum in the back of my throat. "Strange," I murmur.

"Would Your Highness prefer another treatment?" Amelda asks from her kneeling position on the side of the open bath.

I shake my head and let my hair drop. "No, that's alright," I say. "It's not worth the trouble."

"It is no trouble at all," Amelda insists, but still, I shake my head.

"No, we should hurry up," I say. "We've been far too long as it is."

With that, Amelda produces a stack of freshly cleaned drying sheets. Together, Celine and I get out of the bath and dry off before I'm once again placed in front of a mirror as Amelda and Celine hurry about—Celine trailing her Bartoli counterpart as she hurries to find what she needs to attend to me.

Unease swarms my mind. It appears that weeks away from the constant of attendants and servants at every waiting moment has taken its toll upon me. It feels wrong to sit and be waited upon now that I know there are things I can clearly do for myself. Still, though, I sit and I don't move. It wouldn't be good if I were to offend Amelda now. Servants talk, and so often their Masters listen.

As their ministrations finish, I look in the mirror and find that I've changed once again. A reflection is meant to show the impression of a person, but just as much as my mind has changed, so too has my outside.

Mere months ago, I'd looked into a mirror and seen beauty. Now, I realize that it'd been a child's vainness to focus on such exterior qualities. My hair falls in softly dried waves around my face and shoulders—shorter than it has ever been before. My skin is still the same tone, though a bit lighter now that it's been cleaned. Dark circles plague the space beneath my eyes while lines crease around my lips and between my brows. No amount of forcing myself to relax gets rid of the pain of the past that draws itself so clearly on my features.

This, I realize, is as good as it will get for now.

"Your Highness?" Celine bends at the waist as she, too, gazes into the mirror with me. "Are you ready?"

I nod. "Yes," I say as I take her hand and stand. "I am."

<h1 style="text-align:center">3
SOLOMON</h1>

"**D**on't you look handsome," Argyle taunts as he finds me sequestered in the back of the glittering banquet hall sometime later. The Bartolis are known for the gold mines within their desert lands so it comes as no shock that the entire throne room and banquet hall is decorated from top to bottom with shining gold accents. The floors are so smooth they reflect the light hanging from the candle chandeliers above.

Argyle flicks a dangling piece of the suit I'd been given to wear to dinner with an amused chuckle. With a long exhale, I swat his hand away. "Try that again, and I will remove your hand from your body," I tell him.

Instead of being frightened by my threat, however, Argyle chuckles and shakes his head. "It is the culture of the Bartoli people to preen themselves like great big birds."

"We look like turkeys decorated for a feast." I gesture at my outfit. It would be a fine suit if it wasn't adorned with so many additional swinging charms and golden embroidery. Every step I take makes me sound like a wind chime taken up in a gust of wind. It's exasperating. Are one's metals from war not enough? Is it necessary to add what has no purpose other than for supposed prestige? Bartoli customs truly bewilder me.

Argyle stretches, running a hand over his stomach with a grin. His ensemble is made up of dark trousers and a nearly sheer shirt with the same assortment of clacking metals along the back of the sleeves. Surprisingly still, we're of the more moderately dressed crowd amongst the banquet attendees.

"We certainly look delicious," Argyle comments lightly as he plucks two glasses of sparkling wine from a passing servant, carting around a heavy metal tray stacked with crystal glasses. "I'll be shocked if one of these ladies doesn't offer to eat us by the end of the night."

I take the drink and relish the chill of the glass against my palm, cringing when the movement causes a commotion amongst the charms. Sipping the bubbly liquid, my eyes travel across the room. Sconces are lit along the stretching walls of the banquet hall and chandeliers of candles hang over the center of the room. Shadows dance in the corners, which are perhaps the only place guests have yet to wander. With more wine, however, I'm sure that will change.

There's tension in the air. One I'm not unfamiliar with, but in Rozentine, I believe it meant something completely different. Here, in Bartoli, I catch several gazes boring into not just myself, but Argyle as well, regardless of his lack of title. Women lick their lips and suggestively position themselves with their breasts jutting outward as other men pass by and appreciate their figures. Never having been to Bartoli myself, I have been only vaguely aware that their practices of social etiquette are different, freer in many senses through gossip. This, however, seems to be the precursor to something I'd rather skin myself alive than allow Devonry to be exposed to.

"They look like they're preparing for an orgy, don't they?" Argyle's question is both amused and disgusted. It's as if he's reached inside and plucked the thought right from my mind.

Others stand in small groups of twos and threes, much like Argyle and I. All of them glance our way before whispering furiously. I shift, wishing I had escorted Devonry here. "I'm sure they'll maintain propriety for a while yet," I reply coolly.

"I'm sure your Princess will be quite shocked by their forwardness," Argyle says.

I stiffen and feel the pulse of bloodlust rush through my veins. More than anger and rage, a violent creature opens its eyes, and claws stab at my guts. Seeing her clean for the first time in weeks made me realize just how much she's changed over all that time. No sooner had the four of us bathed, however, than we'd been hurried to our chambers —near the Rozentine Ambassador, of course, who we all had yet to meet—and then ordered to prepare for this farce of a banquet. *Ridiculous and frustrating.* Once more, she is out of my sight and my discomfort with that mounts with each slowly passing minute.

Should one man even *attempt* to lure her out of my sight, I will rip his cock off and feed it to him. "She is a royal," I grit out. "Even if she's shocked, she will be fine."

Argyle's gaze burns into the side of my face, but I refuse to meet it. "So protective," he murmurs. "She might start to resent you if you stand in her way of getting what she needs, old friend. What if Prince Enver wishes to hasten their marriage as collateral for helping her with Nasir?"

The thought of Enver and Devonry does something to

my insides. If Prince Enver tries to pressure her will, then he, too, will perish under my fangs and blade, I think to myself. Unfortunately, however, I'm not in a position to say as much. Instead, I switch topics. "What can we expect from this banquet?" I ask, in lieu of answering him.

Argyle allows the change and straightens. "When the King, Queen, and that"—Argyle's voice lowers to a whisper—"*brat*, Prince Enver, finally make an appearance, they'll want Princess Devonry to press their fingers to her cheek, starting with the Queen, then King, then the Prince. It's a sign of respect, a royal tradition here, and they *should* return the gesture."

"Press their fingers to her cheek?"

He nods.

More people filter into the room. A woman showing more skin than gown watches me as her gold-dipped fan flutters over her buxom chest. When she notices that I've caught her staring, her face reddens and her fan moves a little faster. What would Devonry have done had she caught me staring? The thought suddenly crops into my mind. She likely would've checked around her to make sure she wasn't being watched before sticking her tongue out. Or perhaps rolled her eyes. Instead, she's not yet here and I'm left to contend with the courtiers of the Bartoli Palace. What little smile I'd worn is quickly melting from my face. All of these Bartoli citizens look at me as if I am little more than a side attraction. They are all so small that it is a wonder they have any kind of military power at all. My hand moves to my hip, settling on the pommel of my sword though there is nothing I can do with it to save myself from wandering eyes.

"Makes one wonder if they're afraid they'll get sick if we all kiss their rings. Though I wouldn't consider that appropriate for our Princess to do. She is above that, no?"

He tips his glass, the contents quickly disappearing with each bob of his throat until the glass is empty. "Oh, I should warn you about the dancers."

I pinch the bridge of my nose feeling a headache forming. "Dancers? During the banquet?"

"Mmmm, they have even less clothing on than these fine women here, if you'll believe it. When they move, their breasts"—Argyle's eyes roll to the back of his head for a moment—"don't let the Princess catch you looking at their breasts. I'm sure she'd be quite upset. I, however, will definitely be partaking in the sights."

I level him with a look. "Fill your gaze to your content, but remember why we're here," I tell him. "Don't wander too far and don't get caught up in anything that could threaten the Princess."

Argyle's lips twitch. "I'd never consider endangering your princess, *Lord Blood General.*" His teasing intent is clear and perhaps it's a distraction from something else.

I lean back, my fingers playing along the glass in my fist as I peek at him out of the corners of my eyes. "It's a wonder that you seem to know so much about Bartoli, considering you've never mentioned visiting before," I say. Another scantily clad woman passes and bends her head in our direction. Large breasts lift up as she inhales quickly and her eyes widen as he tips her face up to our height. With a scowl, I divert my gaze. Trouble. Tonight will no doubt be nothing but trouble if this is any indication.

Argyle shrugs. "Guess I just picked up on it from travelers who gossip."

I arch a brow at him. "Travelers from Bartoli?" *Ones who specifically would know about the customs of the royal family?* Doubtful.

"Sure. Would you like another drink?" His glass is empty while mine is only missing a few sips. Before I can even shake my head, he's moving to find another servant. I let him go. I know better than most that Argyle is a man full of secrets. If he wants to keep them for a while longer, so long as they don't place Devonry or me in harm's way, I'll let him.

No more than two blissfully silent heartbeats pass before two men along with fluttering beauties appear at my side. One man stands before me with his black hair slicked against his scalp. He cranes his neck up at me and then clicks his tongue. His associate stretches up on his toes, lifting his chin as if that might help him grow another inch or two.

"May I help you?" I ask blandly.

"You're so *big*." The first man crinkles his nose.

I blink, wondering if there is more to the statement, but when nothing further comes, I manage to give him a nod. Compared to the people here, I suppose I can understand that. Argyle is perhaps the only person taller than me in the entire room. Everyone else is a head shorter or more.

"What kind of foods do you eat?" the second man asks, and the woman on his arm leans a little closer.

"Is it natural to be so … robust?" she inquires.

"Excuse me?" A slender hand finds my bicep and I freeze. The woman, as if she doesn't realize the insult, gives my arm a squeeze before giggling and turning to whisper into the man's ear.

"It's a curiosity," the first man states. "We so rarely have Rozentine visitors outside of House Daemonium, and they're nothing like you."

"House Daemonium are not soldiers," I grit the words out.

"You look utterly barbaric," the second man says with a shake of his head. "I'll bet they had to specially make that suit for you. I'm surprised it isn't bursting at the seams."

Words fail me, but it doesn't seem as if I need them when the other woman chimes in. "Do you think his … you know … is just as big?" She touches her translucent, bejeweled gloves to her lips.

"It must at least be proportionate," the other woman replies.

The open contemplation of my size is more of a shock even than the clothing choices of the Bartoli nobles.

"*Mighty* intimidating," the second man chortles, sending the women into another fit of giggles before he barks at me like a dog and growls with a show of his teeth.

I swear my eye twitches. These people seem to openly view Rozentine citizens as little more than animals on display. My hand moves to the hilt of my blade and tightens.

"I think I could still take him." The first man makes a show of shoving up his sleeves, not even noticing the way his own dangling jewels and tassels clank and clatter. "No doubt all of this brawn has nothing to do with his brain."

My lips stretch into a smile and my fangs slide down. The man pauses, his eyes widening. "Should you wish to die," I say quietly, "I'm more than happy to oblige."

"And that will be quite enough!" A familiar figure appears between us. "Thank you all for your warm welcome, but I must steal my friend away. *Now*." The girls gasp as Argyle swoops in with two new glasses in hand and nudges me away with his elbow. "Solo, *move*."

I don't. Not immediately. Instead, I stare down at the little man on the other side of my friend who has now directed his shocked attention to Argyle. As if he senses my focus, his head turns and he captures my gaze. I bend and he scuttles backward a step. "I would advise you to keep your inappropriate thoughts to yourself, sir," I say with sinister quiet. "Many Rozentine soldiers would have sliced you from throat to groin for your insults. Be grateful that you have been spared. Desiring battles you have no chance of winning will end with your death sooner or later."

The man doesn't get a chance to respond as Argyle shoves the glasses of liquor into one of the women's hands and then grabs me and drags me away. Even as we retreat to another portion of the banquet hall, the rage of insult remains burning hot inside my chest.

"What in the name of Levim was that?" I snarl, keeping up with his long strides.

"That would be the Bartoli nobles," Argyle answers with a sigh.

"These people have no sense. The men wanted to fight me and the women were practically taking bets on the size of my manhood."

Argyle casts me an amused smirk. "To be fair, it is quite large."

I pause, prompting Argyle to lift his brows. "And how would you know that?" I shake my head. "Never mind. I don't want to know."

"Drinking will make you feel better," he says. He taps the bottom of my still-full glass. "Or, at the very least, it'll make tonight more bearable." An odd ache settles in my chest, but I nod and follow him as he leads me further away from the Bartoli nobles.

Two tables run parallel at the foot of a dais where another table, intricately carved from dark wood, waits for the royal family. Empty plates glisten before even emptier chairs. My stomach rumbles. Surely, this farce of a banquet will begin soon.

"I suppose," my friend continues as he procures

another two glasses from a waiting table full of liquors, "Bartoli nobles can be a bit risqué."

"Hence the scandalous clothing?"

He nods. "They're not particularly kind people. They take offense rather easily and are overindulgent in acquiring baubles and fashions." I drain my last glass and set it amongst the full ones before I take a second glass Argyle offers me. "They're cruel to their servants and even crueler to people who cross them. I'd hate to see such a wonderful man such as yourself at the end of any of their wrath."

I snort. "They're arrogant." And seeing how easily they risked their lives to impress women only makes me realize just how cunning Nasir had been. He played the part of the amiable royal well, though it was clear that wasn't where he'd come from. He'd been so inadvertently benign that not even I had realized his intentions until it'd been too late.

"You'd be surprised at what these people are capable of." Argyle eyes the crowd over the rim of his glace, glaring as though he knows firsthand the dark deeds of the people of Bartoli.

"No," I say. "You're right." Nasir had proven that the Bartoli people are not to be trusted. Our public arrival has awarded us a modicum of safety, but something tells me the moment the Bartoli Royal Family gets what they want, that will change. We just need to find out exactly what it is they're willing to trade to return Rozentine to its true heir.

The cold awareness slips from Argyle's features, his mouth rising to that familiar smile once again. "Enough of this seriousness," he says, tapping the underside of my glass. "Drink up." He raises his own glass to his lips. "You're going to need it to get through this night."

This night and every night that follows so long as we're

in enemy territory, I amend silently. Instead of saying as much, though, I do as he wishes and drain my glass. The buzzing sensation of the sharp liquor sliding down my throat does little to soothe the tautness in my muscles. Turning my head from Argyle, I scan the banquet hall, searching.

Where in the bloody name of the Gods is she?

"Fucking idiot!" I turn my head at the sudden shout from a nearby noble and watch in silent disgust as a fat ruddy-faced man backhands a servant. "Look what you've done. Do you know how much this costs?!" The Bartoli noble continues to scream at the teary-eyed youth who bends himself nearly in half to show his subservience.

I grit my teeth as Argyle sets a hand on my arm. "Don't," he warns me with a shake of his head. Is this what he meant by cruelty? Openly abusing servants at such a grand event? It's repugnant. "Solomon…" Argyle's voice is as firm as his hand, but we both know that if I truly wanted to, he wouldn't be able to hold me back. The only reason I do so now is because of how important I know it is to Devonry that I remain appeasing and polite during our stay here.

I hope she arrives soon, I silently pray. *Now would be the perfect time.*

No sooner has that question permeated my mind than a hush falls over the room. As if my wish has been answered. A new face, dressed in the same servant's uniform as the poor boy being yelled at appears at the open doorway to the banquet hall and nervously clears his throat. "Announcing Their Royal Majesties, King Florian, First Queen Helena, and Crown Prince Enver." The servant bows and sweeps his arm to the side as he hurriedly moves out of the way to reveal the Bartoli Royal Family.

Just like that, the furious noble quickly averts his attention, allowing his target to scurry away.

Argyle stiffens at my side and though I cast him a glance, his enigmatic expression is sealed shut. I return my attention to the front of the hall. The King strides in first, a man of short stature with his head weighed down by an adornment of gold foliage circling his skull. The showy crown appears heavier than any I've ever seen in Rozentine.

Queen Helena moves into the room at his back and quickly reaches his side where he takes her arm and weaves it with his own. Long dark hair hangs in a singular braid down her back, decorated in ornate gold and pearl pins that appear like little suns sewn into the strands. As she moves, the lavender fabric of her gown splits up each of her thighs, revealing charms that wrap down the length of her legs. As she and the King move through the room, nobles lower themselves into intense bows and deep curtseys.

It's like watching a play that might have been enjoyable were it not for the fact that both Argyle and I seem to be unwilling cast members without a singular line of script to go off of.

King Florian steps in time to the chimes of his Queen's jewelry. His dark blue pants complement the softer colors of his partner. Metal charms jingle against the King's loose top. It's little more than a vest made of the glistening charms, revealing dark curling hair over his olive skin. So this is Prince Nasir's father. There's no denying the heritage, not with the similar sharp features of his nose. The two are very much alike in physicality.

I stiffen as the King strolls down the hall with his Queen because a moment later, a new figure appears in the mouth of the doorway. *Enver.*

"Careful there, Solo." Argyle's warning whisper slides over my ears, reminding me of where we stand. "Bow your fucking head. Don't draw attention, not yet."

My gaze snaps to him, but Argyle's attention is focused solely on the man who enters the banquet hall. His head is lowered, but his eyes are centered upward as he stares out from beneath his brow. I look back to the man—Devonry's *betrothed*. Even unspoken, the word is vile in my mind. So much mystery has surrounded this man—the one who has ignored her for years and passed off his responsibilities to her to his younger sibling. A sibling that betrayed them both and slaughtered my King.

My hands clench at my sides. Unlike his brother, Prince Enver's hair is cut short around his head, cropped close to his scalp, leaving only the top long enough to fan across his forehead under the gold crown. As he moves, he keeps his head raised. The sign of a man who's never had to lower his gaze to anyone in his life save for his father and mother. While he stands slightly taller than his father, I size him up as he passes me. Were he and I to cross swords, I would win. That, more than anything, gives me some sense of relief.

Another note of interest is that—unlike the nobles surrounding us—Enver wears more clothing. A vest as gold as his crown fits his slender frame, and the collar of a white linen shirt peeks out from beneath it with long white sleeves fitted over his arms. No added jewels or pageantry. *Intriguing.*

The Bartoli Royal Family makes their way to the dais, and as they do, the nobles begin to rise. Argyle and I straighten with the rest of the room. My grip on my glass is frighteningly tight, so I turn and place it on a nearby table. The room is ripe with anticipation. Eyes bounce from the

King and his party to Argyle and me—few doing much to conceal their curiosity and awareness.

"My wonderful court, I am so very thankful that you all could join us on such short notice for this joyous occasion." Despite his size, King Florian's voice booms through the room with authority.

Joyous? I bite down on my tongue to keep from reacting to that. His words are blatant disrespect.

"It is with a great deal of excitement that I present to you our guest of honor, my son's betrothed, Princess Devonry of the Rozentine Kingdom."

All heads turn toward the open doors as he gestures to the back of the banquet hall. A small figure stands there with her head raised high. My body heats. Awareness tingles across my back. She doesn't look at me. No, she shouldn't. Instead, her gaze is trained on the King. For a brief flicker, she glances to either side, looking first at the Queen before landing on Prince Enver. Devonry doesn't show any emotion as she steps into the hall; she's too well-educated and too accustomed to court life to let her thoughts show at a time like this.

Hot air pierces my lungs, invading. Sharp stings press against my chest as I watch her move forward. Her slender body has changed. Her skin shines brighter, filled with warmth, but her eyes tell a different story. They're harder than they've ever been. Steel pressed into twin irises of cautious blue.

Alone at the mouth of the room, she appears almost lost at sea and I want to go to her. I take a step forward to do just that, only to pull up short when a hand grabs my arm. "She has to finish the ceremony," Argyle says. "Don't interrupt."

Finish the ceremony? When she looks like an outcast

being sent to the gallows? Heated rage burns up my spine. "She—"

Argyle's hand tightens and his eyes flash—one blue, one brown—as his upper lip pulls back over his teeth. "I warned you," he hisses. "The Bartoli's take offense easily. If you fuck this up, it will spell disaster. You're the fucking Blood General, keep your wits about you, damn it."

His words slam into me. Insulting, enraging, and … utterly valid. With gritted teeth, I carefully pull my arm from his grip and stand back as Devonry continues through the room. Her hair has been washed again, yet despite that, there remains some hint of strawberry in the once white tresses. Still, the trace of the dark dye that made her look like a stranger is gone.

Bold crimson material covers her, swirling around her chest and waist, draping over her shoulder down to her backside. The flesh of her legs is revealed with each step she takes as the gown splits apart before coming together again and again. My groin tightens, my cock stiffening despite myself. Gold chains circle her neck and waist dangling down her hips and between her breasts, glinting under the light.

Exquisite. It's the first word that comes to my head. Followed by a litany of others. Alluring. Ethereal. Divine.

"She is." Argyle's agreement makes me frown until I realize I'd whispered the first word aloud. I shake my head and turn back to the hall. The beast within opens its eyes and feasts his gaze upon her. My thoughts roll with dangerous intention and desire. Argyle's attention stings. I can sense his stare as it shifts between the Princess and I. Calm. I must calm myself.

For a moment, I close my eyes, recalling an old memory. The one thing that is guaranteed to pull the beast back from its desire to take her, even if it means cutting through the people that surround us now and throwing away the façade of humanity, never to return. In my mind's eye, I see the dark shadow of a crow flying overhead as I stand coated in the blood of my enemies and soldiers alike. Death. Battle. War. If we're to avoid it again, I must do my utmost to ensure Devonry's plans come to fruition.

Once that is established and the beast grumbles its understanding, I reopen my eyes and refocus on the scene before me. A man steps from the crowd of nobles, skin paler than the others around us, but his attire similar in tone. White flowing fabric pants and a matching top with a gold embroidered vest glint under the candles and wall sconces. He offers his arm, and Devonry pauses to take it. My chest tightens and I jerk my head to Argyle. His face, however, has darkened. Recognition? Or something else?

She must have been informed of the ceremony and practices, however, because Devonry doesn't resist as she allows the man to guide her forward to the royals' dais. The man turns his head, glancing back, and I catch sight of the lavender irises. My body immediately softens. Purple eyes are a sign of House Daemonium. He can be none other than the Rozentine Ambassador.

It's strange how I hadn't noticed him before. My gaze narrows on the slender, well-dressed man. Though it's apparent by both his purple irises and his lightened skin that he's not a native of Bartoli, his attire and mannerisms are just as opulent and overextending. He turns back to the King and Queen, leading Devonry to the edge of their seats. To be presented to her … *intended.*

Blood rushes in my ears. I close my eyes as I feel the burn of it through my limbs. My tongue swells as saliva collects. Hunger races through me, but I tamp it down. How long has it been since I last had blood? A few days, at least. Not since the boat where I could pay a crew member for a few minutes of their time. My bloodlust isn't quite as strong as it's been, but it's still there.

When the two slow at the front of the dais, the Bartoli Queen steps forward. She lifts her chin and stares down her nose. Pride fills me as Devonry lifts her own gaze and refuses to lower it. She is just as much a Queen in her own right—despite the traitorous actions of their Prince. A moment of tense silence passes and then the Queen reaches out her hand. Devonry releases the Ambassador and takes it, pressing her fingers to her cheek in a sign of respect. Respect unearned, in my opinion. Then the King stands and moves forward to repeat the action. Then, finally, Prince Enver.

Towards the end, however, Prince Enver bends and says something so low that even I can't capture it. Devonry's face tilts up again and she offers a smile at whatever it was. Bitterness seeps into my chest and I bite back a growl. Then, without further formality, he offers his palm to her once more and when I expect him to press her fingers to his cheek as Argyle had mentioned, instead he guides her to the steps and up onto the dais with himself and his family. The Ambassador bows and then steps back into the crowd.

My gaze seizes on him and I lean closer to Argyle. "Get more information on the Rozentine Ambassador," I practically snarl, struggling to repress the strange sensations colliding within me.

Argyle passes me a glance but responds with a silent nod.

"Tonight!" Prince Enver calls over the room, holding up his intertwined fingers with Devonry's. "We feast to the promise of our allied nations. We lift our glasses to my soon-to-be bride and the mother of our future King."

My stomach drops. My throat closes. Violence. Hatred. The rich cast of pain boils under my flesh, threatening to rise to the surface and rip from me. All around me, hands lift in the air, drinks being raised, cries of happiness, cheers. My claws ache to cut them all down. To slice through skin and bone, to see their blood pooling in the center of this gaudy hall.

Instead, I feel Argyle shove a new drink into my hand. I hear him speak, but the words don't reach me. Movements stiff, the glass lifts toward my lips. Across the room, Devonry's gaze meets mine. No joy. No happiness. Mere resignation reflects in her gaze. I drain my drink, her late father's words still ringing in my ears.

I am not for her. She is not mine. This is her destiny.

I repeat them over and over again. Unlike when I was a child, though, the words don't sink as deep this time. Instead, they bounce from my mind and are quickly replaced by the burn of hatred for the man currently holding her hand. The glass in my hand cracks. Argyle rips it from my grip and steps into my line of vision—blocking me from her.

"Don't, Solomon." I hear him, but it takes a moment for the words to sink in. "Now is not the time. No missteps. No scenes. Just keep her safe."

Right. Keep her safe. He's right.

I am not for her. She is not mine. This is her destiny.

Over and over again. Even if she's not in my sight, that doesn't make the words any less a lie than they've always been.

4

DEVONRY

I'm trussed up like a celebratory bird meant for slaughter. Yet, I feel that if I had feathers, they would cover more than this bright red monstrosity that now rests upon my skin.

"You look … quite beautiful," Celine offers as if she senses my impending tirade that I'm only managing to stave off by sheer force of will.

I resist the urge to rip the dress off and burn it to a crisp. "I look like a prideful, bloodied peacock," I mutter.

Celine presses her lips together, but I spot the amused smile before she can manage to hide it completely. I can't even be mad. Were I in her position, watching this farce of an introduction ceremony, I'd be laughing at myself. My gaze moves down to the sheer skirts that swish about my thighs and ankles. The presence of such transparent fabric makes no sense to me. What's the point of it if it leaves nothing to the imagination? The skirts hardly touch me, and even when they do, they split open to reveal long stretches of my legs along either side. My stomach is left bare save for the wrap that Amelda had taught Celine how to weave around me. Still, though, the wrap is also little more than decoration for the dress.

As I turn from side to side, unused to the strange sensation of such an unusual dress, I have to admit that despite the pomp and circumstance of its design, it is quite airy and comfortable. *Is it because of the heat of the land,* I wonder, *that the style of clothing here is so free?*

The dress itself is beautiful, but the accessories are what frustrate me beyond belief. The weight of them drags down my shoulders and makes me feel as if I am a jingling bell with each step I take. Gold bands circle my throat and from them, long golden chains dip over my chest and between my breasts. The earrings I've been given do the same, dipping down, and down some more until they reach past the ends of my hair and even my shoulders. The matching gold belt that keeps the skirt's waistline from being visible feels cold against my skin.

They're all beautiful, glittering in their luxury. Gold manacles binding me into a place I never thought was confining before. The cleverest way to keep someone chained is to convince them that they're not imprisoned at all.

"I am sure it is different than what you are used to, but this is considered quite the ensemble here in Bartoli," the maidservant who had attended me after we'd left Amelda states. She is an older woman with graying strands straightened and flattened down to her scalp, creating a rather severe look that no doubt makes others afraid to contradict her words.

"It's very … shiny," I say, unable to come up with another word for the whole look.

"Prince Enver picked it out himself," the maid says, sounding rather proud.

I blink and glance up quickly at her. "Is that true?"

She nods, her thin lips stretching into a pleased smile. Perhaps, before, her words would have made me feel loved or even honored. Now that I know these accessories and the dress are from him, it makes me feel as if I'm being forced to remake myself in the image he expects or wants. He knows nothing of me yet has the confidence to choose my attire. A farce, indeed.

"You will make a striking entrance with this," the maid says.

I suppose that is something we can both agree on, although she likely views it as a compliment, whereas I see it as little more than a potential threat hanging over my head.

A knock sounds upon the chamber door and I turn toward it as the maid calls out. The door opens and a tall man dressed in long dark tan trousers and a white vested shirt embroidered with gold and the Bartoli Family Crest enters. The attire is an exact replica of the guards I'd seen stationed around the palace grounds.

"I'm here to lead you to the banquet, Your Highness," the man says, bowing low. He doesn't stand back up immediately but rather keeps his head down as he awaits my acknowledgment.

Celine and I both exchange a look. There's no stopping this now, I suppose. Even if it means I'll have to appear dressed like this, the fact remains—I have to see and speak with the Bartoli Royal Family. I have to make them understand the gravity of my situation, of the situation caused by one of their own.

"Thank you," I say. "You may rise." His head lifts as I hold my hand out to Celine. She helps me down off of the dressing dais. The flat sandals of the outfit feel odd, but at least they, too, are comfortable. "Let's be on our way."

The guard nods, and together, Celine and I leave the dressing chambers to make our way into the hallway. The man strides ahead rather than behind or alongside us, but I don't say a word. What little I know of the Bartoli Empire and their culture does not include whether or not his position is one of respect or insult. Celine casts a look at me as we walk, with her steps slightly slower than mine.

Knowing where she comes from and the fact that the House of Ravens is unlike any other House—one made up of fallen nobles and illegitimate children—she acts with far more grace and knowledge than half of the court ladies I knew in the Sunfire Palace. I suspect her original House kept her around before casting her out. Otherwise, she would never know the things she does. Regardless of how she does, though, I find myself grateful for her presence.

Celine and I follow the man into a corridor and down a flight of stone stairs. The closer we draw to the banquet hall, the louder the sound of conversation grows until it's a dull roar in my ears. Once, I was used to this. Once, I felt accustomed to being presented to people, but right now, I would give anything in the world to go back to the forest where it was just Solomon and me in the quiet of nature.

The guard stops well before we do, his longer legs having carried him further ahead. Celine steps back, sliding to the side as he gestures to the solid white oak doors with yet another crest of the Bartoli Royal Family embedded into its surface. My spine stiffens and I lift my head. The crown I was given, slender as it is, feels heavier than ever before. It rests against the top of my head, an awkward trinket.

It's a constant reminder of the fact that here, in Bartoli, I have no power. Even the clothes and crown I wear aren't mine. Merely borrowed. But I'm here for a reason. To make sure that this hollow crown is not the last that sits upon my head.

My heart races in my breast. My throat squeezes until the barest sliver of air can hardly make it down into my lungs. I clutch my hands together in front of me to keep them from shaking. This is it, I realize. The moment I have looked forward to my entire life—the moment I meet my fiancé.

I never expected that it would happen quite like this— in the shadow of his brother's betrayal and my father's death. I find myself different in both body and mind than I had pictured. My insides expand with air, and I feel just as cold as the Bartoli Palace. Empty of emotion save for anger and mounting desperation.

Seemingly ever watchful and knowing, Celine leans forward, her voice dropping as she speaks. "Don't forget," she says. "Start with the Queen, fingers to cheek." I look at her and she offers up a smile, though it, too, seems as stiff as I am. I nod my understanding and return my gaze to the doors, gesturing for the guard to continue.

He steps forward and opens the doors, which I realize are only the first set of two. The second set, however, is already open—allowing me a moment to gaze beyond and into the main hall where the crowd of people—Bartoli nobles—part to make way for my entrance.

Hundreds of eyes turn and lift to where I stand. The sensation of air fluttering over bare flesh reminds me just how unclothed I am. Thankfully, even with the bright red of my gown, there are nobles even far more outlandishly dressed and undressed, depending on how one looks at their attire. My relief is short-lived, however, as a deep voice booms from the other side of the hall.

"It is with great excitement that I present to you our guest of honor, my son's betrothed, Princess Devonry of the Rozentine Kingdom." My stomach cramps as King Florian lifts his meaty fists toward me in a come hither gesture. If there was a singular noble not aware of my presence before, they are now.

As I move toward the center, a figure moves away from the line of faces. As I lift my gaze and meet his, the glow of amethyst-colored eyes tells me exactly who he is. The Rozentine Ambassador. He raises his hand as I pause alongside him.

"Your Highness." He offers his hand. It's been a long time since I've seen him. So long that his appearance rings no bells, but I know that, in the past, I'd been at a ceremony that honored his travel to the Bartoli Empire years before. Even if we're little more than strangers from the same Kingdom, just knowing that someone from my country is alongside me eases the tightness in my chest a bit. I take it as he bows down low over my knuckles, and the movement gives me further opportunity to examine him.

Though he is taller than me, his shoulders are narrow beneath the white and gold suit he wears. His fingers are long as they grip my own, and when he raises back up to meet my eyes, I can see that he's got hints of gray in his ink-black hair. The strips of salt linger at his temples and in the beard that covers the lower half of his face.

"It's an honor to see you again, Your Highness," the Ambassador states. "You likely don't remember me, but I am Lord Byron of House Daemonium."

I don't remember him well, but the purple eyes of House Daemonium are distinct. I nod. "It is a pleasure to see a friendly face here," I say, meaning every word. Even as I resist looking around, I'm distinctly aware of the foreign eyes on me, picking apart every move I make.

"I shall be your escort this evening, Your Highness,"

Lord Byron says, folding my hand over his arm as he turns to stand at my side. "Shall we proceed?"

I know the question is merely a formality. The only answer available is yes, so I merely nod in lieu of a verbal answer and keep my lips pulled into a polite, agreeable smile that I don't actually feel. It would be an insult to refuse now. Not that I would even if I could. No, I have to face the Bartolis. I have to gain their sympathy and their aid. In the end, my life is not the only one that hangs in the balance.

Lord Byron's grip is gentle, almost too loose, as he leads me further down the banquet hall between the twin lines of Bartoli nobles. I keep my head high, focusing on the steps in front of me rather than the rapid pace of my heart as it threatens to burst from my ribcage. Though I want to, I don't glance back. Yet, still, I can sense Celine's familiar presence and her gaze upon my back.

Instead, I scan the room as I walk, searching for a particular pair of blood-red eyes. Seconds tick by and I worry that I've already passed him. Then, finally, I see a familiar gaze of crimson amidst the crowd. Somehow, just glimpsing them as I stride through the hall is enough to give me strength. Solomon and Argyle each drop into deep bows as Lord Byron marches me past them and right up to the head dais at the very back of the hall.

Queen Helena's outstretched hand awaits. Her rings sparkle under the light of several large sconces on either side of the room. Trying to find the balance between a firm touch and a gentle one, I take her hand and press her fingers to my cheek. Her skin is ice cold against my own. Those soft features of hers remain impassive even when I move on to the King.

King Florian smiles at me through our brief interaction, though I struggle to find the same warmth in the dark depths of his eyes. Sweat gathers in my palms and heat courses through my veins as I finally stop to stand before my betrothed. Prince Enver looks much like his mother. Brown eyes rimmed with thick lashes, a rounder face giving him the appearance of boyhood, though the shadow of a beard trails his jaw. Strands of onyx hair fall over his eyes as he leans forward. I take his hand pressing his fingers to my cheek.

"It is so lovely to finally meet you, Princess Devonry. You look stunning." He nods before his hand finds mine. "Shall we?"

A nervous laugh bubbles out of me. Prince Enver only smiles wider, leading me toward the dais steps and up to his side. He turns me toward the crowd and interlaces our fingers. His touch is smooth, soft, and blatantly clear of calluses. So much different than Solomon's.

"Tonight," Prince Enver holds up our joined hands, "we feast to the promise of our allied nations. We lift our glasses to my soon-to-be bride and the mother of our future King."

Those gathered raise their glasses, several letting out a cheer. I scan the crowd finding more available flesh than I'd ever seen before. My attention settles back on my guard. His lips are pursed with new vigor and those crimson eyes are locked on the Prince and me. He downs the last of the contents of his glass, murmuring to Argyle. I wish I was good at reading lips.

Heat burns up my neck to settle on my cheeks. I turn my attention to Enver, forcing myself to appear grateful. The Prince drops my hand only to pull my chair back for me. I tuck the assortment of fabric under me, adjusting it to hide what skin I can as I lower myself.

"I hope your recent submersion into our culture hasn't been too terrible for you, Princess," Enver starts, taking his own seat and finding his waiting glass of wine. "I'm sure it's much different than learning about our customs from books."

"It is." I lift my gaze to his warm caramel eyes, close enough now to see the dark ring of black that circles his irises. "But oh so beautiful. Everywhere I look, there's something splendid to entertain my attention."

He tips his head to the side, eyes dancing from my lips to my eyes. "I don't think I've ever found something as splendid to hold my attention until now."

"You flatter me." My smile starts to fall, but I force it back up.

Shouldn't my heart be skipping a beat? Where is the flutter of my stomach?

Enver leans close, his voice dropping into a deep whisper. "I aim to." The low chatter that fills the room as guests find their seats nearly swallows up his words and I have to look away.

Settling at the end of the table farthest from me, Argyle and Solomon watch us. The distance creates a growing unease low in my belly; the sensation only furthers when a woman draped in sheer white fabrics hurries into the spot left empty at Solomon's side. His eyes widen and his mouth curls as she leans into him, whispering something that causes his face to turn a dark shade of red.

Servants flood the room with plates overflowing with steaming food to set before us. Several gold forks, knives, and spoons wait on either side of my plate glistening in the flickering light. I stare at them, remembering all the times I've eaten half-cooked meat with my bare hands since my coming-of-age party.

It's Enver who fills the silence. "We have the finest chefs in all of Bartoli. Make sure you try the gravy." He points his fork at the small bowl next to the lamb.

"Of course." I blink at the yellow mixture.

Music picks up somewhere in the room, a reedy sound blown through a long tube of a strange instrument that lilts up and down in tone, something unfamiliar that reminds me of what snake charmers in markets might use. The musician stands at the entrance, women entering at his side and surrounding the guests. Small scraps of material cover their breasts, and an even smaller piece hangs between their legs. I feel my mouth go slack as the women's hips begin to twitch, and their stomachs roll in time with the music. Several shake their arms, creating soft jingling sounds from the charms on their wrists. They run their fingers over the shoulders of guests and writhe to the beat of the music. The Bartoli citizens clap and cheer, shouting louder when the women fall into their laps.

No amount of studying about Bartoli customs could have ever prepared me for this.

Prince Enver chuckles. "Yes, the dancers are quite a sight to see. I tried to tell my father they weren't necessary tonight because nothing could outshine you, but he insisted we dazzle our guests with our finest entertainment."

The strong scent of a rose soap momentarily drowns out everything else when Enver casually drapes his arm over the back of my seat and leans close; it's not an unpleasant scent, but it is strong and heavy. "I hear the Rozentine people are quite adept at entertainment, Princess," he says with a grin. "I've heard there's a special dance—something to do with a sword and fire."

His eyes connect with mine, direct and probing. A sinking feeling weighs down my gut. "Yes." I straighten.

"It's a ceremonial dance meant to bring great honor to the Goddess Aerea."

He nods and places his hand on the table in front of us, trapping me in my seat as he bends even closer toward me. My spine presses into the back of the chair as I feel his arm over my head. "The Royals of Rozentine are said to be descended from that Goddess, yes?"

"That's correct." I'm acutely aware of our nearness and more and more bothered by it than I ever thought I would be. I turn my head away, seeking out someone nearby to save me from this discomfort. Before I can find anyone, however, King Florian speaks.

"Entertainment and dancing is one of the best ways to honor the Gods." As he speaks, his words slur slightly. "Someone should show us this dance!"

For the first time, the Queen's face peers past the King and Prince. Her thin lips twist into a smirk that lifts her otherwise stoic features. "I agree," she says. "Princess Devonry, I would personally *love* to see something of your culture. It's been many years, but there was a time I once visited Rozentine before I was Queen, and I was able to see —I believe it was your mother, the Saintess—perform your little fire dance."

Little fire dance? The insult burns into my chest. The tradition of that dance is monumental, spanning back centuries. It had taken years of practice with my mother and then even more once she'd been gone to even come close to perfecting it.

Appearing completely unaware of my mounting irritation, the Queen continues. "It was quite the spectacle, if I remember correctly. The Saintess was a powerful young thing then, with all that fire, though I heard she refused to use it even in defense. Please give a demonstration to our court how you honor your Gods."

She's doing it on purpose, I suspect. Her words are little digs and barbed spikes cutting past my polite façade. When I smile her way, it's all teeth and venom. "I don't think—"

"Yes!" Enver agrees, removing his hands from the table and my seat to clap them together so that several heads below the dais turn our way. Heat steals across my cheeks, burning hotter with each passing second. "Showing us the ceremonial dance of Rozentine would be the perfect welcome into our country." He turns to me and my muscles tighten across my back as his fingers drift over the bare skin of my shoulder. Thankfully, since he doesn't seem put off, I must manage to maintain my calm disposition.

I set my fork against my plate with a bit more force than necessary and it falls with a violent *clunk*. "I don't think that would be appropriate."

"If anything, this is the most appropriate time!" King Florian bellows. His voice echoes across the room, causing several more conversations to stall or stop altogether. More attention shifts to the head table, everyone watching on with interest.

Something vicious and wicked curls around my throat, squeezing the air from my lungs as I lift my head and look out over the crowd. A familiar pair of red eyes meet mine. Solomon is watching us—me. I can feel the warm, tingling sensation of his attention on my face. Even though the Bartolis have seemingly, intentionally, called more attention to our conversation, there are still a few women dancing suggestively across the banquet hall.

Even as Enver's body heat lingers around me, I can't pull my eyes from Solomon's. Not until one of the dancing women moves close enough to flick him with the edge of a feathered wrap. His face twists in disgust before evening out once more. I try not to look too deeply into the relief that fills me at his reaction to the woman.

"Please, *Princess*. I would be so honored to witness just a taste of your family's famous abilities," Enver says, whispering the words into my ear as he reminds me of his presence.

Abilities. What confidence have I for standing before these people as little more than their next source of entertainment wavers? Born with the power of Aerea in my very veins, yet what do I have to show for it? An inkling of her flame? A warmth in my body? What little I have, I have even less control of.

"The fire dance is traditional," I say evenly. "It is meant for ceremony, not entertainment."

"This *is* a ceremony of welcome," the Queen replies. "We insist." I cut my eyes toward her and she smirks again as if knowing that a mere refusal to their request will put me in an even deeper corner than I've already been backed against.

"Come, come, Princess. Grace us with your talents." Florian waves a hand over the crowd. Without waiting for another word from me, Prince Enver stands and offers me his hand. "The Princess would like to share with us a dance of her people!" King Florian calls out.

Fingers trembling with barely repressed rage and indignity, I can't decline this request now that they've drawn so much of the banquet's attention. Plastering a cordial smile on my face, I rise with Enver's urging and move down the dais.

Taking the movement as an opportunity to glance at where Solomon stands, I notice that even Argyle's expression is wide-eyed with shock. And Solomon … Solo looks as if he might jump from the table and rip the royal family to shreds at any moment. Yes, he understands—even if no one else in this room does—how disrespectful the Bartolis' demands are.

To them, it appears, I am little more than a dancing monkey meant to entertain. *Well, fine,* I think to myself. I shall entertain them. Captivate them. Beguile them. If I have to play this part, then I will ensure that there can be nothing except awe and enthrallment left at the end.

5
DEVONRY

The attention of the crowd gathered within the banquet hall burns into my exposed skin. With slow, careful movements, I remove the wrap that covers me and hand it to a servant who steps forward to take it. Without it, I feel more exposed, but such is expected in the traditional form of this dance—the clothes are not the focus. I pivot my body until I face the crowd. Glancing down into my empty hands, I frown when I realize a piece is missing. I can't perform this dance without the most essential prop.

Twisting back to Prince Enver, I bow slightly, clenching my hands into fists as I force the words to come out in a respectful tone rather than one of irritation. "If you will allow me to make a request," I say. "I require a certain item to perform this dance."

"What is that?" he asks.

I lift my head. "A sword." Not just any sword, either. "May I ask my guard to allow me the use of his?"

Prince Enver looks to his father and the King nods his acquiescence, appearing very much red-faced and intrigued. I wonder if this is how others felt when they bowed before my father. I should hope not. This obvious symbol of my lack of power leaves my insides churning with humiliation. But I swallow it down. I'll do this and far more if it means gaining the aid I seek.

Once I've been given permission, I scan the crowd again for Solomon. There's no need to search for long. Solomon makes his way out from the gathering of onlookers. His red gaze bores into me as I step toward him, moving across the cold tiled floor. Nervousness steals into my veins, but I shove it down. As angry as I am and as frustrated by the Bartolis' lack of respect for not only me but my culture, if this is something I must do, then, at the very least, I will do it with a piece of him in my hands.

"My Queen." Before everyone, Solomon goes to his knee, bowing his head as he reminds everyone in the room that I am no longer the Princess they've continued to call me, but I am the rightful Queen of Rozentine. I am a royal like those sitting upon their dais, watching on as curious as everyone else.

"Solomon." I hold my hand out. "May I please borrow your sword?" He reaches down to his side, untying the band that holds the sheath of his sword before he presents it to me, holding it flat in both palms raised above his head as his eyes remain downcast.

Why, I wonder, did it used to feel so good to see him bowing before me? Now, it feels *wrong*. My childish smugness and pride are gone. In its place is the desire of a woman to see the man whom she has relied on for survival, for connection, for aid, to be recognized for his achievements. His accomplishments. I did not save myself from Nasir's clutches. *He did.*

"Whatever I possess is yours to claim," Solomon says as he offers up his sword to me. "From my blood to my life, my Queen, both I and my blade exist solely for you."

My tongue thickens, swelling inside my mouth as all of the saliva I possess evaporates in a sudden burst. My gut churns as I stare down at him, Solomon's dark head bent down low enough that I can see the vulnerable backside of his neck. It is a sign of trust; to bend so far for one's master. Even though I knew I would someday stand above him like this, I'd never expected how easy it would seem to him to take to his knee before me in front of so many. Somehow, through the riot of my emotions, I manage to reach for his sheathed blade and remove it from his hands.

"Thank you, my Lord," I reply, forcing the words out, "for your allegiance and continued loyalty to the Rozentine Crown."

"To you." His response stops me when I mean to step back and release him. Solomon's head lifts and his gaze connects with mine. "My allegiance and loyalty will always be to you." A soft pause lingers between us and a moment later, he finishes with a quiet, "My Queen."

I don't know what to say to that, so I say nothing at all and after a beat of silence, Solomon breaks the strange spell he's woven over me. He lifts back to his feet, towering over both me and the majority of the Bartoli nobles in attendance. It's quite obvious, too, as he strides back to where he'd been standing before that he's captured the interest of several more women in attendance than those who'd already shown interest. As if he didn't already stand out enough.

My chest tightens into an unusual coil that winds around and around until an aching pain begins to form. With the flat of my palm, I rub against the place between my breasts, trying to ease the strange sensation to no avail.

"I look forward to seeing your performance, my love," Prince Enver calls from behind me.

My love? I turn back to him with narrowed eyes but say

nothing as I unsheathe the sword and hold it up. The flat, slightly curved metal gleams beneath the glowing lights of hundreds of candles lit and descended from above in the chandeliers that hang above our heads. A pair of familiar blue eyes reflect back at me on the surface of the weapon. The blue swirls like dark oceans and then flashes bright gold for a singular moment as I feel the pain in my chest quickly turn sharp and then fade away. I blink, and the color disperses as if it was never there.

Sweat gathers at the low hollow of my back as I set the sheath within the waiting servant's hands. They quickly take it and back away as I stride forward, right into the center of the banquet hall. The heat of the burning gazes settles over my flesh. The once stagnant air in the room seems to disappear as whispers cease and breathing comes to a standstill.

A fresh hush falls over the crowd. My fingers twist around the hilt of Solomon's sword as the musician strikes up a harmonic timbre, filling the otherwise silent room. I can dance to any song if needed, but thankfully, the musician keeps the tone simple and smooth. It begins slow, and I turn, cutting through the air in front of me with the blade as I follow the rhythm.

My eyes slide shut at the hovering note of a bow being drawn across a string echoes up my spine and through my skull. The reverberations move into my limbs and down more, to the metal in my grasp. The blade swipes back and forth, the handle turning over my knuckles as I spin it with the movements of my body.

My hips sway from side to side. Silver white spots flash behind my eyes, molding into gold sparks. I open my eyes, my lashes lifting to see nothing before me but a cloud of white. Distantly, I know I haven't moved far. I'm still in the banquet hall, surrounded by foreigners—unknowing yet if they are enemies or allies. But here, at this moment, this dance of my people becomes more than a silly little taunt from the Bartolis.

The music grows louder—the drag of the notes echoing longer. I twist and spin. Feet pressing into the ground beneath me, toes curving down as I lift my heels and turn. One leg arches into the air, skirts sliding along my calves as I allow my body to take command.

Hollow voices—both male and female—hum in my ears. *Strange,* I think. *There were no lyricists before.* But these voices don't make words, only sounds. Softly, at first, then louder as the seconds tick past. The tune of their vocal chords pull tight, urging me to move faster.

Ironically, despite my earlier reservations, the lack of fabric twisting around my legs makes the flow of my movements that much easier. It's simple, I find, to allow myself the space to breathe and move as my limbs want to. The room is fading away, and the rapt attention of eyes on my flesh goes with it. Until it's just me and the dance and the sword.

My bones ache and sing with each step I take. The hilt of the sword burns hot in my grasp. Light wars against a darkness that festers inside of me. Anger, intimate and seething. The humiliation of being forced to perform, to act as a jewel upon display for these people, swells in my breast. This is nothing but a mockery made of the Rozentine culture.

I clench my teeth, forcing myself to continue when all I'd rather do is take this blade in my hand and swipe it across the necks of those who might be leaning too close as they gape and gawk at me. As if I am little more than an animal meant for their pleasure.

Calm, a voice inside of me warns. My steps stutter at

the shock of the unfamiliar, feminine tone. It's not mine. Yet, it feels familiar.

Thankfully, despite the almost stumble, I manage to evade falling and instead turn the movement into yet another turn in the dance. I blink and the fog around me disperses, revealing empty eyes all watching me.

Around and around, I go. I strain my ears, trying to catch that voice once more. For a long while, I swear I must have imagined it.

I focus on the sword in my hand. It's heavy, the hilt thick, but the blade thin. A veritable weight that drags me into a slower movement than I want to have. Its sharp edge cuts through the air—one way and then another. Up and down. Side to side. It's sharp, glistening under the flickering candlelight. This sword is unassuming to the untrained eye—a piece of beautiful artwork that could slaughter thousands. Much like its owner.

Solomon. Solo. Powerful. Strong. My weapon. My guard.

My bones tremble as I slam my foot down hard and lift the other high into the sky, splitting my legs apart as I twist and turn in time with the rising crescendo of the song. My gaze is so trained on the silver flash of the sword's metal that it takes several moments and more than a few gasps from the crowd for me to realize that the sparks flickering in the edges of my vision aren't the candles.

A haze of gold and red licks up my calves and thighs, surrounding me. The heat is real. The fire in my mind has somehow come to life. My breath stutters to a halt in my chest, but before I can drop the sword and scream as flames consume my body, the voice comes back.

Keep going, daughter mine.

An invisible hand pushes me, forcing me to move. Faster than before, I turn and spin, taking step after step as

I twist my head from left to right, searching for the owner of the voice.

I see nothing and no one save for the shocked faces of the Bartolis and their nobles. The flames take on new life and instead of following me, I find myself trailing behind them with each sway and movement. Tears burn at the backs of my eyes.

It's real. My heart shudders. The Awakening is real. If only my father could have seen this. Pain slices through my chest as real as if the blade in my hand had pierced my heart, but no blood flows down. I blink back the tears, and that invisible hand from earlier comes back—soft fingertips brushing across my cheek as if to soothe my agony.

The unseen presence remains with me, at my side, for the duration of the dance. Until my thighs shake with strain and sweat coats my skin from fingertip to face. The music gradually stops, and as it does, so do I. The sword comes down hard, the tip slamming into the floor so harshly that a crack forms within the white tile.

The flames disperse and panting, sweating, I lift my gaze to Prince Enver. I don't have to look in a mirror to know that my eyes are not kind. They are accusatory. I swear it, now, as silently as I watched my father's death—if he or his family had anything to do with Nasir's betrayal, I shall kill him, *them*, myself.

And I shall leave the regret to those who have the luxury.

No, my daughter, the voice says, brushing her hand over my shoulder. *Not now. Soon, you will have to make the choice—a choice of sacrifice—but not now.*

A part of me longs to believe it is my mother's voice in my head, but something tells me it's not. Something inside of me says it's grander, more powerful. The voice and her words are of a stronger essence.

For a brief moment, as the last note of the stringed instrument filters over the air, there is nothing but silence and heat. Then, slowly, the crowd begins to clap.

The sound of applause grows louder and panting, I take the sword in hand, removing it from the crack it formed and lowering it back to my side, my grip tightening as Prince Enver approaches. Even as he does, I turn my head to the side, gaze seeking. Solomon meets my eyes and moves, easily slipping through the crowd like water finding any available crack. His massive frame taking up as much space as possible between them, like a ship cutting through thin waters.

"That was beautiful," Prince Enver says, recapturing my attention as he comes to a standstill.

"I hope you were pleased by it, Your Highness," I say, bending my head slightly before lifting back up. Try as I might, no smile comes to my lips. The dance, though liberating in its own way, serves as a reminder of all I've lost. "Perhaps, now, you'll give me leave to speak with you about more important matters."

The dark curls at the sides of his temples shift as Prince Enver throws his head back and laughs. The sound hurts my ears and I wince as it pierces through the air. A shadow falls over my side and I don't have to look to know that Solomon is there. Looking at the face of my betrothed, Enver's features are angular. Somewhat similar to Nasir, although still different enough. Compared to Solomon, however, he appears far less imposing. Skinny in comparison despite the light definition of the muscles in his arms and chest revealed by his clothing.

"All in due time, Princess Devonry," Enver says as he reaches out, offering his hand.

All in due time? I stiffen. *Is that the Bartoli fucking motto?* My upper lip curls back and my palm tightens on the sword still in my hand. As if he senses my rising anger, Solomon reaches out and captures my wrist.

"My sword, Your Highness," he says, reminding me that I'm still holding onto it in the presence of another royal. A silent threat. "Shall I take it back?"

Enver's eyes brighten upon where Solomon's hand is on me and before I can open my mouth and say anything, he steps forward—deftly cutting between us in a way that forces Solo to release me or risk touching the Prince.

"It would do you well to remember that you aren't to touch a royal without permission, Lord Solomon," Enver states as his fingers drift down my side.

The creeping feeling of his touch distracts me from the meaning behind his words. My brow puckers, but I don't resist as he takes the sword from me and offers it back to Solomon. Just as Solo reaches to take it, however, Enver's fingers part from the handle, and the sword drops—clattering to the ground between them.

The shock of the insult takes a moment to penetrate my mind. Solo, for his part, though, doesn't react. His face remains unchanged as he stares back at Enver. "My apologies, My Lord," Enver says casually. "My hands must have been too weak to hold such a barbaric weapon."

His hands are too weak? But mine aren't? I grit my teeth as tense silence spreads through the space between the three of us. My chest rises and falls. I can't say anything because I fear if I do, I'll do something I'll regret … perhaps even strike this pompous ass of a Prince.

"No apologies necessary, Your Highness," Solomon replies smoothly. When he shifts his attention slightly to me, my heart reacts to the dead look in his eyes. It's as if he's stepped back in time and become the same boy he was when he first returned from battle. Ice practically drips from his tone. "I'm sure any man near my Princess would be nervous. Sweaty palms are to be expected and weakness is nothing to be ashamed of."

Prince Enver's jaw clenches at Solomon's words, but it's only what he deserves. It doesn't escape my notice either though, that he said 'my' princess as if I'm something only he can claim ownership of. That small word should not heat my insides the way that it does.

Enver harrumphs and turns back to me, effectively dismissing Solo as he bends to pick up the sword. "Come along, darling," he says, sliding his hand along my arm and hooking my palm around his spindly forearm. "Let's return to the dais. The King and Queen would love to express their pleasure at your dance."

Pleasure? I tip my head back. Even knowing that I have no right to refuse, a sinister, vile desire blossoms within me. No wonder, I think. The House of Ravens must see all royals the same. They must see us as I now see the Bartolis —childish, unintentionally cruel, and more than anything else, selfish.

Enver tugs me with him as the servant from earlier appears, handing him the sword's sheath. Like it or not, this world is full of status and Solomon and I are on two separate levels. Whereas he can remain here on the ground, I must follow the steps and rise to the top … if only to protect those beneath me.

6

SOLOMON

My gaze bores into Devonry and Prince Enver. A wicked creature awakens within my chest, swallowing all of my logic. I don't like it. His eyes on her. Him touching her. I don't like any of this. The crowd. The fanfare. The way she's practically on display for the crowd of Bartoli nobles.

The beast within me growls in agreement. If it were left up to us, Devonry wouldn't have to worry about any of this. She'd be sequestered away somewhere. Her very presence is not meant for the eyes of those who can't even appreciate the Goddess standing before them. I want her to be mine and mine alone.

Jealousy is a rather ugly creature, but at least it knows my true desires.

Argyle moves to my side as I take my place back within the crowd. He's practically buzzing with energy as he flicks his gaze back and forth from me to the Princess. The cutting insult from a man such as him bites into my pride. I may not be a royal or a prince, but at the very fucking least, I'm not a man who ignored his betrothed until she was *forced* to make the trek to his country because of his brother's betrayal.

"Careful there, any longer, and the Princess' face might burst into flames from how sharp your glare is."

I cut my eyes back to my friend at his words. Argyle's face is twisted into a mask of amusement. "You saw what I saw," I say. "She's definitely Awakened."

"That she is," Argyle agrees with a nod before he, too, turns to gaze up at where Devonry sits on the dais next to Prince Enver. Her brow is puckered and I have no doubt she is attempting to speak to him on behalf of Rozentine, but it appears that neither he nor the King and Queen of Bartoli have any interest in discussing the actions of their youngest Prince.

Why would they? If things play out in their favor, they still maintain the possession of Rozentine—regardless of which Prince Devonry marries. *This was a terrible idea,* I realize belatedly, *coming here.* If they refuse to help us or send aid to Rozentine, what else are we to do?

"People are talking," Argyle says, his gaze scanning the room as the roar of the crowd ebbs and flows. There's so much stimulation, it's making me a little dizzy. The music. The dancing. The laughter. I could hardly stand the celebrations and balls back in the Sunfire Palace, but at least there, I'd felt at home. Here, we are like strange artwork displayed in a roadside entertainment booth. "I suppose the rumors that the Princess was unawakened will be replaced by the rumors that she is, in fact, Awakened now."

"Do you think…" I hesitate to say the words even though there is a cruel hope blossoming in my chest.

The burn of Argyle's attention touches the side of my face, but I refuse to look at him. No, my sole focus is on the woman on the dais. Her blonde hair is slightly redder than it was when she first walked in. While it could have been because of the dye before, now I know that it's more likely a sign of her increasing powers. Now that the goddess Aerea has graced her, she will change more and more. Maybe, if the Gods are merciful, she will realize, too, who I am to her. Who we are to each other.

"She will need training," Argyle says, not bothering to help me finish my earlier question. "Her power will be potent, especially because of which house she comes from."

I look at him. "Are you offering yourself up for the position?" I ask.

He snorts. "I believe you are more suited to be around the Princess," he says.

"You have more experience," I remind him.

His smirk falls as he realizes I'm serious. "You are the Gods damned Blood General, Solomon," he says, pivoting so that his back is to the crowd. "Don't tell me you are frightened by a small woman."

"She is not just any woman," I reply, gritting my teeth. "She is—" My everything. The mate that my soul cries for. I clear my throat and start again. "It takes a certain level of objectivity to train a newly Awakened."

Argyle curses beneath his breath. "You cannot be serious. You want *me* to train a Princess? Not just any Princess, but the future Queen of Rozentine?"

"She needs to be trained sooner rather than later," I continue. "You're right, her powers will be strong. If they get out of control…" I don't think I need to explain to him the dangers of an untrained Awakened. If anyone knows the consequences of an Awakened with no knowledge of how to control their abilities, it's Argyle. He's trained enough of the House of Ravens to know that the kind of accidents an Awakened can cause are almost always bloody.

"Fuck." Argyle scrubs a hand down his face before cutting a dark glare my way. "You are the most aggravating son of a bitch, you know that?"

Despite their insult, I straighten my shoulders and find my mood slightly improved by those words. My lips curl up slightly. "Ugh." Argyle scoffs. "You're proud of that, aren't you, you bastard."

"Shall I take that to mean you'll do it?" I inquire.

"Fuck you." In the language of Argyle, I take that as a 'yes,' though an unhappy one. Regardless, it's what I wanted and it's what *she* needs.

The banquet drags on, and the later it grows, the more I take to the shadows and sidelines, playing the observer. Argyle ambles away, distracted by the woman who has trailed us from Carrion City. Celine, though polite and obviously loyal to Devonry, appears much less impressed by Argyle and his attentions than the other ladies in the crowd.

"My Lord?" I close my eyes as the scent of peonies nearly overwhelms my already sensitive nostrils. When I reopen them, the sight of Argyle and Celine is disrupted by a woman with fluttering lashes and a pink feathered fan swishing back and forth before her face, wafting more of that sickeningly sweet scent into mine.

"What?" I bark as I turn my head to alleviate the stench.

She pauses as if confused by my sharp tone, but if that was enough to ward her off, then she wouldn't have approached me to begin with. The fluttering and swishing start back up, slightly faster and more annoying than before.

"This is the first time that we've had more Rozentine

citizens visit us in our court," she says. "Certainly no one as … warrior-like has ever graced our side before."

"House Daemonium are just as warrior-like, my lady," I force the words out through clenched teeth, trying not to breathe even as I shift and turn my gaze back to the dais. Blinking as I spot the empty seat next to Prince Enver, my heart jerks within my chest.

"Oh, but Lord Byron is not as large as you are," the woman says, a sigh in her voice. She reaches out as if she means to touch me. Without thought, I grab her hand, stopping the movement and causing her to jump in surprise. "Oh my, your hand is as big as a bear's paw!" she exclaims.

With a scowl, I toss her hand to the side and turn away. "Excuse me," I say, not offering any further justification for my departure. All I know is that if I do not get away from her heavy perfume, I may vomit. Instead, I go in hunt of my charge.

The lights of the banquet hall have dimmed as the night has dragged on and there are darkened corners now filled with couples in various forms of embrace. Argyle hadn't been joking when he'd said that the Bartoli court is freer with their expectations of people. Soft, muffled cries lilt over my ears, churning my blood as I search for Devonry.

The fires of her dance, the way the flames had curled around her limbs—sliding along her flesh—reappear in my mind. Amid her performance, I'd found myself more entranced than ever before. I'd imagined that it was my arms around her, grasping her waist and lifting her into a circle. I'd craved the feeling of her flesh against mine. Unlike the woman from before, Devonry's scent is never overwhelming. Right now, I find myself craving it.

The sparkle of gold catches my eyes as I bypass a pair

of glass doors half-cloaked in thick heavy curtains. I pause and peer through the windows. Even with her back to me, I can tell that I've found my goddess. Turning my cheek, I stop a passing servant and grab two glasses from his tray before gesturing him on his way.

Wrong though it may be, there is a wish in my heart that clings to my mind. Now that she is Awakened … maybe, just fucking maybe she will know the truth.

DEVONRY

The air is thicker outside than it had been in the banquet hall, but somehow, it's easier to breathe. I lift my face to the sky and take in the fresh sights before me. Behind me, the Bartoli musicians play a jovial tune as the nobles and their partners dance and drink with merriment. I never thought I'd be disgusted by something that used to be so normal to me.

Now, I can't help but wonder about my home. Is Sheza okay? Is she still alive? What of the others still within the walls of the Sunfire Palace? Or the citizens of Rozentine? Lord Ahren and Lady Marjorie? Lord Frederic.

Each passing second fills me with an anxiety that is so fresh that it overwhelms me with fear. What if I fail? I look down at my hands, turning them over so my palms are facing upward. If I'm really Awakened, does that mean that Aerea has finally recognized me as her heir? After everything that I've lost and been unable to protect, how can she?

The sound of light-hearted conversation and the fresh notes of music lilting through the air alert me to an intruder during my solitude. I curl my fingers into my palms before dropping them to my sides and turning to greet whoever it is with a fake smile plastered to my face. The second I see who it is, however, my shoulders slump and the smile drops. Solomon's ruby gaze meets mine as he lifts his chin and then closes the door behind him, letting it snick shut. The sound isn't cut off, but it is muffled slightly.

"You know it's not appropriate for a noblewoman to be alone with a nobleman without a chaperone," I say sharply.

He arches a brow before taking a step away from the doors. "We're not in Rozentine anymore, Princess," he replies, "and I don't know if you've noticed, but I don't think the Bartolians are as reserved as we are."

My eyes move past him to the people beyond the glass doors. He's right about that. The amount of flesh and outright sexual tension that filled that room was damn near suffocating. Though a part of me admires them for their freeness, I am simply not accustomed to it. Finally, I turn my attention back to the man who's now walking toward me, and more directly, on the twin flutes of bubbly liquid held together in one of his hands.

"I thought you could use a little liquid relaxant," Solomon says as he offers the drink to me. I take it without hesitation. Alcohol used to simply be a means of amusement in Rozentine, but now, it feels like so much more. It's dangerous to let myself use it in this way, but I can't stop myself. I need a distraction, a dulling of my senses, something to take the edge of the world off.

"How is it," I start, "that despite your dislike of me, you still always seem to know what I need?" Putting the rim of the glass to my lips, I tip my head and drink.

"I don't dislike you."

Choking as the bubbly alcohol somehow tries to follow

the wrong path up my nostrils instead of down my throat, I jerk my head back down at Solomon's words. "What in the world do you mean?" I snap, coughing. "Of course you do. You've been an absolute monster to be around ever since you returned from battle years ago. It's like you went away my friend and returned a cold…"

As I speak, Solomon draws closer and closer. Each step brings him toward me and as he dips his head to keep his gaze on mine, it shadows his features until all I can see are the clear glowing depths of the twin pools of his bloody irises. My words seem to swallow themselves, captured by the wind as they drift away. Silence falls between us. Tense, cool silence that I've become all too familiar with but until this moment has never felt quite this heavy.

My chest rises and falls and I am imperceptibly aware of each breath I take. My sight is filled with him as my back meets the half-circle of a stone railing that encloses the balcony. "S-Solo?"

"I have never once *disliked* you, Devonry," he states. "You have been the sole reason for my existence from the very moment we met. Before I ever became your guard, I have been yours. Dislike? That was never possible. Not from me. Certainly not *for* you."

Little tingles of heat creep up along my bare arms. Across my stomach. Down my legs, where the skirts of my dress split open. I tighten my fingers on the glass in my hand and then, before I can think better of it, I throw back the last of the alcohol in it and set it on the edge of the railing before reaching for Solomon's glass as well. With an enigmatic expression that I can't decipher, he allows me to take the second glass, and that, too, I drink.

Once I'm done, I feel a flush of heat in my face, but I'm not quite as uncomfortable as I was. With how little I've had to eat since we arrived, the alcohol works quickly. I go to set the second glass next to the first but accidentally push it too far and send both over the edge and into the darkness below.

"Oh!" I reach out, but Solomon stops me, capturing my hand as the sound of glass shattering on the stone ground below the balcony echoes back up to meet our ears.

"I..." More heat fills me. "I didn't mean to do that," I say, the confession slipping free.

"I know." The deep rumble of his words slides along my spine. He's so close—too close. I can't think when he's touching me. I tug my hand back, but his fingers close down harder on mine, refusing to free me.

"Solomon..." Turning my head, I look up at him. "Why are you out here?"

"You've Awakened," he says as if that explains every-thing when it doesn't. Not to me.

"Yes?" I continue to look at him, waiting, but he says nothing more. Instead, he turns his gaze to where we're connected by our hands. His fingers loosen their hold as he twines them together with mine. Heat encompasses me, surrounding me and burrowing beneath my skin and it all connects back to where our skin touches.

I follow his gaze. His hand engulfs my tiny palm easily. Yet, despite the scars that litter the backs of his knuckles and up his forearm, I trust these hands. I trust *him*. Implic-itly. His gaze and mine have fallen on the same thing. Our hands clasped together. It's like two pieces of a very old puzzle have been placed together, their parts fitting right into the perfect grooves.

My chest tightens once more—that strange feeling coming back. A yearning I don't want to admit is as familiar to me as breathing. It's like all of the feelings I had for him when I was a child have resurfaced, as if they've been waiting for the chance to see him again. My head is a mass of flames and confusion. When Solomon finally speaks, it's to ask me a question. "Do you feel any different?"

"Different, how?" I reply.

"Do you feel any … desires you didn't before?"

Frowning, I turn to meet him, tugging harder until he's forced to release my hand and we're finally back face to face with my back against the railing and his chest nearly pressing into my own. "I don't know what kind of desires you're referring to, but it's inapprop—"

"There are always conditions to the powers gifted by the gods," he interrupts me.

"Conditions?" I repeat.

Once again, I find my hand captured by his, and this time, instead of twining our fingers together, he lifts my palm to his face. I frown as he turns it over and then gently eases my wrist to his mouth. A gasp leaves me as a sharp prick scratches along my flesh. There's a pulse within my chest, my heartbeat leaping against the prison of my insides, wanting out, wanting freedom. Solomon's eyes glow brighter as my gaze falls to the sharp point of his canines as they touch where my pulse beats a rapid cadence.

"Do you know why the House of Blood is named what it is, little Princess?" His words are low, deep. They reverberate through the air between us, a warning and an enticement all at once.

"Each House took on the name given by their ancestral God," I say, my voice barely above a whisper. I can't do much more than that—whisper—because it feels as if all of the air in my lungs has been stolen right from my chest. I'm afraid to know the reason and yet, at the same time, I think I have always known. A deeply rooted truth that I refused to acknowledge for so long. Why? For stupid, childish reasons. Because I was angry. Because I was hurt. Because I was scared that I was wrong.

"And do you know why Levim gifted us with the name of Blood?" Solo presses.

I couldn't tell him my own name right now if he asked. Not with the way his teeth slowly drag back and forth over my sensitive skin and my heart seems to leap with each pass. I shake my head.

Solomon lifts his head slightly and his upper lip pulls back, revealing twin long fangs. Fangs I've seen before. They are part of his Awakened form. As I think that, his body seems to grow larger. He shifts from towering over me to completely encompassing me in his shadow. My back presses harder to the railing and his hips move forward, against my stomach until I swear I can feel something there that has my pulse racing even faster than before.

I think I know what he's suggesting. There have always been rumors, quiet rumblings of the exchange between the Awakened and their Gods. His fangs, the glowing red of his gaze—he's hinting at something, at *his* desire.

"S-Solo." I say his name and then pause with a gulp. Try as I might, I can't stop watching the way his fangs drag along my skin. He never penetrates my flesh, but with each passing second, I start to wonder what it would be like if he did. "W-what are you doing?"

"Each ability gifted by the Gods comes with strings attached, Devonry," Solomon says, not answering my question. "The more you use your abilities, the more you crave something to replenish the energy you've used. There is always a downside to power, a price to be paid. There has not been an Awakened Sunfire since the Saintess Queen and she was gone too soon to teach you."

The mention of my mother makes me stiffen, but he doesn't let me pull away. Solomon reaches up with his other hand and captures my chin, tilting my face up so that I am looking squarely at him. My lips part. The red of his eyes is shifting. The different shades are slithering back and forth over each other like a thousand tiny blood snakes. It's as frightening as it is beautiful.

"I don't have any strange desires." Even as the words escape my lips, I know that I'm lying. I *do* have a strange desire. Right now, the thing I want most in the world is something I should never hunger for. I should turn away from him, demand that he release me from this strange hold, yet I don't.

I *want* to kiss him. I want Solomon Winett to take me in his arms, and I want him to devour my mouth the same way his sword devours the lives of his enemies. My head swims with the alcohol in my system. I sway into his chest. There's no more energy or effort to pull away.

Solomon's head dips down and I feel the heat of his breath upon my face. So close. I close my eyes, waiting…

"You will," he says. I blink my eyes open, frowning as he pulls back. "Eventually, the more you use your abilities, you will start to see changes. I can't help you if I don't know of them. Please keep me informed." His hands leave my skin all too soon and somehow, I find myself colder than before he came out here.

"That's it, then?" I ask, startled as he turns away from me. His back is massive, blocking out the sight of the glass doors that lead back into the banquet hall.

Solomon doesn't answer right away. In fact, he remains quiet for so long that I start to wonder if he ever will or if he'll turn into a statue right there. Finally, when he does speak, he turns his head and looks back. His eyes illuminate, a deeper color than I've ever seen before, gleaming from within. My throat dries up. There's something unnerving in that gaze of his.

More than hunger, it's longing. A voracity that I've never seen in him before. Or perhaps I had and now it's no longer hidden from me. Between my legs, I feel something wet slick down my inner thighs. I press them together as I place a hand over my lower belly. Butterflies awaken within and take flight. My body responds to that look of his, craving something I'm unfamiliar with. Needing something that just isn't possible.

Thoughtlessly, my lips part and my tongue comes out, swiping across the lower one to wet it. A low, rumbling growl sounds, echoing into the dark sky above. I blink. One second, Solomon is standing a few feet away, his back to me even if his head is turned in my direction, and the next…

A shocked gasp is ripped free from my throat as hard hands find my hips, lifting me onto the railing at my back. My ass lands against the stone as a warrior's body finds its way between my legs, pushing them wide so that the skirts part and one leg is entirely bare up to my hip. Solomon covers me from hip to shoulder. His chest pushes against mine as he grips me tightly.

One of his hands leaves my side and comes around, gripping my hair as he pulls my head back. When I stare up at his face, now revealed by the light of the moon, I see him as something different than the man I've come to know. His features are twisted. Darker. His gaze unsettled and clouded over with lust and yearning. I wince as his hold on my hair tightens and he cranes my head back further. His eyes rove downward, over my throat. I swallow, sure that he can sense every pulse of my heart and how fast it's currently racing, but I don't stop him. Even if I wanted to, I don't think I could get the words out.

"I don't dislike you, Devonry Estand." Solomon's words remind me of the start of our conversation. They're gruff, a low thunderous sound coming from his throat. "However you are and always have been my affliction and my addiction. Every piece of you, from your body"—He releases my hip finally and trails his fingers up my stomach in such a light touch that it makes me suck in my belly at the strange sensation. He doesn't stop until he finds my mouth and presses his thumb against my lower lip, pulling it slightly down, revealing my teeth—"To every word that escapes this provoking little mouth, has caused me the worst kind of misery and the most sublime bliss."

Confusion swarms me. "Then ... why?" I whisper. "Why did you change?"

"Everyone changes, love," Solomon replies. "War. Blood. Loss. Battle. It changes a man."

"I thought you hated me," I tell him. "I thought you blamed me."

"A part of me did," he confirms. Tears burn at the backs of my eyes as he confirms that fear. Before a single one can fall, however, he distracts me by tipping my face back even more and forcing me to meet his eyes when I hadn't even realized I'd dropped my attention to his chest. It's so much closer and it hurts my neck to look up at him for so long, even if he is leaning over to make it easier.

"You *are* to blame, Devonry," he says, stabbing my heart with his words. "You are to blame for every damned desire I've ever had since the day you were born. So, this..." He leans down more. "This is your fault."

As the accusation and blame leave his mouth, Solomon covers me completely and his lips come down hard upon my own. Shock fixes me to the spot. His lips are far softer than I expected them to be. I should push him away. I know it. It's inappropriate. It's wrong. We are here, in a country not my own, at a party where my *fiancé* is. I know all of that. Yet, I find myself unable to move. Unable to do anything but reciprocate this kiss.

I close my eyes and lean into his hands. Lightning races through me as with that last barrier gone, I take his kiss and make it my own. All of the anger and exhaustion from the past several weeks boil up and over like a kettle of tea left on the fire for too long.

This kiss is like molten fire, liquid and heated. My lips part as the need for air becomes too much, and his tongue takes advantage. He slithers into my mouth and twines his tongue around my own. The butterflies in my stomach are circling, moving faster and faster as something hot and hard rubs against me.

Cool Bartoli air slides over my bare leg as it arches around his hip and he lowers one hand to the small of my back. *More. More. More.* I shiver and seek him out. My hands creep up along his arms as I kiss Solomon Winett. Our chests are pressed to one another as his lips work against mine. Something curls in my stomach. I feel empty, as if I'm missing a piece of the puzzle.

"Solo." I moan against his mouth, gasping, panting.

"Open for me, Devonry," he says. "Let me taste you."

A whimper escapes my throat. That phrase—let me taste you—niggles at the back of my mind. Reminding me of something, but I'm too distracted now by him to think too hard on it. Solomon pushes my legs wider as one of his creeping hands makes its way over my stomach and then down. He presses the fabric of my dress against the place between my thighs and a sharp bolt of pleasure lances through me.

I cry out, clutching at him as I hold on for dear life. "Solomon!"

"Hush, love," he says. "Not too loud."

I can't help it. It's something I've never felt before. This is … it's… "Solomon, what…" I open my eyes again and gaze up at him in wonder. "What…"

Thick fingers delve beneath my skirts, sliding into the slit at the side, not stopping until they come across the wetness I've been so viscerally aware of. My eyes widen and I jerk my head back, gazing up at him.

"I-I don't know why—" I start to say only to be stopped by Solomon as he kisses me again, swallowing my words.

His fingers, like his tongue, begin to move. Slowly at first, and then faster as each beat passes. Solomon strokes along my entrance with two fingers. Up and down in gentle passes before he stops and pushes them inside. Unconsciously, I tense up, a whine pouring out from between my lips as my muscles clamp down around his digits and my nails sink into his arms.

"Wait." I gasp. "It's too much…"

Solomon doesn't stop, though. He presses forward, sliding his fingers into my channel before withdrawing them. More wetness forms as my face heats to impossible levels. If it were possible to combust simply because a man is putting his fingers inside me, then I would do so now. Unfortunately, I remain completely whole and unshattered as he powers forth and repeats the process.

"It feels strange," I say. "I-I don't know—"

"Does it hurt?" Solomon asks, cutting me off.

I shake my head, pressing my face into his chest as his hand continues moving. It doesn't hurt. It's quite the opposite. There's a bizarre thrill inside of me that's growing. A bubble of pleasure that's quickly filling, swelling larger and larger the further he goes. Tears leak out of the corners of my eyes—a fact I should be ashamed of as I lift my face back to Solomon's, seeking comfort.

Solomon takes my silent plea and acquiesces. His mouth covers mine once more and his tongue presses inside. He kisses me as I ride his hand. That pleasure grows with each stroke and thrust. I must be soaking his fingers, my wetness gathering as it drips down my inner thighs, smearing all over my flesh. One wrong move, and I know I could accidentally go flying off this railing, but Solomon is nothing if not careful. So, I don't care. No matter where I am or what is happening around me, I know he'll protect me.

"You're so tight, love," Solo groans. "Yes, just like that. Did you know your hips are moving in time with my movements?"

I'm moving with a fog over my mind. His words sink into me, but they elicit no reaction other than to seek out his dangerously talented hand more. He nuzzles against the side of my face as I pant, my chest rising and falling in fast movements.

"Come, little Princess," he whispers against my temple. "I want to feel your pussy squeeze around my fingers. There you are … yes, fucking Gods … so fucking tight."

I muffle my cry as the thrill reaches its crescendo and bury my face right into his chest as I stop moving altogether. My body twitches, tightening and releasing as the roll of pleasure sweeps through me. Sweat gathers at the base of my spine and in beads across my chest as I pull away. I shiver as the cold air finally slaps me in the face reminding me of where we are.

Solomon doesn't change as my expression morphs—no doubt showing just how hard I'm crashing back to reality. Instead, he slips his fingers free of my—what had he called it?—pussy, and then lifts them to his face.

Horror descends as I watch with wide eyes as he pulls his fingers, glittering with my wetness in the moonlight, to his face and then sinks them into his mouth. His tongue flicks out, licking between them as he sucks it all off. His eyes burn into me all the while. The ruby irises glow dangerously in a way that sucks my very soul from my body and forces it to collide with his.

Too late. It's far too late.

I blink and the world shifts back.

Solomon's hands are in my hair and he's staring down at me with an enigmatic expression. My thighs press together beneath the skirts of my dress and I feel a telltale sign of wetness leaking down. But Solo's hands are in plain view. They're neither beneath my skirts nor coated in my wetness.

What….?

"Devonry?" His voice is deep and tinged with the lilt of concern.

I return my gaze to his. Had I just … imagined all that? Him with his fingers inside me? The look of utter devotion? I reach back and pry his hand from my hair and lower it to our sides.

"You blame me…" I force myself to speak because I don't know what else to do, and I can't let him know what just went through my head or … how real it felt. "For what, exactly?"

Solomon continues to stare back at me as if he can penetrate my skull with mere intent alone. A shiver slithers up my spine and I cross my arms around my body, hugging myself tight to keep myself from touching him again. I fear if I do, that strange imagining will come back.

"It doesn't matter anymore," Solo finally responds with a shake of his head.

Irritation blossoms in my chest. It doesn't matter? It doesn't fucking matter? Then what was the point in bringing it up in the first place other than to make me feel inferior or like I'd done something to warrant his hatred?

A scowl overtakes me and I jerk away from him. "If you want to blame me for your hatred, then do so at your leisure," I snap. "But we have a job to do here." I turn to go and freeze when I feel his palm on my arm once more.

"Don't do that," he says.

I twist around, deftly pulling myself from his grasp as I feel a bolt of fire skitter beneath my skin where he touched me. *Something's wrong with me. There has to be. Why the hell would I be reacting to him like this?*

"I'm not *doing* anything." I take a step away from him and another and another until I'm as far from him as this balcony will allow.

"You are," he insists, his red gaze darkening. "You're running, Devonry."

I bristle, setting my hand back on the balcony's railing, needing something to keep me grounded in the here and now and not back into that damnable fantasy that had attacked me. There's no way Solomon would do that to me. Even if he doesn't hate me, he certainly can't find me attractive in that way. Can he?

I shake my head. These thoughts are doing me no good. "Then stop pushing, damn it!" I snap out, replying to Solo's accusation. Fire stretches a path beneath my skin, spreading out like rivers flowing into my veins. Anger. Heat. Untapped potential. It's so hard to keep it under control.

"No."

I blink as that one syllable comes out and slaps me in the face. "No?" I repeat the word, feeling it over my tongue and how ... *wrong* it is. I lift my head and gape at him. When had I looked away? I don't remember. But what I do know now, is that my fury is dulled by the shock of his refusal.

Solomon stalks forward, following my footsteps until he stands before me, blocking out the scenery beyond the balcony. Our bodies are so close I can feel his heat and my imagination latches onto it. My limbs grow lax, and I must force my fingers to tighten over my own arms in order to keep them from dropping. No, not again. I won't lose myself to the blur of what isn't real again. This is real. An angry Solomon in front of me, glaring down at me with those twin pools of burning flames.

"I will never stop pushing you, Devonry," he swears. "It's my job to push you."

"Your job is to guard me," I tell him, proud of the way my voice remains steady when it feels like all of the breath has been pulled from my lungs.

His attention is penetrating, and I swear he can see right into my mind—past all of my barriers and into that place where my imagination had taken over. I'd practically felt the two of us … his fingers inside me. His tongue on mine. His desire for me sits between us like a mirage, and I'm not sure if it's just me or if it's real.

"My job, Princess, is to ensure your safety," he says. "To do that, I have to push you—to new depths, to new heights, to places you didn't even know existed. One step could cost you your life and I refuse to let that be a possibility. My job is to push you to be better, to be stronger, to protect yourself because if, Gods forbid, I'm no longer here, I want to ensure that you will survive."

"Survive?" I gape at him. "You act like you might die."

As soon as the words are out, I realize that that's exactly what he means. Solomon *could* die here, in Bartoli, or back in Rozentine. If I live past him, what will that mean for me? Horror fills me and as if he can read my thoughts, Solomon reaches forward and gently pulls my hand from my arm. He holds it up and bends down. His lips hover briefly over my knuckles before he presses a kiss there, the sign of respect to royalty. My breath catches and my heart hammers against my ribcage.

"It is my honor and my purpose," he says quietly, lifting his head, though not his face. "To push you to be what you were meant to be. *My Queen*. I will protect you until my dying breath."

His words are breathed out over my flesh and when he's done, he doesn't spare me a glance as he drops my hand, standing back to his full height, and then turns around and re-enters the party. I'm left standing in hot Bartoli air, feeling like my lungs have been compressed and my soul has been stolen from my very breast.

He was right, I realize. There's no denying it any longer. I *do* have desires and all of them seem to center squarely on the man I thought hated me for years. My desires are focused on none other than Solomon Winett, himself.

8

DEVONRY

For several days after, I walk around the Bartoli Royal Palace trying to find anything and everything to keep me busy or at the very least to keep me from remembering that night on the balcony. I'm given a tour of the Palace grounds by Prince Enver, himself, and meet with the Queen for a rather dull tea time. In both instances, I'd try to broach the topic of Nasir and Rozentine, and both times, I've been quieted by assurances that King Florian will call for me when he has a solution.

Since nothing is getting done, my thoughts instinctively revert to the night of the welcome banquet. What should have been a night of humiliation as I'd played the part of the dancing monkey for the Bartoli Royals had become something different altogether. I hardly recall the dance anymore. The only thing I think of when that night comes to mind is the way Solomon looked at me in the hot air with the moon and horizon at our backs.

Unfortunately, that also means that anytime I see Solomon, himself, those memories return as well. So, anytime I catch sight of him—either in the corridors or in the training courtyard—I find myself fleeing like a scared field mouse.

Finally, on the third day, I decide that enough is enough. Solomon hasn't mentioned what transpired between us. Not the argument, of course, and not my delusional daydream. *That* he, thankfully, remains blissfully unaware of.

After dressing and preparing myself for the day, I stride out into the corridor and follow the sweet scents of a sugared breakfast, certain I'll find a few others in the banquet hall. Now that the welcome party is over, it's been turned into a large dining hall for the nobles of the Palace.

The sound of other footsteps echo down the corridor and my stride falters, eyes sweeping over the polished stone and gold that makes up the Bartoli Royal Palace decor. I pause and look back, half expecting Solomon to appear before me, familiar glowing red eyes and all. It's as if the guilt of having that involuntary fantasy about him is shadowing me.

The footsteps grow closer, louder, and then turn the corner. Instead of the hulking, dark form of my bodyguard, a different face appears around the corner. Dressed in a casually ostentatious suit embroidered with gold filigree, Enver smiles as he turns the corner and looks up to spot me waiting just outside the dining hall. He continues on his path until he's a few feet in front of me and only then does he sweep his arm down into an overly dramatic bow. I simultaneously relax and tense at the same time.

"Darling." Enver smooths a hand over the silken jacket of his suit and straightens. "The Gods must have blessed me with good fortune to have my sweet betrothed in front of me so early. I fear your presence here is already spoiling me."

His words, though pleasant, ring in my ears with a note

of duplicity. Instead of lingering on them, though, I offer him a small curtsy of my own and a forced smile. "You speak too highly of me, Your Highness."

Prince Enver's gaze trails down my face to the split of fabric at my chest and then lower still before returning to my face. "Nonsense, Princess. In fact, I've been *most* jealous of your guard."

Breath is caught in my lungs. Unwanted heat sears down my neck and spreads to the tips of my ears. "I'm sorry?"

"Lord Solomon has had such privilege escorting you here. I fear he, too, may be a bit infatuated." Enver's words penetrate yet the meaning eludes me. No, rather, I force the meaning behind his words away, unwilling to admit to them.

A ripple of emotion passes through me, unease and irritation. Enver's words cast a dark cloud over my thoughts.

"Solo has been with me since I was a child." My words are sharp and I try to soften them a bit by giving him another smile, hoping this one seems more sincere than the last. "I assure you, he has no such thoughts."

Prince Enver rocks back on his heels and hums in the back of his throat as if he doesn't quite believe my words. Instead of saying anything further, though, he merely smiles and offers his arm to me. "I digress," he says. "I'm sure you're famished. Shall we walk in together?"

Etiquette dictates that I can't refuse, so in place of a verbal answer, I take his arm and together, the two of us step into the dining hall. Platters of steaming food await, scattered over a single long table with other empty tables spread throughout the room. The few bleary-eyed servants who anticipate the chance to serve straighten the second we enter, their eyes widening as they spot the two of us, arm in arm. No doubt, rumors of our *good relationship* will spread before the end of the day.

And as if that's exactly Enver's goal, he gently leads me down the line of tables before carefully helping me to a spot he finds appropriate and takes his own seat alongside me rather than across from me. My spine stiffens. "It's truly a blessing to have you visit the Bartoli Empire, my future Queen," he says, reaching up to toy with a strand of my hair that's fallen over my shoulder. "You're far more beautiful than I was led to believe."

I cut a look at him from the corner of my eyes. Is that supposed to be a compliment?

"Had you visited Rozentine at any point during our betrothal, you would have known just how beautiful I am." The words are out before I can stop them, but once they're free, I find that I don't regret them. It's the truth after all.

Enver chuckles as if he's been well and truly chastised and pulls his hand from my hair. "Right you are, darling," he agrees.

I turn my head, narrowing my gaze on his face as he turns it away and snaps his fingers at a nearby servant. A tall lanky dark-haired boy quickly hurries forward, nearly stumbling over himself to get to the Prince and me before any other servant can think to take a step away from the wall.

As Enver relays which foods he desires to the servant, I spare a glance around the room. It's a curious thing, I think to myself, why there seems to be no one here. It's hardly early in the morning, but over the past few days, each time I've come, it seems that this is the case. There are mountains of food piled on the center table and only a couple of Nobles sitting at various tables.

"Some call the Bartoli Empire the land of Midnight

Suns," Enver says, pulling me away from my thoughts as the servant scurries away to do his bidding.

I turn to him. "Does that have anything to do with why there's hardly anyone here?" I ask, curiously.

He chuckles, nudging the underside of my chin with one of his fingers before he nods to the rest of the nearly empty dining hall. "Bartoli days are spoiled by the heat of the sun beating down on our desert lands. Many nobles prefer to do their work at night, so few of them ever actually rise before noon. My father and I thought you and your companions would feel more at ease if we offered a larger spread for morning breakfast since we anticipated that you would not be used to our way of life yet."

Well, that explained the lack of people. "Doesn't that seem wasteful?" I ask.

Enver throws his head back in a great laugh that bounces off the walls of the banquet hall. Several heads turn and I'm struck stupid as I don't understand what I could have said to make him laugh so wholeheartedly.

"You are so adorable, my love," Enver says after a moment as he rights himself and wipes a finger under his eyes. "Nothing is wasteful when it comes to you."

I stare back at him rather blankly, but if he expects a response to that comment, he doesn't get one. The servant returns, a full tray of food set down before us piled high with scones, berries, fruits, and other treats that make my stomach curdle. Especially since just minutes before I'd thought myself rather hungry.

To avoid talking any further, though, I snatch a few things and put them on my plate. Enver watches with a semi-amused smirk that leaves me feeling rather annoyed. Several more minutes pass in blissful silence as I force bite after bite down my throat, trying to hurry this meal along without seeming like I'm rushing.

"You know," he finally breaks the silence as he licks red berry juice from his fingertips. "Becoming infatuated isn't difficult when it comes to beauty. Even barbarians are capable of harboring such desires." He pauses and then smiles at me. "I may even find myself trapped in my own infatuation."

I reach for the glass before me, pausing when I realize it's empty. Before I can lift my hand, Enver notices the issue and barks at one of the servants. "You!" He points at the boy from earlier, who's stationed back against the wall. "What kind of imbecile forgets to fetch water?"

"I-I am so sorry, Your Highness. I'll grab that r-right away—"

Enver sneers and waves his hand and I jump when two of the soldiers stationed at the furthest side of the dining hall peel themselves off the walls and march forward. The boy's naturally tanned face goes sheet white. "Y-your Highness!" He stumbles back as he cries out.

"Take him away," Enver commands. "Have him thrown out. You—" Enver points to a new servant, a robust woman with thick hair draped in a long braid over one shoulder. "Grab the Princess a glass of water."

The guards grab ahold of the first servant and drag him from the room before I can gather myself to speak. It all happens so fast that I'm left reeling by the sudden viciousness of Enver's actions. A moment passes and the female servant returns hastily with water that she places in front of me before bowing low and keeping her head down as she backs away.

"Now," he says, turning back to me as if nothing had occurred. As it stands, I glance around the room, noting how none of the nobles seem particularly surprised or even all that concerned about the servant's sudden departure by way of being dragged from the room by Bartoli Royal guards. "What were we saying?"

"N-nothing." My voice is almost breathless as I force the word out.

Is this how he truly is? I try to recall what information Nasir had given me about his brother over the years, but it's all fogged over with other, darker, memories that I don't care to think about.

"Hmmm." Enver reclines in his seat before he begins talking again. "I'm joining my father on a hunt along the coast today. It's prime migrating season for some of the birds. They're quite large and colorful and their feathers make the most gorgeous accessories. Perhaps you would love to have tea with my mother; I know she would be happy to have you. Or you could take a day trip into town if that would please you. Is there anything you'd like to do? I'm more than happy to set it up for you."

Gritting my teeth, I set my hands in my lap and swallow down the harsh taste of bile. "Actually," I take a breath. "If you're offering to set something up for me, I'd appreciate it if you could set up a meeting with the King. I think it's time we discuss the actions of Prince Nasir."

He lifts a full glass of wine to his lips, blinking slowly as if he is unsure where this is headed. I don't even bother to question why he's drinking wine so early in the day. What little I've managed to eat is already souring in my stomach. My fingers curl into my palms.

"I prefer not to talk about Nasir." Enver's tone is dry and ripe with disinterest.

My lips twitch and I fight back a scowl, pacing myself through the anger that rises within me. "He—"

"He is one for dramatics, is he not?" Enver interrupts. "But what my little brother does is not of much consequence. I'm sure whatever trouble he's caused can easily be smoothed over."

Not of much consequence? My nails stab into my flesh as I curl my hands into tight fists. Fury fogs over my mind. My father is dead. Slaughtered at the hands of Nasir. The urge to wrap my hands around Enver's throat and strangle the life from him—to watch the light in his eyes bleed out as I cut off his airflow—rises like an all-consuming tide. I fight it back, breathing in slow, methodical movements.

"Prince Nasir murdered—"

"Do you like shopping?" The question comes right before Prince Enver takes a bite, chewing with the same leisure as he seems to take this whole conversation. If he notices the rigidness of my body or my mounting frustration, he doesn't show it.

Inhaling, I try again. "My entire reason for coming here is because of your brother," I state, my tone frigid.

"Yes, and I'll have to thank him for that, truly," Enver replies. "However do you really think now is the time for such unfortunate discussions?" He sighs and waves a hand through the air and several servants fall back upon us, lifting away the tray of food as well as our plates and glasses.

Thank him? He'll *thank* him? Enver's dismissal sends bites of rage throughout my body. A dark warmth settles in my palms. I lower my gaze, folding my hands in my lap, trying to breathe through wave after wave of the fury assaulting me. Enver takes advantage of my silence, shoving away from the table and standing abruptly. The raw emotions flooding my body ease slightly at the newly created distance.

"Now, if you'll excuse me, darling," he says. "I do have to be on my way. Please have a servant fetch me if there's anything you need." He bows shallowly and disappears from the room, leaving me feeling as if the only way to cool my animosity is by an act of defenestration—more specifically, performing such on Enver himself.

Every word a Princess shouldn't say comes to mind. For a heartbeat, my head is a cacophony of curses and phrases learned since escaping Nasir, vile swear words born in the slums I'd traveled through and heard from more than one sailor. In my time here thus far, I've been laughed at as though my concerns are a joke, I've been sent away like little more than a servant, and my father's death has been disrespected at every turn. The longer I'm here wasting time, the stronger a hold Nasir is gaining on my kingdom.

Huffing a breath, I push away from the table. Servants scoop up our plates and make a point to give me distance as I stride from the room with violence on my mind. The halls blur as my vision grows hazy with tears that prick my eyes, though I won't let a single one fall. Someone has to listen. Someone is *going* to listen.

Finding my way back to my room, I throw open the door and step inside toying with the idea of screaming into my feather-stuffed pillows. Two bodies lounge and stretch across the small sitting area just inside. A muffled gasp spills into my palm as I slap my fingers over my lips at the sight of them.

When I realize that they're both familiar, the tension in my body eases and irritation comes galloping back. "Argyle," I state before turning to the second man. "Solomon."

"Hello, Princess," Argyle replies with a grin.

"Why are you in my room?"

The warmth of Solomon's attention on my skin reminds me how, only moments ago, I'd had a different set of eyes not nearly as pleasant on me as well. In contrast to

Enver, a single glance from my guard has goosebumps rising all across my flesh. Unable to meet Solo's gaze, I focus on Argyle.

"Your couch is so much more comfortable than mine." Argyle makes a show of cozying further into the cushions. "These rooms are much better than ours too, don't you think, Solo?"

"Very cozy." Solomon's boots are propped up on the small table at the center of the arrangement. Despite his feigned casualness as he tucks his hands behind his head, his features are drawn tight, suggesting that he's not as *cozy* as he says. My gaze trails down the dark tunic and leather trousers that encase his long legs to the scuffed boots resting right on top of the, no doubt, expensive table.

I fold my arms over my chest. "Don't you two think you're a little too comfortable around me? I miss the days when you'd refuse to even have a conversation with me because it wasn't *appropriate*." I direct my glare in Solomon's direction but only briefly.

"Those were the days." He tilts his head, watching me with an unreadable expression in his eyes. Despite that, the corner of his lips curls upward just the smallest amount when his eyes meet mine.

"It's hard not to become quick friends with those you've traveled with over sea. Cramped quarters and all. Nevertheless, Princess," Argyle points a long, slender finger toward me, "we're here for more than the joy of your welcoming presence."

"I sense that," I say, unable to move away from the door.

"A quick wit, that's what I like about you." Argyle groans as he sits up, stretching his arms overhead until the edge of his shirt lifts to reveal his lower stomach. "Seriously, my bed is like sleeping on rocks. Bat your eyes at the Prince on my behalf, would you?"

"Trust me, if batting my eyelashes did something to sway him, I'd already have done it." I sigh. With careful steps, I stop behind the chair opposite the men and grip the back. "We've been here for several days now and every time I bring up Nasir, they treat me like an absolute farce. Just this morning, Enver practically sprinted from the room when I tried to broach the subject. He didn't even finish his breakfast."

"Well, we have the perfect thing to help get this off your mind."

"Does it include getting my kingdom back?" I deadpan.

His response is enigmatic. "In a way." He stands, sparing a glance at Solomon who still sits leaned back and as relaxed as a man with a perpetual stick up his ass can. "Your abilities cannot, and should not, be ignored any longer. You need to learn how to keep the power you're developing in check. It would be a shame if you accidentally set the Bartoli Palace on fire." The way he says that last sentence makes it imperceptibly clear that he couldn't care less if I set the Bartoli's Palace aflame.

And as if to punctuate Argyle's words, Solomon snorts. "A real shame," he agrees blandly.

I grind my teeth, flicking my attention from Argyle to Solo for the briefest of seconds before planting my hands on my hips and settling my full attention on Argyle. "And who will be teaching me?"

Argyle waves a hand between himself and Solomon, whose mouth lifts in an annoying little smirk that makes me want to scream. Definitely not.

"I don't need two teachers," I snap. "You'll do it." I point at Argyle. As if he was expecting my response,

Argyle straightens and lifts his head, swinging it from me to Solo and back again, preening like a prized bird.

"I am a fantastic teacher, you'll see," he says as he pushes to his feet. "Come, let's get started."

"*Now?*" I blink.

"*Now,*" he repeats, mimicking my tone. "Unless you have something better to do?"

"I'm sure Queen Helena would be delighted to have you sipping tea and sewing handkerchiefs for her son." Solomon's boots hit the ground with two solid thuds. Irritation floods my system. Right, because sipping tea and sewing is the only thing noble ladies are interested in. Solomon leans forward, propping his elbows on his knees. "Soon, the two of you will be making cute little garments for your future babies."

I bite down on my tongue before I bare my teeth at him. "Do I detect a hint of jealousy, Solo?"

He clicks his tongue against the roof of his mouth. "'Course not, Princess. What is there to be jealous of?"

My hands ball into fists. Perhaps learning how to harness my newfound powers is best. Maybe one of these days, I'll learn how to conjure something to scorch the annoying smirk Solomon tosses my way right off his stupidly handsome face.

Argyle claps his hands together. "Alright, enough flirting, you two," he says. "Let's go."

"We weren't—" The denial rings out on my tongue, except Argyle is already moving across the room, closing the space between us. Those mismatched eyes twinkle with clear mischief as he swings an arm over my shoulder and turns me toward the doorway. I swear the grin he wears seems permanently stitched to his face. It only widens as he turns his head back. "See you in a bit, Solo."

"Hey!" Argyle guides me toward the exit, showing no

sign of noticing the stiffness in my body and refusing me the chance to turn and give my guard one last look.

"Don't look back, Your Highness," Argyle's voice dips low into a whisper. "My first lesson is this—always keep him guessing."

I scoff, waiting to respond once I know we're far enough down the corridor that Solo won't hear. "Solomon doesn't care what I do or with whom," I tell him.

"Oh?" Though he slides his arm off of my shoulders, Argyle's eyes are like twin daggers, burrowing into my flesh. He walks with an ease that suggests a familiarity that even I can't fake while here in this castle. I open my mouth to refute the disbelief in that singular word, but instead, I just let it go. What would be the point anyway?

Argyle hums a joyful tune as he walks, releasing me, and only occasionally looking down to make sure I'm still at his side. The humming pauses as we pass a couple of Bartoli guardsmen, then quickly resumes again when they are out of earshot.

I clear my throat and peek at him out of the corner of my eye. "So … how are you liking Bartoli?"

He chuckles. "No need to make small talk, Princess. I'm comfortable in silence, but to answer your question…" Argyle looks over his shoulder before facing forward again. "Bartoli is nothing like home. I find myself missing the bowels of Rozentine." He shoots me an easy smile, "But I'm sure we'll be back before we know it."

"I miss it as well." The all-too-insistent hurt in my heart throbs in time with my words. After a lifetime of being raised to care for and reign over a nation, it comes as no surprise that—even with the adventurous trip we've taken over the seas—I want nothing more than to be home in the Sunfire Palace. I want to feel the breeze on my face as I stand in the courtyard facing Sanctus City. To smell the sweet scent of roses in the garden and see the glimmering flag of my Kingdom flying high. "Though I'm not sure there is much to be missed in the 'bowels' of our country."

"There is beauty to be found even in darkened corners, Your Highness," Argyle replies.

I shudder at the memories of peeling paints, faded signs, the wreak of body odor, and blatant prostitution. All things I saw while on my travels to Carion City. I'm sure to Argyle, though, who grew up in such places, there must be good memories attached, not ones of fear and racing away from danger. I try to push my thoughts away as quickly as they come. Just another reminder of all there is to do in my own kingdom after I get Nasir taken care of.

As if he can read my thoughts, or perhaps it's all there plain as day on my face, Argyle begins talking again. "You're used to seeing the world through the eyes of a royal. Sure, there is plenty to be improved, poverty to be amended, hungry bellies to be filled, but you're missing all the joy there is in the life of a commoner. Commoners are free in a way you may never be." My lips part in surprise at the truth of his words. I want to deny them, but I can't. He offers me a sincere, if wane, smile. "I apologize if I'm being insensitive to your position. There is plenty of work to be done in Rozentine but I still hold much love for our home."

The grand halls give way to stone pathways as we step out into the morning. The gardens still glisten with dew, not yet dried from the rising sun. A guard straightens near the door, watching us intently as we move by.

"No apologies needed," I say. "But do tell me something. You met Solomon in these bowels, didn't you?"

He nods with a slow-growing grin. "I did. Your bodyguard and I enjoyed many nights deep in the Rozentine countryside. He really isn't as much of a prude as he appears to be when he's with you."

"I find that hard to believe." Though the memories of our camaraderie in our youth are simply too easy to bring forth, it's hard to imagine a simpler, easier-going Solomon now. "After he went away to battle and then returned, it was clear he no longer cared for me in any way. It changed him into someone I no longer knew."

"Battle does that to most," Argyle replies. "It changes many, although trust me when I say it did not change his true feelings for you … only how he portrayed them."

"I—" Only what words sit on the tip of my tongue are too hard to speak, so I swallow them down, desperate for a change of subject. "You said once that Solo saved you?"

"He found me at the bottom of a bottle of whiskey … well, several bottles of whiskey. Helped me clean up my act because the path I was on was only going to lead me to a slow death. At the time, I thought that's what I wanted."

"It isn't now?"

"I drink responsibly now." He chews his lip to subdue a smile. "Most of the time."

The garden path ends, and he walks me further out into the courtyard toward a grouping of trees. I follow, lifting my skirts to keep them from dampening. My slippers quickly darken as we traipse through the grass, leaving me wishing I'd slipped into a pair of riding boots or something better suited.

"May I ask what was so terrible to make you drink so much? Most people don't just take up ruining their livers for the fun of it."

"No, I suppose they don't," I agree.

Argyle's attention lifts to the trees. His ever-present smile flattens as his eyes glaze over. It's only a moment before he speaks again, though quieter. "Joining the House of Ravens is a rough transition for nearly all of us. My relations with my family abruptly ended. Someone I cared very deeply about was…" He pauses, clapping his hands together as we stop under the trees. "You know what, let's not get into that. Wouldn't want to ruin your day with my tales of woe."

"It's admirable how you've survived through it, though." *Whatever it was.* "I can only hope that I can maneuver through these terrible times with as much grace.'

His chuckle releases some of the tension building in his shoulders, but it feels forced. Somehow, I wish I knew exactly what to say that would give him genuine relief, but in fear of saying the wrong thing, I opt to say nothing at all.

"I would hardly call becoming a drunk graceful," Argyle muses. "Nevertheless, I appreciate the kind words. Shall we move on to some formal training now that we are far enough away not to burn down our host's home?"

"Yes, of course."

"Perfect. Now in the early stages of Awakening, it can feel unpredictable or hard to find a mental link to the power that is waiting just under the surface. It's important to help you gain some control now because your abilities will only grow stronger whether you learn to control it or not."

What little warmth the sun provides is trapped above the treetops. Shade washes over me as we step into a veil of trees, bringing with it a slight chill that raises goosebumps on my arms. I rub my palms over the exposed flesh. My dress, while more modest than what I'd worn to dinner several nights ago, is still much different than the full-coverage gowns of Rozentine.

"What happened," I begin slowly, "during my fire dance was certainly unexpected. One minute, I'm begging

Aerea for some small sign of my Awakening, then the next moment I'm coated in flames. It was exhilarating and terrifying at the same time."

"Not exactly what you want when you need to be in control." Argyle folds his arms over his chest, leans into the trunk of the nearest tree, and crosses his ankles. "Sparks of emotion can be helpful in the early stages. Anything particularly irritating about your current circumstances that might help?"

"Too many to count." I breathe a laugh, wrapping my arms around myself. "This *family* is currently at the top of my list. I don't understand why they are so apathetic toward it all. Nasir is the entire reason we are in this mess in the first place." Fingers curling into my flesh, I don't stop until I feel the pain of my own grip. "Prince Enver is quick to call me love, to flirt, and to charm me, although in the next breath he is dismissive or spiriting himself away for his next bit of fun."

"Royals have hard heads. Sometimes they are so caught up in their own world that they can't see the reality of their actual situations." Those mix-match eyes examine me with the level of scrutiny I'm used to from Solomon.

Pinned under his attention, I force myself to uncurl. My shoulders pull tight and I lift my chin, determined to become exactly the person I know I'm meant to be. A woman who leads. A Queen who faces the worst of the world so that her country can persevere and thrive. "We aren't that dense, are we?"

"You've had plenty to shake you from your stupor, but the Galeanos? They haven't." Argyle pushes away from the tree. "They have no reason to help you. You know that, right?"

"Nasir is one of them. They have every reason to help

me." I lower my arms to my sides, fingers curling into my palms.

"No." He shakes his head. "They don't. Nasir isn't creating waves here in Bartoli. The problem isn't on their land. They don't care, and in their minds, they don't have to. You, your Highness, need to make them listen."

"How exactly am I supposed to do that? I've tried. *I'm trying.*"

"You are a queen in your own right; use the power of a queen." His gaze shifts over my face.

Perhaps if they don't perceive the problem as their own due to proximity ... perhaps ... Perhaps I'll become their problem. I'll make this a problem they can't look away from.

"Okay, I hear you. Now, how do I harness this ... emotion? How do I turn this into control? I show him my hands and the heat that builds in my palms glows a soft orange. No flames, but a swirling energy already budding.

I stare at my palms, waiting for something more. *Is that it?* I think. *Just heat?* That can't be it. *There has to be something more, doesn't there?*

"Start with something that brings your emotions to the surface but on a smaller scale." Argyle's attention lifts over my head and settles behind me. I turn, sheer skirts twisting around my ankles.

Solomon is propped on the tree behind us, his elbow holding up his broad frame as he lifts his brows and allows his gaze to slide up and down my body. A different sort of heat runs through my veins settling in the apples of my cheeks.

"By the gods. Has he been here with us this entire time?" I point an accusatory finger in Solo's direction but give Argyle the weight of my narrowed glare.

"He could have been." Argyle shrugs. "Or he could have just appeared at the most opportune time."

"You really should work on your awareness of your surroundings, Princess." Solomon stalks forward until I'm sandwiched between these two men.

Argyle clears his throat, retreating to his own tree for leaning. "I've noticed that Solomon has a particularly useful talent of getting a rise out of you. Be it good or bad, it doesn't matter. His *influence* on you is a safe medium for us to test you under."

"No." I shake my head. "No, absolutely not."

Please no.

Not when I can't trust my traitorous body around him. I'm betrothed to a Prince, yet I'm unraveling at the slightest touch of my bodyguard. This—whatever it is— is a danger to the peace of my country. Solomon makes me a danger to myself.

Solomon bends until his height matches mine. His fingers brush something off my shoulder as he brings his mouth lower until I can feel his breath against my neck. Only by sheer will do I stay standing in that spot instead of sprinting as far away from him as possible.

"I see I'm already doing my job here. How easy it is to push all your buttons, little Princess…"

Something flutters in my lower stomach. My lips twitch into a sneer as I refuse to give him even an inch. "Don't you have better things to do than harass me? Or am I just that hard to stay away from?"

A smile brightens his features. The fingers that brushed my shoulder drift to my neck. Solomon traces a line along my exposed skin, from jaw to collarbone and over my shoulder. "You have no idea."

My heart stutters in my chest. The racing of my pulse is loud in my ears, something I know he can easily pick up on.

"Argyle, this is not going to work." I turn away from Solomon. "This is going to turn into us killing each other."

"There. No, it's there. Can you feel it?" Argyle waves a hand at me. "Your eyes. I can see it."

I don't feel anything other than the distinct need to run away.

"Here." Solomon's body aligns with my back. His touch slides down my arms, smoothing over my burning flesh until he finds my hands and lifts them.

My vision flashes gold. Green leaves and long dangling limbs turn into glittering sparks of light all around me. I blink rapidly, until the light dies down, and turn my attention to the way he holds my hands in his.

"Harness that energy. Be it hate, or anger, or something better. Take it, Devonry. Take whatever you need from me."

Argyle is silent, one hand pressed against his lips as he surveys the scene. A shiver passes down my spine. Solo's touch tightens for a sharp second before it's startlingly gentle again.

"Use me," he hisses in my ears. "Use me for whatever you need."

Each inhale feels shallow, unable to slow the ever-growing fire inside of me. Gold floods my vision again as I stare at Solo's hands wrapped around mine. His thumb draws a circle against my wrist, coaxing more fire. The light in my palms brightens.

I gasp. Solomon pulls me closer still. "Don't fight it. Feel it. Let it build, but don't let it consume." His voice is rough, lips brushing near my temple.

His nearness draws the betraying desire down until it dips between my legs. Solomon takes an exaggerated slow breath in as if he can smell my own confusing want. I shift in the circle of his arms and close my eyes, feeling my abilities clear down to my feet.

"Don't tease me, Dev," he whispers too low for Argyle to hear. "I can feel that power flowing through you right now. I can feel it grow every time I touch you. Do you like how I touch you?"

My inhale is ragged. Where our bodies align, I feel as though I'll burst into those all-consuming flames.

Let it build but don't let it consume.

Closing my eyes, I release some of the tension in my muscles. Easing against Solomon's solid frame. There is safety in the circle of his arms, but so much is unknown. Biting into my lip, I let the feeling stretch until it touches the tips of my fingers and reaches the ends of my toes. The sensation of these abilities—a living, swirling thing inside my veins—takes to my silent command. My mind reels to follow it and guide it forward, though it flows in all directions from the pulse of it in my chest.

Solomon strokes his thumb against mine, coaxing the fire within me. Each strand of power forges a brazen path through me, rushing too quickly for me to keep up with. A smoky scent lingers with every inhale, the taste of it thick on my tongue. My skin warms as gold deepens in my vision and my mind conjures images of his fingers stroking other more forbidden places on my body.

"Yes, Devonry! Yes!" Argyle shouts.

I open my eyes, blushing at my own wicked desires. Within the palm of my hand, a flame flickers in the breeze. It's small, no larger than a wine glass, but it's there.

"Shit." Argyle hisses in the next heartbeat.

There is no stop to the cascade of my abilities as it reaches the end of my physical being. Fire licks at the grass, eating rapidly into a growing circle around us. I grit my teeth to try and staunch the flow.

Solomon drops his hands from mine and stomps a heavy boot on the flame, dragging the tip of his toes through the dirt. Without his touch, the flames within me start to recede, followed promptly by my shame and the taunting knowledge that I'll use Solomon for my own needs and the needs of my kingdom. And he deserves far more than that.

What flames remain are cast in the darkness of night that quickly smothers it. Argyle waves his hand and both the shadow and fire are gone. My gaze jumps to him.

He only shrugs, pulling the slip of shadows back into him. "I suppose the gifts of my family are good for something."

All the air in my chest leaves me in one solid exhale. I tilt my head back, settling it against Solomon's shoulder. His chest rises and falls with the same exhilaration that's taken hold of me. When I look up at him, his red eyes glow bright, fangs poking out against his lower lip, and he holds my gaze.

Several long seconds pass before Solo curls his fingers against mine, closing my hand into a fist. The fire dissolves with a small puff of smoke.

"Keep trying, you'll figure it out," he says, slowly pulling away. "And, Devonry, no more avoiding me." Some of his icy exterior drips back into his tone. "We need each other more than ever."

Shame and guilt are quick to dampen my spirits. Dipping my chin in agreement, I take several steps away. In my success, I am still a failure. A small part of my confidence withers away at the thought. "Thank you for helping," I say.

"I am at your disposal." Solomon bows with a mocking grin.

"And now we just need to recreate that again and again

until you don't need him here to do it and you don't accidentally set the world ablaze." Argyle claps slowly.

Do this again and again? How many times can I survive Solomon's touch before I'm burning alive and taking him with me?

9
DEVONRY

What power does a Queen have when she no longer holds a throne? I run my fingers over my gown and tuck my hair behind my ears for the millionth time. My eyes burn with the need for rest, my body sluggish and slow, but my mind … it won't quiet. I can't let another day come and go without the reason for my visit being addressed. The longer we wait, the more it eats away at me.

Heat comes easily to my palm. I circle a finger over the soft glow, remembering how Solomon's thumb had grazed my skin. The light grows as I get lost in the memory, but it never turns into flame. I sigh at my own haggard reflection. Training is hard. Trying to ignore the way my body begs for Solo is harder.

I place the simple gold crown on my head; compared to the others I've worn in my lifetime and those worn by Prince Enver and the King and Queen of Bartoli, it's far more subdued and plain. It's a reminder of my position to not only myself but everyone else. I turn from the mirror forcing myself to forget about today's session, to focus on what's important.

As far as the Galeanos are concerned, I'm only here to further solidify my betrothal. No matter how often I broach the topic, I'm met with dismissal. The longer I'm here, the more I can't even fathom how this alliance is even salvageable. There is no respect for me, my family, or Rozentine. To the Bartoli Royal Family, I'm merely a game to be played.

Maybe Argyle is right. The problem isn't on their shores. I am. And they don't see *me* as an issue. They don't see my kingdom's grievances as their own.

Not yet, anyway.

How can I make them see?

I am capable of causing a commotion, of bending the rules to get my way. Solomon knows that firsthand. My skills only need to be applied here to this situation. I pace before my door trying to find the words that will get through Prince Enver's thick skull. My requests to meet with the King and Queen formally have all been denied. If I even mention Nasir to Enver, he runs from the room as though it is on fire. I need him not to run. But trapping my future husband is not something they taught me how to do when formally training me to be queen.

Argyle's advice repeats in my thoughts again and again. *Royals have hard heads. Sometimes, they are so caught up in their world that they can't see the reality of their actual situations.*

As much as it pains me to admit, he's right. I never saw Nasir's true motives coming. I was so caught up in my day-to-day life, of the excitement of something … anything … to distract me from how very alone the castle can feel that I was blind.

The reality is that Nasir's actions could potentially send the entire continent into a war. What peace we've been able to build for our countries is threatening to topple, but a royal's blood won't be the only thing to cross a blade if this escalates. A war would kill hundreds, if not thousands. People I've sworn to protect. In the end, I would be the one to make that decision. To go to war or not.

So, even if I want Nasir to pay for his crimes. War is not what I want. War is the furthest thing from my mind as I stride from my chambers into the corridor of the Bartoli Royal Palace. He's avoided it thus far, but I won't allow Prince Enver to keep dismissing the effect of his brother's actions. He needs to be the one to bring it to King Florian since it's clear that the King and Queen won't meet with me unless Enver is there.

I pause, turning my head to peer out of a window beyond the dunes in the distance. Even though night has fallen, the air remains hot and humid, only marginally better than it is during the day. The few sconces left burning on the stone walls light my way, leaving the rest of the corridor shrouded in shadows. The air outside my room is stagnant and there is no evening breeze.

As I head down the hallway, recalling the brief tour I'd been offered not long after my arrival, I'm cast back into my memories. This place, though very different from the Sunfire Palace, reminds me of a time when striding through luxury didn't make me feel so alone. When it was comfortable rather than unnerving.

I pass by an opening leading into a central courtyard. The hedges inside the alcove are trimmed to perfect spheres, and the golden crest of the Bartoli Royal Family is laid out in the stone walkway. Enver had been proud to show me all of the places their crest is embedded. It seemed almost as if they were frightened that if they didn't label every damn thing in this palace as theirs, someone might mistakenly walk off with it.

More excruciating than smiling and allowing him to prattle about himself for hours had perhaps been the very end of the tour when he'd shown me to his bed chambers. Now, though, I'm grateful for the knowledge since this may be the only time we can talk without wandering eyes or ears getting too close. Maybe without the concern of others—servants and nobles alike—flitting about, Enver can be honest with me. Perhaps we can discuss truths and issues rather than irrelevant conversation filler.

My slippers whisper over the marbled floors. Not a soul greets me, and surprisingly, there aren't even any guards as I climb a flight of stairs holding the solid gold railings. My footsteps slow as a giggle echoes from the shadows. Prince Enver's chambers are so close—right around the corner.

And as if the thought conjures him, Enver's voice slips from the darkness. "My dear, you're so ready for me." A soft, feminine gasp reaches my ears in response. My stomach knots as the woman moans. Wet, slick sounds follow. Kissing? Something more?

"Y-Your Highness … oh please, Enver…" The knots turn to stones that sink to the pit of my stomach. I turn and press my spine to the side of the stairwell. There's not even enough energy to feel hurt at this discovery. I shouldn't be surprised. Part of me isn't. Humiliation, though, that I have in spades. And anger. Plenty of anger.

I grind my teeth together, trying to stifle my frustration and the flood of dangerous emotions that threaten to overtake me. Perhaps, before, I might have run away in tears and tormented myself with the fact that my betrothed seems to be a self-serving womanizer. Now, though, it doesn't matter to me.

With renewed determination, I back down only a few steps so it will seem more natural when I appear around the corner. I begin my advancement to Prince Enver's room, making sure my footsteps are loud enough to hear.

I step into the hall and stop, spotting the two huddled bodies pressed against a wall. When I expect Enver to shove away from the Bartoli noblewoman whose luxurious dress appears half undone, he surprises me further by lifting his head and turning it in my direction.

Dark eyes framed with long lashes meet my gaze. Enver's expression is partially obscured in shadows, but the lift of his lips is still visible. The woman, either uncaring or unnoticing of my presence, continues to writhe against the wall and him. The material of her gown is gathered between them. Her skirt drapes around where the Prince's arm disappears beneath.

"Like what you see, Princess?" Enver calls.

In response, the woman's eyes open. The 'o' of her mouth widens as she glances to the side and finally sees me. Her jaw drops. Prince Enver doesn't even so much as shift when she starts to push her dress back into place. "Ah, I'm not done with you yet, darling." He nips at her ear. "Don't move."

Ice fills my veins. "We need to speak." I fold my arms over my chest.

If he's surprised by my lack of reaction, he doesn't show it. Instead, he grins and replies, "I'm listening."

I glance at the woman in his arms. She licks her lips rather nervously, darting looks between the prince and me. She's a beauty with her cherry lips and her hair in black waves falling to her waist. That doesn't make me feel any better. "We need to speak, *alone*," I clarify. "Send your mistress away."

"And spoil my fun? Why would I do that?" His light, playful tone starkly contrasts the devilish look darkening his face. Something dangerous flashes behind his eyes. "I'd much prefer you join us, Princess. She's a darling girl, and I assure you, she'll please you as well as she pleases me."

The woman doesn't respond to his claim but sinks slightly against the wall as if humiliated. I almost feel sorry for her. *Almost.* I'd hoped that when I captured Enver after dark and away from prying eyes, he'd be a better man than I'd started to believe him. His lustful gaze has now crushed that hope as he roves down my body with a smirk.

"I'll have her hung." I don't even recognize the words leaving my mouth, nor do I believe them. I feel like a fake, trying to stand my ground against this man who is used to walking all over others. Still, I know I can't back down.

Enver chuckles and arches a brow my way. "On what grounds?"

I step closer, gaze focused on his half-lidded expression as the woman's face pales. "Threatening the Rozentine-Bartoli alliance, of course." My voice comes out even, despite the fact that I feel anything but calm.

"Fine." Prince Enver grins, his hand moving under her skirt though she isn't so much as breathing right now, much less reacting to his touch. "Hang her. I'll be done with her by the time you return with guards, and then I'll find another."

Damn it. I tilt my head to the side. I don't really want to kill this woman. Even though she seemed fine fucking a betrothed man until I arrived, I don't think she deserves to die for this mistake. Enver knows that.

"Fine," I say. "Then let her stay. If you wish for her to hear about Nasir's—"

"Dear Gods," Enver mutters. "Not even married yet, and you're already a nag. My brother didn't warn me about that." A sigh escapes him as he pulls his hand from her dress. He glares at me and then, with the tilt of his head, sends the woman scurrying down the hall.

The entirety of his attention falls on me. "Thank you." The words come out through my clenched teeth. Grateful is not something I feel right now.

Enver clicks his tongue while wiping his glistening fingers against his pants. "I don't like my family being the fodder for gossip. You have my attention, Princess. Get on with it."

"If you don't want to be gossiped about, then why make it so easy to find you *playing* in the hallway?"

"Let me make one thing very clear to you, *dear*. You and I"—he steps closer—"are nothing more than an arranged marriage. Our fathers' politics are what will bind us, nothing more." His smile melts into a grimace of annoyance. This is the real Prince Enver. "You were born for breeding. We'll marry, and then I'll fuck you until your belly swells with my child and our Kingdoms have the heirs they desire. I do not appreciate being interrupted." He stops only inches away.

The thought of this man putting himself inside me makes me want to vomit in disgust right before I punch him in his conniving face. I repress the urge, but just barely. "Whether any of that is true or not, you still need to respect the alliance as is your duty as a Prince of Bartoli."

Enver mocks a bow. "You're putting on a good show." He straightens. "But I'll do as I please—as only a Prince can." I lower my hands to my sides, fingers curling into my palms. He chuckles. "Let me give you some advice. It would be silly of you to expect monogamy. Kings take mistresses all the time. My father has three at his disposal as we speak. Princess, you're good for stock and blood ... a future heir for both our countries. Never in our contract, though, does it suggest that you should expect my sincere love."

"I am not here to discuss *love* with you, Your Highness."

My words are cutting. "As it currently stands, my love for you matches yours to me—which is to say, *there is no love*."

He cracks a smile, lips parting as I'm sure a snarky comment is ready to fly. I don't let it.

I step closer, closing the distance between us further. "Your brother's actions have risked the lives of my people," I snap. "And you and your family don't seem to realize this."

Enver groans, his fingers rubbing tiny circles against his temples. "My brother is not my problem."

"That's *exactly* what he is." Heat swarms beneath my skin, seething and growing hotter. "Talk to King Florian, make him see that—"

"Devonry." My name on his lips calls a stop to my demands. He blows out a breath and shakes his head. The annoyance from only seconds ago begins to melt as a new mask is quickly implemented. "If you were looking to gain my father's attention or seek his aid, I'm afraid you've come to the wrong place. Maybe tomorrow night, slink over to his chambers." Enver's eyes find the curve of my breast where it pokes out of my dress collar. "I'm sure he won't refuse you." His gaze moves back to my face. "Though I warn you, you'll have to do more than glare at him for help with Nasir."

"Why do you think I came here?" I demand.

He chuckles. "Obviously for safe haven," he replies. "Who else would you come to but your darling fiancé?"

Bile burns in the back of my throat. "Nasir is just as much Bartoli's problem as he is Rozentine's," I growl.

Enver shakes his head. "Any decision regarding aid is up to my father, not me."

"You are the crown prince. You have power, Enver."

I take in a carefully measured inhale as he leans in and pinches a strand of my hair between his fingers before gently twisting it. "Until my father dies—and he has many, many years ahead of him—I'm content." He drops the strand of hair. "You're right. I am the crown prince and as such I have many luxuries at my disposal. The life of a king is hard, to say the least. Until I'm forced to take that role, I'm quite happy living *this* life."

"You're disgraceful."

"No, I'm a royal. And from what my brother told me about you, I'd thought you were the same. You don't appear at all the naive-headed, pretty-faced Princess he described. Clearly, he misread you. Either that or you've forgotten your place. If that's the case, then I certainly hope you come to your senses sooner rather than later. It would behoove you, don't you think, to seek what you want in the best way that women know how." His grin is lasciv-ious as his gaze pans down to my breasts for several long beats. Never before have I wanted to claw someone's eyes out. The meaning of his words is not lost on me. Even if I'm a royal, using one's body is still a version of prostitu-tion I won't lower myself to if I can help it. I'll hold onto my dignity for as long as I can, and in the end, if I'm forced to give him my body in return for my Kingdom's salvation, I'll make sure he fucking pays for it. That much is for Gods damned sure. "I'll be waiting for you to come to your senses and use what you have to get what you want. When you do, you know where to find me."

With that, he spins on his heels and strolls the last few feet to his bedroom door. The soft thud of its closing signals the true end of our conversation.

Gold blinks in and out of my vision. Hatred. Anger. Pain. It soars through me. I press my hand flat to the stone of the wall, feeling the fire inside of me gain momentum. Try as I might, no amount of deep breaths alleviates the symptoms.

A burst of light flashes beside me, and I yelp, yanking my hand away from the stone to see its now charred surface. Tiny sparks dance at the end of my fingertips as I turn my palm over and gape down at it. I thought that once Awakened, I would have more control over these abilities, but it appears that's not the case.

With uneven breaths, I stumble backward. Goosebumps rise over my flesh where a shiver of power moves like liquid under my skin. Violence sings in my blood. Powerlessness heightens everything from the prickle of heat over my forearms and the nape of my neck to the cold of my hands. If Enver's words have taught me anything, it's that I have essentially nothing here in Bartoli. No power. No authority. I have nothing I need to save my Kingdom and my people.

Turning away from Enver's chamber door, I start walking and don't stop ... not until I'm back in my own room with the door shut behind me. The four walls of this luxurious bedroom feel smaller and tighter than ever, and inside, the flames roar on.

10

SOLOMON

Fire arches through the air and lands against the sandbags stacked high enough to mimic a human figure. Most of the burlap has burned away, leaving just a sad pile of sand. The ball of flames bursts into smaller sparks before it dies away entirely.

Another perfect hit. They're getting more frequent now. Along with the dark circles under Devonry's eyes. That isn't even the worst of it though. She seems more different than I've ever seen, a mixture of determined and resigned. Neither of which would be a bad thing if I didn't suspect she was sneaking out of her chambers at night and losing sleep.

I watch her now, noting the minor wounds on her fingers as she lifts her hands and tries to summon another fireball. Her abilities appear to be growing in strength, but even so, as she focuses her gaze on her palm and flames come to life at her fingertips, her face blanches white for a moment and they flicker.

I've seen her hungry and tired. I've seen her angry and bitter. This girl, the one who schools her face into neutrality while something dangerous burns in those gray-blue eyes, is new. She is forever changing. Unpredictable. As concerned as I am, I am damned to do anything unless she comes to me.

Somedays, much like today, I feel like I'm running to keep up with her. The swinging pendulum of her mood, the hot and cold feeling of being near her, it's confusing. Jacin would know what to say. He'd have told me just how to fix this—whatever it is—between us.

Ignoring the heartache in my chest, I turn to Argyle, who nods approvingly as her fireball disintegrates into sparks. He grins. The man is damn good at acting, I'll give him that. I, however, have never been talented in that aspect and Devonry avoids looking my way as she turns back toward us.

Brows pulled low, she runs the back of her hand across her forehead, wiping away perspiration. Finally, crystalline eyes connect with mine, sparks of gold lingering within the depths for a moment before disappearing. "What?" she asks. "Why are you scowling?"

"I'm not scowling."

She frowns. "Well, it's certainly not a pleasant look you're giving me," she snaps.

Argyle jumps in, saving my sorry ass before I can come up with a response. "Your Highness, you and I both know Solomon is smile-challenged. He must have forgotten to practice his big-boy smile in the mirror this morning."

Now, I *am* scowling and directing the full brunt of it at my supposed friend.

"No." She rubs her palms, looking at the yellow glow that is dying away. Her breath is slowly evening. "I know he is capable of genuine expression. Even if he has to break that brooding exterior. Something's on his mind."

She shifts but keeps the distance between us. I know

I've muddied this up. That much she has made blatantly clear since *that* night on the balcony. I'd stood there before her, imagining all sorts of inappropriate things I could do to her out there where no one could see us. My fingers in her pretty pussy. My nose against her skin. The scent of her blood vibrating in my lungs. No amount of teasing or taunting has lessened it.

"What is there to be upset about?" Argyle slaps me on the back, gently shaking me. "Our girl is getting better. Is she not?"

I try not to flinch at the word *our*. Primal instinct rises, but I quickly shove it down.

Control your fucking cock, Solomon. I curse internally and clear my throat.

"She's doing well, but she should be further along by now."

Devonry raises a brow.

"There is always room for improvement, but how so?" Argyle asks.

Inhaling, I glance up at the skies where the sun is decidedly turning for the horizon. Only a few more hours of sunlight left. An evening breeze cooled by the nearness of the ocean manages to break through the circle of trees. My palm finds the hilt of my sword, a comforting measure.

"Have you been practicing your archery, Princess?" I turn toward where I know her bow and arrows lay in the grass. If I'm right about those cuts on her hands, then she is.

"Yes," she says, confirming. Devonry follows my gaze.

"I see where you're going with this." Argyle's long strides eat up the distance between us and the bow. "Excellent idea."

My attention returns to Devonry, finding her eyes locked back on mine. She examines me with a level of scrutiny that leaves me feeling as though I'm transparent. I wonder if, deep down, she's disgusted or perhaps confused by the lines we've crossed together. And yet I'm here, eager for another chance. Desperate to hide all the ways she tears my walls down with just a single look. I swallow and extend an arm toward Argyle. He places her weapon in my hand without a word. The wood of the bow is warm despite the shade.

I take a step in her direction and she takes a step back. I stop and tilt my head, examining the stubborn set of her jaw, hating the way I want to kiss it away. Sighing, I take another step. This time, she doesn't move. Devonry's cheeks darken to another shade of crimson as I reach her.

"Shoot the sand." I offer the bow.

"Easy." She smiles. Just as she can tell when I may not be genuine, I see right through her too. The easy lift of her lips doesn't brighten her face. That grin doesn't reach the torment of thoughts twisting and churning in her gaze.

A twig breaks under my boot as I step away. The sound causes her to blink heavily, but she turns her back to me and faces her target. Muscles that she didn't have before are visible under the thin material of her dress as she raises her arms and sets her bow. She's only been training for a short while—from Lord Frederic's domain to Carion City to the ship and now … here, in Bartoli. Sweat stains through the cream fabric of her clothes, making it practically sheer. She pulls the string back. With a soft *thunk*, the arrowhead sinks into the target.

Devonry faces me, smirking. Argyle claps as she dips down into a curtsy. Stalking forward, I move past her, our shoulders nearly brushing before I grab the fletches of the arrow to pull it free.

"It's a pretty large target," I start, "but I'm glad to see you're not letting yourself get rusty."

She scoffs. "Are you going to give me something challenging to do, Solo? I don't have time to waste."

"I'm getting to that." I stop, half a foot before her.

Lifting her chin, her lashes raise as she looks up to my height. "Get to the point, *faster*."

I truly smile, then. Leaning forward until my lips can graze her temple, I speak softly, aware of Argyle watching us with his head cocked. "I'd rather take this slow." My lips shift into a lopsided grin before I reach for her hand. Devonry stills but allows me to open her fist and set the arrow in her grasp. I straighten. "Wouldn't want you to get too eager and accidentally hurt yourself. I am your guard; I'm meant to look out for you, and you're no expert yet."

"He has a point," Argyle adds. The glare Devonry has fixed on me turns to Argyle in one sharp turn of her head. "Or not." He chuckles.

"Now light your arrow on fire and hit it again." I point at the arrow in her grip.

"You want me to shoot a flaming arrow?" Her mouth flattens to a thin line.

"Yes."

Her shoulders set in that familiar stubborn way. Her skirts flick out around her calves as she twists and readies her stance. Quietly, I move until her back aligns with my chest. Her floral scent deepens with the crisp smell of ash. Devonry stiffens as I run my fingers down her arms to where her arrow is knocked in one and aiming the bow in the other.

"Is this necessary?" she hisses.

"Shhh." My hand closes over hers. "Think of sending your flame through the arrow. Warm your fingers, instead of your palm."

Her pulse hitches higher as I trace over her fingers. Heat blooms, still gathering mostly in her palms but a lick of fire starts at her fingertips. I yank my hand away, earning another chuckle out of Argyle.

"Don't play with fire if you don't want to get burned," he calls.

I hum and nod. Flames travel quickly over her arrow. "Focus on the fire, Princess," I order. "Keep it surrounding the arrow without letting it eat away at the wood."

Taking a long breath in, she locks her gaze. As she exhales and tries to loose her arrow, I blow a slow, cold breath down the shell of her ear and onto her neck. The arrow flies far to the right, missing the target.

"Solomon!" Devonry growls. Argyle closes his fist, suffocating the fire without touching it. "That wasn't fair. You distracted me."

"Oh, so now I'm distracting?" I run my tongue along my lips to moisten them, and her eyes follow the motion before she puts a hand on my chest and shoves me away. I play along, taking a step back and raising my hands.

"In the heat of battle, there will be lots to distract you." Argyle shoos me away with a hand. "I'm sure he was only making a point."

"A point of being an ass." She grabs another arrow and knocks it. Lifting her bow, she faces me, arrow pointed directly at my chest. I don't move. Devonry scowls, flame taking over the shaft of her arrow before she turns.

I exhale and watch as the arrowhead sinks into the sand where one might guess a person's head might sit. Though something in me thrills at her success, I refuse to smile. Devonry lowers her bow before turning to face me.

"Would you look at that," she says.

"I'm looking," I answer, though my attention doesn't drift from her.

Her cheeks are pink from the effort of training. Those eyes of hers are wide as she takes me in, head to toe. She smirks then. A cocky little smile that has my heart pounding and my lips turning up involuntarily.

"One more for good measure? So you can't say that it was all just luck? Mhmm?" She hums. In seconds she's knocked, shot, and lowered her bow. Another arrow just slightly off from the other sends sand cascading down the pile.

From the line of trees, a slow clapping begins. Devonry starts to speak in my direction but stops as soon as she realizes the praise isn't from me. We both glance at Argyle who turns toward the noise.

"Who knew my bride was quite the archer?" Prince Enver practically sings the words. "You know we do have several expert archers in our guard that could give you some pointers."

"Prince Enver." Devonry nods in deference to his appearance before straightening. "To what do we owe the pleasure? You sure do seem to be quite the *busy* man as of late."

Every step he takes toward her, I sense my shoulders rising another inch closer to my ears. Muscles in my jaw twitch.

"I found myself with some time and thought, what would be better than some quality time with my betrothed? Little did I know I'd find you out here, sweating with the staff." Enver gives Argyle and me a sideways glance. My knuckles pop with the intensity of my fisted hands.

The Prince moves closer and Argyle walks to my side. The two of us watch like mirrored images with our arms folded over our chests and deepening frowns.

"I don't like this," I whisper.

"Do you not like this situation, or do you just not like him?" he says under his breath.

"Both. The answer is both."

But Devonry is not a frightened animal under this Prince's shadow. He talks to her in his low, sweet voice, and gives her that all too charming smile. She doesn't smile back. She doesn't wilt, nor does she preen.

Prince Enver runs his finger down the side of her face, finding a loose strand of hair to tuck behind her ear. My Princess shifts away, an expression as familiar as the back of my hand painted on her pretty features. Barely contained anger. The face she'd worn in front of her father or any other member of her court when her buttons had been pushed but she needed to pretend they hadn't … that face. Fake. Her friendliness with him is fake.

"It would appear she doesn't like this much either. Should we intervene?" Argyle asks.

"Not unless she needs us to."

"I would love to steal you away for a bit. Perhaps a walk in the garden?" Enver says much louder, a brow raised in question toward us.

"No," Devonry answers, perhaps too quickly. "Sorry," she amends. "It is important that I practice. I'm sure you understand."

"Most things come naturally to me, so practice isn't something I really do, but what I do understand is how remarkable you look today. My heart might break if you don't allow me but a moment of your time." If I didn't know any better, it might appear that the Prince is giving her puppy eyes. How pathetic.

I wait for her response, teetering on the tips of my toes. Argyle plants an elbow on my shoulder; leaning into me or holding me in place, I'm not sure.

"My deepest apologies for wounding you." She doesn't look sorry at all. "But I'm sure you'll find *something* … to mend your aching heart for you."

His smile fades. "Well, I'll leave you to it then. We can

catch up another time and I'll find a way to soothe the hurt." Enver pats his chest for good measure before briskly leaving the enclosure of the trees.

The red in her cheeks has deepened but Devonry only purses her lips and fingers through the last of her arrows counting them quietly. Before the prince even reaches the steps to the castle she rights herself and sends flaming arrows in rapid succession into the sand.

Thunk. Thunk. Thunk. The arrows hit their target again and again while the air takes on the bitter scent of their wood shafts burning.

"She seems upset." Argyle eyes the castle. "Coast is clear again." I only nod. "What do you think happened between the two of them for her to be so upset and unwilling to talk to him? What could make her angry enough to do this?" He points a long finger in her direction.

"I'm not sure but I'm going to find out." Tipping my head in the direction of the castle, Argyle is quick to take the hint. He commends the Princess on her hard work and swiftly heads away leaving us alone.

The two of us stand watching the flames die. Several silent seconds pass before I move to her side.

"Stop," Devonry says.

"I'm not doing anything."

"I can feel those pretty red eyes judging me, all broody-like." Her proud shoulders curl ever so slightly. The only sign that she's exhausted by all this.

"I don't think pretty is a word you have ever used to describe any part of me."

With a roll of her eyes, she attempts to step away. She doesn't make it far as I move into her path.

"Solomon." Her voice lowers, laced with frustration.

"Devonry." She stares at the ground in answer, so I

keep going. "What happened between you and him? Why the cold shoulder?"

"Oh, he deserves more than a cold shoulder," she snaps. Finally, her blue-gray eyes meet mine.

"Not that I disagree, but for what?"

"I—" Her face flushes further as her lips press into a firm line.

I tilt my chin down trying to get a better look at her face. Sunlight casts itself between branches dotting her cheeks with small slices of light. An emotion I can't quite name teases at her features and I'm torn between demanding what's going on and letting it go for her sake.

"You can tell me anything you know," I say, gently. "I'm listening."

She folds her hands in front of her, sighing. "I went to Prince Enver's room the other night." It's my turn to flush at her comments. Anger is quick to ignite. I straighten but don't move as she continues. "I needed to make him listen…"

I squeeze my eyes shut tightly, my imagination already running away with the worst ideas. Him. Her. Clothes falling away. If he … if he hurt her … Each breath is tight as though I can't quite get enough air. My heart pounds harder and faster.

"Did he touch you? Force himself on you?" It's a wonder she can understand anything that I've said with my teeth grinding together so roughly. Still, she blinks several times, her hand drifting to her chest. "I swear to Levim—"

Her skin is warm, still damp with fresh sweat but my hands rove over her arms looking for any signs of bruising. I tip her chin next and push her hair back to get a good look at her neck. I'd keep checking too if she didn't swat me away.

"No. Solomon." The delicate circles of her hands take

hold of mine, gripping them with no signs that she'll let them go. "He didn't touch me."

Releasing all the air in my lungs, I look for any sign she's lying. Devonry stares back, unflinching. Truth. She has to be telling the truth.

"Do you swear it? If he put his hands on you, tried to get you into his bed—"

"Even if he did, he is my betrothed. What could we even do about it? Everyone would see it as his right."

"Not until you are lawfully wed." *Because until then you're mine.* "If he does anything without your consent"—I swallow past the lump in my throat—"before your wedding night, I'll kill him."

"Solo." Her attention searches the land around us frantically. "You can't say things like that. Not here."

"I mean it." A growl rumbles up my throat. The thought of Enver with Devonry makes my body burn with disgust, with hatred. My jealousy is a form of fear built on the spine of reality—what if … he makes her happy? Then what? Must I let her go? For the sake of Rozentine? I don't want to. My inner beast rebels at the mere thought. She is mine—ours. She just doesn't know it yet.

Then her hands are on my face, thumbs moving in soothing strokes over my jaw. My vision is cast in red, though I try to shove my power and the growing dark feelings rising up inside of me back down into my gut. My fangs lower but don't quite press into my lip.

"He didn't touch me," she whispers. "Listen, he didn't. He didn't touch me. I'm fine. I swear it."

I nod, although her repetition only makes me question the validity of her statement. I hope to the Gods she's not trying to protect him from me. If I find out he's hurt her … if he's forced her to do anything indecent as a favor to gain power, I'll fucking kill him myself. And I will take pleasure in doing so.

"I went to his room to talk, only talk. But when I got there, he was..." My Princess chews at her lip. "He was hands deep in a woman's ... well, I'm sure a man with your experience can figure it out. They were out in the corridor, not even behind closed doors. She, at least, was nervous about getting caught, although Enver seemed to enjoy it. Like he wanted me to watch, to know."

Red dissolves from my vision. However nothing quells the wave of disgust that crashes into me. I cup her hand, pressing it to my cheek to savor every second of her touch. Her palms have become calloused, leaving them rough. Guilt descends upon me. Her hands, once soft and smooth, are now harder. Though I know, deep down, that it is a necessary change that doesn't erase the wish that she could still be the innocent and protected Princess she once was. If I could turn back the clock, I would ensure she never had to suffer the pain of loss and the sharp knife of betrayal—even if it meant King Vernon was still alive. Even if I would have to give up everything we have been through over the last month, including the closeness we now share.

"Like he said, our marriage is only a political one. There will be no love between us, only what is required to produce an heir. Kings take mistresses all the time, right?" Even as she speaks the words, I can tell by the twist of her lips that she detests them. Devonry lifts her face, her lips awkwardly tilting up at the edges by pure force. She looks at me ... for what? Comfort? Yes, that's what she needs now. Comfort. But am I truly the person to give that to her? I want to be. Damned though it makes me, I want to be everything she needs. All these little moments of desire mean everything to me, but this is something more. This is real, raw, and vulnerable.

After returning from battle, I mocked her naiveté for a while. The real world is a cruel place, and she was bound to find out sooner or later. I'd just hoped it wouldn't bring her this much pain. She had to learn what this marriage would be at some point. The truth of her situation is finally clear. She'll never be allowed certain freedoms while her husband can run around sampling the staff like they're his personal buffet.

"It's not unusual for a King to have a mistress or two," I admit, though the words taste like bile on my tongue. She flinches. "But Devonry, listen to me, you deserve more. You deserve someone who is devoted to you. Only you. You deserve more than this boy who waits to play at being a king." I mean every word I say to her, and I pray to the Gods she believes me.

For this minor bit of time, there is no hate between us; there isn't even lust, only sorrow. I don't have to pretend I hate her or pick at her to get any sort of reaction. For now, it's just us—who we are at our core. Two souls lost and trying to hold it all together. I'd do anything to keep us here, to not let this moment go. If I could change things, if I could fix this … Gods I wish I could.

Still holding my attention, she drops my hands, leaving my skin cold. I fight the way my body leans toward her, trying to give her the space she seems to want.

"Don't pity me." Her words are sharp, but as I watch the play of emotions over her face—first pain and then resolve—I realize she's not only talking to me but to herself as well. She doesn't want anyone's pity, least of all her own. "I'm going to change things." Devonry squares her shoulders and inhales, breathing so deeply that it lifts them. "There is no way I'm going to allow myself to be shackled to an idiot Prince who only cares about chasing skirts and drinking."

Pride swells within me. "No, I know you won't." My palms itch with the desire to reach out to her, but I curl my fingers into fists and remain still. As much as I hate to admit it, there are times when one needs to find their determination on their own and now might be such a time for her.

"I can do this," she says, jerking her head up and down as if punctuating that statement.

My lips lift into a smile. "I've never had any doubt." It's raw, pure honesty. So long as I've known her—even as a child—I knew … I know … that she'll rise to where she's supposed to be. Damn the obstacles.

Devonry looks back at me once more. "I…" She blinks and then shakes her head. "Thank you," she says quietly.

"I did nothing."

"No, Solo." Her hand raises once more and the soft glide of her fingers down my jaw makes my insides clench with need. "You've done so much, not the least of which was getting me here safely. I can take care of the rest. Trust in me."

"I trust you," I admit. With my heart, my soul, my life, and all of the ones after this one.

She chuckles and shakes her head, negating my words. "I don't think you do," she replies. "Not yet, at least. Not the way I want you to, but you will. *Soon.* You will." With that, she slips around me and heads toward the castle.

11

DEVONRY

Celine's hands slide through the strands of my shortened hair, soap falling from her fingertips and landing in the pool of water surrounding me. As she washes away the sweat of the day, I find myself sinking deeper and deeper into both the water and my thoughts.

It's funny how a few short weeks ago, this was a regular occurrence—someone else washing me, dressing me, and taking care of me as if I was physically incapable of doing the same activities as the rest of the world. Now, I find discomfort in what was once the standard. To say as much would hurt Celine's feelings, and if I'm being honest, it's been nice having another woman around, so I remain silent and let her perform her self-dedicated duties.

Unlike me, Celine is older and wiser. She's not nearly as old as Sheza but a woman in her prime. Someone close enough to me in age to understand certain things and yet also wiser by many standards. I peer back at her as she moves away from the edge of the tub to the table of soaps and other baubles used in the bathing chamber.

There's no telling Celine's actual age. If I had to guess, I'd say she's only a few years older than me, but she's so good at everything she does—so graceful in the way she moves—so natural in every aspect of her life that it makes me feel like she's eons ahead of me.

When she turns back toward me, I flip around and sink deeper beneath the water until my lips are barely above the surface and the strands of my hair fan out around my neck and shoulders.

"Your Highness?" Celine's voice echoes through the room and I squeeze my eyes shut. "Are you alright?"

Damn me, I think to myself. There's no place for petty inferiority in my life, and yet … I can't help but think that if only I were more like her from the beginning. Would I even be in my current predicament? Could I handle Enver better if I was?

"I'm fine," I lie and sit back up again as she approaches the tub.

She goes to her knees, and one long, slender hand moves over the rim into the water as she lets a few colored salts drop into the liquid and then stirs them around. "Is there something on your mind?" It's a calm question, asked in a carefully composed tone.

The answer, though, causes a riot in my head.

There's so much on my mind that if I were to part my lips and try to let it all fly out, I'd likely vomit up the contents of my stomach along with it. Instead, I shake my head and turn away as she lifts a cup and pours a hefty amount of water down the back of my skull, drenching my hair and rinsing the soap from the strands.

Celine hums in the back of her throat, a soothing sound. She has a beautiful voice, I realize. I wonder if she's ever sung before. "You know," she begins, "I never thought I'd be here like this."

I hadn't even realized my eyes had closed as she'd rinsed my hair until they popped back open. "Here?" I ask, curious. "You mean in Bartoli?"

"Not exactly Bartoli, but here with you, Your Highness," she admits. Celine's touch is gentle as she smoothes the water still clinging to my hair with her fingers, squeezing it out gently. Her attention is solely focused on the task, and perhaps that's by design because it makes her next words easier to consume.

"I'm a bastard," she says. "An unwanted daughter of a rotten branch of a lower noble family."

A rotten branch of lower nobles? *Which family?* The question sticks in my throat. It's inappropriate to ask, but at the same time, I want to know so that I may punish them accordingly once I've regained my throne. Even though I've only known Celine for a few short weeks, her loyalty and kindness have been a saving grace. I bite down on my lower lip as she moves her hands across my scalp. The pressure relaxes my muscles, making me sink further beneath the water with my head back.

It takes considerable effort to reply to her comment. "I think…" I sigh as she hits a rather sore spot. "I've started to realize that nobility has less to do with blood and more to do with personality."

Celine smiles. "My mother said the same thing," she confesses. "She was a maid and died when I was very young. Before she passed, she instilled within me the knowledge that nobility had little to do with one's lineage. Dignity isn't passed down by the Gods. It is earned— through blood, sweat, tears, and hard work. I've lived by that understanding ever since."

I blink at those words before looking at her. Her face is placid. How she does it, I doubt I'll ever know, but she's good at hiding her emotions. Not by a singular flicker of her eyelashes can I determine what she's thinking as she lifts her gaze to mine.

"Your mother sounds like a strong and intelligent woman," I say.

"She was." There's a wealth of pain in those two words. Sadness. Pride. Resignation

"I'm sorry you lost her." The words I say feel pathetic in the face of her admission. "How…" I stop myself before I ask something offensive.

As if she can read my thoughts, Celine's face finally changes and softens once more. "It's alright," she says, her movements continuing as she dumps more water over my hair and shoulders, careful not to pour it directly into my face. "I've come to terms with my station."

I consider her words carefully. She continues to work, her movements soft and unhesitant as I gather my thoughts. By the time I think I know what to say to that, the bath is over and I'm standing for her to wrap a long cloth around my body. I tuck the corner against my breasts as I step out of the tub and onto the cool, tiled floor.

"I think your mother was right," I admit. "In terms of what the nobility should be—dignified, kind, worthy— those things aren't reserved for those of us descended from the Gods."

Quiet follows my statement and I look up as I follow her out of the bathing chamber into the main dressing room. Celine comes to a stop by a vanity before lifting a brush into her hands.

"You're good at everything I've seen you do," I tell her honestly.

Celine's face blanches in shock. Why should she be surprised, though? I've only spoken the truth. I move to the vanity and take a seat, but instead of letting her attend to me, I take the brush from her hand and start at the ends of my choppy hair as I look into the mirror.

"If I'm honest," I say. "I'm jealous of that. It seems so silly to me now how I'd become accustomed to people doing such mundane tasks for me—day in and day out—so much so, that it was, at first, a struggle to figure out how to do the things for myself without help." I look away.

"That's not through any fault of yours, Princess," Celine protests.

"Maybe not," I agree as I yank the brush through the strands of my hair. "But the fact remains, I was complicit in *my station*." Because being a Princess was easy … or so I'd assumed. I thought being royal meant that I would have to sacrifice larger-than-life things—like true love. I had no clue what things those beneath me had to sacrifice. Life. Love. Safety. All for the sake of survival. "I didn't try to learn more; I didn't try to do things for myself until I was forced to," I say.

Silence falls over us at that statement. I finish brushing the knots from my hair and set the brush on the vanity. Celine remains still and silent as I stand and move across the room again. I let the towel fall away as I pull on the thin night chemise and then wrap a silken robe around it. A gentle breeze fills the room from the open window—a necessity for keeping these chambers cool after the hot baths.

I stride over to the window and look out over the land that is not my own. Stars glitter overhead, surrounding a fat white moon as it shines across the sands and ocean.

"Things are going to change," I inform her. "I've changed and so must Rozentine. You're right. Being born noble doesn't promise dignity. Just as being born a bastard or peasant doesn't promise powerlessness." I turn back to her as the words leave my lips.

Her eyes are red-rimmed, I realize. This is the first time I've seen her expression shift and change in a way that I know isn't intended or allowed. Her gaze is watery and when it meets mine, she falls to her knees, bowing her head. I inhale sharply at her sudden position.

It's a natural inclination now to order her to stand. The discomfort I feel at seeing her bow before me is fresh, but it's there for a reason. It's there because I no longer see her —or anyone—as different from myself. Status. Classes. Noble station. All of it is irrelevant in the face of betrayal and death.

"Your Highness," Celine whispers, her voice choked. "Please forgive me for speaking out of turn. I didn't mean to make you feel—"

"Stop." Though she can't see with her head bowed the way it is, I hold up a hand as if I can halt her words with a singular movement. "Don't apologize."

Celine's head tips back and her teary eyes meet mine. I lower my hand back to my side and leave the window, striding across the floor until I'm standing before her. Once there, I crouch down to meet her gaze more directly.

"There is nothing that you have done that warrants an apology," I assure her. "If anything, I should be the one apologizing to you."

She frowns. "I don't understand."

I sigh and take her hands, helping her back to her feet. As she stands to her full height, though she's only a few inches taller than me, I have to crane my head up to continue to meet her eyes.

"I have been a pathetic excuse for a royal," I tell her. "Until I was chased from my throne and palace, I had very little practical knowledge of how my people live and how they are treated in Rozentine." I *was* the naive-headed, pretty-faced fool Nasir told Enver about. "For that, I'm sorry, Celine. For that, I promise you that things will change. I am changing, and as the heir to Rozentine's throne, I swear to you that people like you—children of nobles cast out of their homes and lineages simply because of the status of one of their parents—will be welcomed into the new Rozentine with open arms. As will anyone of any status."

I've already thought about this long and hard, and as I speak the words, they feel right. They feel like the truth. The time for change is upon Rozentine. I'm only ashamed that it's taken so long.

"Your Highness…" Celine's voice is breathless.

I shake my head and offer her a smile. "Please," I say. "I think you only need to refer to me by my title when we're in front of the other nobles or royalty. When it's just the two of us, Celine, I'd like for you to call me Devonry. I'd like for us to be friends."

"Friends…" She sounds shocked and I can't blame her. If her life is as I suspect it's been, then the idea of a Princess befriending the half-blood child of a noble house is likely preposterous. But I don't care anymore. There are a lot of changes coming that people will look at as insanity. Celine doesn't say as much, though. Instead, she composes herself quickly and then offers me a smile of her own. "Yes." She sniffles. "I'd like that … Devonry."

I press my luck further. I keep her hands locked in mine when she tries to pull away. "I hope, too," I tell her, "that someday you'll be able to tell me more about you—about your past and your life. Everything about you."

Celine blinks at that statement and then after a brief moment, she gently shakes her head. "I would like that too," she says, "but not tonight. Tonight, you need to rest."

Her hand lifts from mine to press her fingertips to my cheek. "You have shadows under your eyes. You're tired."

Tired is an understatement, but I'll let her have it. I release a breath I hadn't known I was holding and turn away. "You're right," I admit again, "and I'm ready for bed."

Less than an hour later, I'm ensconced in the private chamber provided to me by the Bartoli Royal Family, staring up at the intricately designed ceiling beyond the gauzy fabrics that linger over the four-poster bed I'm lying in.

I turn on my side and shut my eyes. Seconds pass and then minutes. Still, I remain awake. Celine was right—I'm exhausted. So much has happened in such a short amount of time. I assumed I'd fall asleep the second my head hit the pillow, but that has yet to happen.

Closing my eyes once more, I begin to count backward.

Ten. A flash of white dances behind my eyes.

Nine. I ignore it.

Eight. It comes back.

Seven. The white turns into a shimmering gold.

Six. There's no more ignoring it as it grows brighter with each passing number.

Five. I give up the game.

There is no making it down to 'one' because the moment I open my eyes I realize I've achieved my purpose.

I'm asleep—except instead of the bottomless slumber I'd anticipated and hoped for, I'm dropped into yet another dream.

I'm back in the field of clouds, and as always, I'm not alone.

With a groan, I turn away from the man who looks just like Solomon. "What is wrong with me?" I mutter to myself. *Why is it always him in these dreams?* It's as if my mind cannot bear to be away from him when I know such a thing is impossible. There will soon come a day when he is finally free of me and I of him. However, the more time we spend together, I'm starting to wonder if that frightens me more than it relieves me.

12

SOLOMON

I know, even before I open my eyes, that this is not a normal dream. It's a connector — part of the thin link my soul still has to my past. To Levim. I shouldn't, but some days, I live for these dreams. Where I close my eyes and open them to see her smiling face.

This is a place where Devonry and I are unbound from the laws of the real world. Back where we started at the beginning of time. Her as Aerea and I as her lover.

My eyes open and take in the surroundings; sheer slivers of mist drift around me. Clouds encroaching, dark at their edges and growing lighter the deeper in they go. Prisms of light shatter the sanctity of the space, illuminating the woman who walks through it all. *Her.*

Even in slumber, it seems, I can't escape my sinful desires. The second I see her, my cock hardens and throbs. The same muscles that had ached with soreness and tension in the waking world now bunch up once again. I want her. Need her.

I sit up from where I'm lying and she pauses, mere feet away. "Love?" I reach out my hand. Aerea always takes it.

Aerea isn't frightened of what she feels for me. After all, we're meant to be. It's only Devonry, who doesn't quite remember, who doesn't understand the ties that bind us, that would recoil.

I expect Aerea's face to spread into a serene smile as she comes towards me, but instead, her brow furrows, and her lips part in confusion. As if she senses my internal hunger, she takes a hesitant step back—away from me. The small movement causes the beast within me to shift. This is not Aerea. It's her. It's really her. *Devonry.*

Her confusion is clear in her expression and the tightness of her body. Her shoulders are ramrod straight and she half turns as if she means to flee. I won't let her get far. Perhaps in the waking world, I must obey her commands, but here … here she is meant for me.

I'm on my feet and towering in front of her—closing the distance between us in the blink of an eye. A startled yelp lets loose from her lips and she stumbles back, nearly falling. I catch her by the arms and pull her closer. "Wait!" Her wide eyes look up into my face, fear and bewilderment warring for space beyond her blue irises.

I bend closer, inhaling her sweetened scent. She shivers as my breath touches her face. She smells so fucking good, I want to taste her. She's safe here, but more than that, it's the only place where I can truly touch her without consequence. Where I can finally—blessedly—give in to my desires.

Silence slips between us, growing louder and louder with each passing second. My insides tighten and contract. Finally, I've had enough. "I'm waiting," I say, breaking the quiet. "But for what?"

Her chest pumps up and down, swelling her chest with the movements. Shakily, her hands lift to my chest, brushing against my muscles to push me slightly back and then she seems to realize something. Her mouth parts, forming the perfect 'o' shape and her eyes dart down to find what I've known all along. That I'm naked.

My lips twitch with amusement as her gaze lands squarely on my cock. "Gods…" Her breathless voice trails off.

Unable to stop myself, I wrap my fingers around her wrist and drag one of her hands downward. "Would you like to touch me?" I ask.

She doesn't respond, nor does she fight me as I take her palm and place it directly on the pulsating shaft that bounces against my lower abdomen. "I-I…" She shakes her head, and when I feel her try to retract her hand, I grip her wrist tighter, keeping it pinned against me. Her eyes flick back to my face.

"Touch me," I command.

"N-no. I don't know what I'm doing here. Gods, this is a dream. This is another dream." Devonry shakes her head hard enough to send the tendrils of her hair fluttering over her cheeks.

I bend my head and press my lips close to her ear. "That's right," I assure her. "This is a dream, Princess. Just a dream. You can do anything you want here. There are no consequences here."

Devonry goes silent, and against my cock, her fingers tremble. It's wrong of me, perhaps, but if fate has already decided to keep us apart, I'll take what I can't have in the light of day by the dark of night.

"Solomon?" I close my eyes at the sound of my name pouring from her lips. Not Levim. *Solomon.* Me.

There is something in the way she speaks my name. A concoction of feelings and all the things that remain unsaid. Fearful yearning laced with tragic regret. My heart thrusts against the cage of my ribs, pounding in my chest. I wonder, if it continues for too long, will the appendage thrust itself from my insides if only to make her notice it?

What an image that might be. My still beating heart lain at the feet of my soulmate.

Say it again, I want to demand. *Let me hear my name pass over those lips again and again.* Even this minimal glimpse at passion is enough to turn my blood into molten, volcanic fire.

"I'm here." There is no more space between us.

Her free hand remains against my bare chest and she's no longer fighting to move away. A blessing. Confusion prickles her expression, forming into little wrinkles both between her brows and at the corners of her lips. "This isn't … real?"

The deep ache in my soul wants to tell her the truth, but I know that she won't be able to accept it. Even if I want her to realize how I feel about her and if she knows that I'm truly here and that we have both been participants in these shared dreams of ours, then once I wake, the whole of our relationship will have shifted. If I'm honest, then we'll lose this moment between us. The one safe space that I fucking need, if only to keep my hands to myself during our waking hours. I can't do it. So, I do the one thing I never wanted to do.

I lie to her. I'll play her fool even if it makes a betrayer out of me. "Of course not," I say. It feels like shards of glass ripping through my vocal cords at just the thought of saying the words. "This is all just a dream." I slide my hand through her hair, pushing it out of the way so that I may cup her cheek and tilt her face up to mine.

I release her hand and she pulls it away from my cock, moving it instead to the vast expanse of my chest as if she's reassuring herself that she's truly seeing and feeling this—despite my words. The tips of her fingers tease at the hair that curls between my pecs. Her gaze is focused. Her lips part and I spot the pink tongue that hides behind her teeth, pressing against the pearly whites.

"How does it feel?" I ask, prompting her.

Her throat bobs and still, she doesn't look at me, but at least she responds. "Smooth," she admits. "Harder than I expected."

I chuckle, the sound a rumble in my chest and throat. "Was my cock also harder than you expected?" I ask.

Her lips clamp shut and she shoots a dark glare up to my face. I grin, feeling lighter than I have in years at the petulant and embarrassed glimmer in her eyes. My hands move down to her waist and I tug her against me, forcing her to feel the evidence of my arousal against her belly.

A gasp leaves her lips and she slaps my shoulder. "Solo!"

This was what I wanted. This ease between us is as natural as breathing. Her taunting and embarrassment. Her honor and love. I dip my head further and set my lips upon her bare shoulder, so soft and delicate. I hug her to me, pressing our bodies into one another. Gods, how long have I craved this feeling? Since my first breath, perhaps? No, since hers.

Since I realized that my only purpose in this world was tied to a tiny, feisty little Princess with more bite than bark.

Devonry's hands press against my shoulders, but she's not strong enough to peel me from her. After a while, she gives up the fight and I feel her hands hesitantly move around me. "Solomon?" she repeats my name and it sings in my chest, making me feel whole.

I don't answer her, not until she speaks again.

"Since this is a dream, I guess … I can tell you the truth." I frown but don't look at her face. Not yet. She sniffs hard, the sound an echo in the vast space around us that's full of nothing but mist and clouds. "I'm scared." She whispers the words so softly that I nearly miss them despite how close we are.

Pulling away from her, I stare down at the heart-shaped upturned face of my most beloved of creatures. Her skin is smooth and soft. The dark circles that plague her in reality are gone. I skim my fingers along her forearms, up to her shoulders, her neck, then cradle her face, holding her as gently as I would the world. Her lashes curl against her cheeks as she closes her eyes and lets out a small sigh.

With one thumb, I stroke her cheek and with the other, I tilt her head to expose her neck and trace the tendon that stretches down the length of it. I lean closer, waiting for her to tell me to stop again. Nervous that the dream will end before it even begins.

"What are you afraid of?" I ask her.

She swallows, her throat moving with the force of it. "This … can't happen," she says. "I can't dream of you this way."

"Why?" My gaze bores into hers. I want to know the truth. I'll beg for it if I must.

The scent of her floods my senses, floral and light. I press a kiss to her jawline, grinning against her when she shivers in response. "Solo…"

"Tell me, Devonry," I plead. "Why can't you let this happen?" Her breath shudders in her chest. I can practically hear the rapid thrum of her heartbeat. My fangs ache to sink into her flesh, to taste the divine blood in her veins. "It's just a dream," I lie again. "Everything is fine here."

"Right," she says, the word slipping out and obviously not meant for me as she continues. "This is just a dream. Of course, it's not real." She shakes her head as if trying to dispel the reservations still clinging to her.

I grit my teeth against her words. If that's what she

needs to believe to allow herself this pleasure, then so be it. After all, I'm the one who started that. I let my desires seduce both of us. Before I have long to mentally flagellate myself, however, her touch distracts me with its soft hesitancy. Lightning pierces me as her tiny little palm moves back down over the ridges of my abdomen and further.

"Fuck." A groan releases from me.

Now that she's seemed to convince herself that this is all a delusion, she wastes no time. Her hand closes around the base of my cock and my head snaps away from her. The tight vice of her grip is a brand on my body. Unable to stop myself, my head slams down and I take her mouth with a force of all of the agony I've been in for the past twenty years.

As though my kiss has given her permission, Devonry's hands move faster, gliding down my length. "I'm still afraid," she admits, even as she pumps my cock in her grasp. How the fuck can she talk when I'm losing my mind like this?

"What is there to be afraid of?" I don't know how, but I manage to ask the question through clenched teeth that threaten to shatter.

"Everything."

A confession.

A plea for help.

"Then let me protect you." The space between our lips is nearly nonexistent. The beast within rumbles, the noise traveling up and vibrating my chest. Her eyes flare. Something wicked in her gaze answers. Heat. Want. Lust. Everything I've longed to see. If I'm not careful I'll lose myself. What sense I have now, little as it may be, keeps me in control.

Now, she is the one closing the space between us and I am at her disposal for however she finds fit to use me. She presses her lips to mine, her arm tightening at my back and holding me closer. Her kiss is gentle, probing, and infinitely curious. My fingers slide into her hair. With a harsh pull, I crane her neck back and force her face upward to meet mine. Her lips part as I kiss her again, licking at the seam of her mouth before I delve inside and steal the stifled moans that threaten to spill out.

Time drifts by, inconsequential. Her body warms as seconds pass. Devonry pulls away, leaving me breathless. She touches her fingers to her reddened lips. "This is—" I don't let her finish. Ripping her hand away from my cock, I turn and the two of us go down in a heap. Our bodies collide with the softness of the misty ground.

Her nipples are pebbled into little rosy buds. As I pin her hands together above her head, I bend and take one into my mouth through the material of her thin shift, laving it with my tongue for several seconds before moving to the second and taking it, too, into my mouth. A cry of pleasure erupts from her throat and beneath me, Devonry's body undulates.

I explore her as I never could in the light of day and when I lift my head, it's to find her eyes squeezed tightly shut and her cheeks a light shade of red. "This isn't real," Devonry breathes the words out again. "Not real."

I don't say it—I can't—but deep in my soul, I scream out. *It is real!* Everything about this is real. My touch. Her pleasure. Our bodies rolling against one another. All of this is real. She does not answer to Aerea nor I to Levim. Here, we are truly ourselves. I grit my teeth. The roiling emotions from before come storming back.

Perhaps she doesn't want to think it's real. The thought stabs into my gut and were it not for the fact that it is an intangible object, I would be bleeding out all over her precious skin.

She's not fully Awakened, I have to remind myself. She won't recognize the truth of who I am. Of who she is. She can't understand the flood of emotion mixed with the primal need that will forever tie us together. Not yet.

The weight of that truth makes my shoulders heavy and my heart burns in my chest. It's been so long since I've been honest with anyone about her, and never to her. The night King Vernon had died, though I'd mourned in my own way—distracted as I was in securing her safety—a small piece of me had hoped … that everything I'd ever wanted would finally come to fruition. That, perhaps, Devonry would Awaken and see…

Now, though, it's become obvious that she is voluntarily blind. Willing to walk through this world with me at her side, but not as her soulmate. Somehow, I manage to keep my mouth closed and the dangerous sentiment to myself.

Even in death, it seems that her father's words and the warning he gave remain a constant chain that binds me. *She is not for you.* I bite down on my tongue until I taste blood as it floods my mouth. Whether he understood the cruelty of telling me that I was not meant for her or not, the words are like bolts through my limbs—weighing me down, even here in what is supposed to be a safe place for her and I to share our love.

Devonry is forbidden to me. A true soulmate would understand that. A true love would be able to stand back and wish only for her happiness. If happiness can only be found without me, though, I don't want it. I want her to suffer as I've suffered. I want her to know this same desire.

As those thoughts consume me, I allow my actions to take on a life of their own. My lips trail her skin. My tongue licks the salt from her flesh.

"Don't stop," she begs softly.

In shock, I lift away, looking down at her as Devonry

bows her forehead against my chest. She presses a lingering kiss against my skin.

Who am I to refuse my Princess?

A growl rumbles up and out of me as I take her in my arms. She gasps. Her small body presses against me, trembling as she wraps her legs around my waist. The heat of her settles against my stomach. Any space between us is damn near too much, a sentiment I believe she shares when she plants her mouth on mine.

Want runs rampant in my veins, all of it heading straight for my cock. When my tongue slips over her lips, I'm already drunk on the taste of her. And I need more. Devonry makes a desperate mewling sound as my hands cup her backside.

The clouds sway, somehow never losing their solidity under our bodies. Wisps of white curl around us. Devonry holds onto me, running her fingers over my skin, nails skimming my hardening flesh enough to scratch but not enough to truly mark me.

I slide my hand up the curve of her body, skimming over her breast, before I push aside the slender straps of her gown. The loosened fabric falls enough to reveal her cleavage. I smile against her lips while I pinch and roll her nipple through the thin material, drawing forth a moan.

"Please," she whispers, sending a thrill through me all the way down to my toes. My cock hardens further, needing her as painfully as she needs me.

"Please? Please, what?" I say between kisses that trail down to the thin material.

"Solomon," Devonry whines when my mouth meets the top of her chest.

With my chin, I nudge the fabric away, exposing her. "Please, what?" I repeat before flicking my tongue over her nipple and sucking it into my mouth. She only answers in incoherent noises as she writhes against me, hips rocking, searching. "Use your words," I encourage with a smirk when her nails start to truly dig into my flesh.

"More, I need more of you."

The words have hardly left her mouth when my fangs extend to their full length. I can smell her blood running through her veins with every beat of her heart and it's as enticing as it ever was. My fangs scrape over her breast but do not puncture, though the idea threatens to end me.

If this is real, if this is Devonry, then she's never seen me feed. She's never had to witness the darker side of my abilities and I won't start now for fear this dream might turn into a nightmare for her. I slide my tongue over my fangs, set on tasting her in other ways.

"As you say." I nudge her legs further apart and run my hands up her thighs, pushing the material of her dress as I go. The desire to sink my fangs into the crease between her thigh and glistening cunt rises with demanding need but I quickly push the thought away.

I lower myself, trailing my nose over her stomach, past the bunching fabric, and to the patch of hair even lower. The scent of her nearly unravels all of the control I have. She's wet, her body practically begging for my touch.

So beautiful. Every single bit of her is utterly stunning.

"Solomon..." My name is more of a question than anything else. I hum against her skin, still finding new flesh to kiss. "Look at me."

I lift my gaze to hers. Her eyes search my face before she nods and smiles. I never look away, keeping my attention glued to hers even when my fingers slide into her, even when her eyes roll back as my thumb finds that bundle of nerves and begins to circle.

She doesn't know that in this world, I truly am me and she is her. That this isn't just a figment of her imagination.

Whatever she is looking for in this moment, I can't be sure, but gods, I hope she finds it.

Settling myself further against the soft cushion of the clouds, I drag each of her legs onto my shoulders. Unable to wait any longer, I press my face between her thighs and drag my tongue up in one painfully slow motion. It's my turn to moan as the taste of her instantly sets my body ablaze.

Within a few flicks of my tongue, I'm able to find that same bundle of nerves and drag my tongue over it in long, powerful strokes. She sucks a breath in, fingers finding my hair again. Her hips move against my mouth as I alternate the flicking of my tongue and sucking against her. Over my shoulders, her legs quake with each second that passes.

I need more. I need more. I need more.

My body screams at me. The head of my cock fucking *throbs* with incessant need.

Devonry squirms as though she can't handle the sensation, but I grab her thighs and hold her against me while I feast. And feast I do. Nothing has ever tasted so sweet.

Her breaths come in uneven pants, as do mine. I can't inhale without my entire body pulsating. My cock is heavy under me, a need I force myself to ignore. The slickness of her coats my cheeks and chin, but even that is not enough. I could drown in it. I could drown in her.

Those long, delicate fingers tighten in the strands of my hair holding me to her and I know she's close. I can feel it in the way she rides my face, in the way my tongue is flooded with her taste.

My growl vibrates against her as I anticipate what's to come. And that's enough. I swipe my tongue over her, never truly getting my fill. Her thighs flex around my face, her back arching as she cries out.

What I think is the start of my name is ripped away as

the world dissolves around us. The clouds disappear, her touch no longer there, but the memory still leaves my skin tingling. Darkness descends, then is blinked away as I open my eyes and find myself back in my room. Alone but with the taste of her ecstasy still on my tongue.

13
SOLOMON

Devonry moves gracefully, wearing an orange slip of fabric dripping with gold gems, at Lord Byron's side, only coming to a stop once they reach a small group of men. She nods to each in turn as they're introduced, giving her the slightest bows of their own. Even at this distance, her eyes manage to find mine, and her cheeks flush crimson.

That's right. Think of me as we were last night. Think of me with my face buried between your legs and my fingers coated in your desire.

Because how can she possibly think of anything else? My own mind is only replaying the memory again and again without leaving much room to think of anything else. It's a wonder I was able to get out of bed this morning after needing to relieve myself of this tortuous lust twice. Okay, three times. And after this, it's about to be four.

Lord Byron reaches out and pats her arm, directing her to whomever must be speaking. She pulls her attention away then. I shift, not liking the way Lord Byron's touch lingers on her arm. My Princess smiles with trained diplomacy as I let loose a breath.

Argyle hands me a drink much more delicate than the mead I'm used to. For the life of me, I can't be bothered to bring it to my lips even when my stomach growls. Not when the taste of Devonry is still evident on my tongue. The scent of her arousal is stained on my cheeks, and I can't force myself to eat or drink for fear I'll wash it away.

"You're different today," Argyle mentions, watching me closely over the rim of his tall, narrow glass.

"Different, how?" I look through the crowd, over bodies already writhing to the pluck of strings on a foreign instrument. Large floral bouquets in obnoxiously large vases on the tables block my vision as Devonry is guided from one conversation to the next.

"For a moment I thought you might be smiling."

Sliding my hand over my mouth, I try to wipe away my expression. What is there to be said? Not a whisper can be uttered about that dream ... quite possibly what most certainly was *not* a dream. At least, not in the ordinary sense. My proximity feeds her growing abilities as hers unknowingly feeds our mating bond. It is not entirely uncommon for mates to visit each other in such a way through our dreams.

But only if both parties are in thought of the other.

"You must have drunk too much already. I am no different today than yesterday," I answer around the tightening of my throat and the lump of hope forming there, waiting to choke me to death.

My friend hums, his eyes narrowing. He doesn't believe me. I don't believe me.

Normally, I'm a better liar than this. *Shit.*

He follows my gaze as it lingers on Devonry once

more. "She is something, isn't she?" He tilts his head in the Princess' direction.

She is everything. I don't scream the thought as the stirring thing within me demands. Instead, I dip my chin in agreement.

"She's growing into herself. Soon to be a political force within the court as well as something to be reckoned with on the battlefields. A strong queen. Well rounded," Argyle continues as he scans the crowd from the dark corner we stand in. "So, you think she'll take to this flaming arrow idea then?"

She'd take to most anything if given the fighting chance.

"Yes. More so if we get her on a horse as well or even get her moving on foot with shifting targets." As if she knows we speak of her, Devonry looks to us for a fleeting second, then turns back to another conversation with a Bartoli noble. The absence of her attention fans the all too frequent desperation to be at her side.

"Are you training her to defend herself, or are you training her for war?"

"Yes."

"You do realize she isn't another one of your soldiers out on the battlefield, right?" He sips his drink, bringing the weight of his attention back to me.

"Why do you say that?" I bring my glass to my nose and sniff but don't bother to taste it.

"She's not expendable. The world will care if she passes. You'll care."

Every cell within my body ignites at his words. My fangs pierce through my gums and my skin burns as my body threatens to shift. "It's for her own safety, Argyle. You know this," I say mostly for my own benefit.

"I know you're fond of fleeting touches and whispering in her ear."

"If you say so." I set my drink on the tray of a passing servant, wanting it out of my hands. A second longer and it might be nothing but shards of glass and spilled liquid. "As far as Devonry goes, I'm happy to teach her whatever she'd like. And maybe…" I chew on the inside of my lips. "Maybe talk of fleeting touches and whispers are not appropriate. We are here to support her, help her as she Awakens. We cannot forget"—*I cannot forget*— "she belongs to Rozentine."

"Actually, I think I might know someone who can help her really dive deeper into her powers. An expert in this sort of thing," Argyle says.

"Wasn't the entire point of collecting you to help her with this?" I ask but don't manage to look his way.

"Actually, the point of collecting me was so that you could use my connections. Remember, I got us on that boat. My talents got us out of Rozentine, and my talents will help get us out of this terrible place when the time comes as well." He taps a finger impatiently against the glass. "Clearly, Bartoli isn't going to help. The Galeanos are playing both sides—Nasir's and hers. Honestly, I wouldn't be at all surprised if they are putting her off in order to send word to Prince Nasir. For all we know, they could be in on this whole thing."

"Argyle—"

"For her safety, Solo." He throws my own words back at me in the wake of my unease.

He might have me there. As much as the idea of letting anyone else near Devonry terrifies me, it could be necessary.

"I want you to dig into this so-called 'expert' before he gets anywhere near her. Find out all his dirty secrets." The smile I may have worn feels long gone now that this new worry sits so heavily on my chest.

"Ah, I was hoping you'd say that. Want to take bets on what I'll find? I'm thinking he has a thing for goats." Argyle fights his own grin.

Across the room, Lord Byron has vanished from Devonry's side though she continues to chat with the Bartoli nobles with about as much interest as she would if she were having a conversation with a broomstick. "No bet," I mumble, looking over all the provocative wear and the citizens who lean into their drinks as if they can't exist without them. The flash of charms on their garments and the excess of gems strung from the ceiling to reflect the light of the sconces is nearly blinding but my focus remains. Lord Byron hovers in another corner, nodding along to a shadow. His lips move in quiet conversation, those eyes of his glowing purple.

"Oh, come on. At the very least, I'm sure he's sleeping with someone's wife."

The chatter sounds distant to me now as I focus on the Lord of Daemonium, our Rozentine Ambassador. He smiles broadly though I can't quite tell what he is smiling about or who it is that he is talking to. I squint, my vision flaring red, then back again only to still find the space next to him very empty. With a glance at Devonry, I find her as she was. Relief is a minimal help.

Argyle, still throwing out ideas, doesn't seem to notice when my entire body tenses. Lord Byron is nothing but a shadow himself as he strides quickly from the room. The hairs on the back of my neck rise. Something is wrong. Very wrong.

And I intend to find out exactly what that is.

"Don't let the Princess out of your sight," I snap, before he can finish telling me of this new fetish with fish oil he's heard of.

"—ah, okay." I don't need to see him to know what little excitement he'd had is quickly fading.

I settle a hand on the pommel of my sword and start to move through the groups of people still avoiding taking their seats at the long banquet tables. My steps move in time with the dark tune being plucked by a standing musician near the head table. Several of the women I pass giggle. One even dares to reach out and grab my wrist. I try my best at an apologetic smile when I shake her off, but I'm sure it only appears as a scowl.

My palm meets the chilled wood of the door and it opens easily as I push my way into the hall. The door closes, muffling the music and chatter, leaving me alone on the other side. I walk a few paces one way and then the next with no clear indication of where he might have gone. Sighing, I pinch the bridge of my nose and turn back.

Cunning dark eyes stare back at me. My vision bleeds red in an instant, fangs and nails extending.

"I never thought you'd be so *jumpy*." Prince Enver chuckles.

"Prince Enver." I grind his name between my teeth, wishing to Levim that it was his bones instead.

"Leaving the party already?" He slides his hand into his pockets, rocking on his heels. The look of innocence on his face is well rehearsed but I see through every second of it. I don't believe Prince Enver to be kind without ulterior motives. Not that he is being particularly kind at the moment.

"No, I'm not leaving just yet." I stand straighter, loving how my height towers over his. "Just thought I'd look around for the sake of the Princess' security."

"I can assure you, my castle is well guarded." The Prince has the audacity to look me over head to toe, still smiling as if he knows something I don't yet.

I stand still, maintaining composure under his contempt. "That is a comfort to hear but I still have a job to do."

He nods, even humming as though he might agree. "You know Princess Devonry is looking for you. Or rather was until you sprinted from the room as though you had a very important place to be." Enver picks a stray reddish strand of hair from his shoulder and lets it drop to the ground between us. "She mentioned something about asking you for a dance this evening. Probably to avoid the many hands of my court, which I don't blame her for."

I will my fangs to retract and breathe through the flash of my crimson vision. She must be desperate for a reprieve if she is actually thinking of asking me for a dance. Not that I would mind, but it's abundantly clear that Enver does indeed mind.

"So you've come here to tell me the Princess would like a dance?" I ask, knowing how carefully this situation must be treated. I'm speaking with her betrothed, even if he's a trollop of a man. "I shall endeavor not to keep her waiting." Before I can even make it a full step toward the door, Prince Enver's hand lands on my chest, stopping me.

"I've seen the way you look at her, *guardsman*." I raise a brow but don't dare to move an inch as he speaks. "Your eyes follow her with much more hunger than a man who only wishes to keep her safe. You watch my future wife the way a man does when he only thinks of her pretty little cunt."

"My relationship with Her Highness is purely … professional." My mind wanders quickly to the night on her balcony. To the nearness of her, the scent of her skin, her warmth, and all those other nights when perhaps I'd been closer than should be allowed for our positions.

"Right. Professional." He pats my chest, the motion full

of contempt. "You see, Solomon. The Princess, by all legalities, is mine. By the standards of her own country, she is to be given to me as a virgin." That dark, plotting gaze roams over me again. "Should she appear to be anything less, the entirety of our alliance may crumble before it's even fully been made. Surely, you are smart enough to understand that?"

Forcing a reassuring smile to my lips, I push his hand away from my body. "While I appreciate your concern for my country, I will remind you that there is only one person here that I serve."

His smile slowly dissolves, moving closer to me still. "I would watch what you say while you are in my kingdom," he whispers. "If I were you, I'd also find a reason not to be so near my betrothed. In my country, it wouldn't look good for her to be dancing with her guard." Enver tugs at the bottom of his jacket, straightening it, and refreshing that same charming smile he likes to wear. "I'm only looking out for her. However, should you have any improper ideas regarding my bride, I will be happy to remind you of the consequences."

If only I could shut myself off to her. If only I could turn off the desire to be everything she needs and more. If only we lived in another time, another world, and a different place … But this time, this world, this place rears its ugly head to remind us—to remind me—of how exactly I should be living.

I hold his gaze. The two of us are silent for several long moments before he chuckles and turns back to the party. "Enjoy your evening, guardsman."

The door closes softly behind him. I close my eyes, trying and failing not to think about my hands around his neck and his face turning five different shades of blue. I would love for Enver to give me a reason to act on these violent delights. And if the bastard has anything to do with Nasir's act of betrayal, well, I'll have every reason to kill them both myself.

14
DEVONRY

Thunk. I jerk another arrow out of its sheath, line it up, and release it again.

Thunk. Close but not quite where it needs to be. I repeat the process another three times.

Thunk. Thunk. Thunk.

The target is littered with arrows at this point and my muscles are screaming at me for relief. Everything aches, from my hands to my arms and shoulders. When I finally lower my arms and look down, I realize that my forearm is striped with red lines and I wince as I touch one.

I've been out here for so long that everyone has since retired. Sweat now coats my skin and I'll likely need to sneak into the bathing chamber before I go to bed so I don't bother Celine in the morning. I've gotten much better at shooting, more so than I ever imagined I would. Now, the bow and arrow don't feel quite as foreign to me as they used to.

It's a wonder I ever actually struck the slave trader back in Carion City. Perhaps it had been the conditions or, more likely, the Gods had been the ones to guide my hand.

As if they were telling me it was alright to make this change. It doesn't feel alright. In fact, it feels like a betrayal. Unfortunately for me, though, I have little choice.

If I'm going to take Rozentine back and free my people from Nasir, if I'm ever going to return to my home and the throne, then I need to be willing to make this sacrifice. My soul for the lives of thousands. It is the price of royalty. My people need a Queen—they deserve one—who is willing to do whatever it takes.

As those thoughts fill my mind, I lift my bow once more and reach for a fresh arrow. I notch it against the bow and pull back, only to pause as a familiar voice echoes through the air. "Out late, Princess?"

I spin abruptly, startled, and yelp as the arrow loosens from my grip and goes flying. Horror descends as it soars through the air, right toward the man who has saved my life more times than I care to admit. Solomon's eyes flash red as I wait for the arrow to strike him through.

It never does.

When he neither shouts nor grunts in pain after several silent beats, I glance down and find the arrow's shaft in his fist. *He ... caught it?* I move my gaze upward to his face.

"I'm sorry," I say, the words escaping on a breath. It's so quiet compared to my racing heart which thuds an impossibly loud rhythm in my ear, that it's a wonder he hears it, but he must because Solo looks down at the arrow in his hand and then back at me before speaking.

"You should be more careful in the future," he states as if he wasn't seconds away from dying a few seconds prior.

"I could have killed you," I say, my voice tight as it grows louder. "*You* should be more careful."

Solomon arches a brow my way. "You wouldn't have hurt me," he replies.

I scoff. "This isn't the place for your arrogance," I snap back.

"It's not arrogance," he says calmly. "There's no possibility of an inexperienced marksman getting the better of me."

Inexperienced marksman? A low growl rumbles up my throat at his words. I know he's right, but it still bites like an insult. Solomon looks around at the empty training grounds before his eyes fixate on the target I've been using for practice. He strides across the open space until he's standing at my side. Once he is, he carefully slides the arrow back into the ground sheath at my side.

I swallow roughly, taking a step back. He's too close. The heat of him, the scent of him—it practically overwhelms my senses and reminds me of those damned dreams I keep having. Dreams where he plays a very particular role ... as my lover. I shake my head, trying to clear the memories away. It doesn't help.

A red glow moves over me and I glance up, realizing that Solo's illuminated eyes haven't yet faded. Normally, they do, but he's still using his abilities for some reason. Why, though, I couldn't say. I'm starting to lose all understanding of Solomon. It's as if the longer we're together, the more his actions confuse me.

"Your hands," he says, and I glance down to note several cuts on my palm and fingers. "You've been practicing too hard."

Subconsciously, I tuck my arms behind my back. *I wonder why I*—an inexperienced marksman—*would practice too hard.* "It's fine," I say. "I need to learn."

"Harming yourself isn't learning," he replies coolly. His tone deepens as if he's upset by that. Why would he be though?

My eyes seek out the ground, dark in the dim lighting

of the training grounds. I can still feel him looming over me, his attention just as intense as ever. My heart picks up the pace and practically gallops against the inside of my chest. My body sways toward him and I have to force myself to move back and stay aware of myself.

Shaking my head once more, I look up at him and frown. "Why are you out here?" I demand. "Just to taunt me?"

He arches a brow and stares back at me, his silence unnerving. My insides coil with unease and something else I don't care to name. I cross my arms over my chest, the bow in my grip bumping against my side as I do.

"I'm not out here to taunt you," he hedges.

"Then, pray tell, what could possibly bring the infamous Solomon Winett out here to toy with an *inexperienced marksman* such as myself?" I bite the words out through gritted teeth.

The ghost of a smile plays at his lips and I have to school my features not to react. "I'd like to offer my assistance," he replies.

I glare at him, but even as he says the words, I dimly recall the last time he'd offered his assistance. I can still feel the warmth of him against my back and side as he helped me lift the bow and aim it correctly. Even if he had taught me a thing or two back in Frederic's territory of Rozentine, getting that close to him again isn't a good idea. We've already come far too close, far too often, to crossing the boundary between a Princess and her bodyguard.

"You're better at hand-to-hand," I remind him.

He nods. "I am," he agrees. "But perhaps a bet would help you stay motivated in your training."

"A bet?" I frown at him and my grip upon my own arms loosens and they move back to my sides. I lift my gaze. "What kind of bet?" The interest of competition spurs me to ask the question, although deep down, I know it's probably a mistake.

"I am better at hand-to-hand, but I'm not unaccustomed to other weapons," Solomon says. "If you can shoot me—or even graze me—before I get to you and take your bow away, then you win the bet."

"What do I win?" I ask, curiously.

Red, glowing eyes land against mine and the racing of my heart suddenly slows. My tongue swells as my mouth dries up. Air squeezes into my lungs. "I'll answer any question you have," he says. "Or you get one wish."

I consider the offer and pull my gaze from his, glancing around. "Where would you start?"

He points to far off in the distance across the training grounds. I follow the length of his arm and finger to see that he's motioning toward the practice poles for swordsmen. It's a good thirty yards away. Far enough for me to have a chance at actually winning the bet. My foot taps against the ground as I contemplate the offer.

"What do you get if you win?" I ask.

His bloody gaze seems to get even redder, and for several beats of silence, he doesn't answer. Then, "That's to be determined."

I shake my head. "It has to be the same prize," I say. "One question or wish."

Solomon continues to stare at me for a moment, his expression shadowed by the darkness surrounding us. I wait with bated breath, wondering if he'll accept. I can't imagine that he won't though. This was *his* idea, after all. Still … I wait.

Finally, he nods his assent. "That's fair," he determines, and just like that, I can breathe again. At least until he removes his outer coat, tossing it into the dirt before rolling up his tunic.

"What are you doing?" I ask sharply, my voice rising in pitch as he stops halfway through rolling his tunic sleeves up and then just as abruptly reaches down and grips the bottom hem before dragging the entire shirt up and over his head. My attention fixates immediately on his bare chest with the lightest dusting of hair in the center. I can still recall how it felt to brush my fingers over that exact spot in my all-too-vivid dreams.

My thighs tighten at the sight of the dips and grooves of his body. Like most warriors, he's in excellent condition. The epitome of health. His muscles are cut into his flesh, with lines that highlight either side of his abdomen where several ridges of abs roll beneath his skin, standing out more than I ever thought possible.

Solomon turns slightly and looks back at me. "I'm preparing for our bet," he says casually, but there's no way I don't notice the gleam of amusement in his eye or the dance of a smirk on his lips.

I blink, realizing that he's doing this on purpose. I straighten my back and tighten my hold on my bow. "Being half naked won't distract me," I snap.

"I don't know what you mean, Princess."

Liar, I internally seethe. He knows exactly what he's doing.

"I'm not one of those fluttering court maidens," I remind him.

"No," he agrees easily enough. "You're not."

With that, he says nothing more and instead, begins to move across the training grounds. With his back turned to me, I watch the way his spine and shoulder muscles flex with each step. The olive-tanned skin darkened by the sun and the curls of black hair at his nape.

I'm not going to actually hit him, I remind myself. *Just a graze.*

He's far too confident for his own good—arrogant, though he claims not to be. If he weren't so then he never would have suggested such a bet in the first place. He must think I'm weak and incapable of ever even touching him. He was close before—that had to be why he caught the arrow so quickly.

"Ready whenever you are, Princess!" Solomon's call from across the training grounds spurs me into action.

"You won't move until I raise my arrow, right?"

He shakes his head where he stands, hands upon his notched hips near the swordsman poles. I inhale sharply and grab a fresh arrow. I keep my bow and arrow trained on the ground as I notch it against the string.

"What if I actually hit you?" I ask.

From where I stand, it's hard to see his expression, but when he speaks, it's in an amused tone. "The likelihood of you actually managing to land a hit on my flesh is the same as the sky falling, *Princess*."

I blink at his words and their meaning before a scowl overtakes me. "I'll make you eat those words, Solomon Winett," I warn him.

He laughs, the sound deep as it echoes across the open space toward me. "I look forward to it. Now, enough playing, loose your arrow and let the game begin."

"Fine, then!" I lower my voice and grumble, "If you're so ready to be hurt, I'll oblige you."

I lift my arrow and pull back as he sprints forward.

Despite the darkness, it's not hard to determine where Solo is with his glowing eyes and skin a stark contrast against the shadows. Even as I aim, however, he moves with lightning speed. I shift my stance, swinging the direction of my arrow from side to side as I try to keep him in my line of sight. He's moving so fast that I'm finding it difficult and with each passing second, he's getting closer.

My breath slides into my throat, choking me, but I quickly push it back out and focus. Solo dodges left and then right and my gaze instinctively follows, but the second I land on him, he's already moving again. He shifts back and forth, painting a zig-zagged path as he races toward me.

I aim and release my arrow, but he dives down, sliding through the dirt, kicking up clumps of it as it flies over his head. Shock rockets through me, not because I thought I'd really hit him, but because I never anticipated that he would move like a serpent slithering along its path.

Hurriedly, I reach for a new arrow and quickly notch it. The time is ticking down. Every second that passes brings him closer and closer to me. I aim once more. He's already crossed half of the distance in such a short time and as he moves, I realize there's hardly a sound outside of my own harsh breathing. He's silent and my heart is pounding.

I'm going to lose, I realize. In fact, I never really had a chance of winning this thing.

He knew it and I was just too stubborn to see it myself.

Despite that, though, I don't lower my arms. Even if I'm meant to lose this bet, then I have to go out with the same grit and fight I started with. It's not over until he touches me and if Solomon can alter his route, then I can alter mine. I shift backward, putting more distance between us as I aim this time and I see the surprise— though not anger—on his face as I move quickly.

The two of us are dancing in this dangerous game. Back and forth, we move—him toward me, but away from my arrow and me … in any way I can. As I move away from a quickly approaching Solomon, I also move away from the ground sheath of arrows. So, that means this is my last chance because if I want to try again I'll have to risk losing to get back to the arrows.

I should have kept them on my back, I think, but it's too late for regrets now. I have to focus.

Lifting my arms once more, I take my aim and pull back. Down the shaft of my weapon, my eyes lock on Solomon's. Determination burns through me. Just a little graze, that's all I have to do to win. He moves back and forth—dodging quickly to keep me on my toes. A cloud of dirt rises behind him.

The steady pulse of my heart thrums in my breast. One. Take a breath. Two. Tighten your grip. Three. Shoot.

The moment I release my second—and last—arrow, Solomon's arm swipes through the air and catches the shaft once again. He tosses it to the side and comes to a skidding halt as my back presses into the target from before. Arrows jut out all around me, and in a last-ditch effort, I reach out and yank one of them from the bale of hay.

"Don't." Solomon's body is right in front of me, only an inch from touching me. The game is still on. He hasn't touched me yet, but neither have I hit or grazed him. My fingers tighten on the new arrow. "Admit defeat."

Jerking my chin up, I glare at him. Before I can deny him, though, his fingers grip mine and he carefully tugs the bow from my grip and drops it to the ground before he performs the same feat with the arrow. Both land in the dirt, and I'm left with my spine against the hay, the ends of arrows jutting out all around me.

He leans closer until the scent of him, combined with his sweat, overwhelms me. I stop breathing entirely as his naked chest touches mine. *"I win, princess,"* he whispers.

We're chest to chest, he and I, and even though he was the one racing toward me, I'm the one panting as I try to catch my breath. He doesn't appear the least bit fazed.

"What…" I start, swallowing roughly. "What is your question?"

"No." He shakes his head. "It was either a question or a wish."

I frown. "What's your wish then?"

Ruby eyes roam over me, seeking something. What, I don't know. Solomon is such an enigma. Even with as long as I've known him, he changes on a dime. Sometimes, he's kind and sometimes a surly bear waiting to be poked so that he can roar his displeasure. I never know what I'm going to get from him.

"To be determined," he finally says.

I blink. "You're not going to tell me what you want?"

"I'll think of something and then let you know." He moves away and I can breathe again, but the shock and irritation he provokes within me still lingers.

As Solomon begins grabbing arrows from the target and yanks them out, piling them in his hand, I settle my hands on my hips and glare at him. "What was the whole point of this bet if you didn't have something you wanted to ask me?" I demand.

"Because it was a spur-of-the-moment decision," he says with a shrug. "I came down here for something else."

I shake my head. I can't believe him. "You never act spur of the moment," I snap. "Don't lie."

"Believe what you want."

I growl. Ugh, he is so fucking frustrating. Turning away, I grab my own discarded bow and arrow and stomp back to the starting point. Once I reach it and put my supplies back, I turn on him as he follows me and returns the arrows to their ground sheath.

"What did you come out here for then?" I demand.

Solomon bends at the waist and picks up the tunic he'd taken off earlier. After dusting the dirt from the surface, he slides it back over his head, that perfectly defined masculine chest disappearing from view. *Thank the Gods,* I think snidely.

"Three nights from now, you and I need to go somewhere," he says before reaching for his outer coat.

I cross my arms. "Where?"

He doesn't look directly at me, but as he tucks his tunic into the waistband of his pants, his eyes finally start to lose their glow. It isn't quite fair that he'd used his abilities to win, but I'm not going to be such a sore loser to bring it up now. It's not like I can say he cheated since we're both Awakened now, but he certainly knows how to use his much better than I likely ever will.

"We're meeting someone," he hedges.

I wait as he finishes tucking in his tunic and then drags on his coat. Still, he doesn't elaborate. "Solo." I huff out a breath. "If you want me to go anywhere with you when we're in a dangerous foreign country, then you need to at least be willing to give me more than the barest of details."

With a sigh, he turns back to me. "I assure you, the person I'm taking you to meet is someone who can help increase your abilities."

"My Awakened abilities?" I clarify.

He nods. "Yes."

I consider his words as I lower my arms and look back to the Bartoli Palace. The training grounds are a good distance away, but the massive building is large enough to block out most of the skyline. Elaborate pillars and artwork are etched into the stone backside of the palace.

"I don't know if the Bartoli family is going to help us," I say. I haven't wanted to make the admission aloud, not without more evidence, but my gut tells me I'm right. None of them seem keen or even interested in the fact that their second Prince has betrayed a Kingdom they are allied with.

"I know." Solo's words are quiet but resigned. "Which is why we need to do anything we can to get ahead." Footsteps in the dirt alert me to his approach a moment before the heat of him touches my side. "We need to start thinking about our next steps as well."

"Returning to Rozentine," I guess. He doesn't say as much, but then again, he doesn't need to. "Fine," I acquiesce, glancing back at him as he stands at my side, staring up at the palace as well. "I'll go with you and meet whoever you're taking me to. Come to my chambers in three days' time. Make sure it's after dark. I'll be ready."

Solo turns and bows his head. "As you command, my Queen."

His Queen ... My insides tremble at the reminder almost as much as my eyes burn at the sight of him bowing before me. It all feels wrong. I hope that when we return to our homeland, something will have changed. Maybe it's me that needs to.

15
DEVONRY

Morning comes far too quickly and with it, increased exhaustion. The few hours of sleep I managed to get weren't enough. So, when my eyes crack open and see the glimmer of the rising sun spreading light throughout the room, there's a considerable part of me that wants nothing more than to roll over, forget where I am, and fall back into perhaps another six months of endless slumber. Unfortunately, that considerable part of me doesn't get her way. A pity for both of us.

Sitting up, I stretch my sore, tired muscles, wincing when new ones strain at the movement. Lowering my hands to my lap, I stare at the red marks on my hands and forearm. They're not super painful, but they remind me of all that's changed. Months ago, I would never even have considered picking up a blade, much less training to wield a weapon competently. Now … I don't have a choice, not if I want to survive. Not if I want justice for everything I've lost.

A light tap sounds on my door a moment before it opens. "Good, you're awake." Celine steps into the room with a small item in her hand. I blink at her appearance and glance from her to the sky, which is still orange and red as the sun rises. I shouldn't be surprised to see her, but the woman likes to rise with the sun. Even now, she appears as if she's been awake for hours—perfectly presentable and dressed, her hair pulled back into a careful chignon.

"Good morning, Celine."

"Good morning, Your Highness," Celine replies as she strides towards the lounge chairs. "I've been asked to deliver this."

I frown as she reaches into a satchel tied around her waist. She withdraws a small white envelope and holds it up for me. I hasten my movements, pulling aside the blankets and forcing my legs out into the chilled air of my bedchamber. Celine clicks her tongue as she hurries to my side. "Why don't I help you dress and call for breakfast first?" she offers.

I blink away the last of the blurry morning vision as she helps me out of bed. As her hands cup my elbow, she guides me across the room to a waiting table. "I'm capable of walking myself across the room, you know," I tell her.

Her lips twitch as she glances at me. "Of course you are," she replies. *Sheza would have loved her,* I think. Almost as soon as the thought enters my mind, I realize my error. *No,* I amend. *Sheza* will *love her.*

Celine holds out the small envelope. "Here," she says. "It was brought just this morning."

As soon as I take the envelope, Celine moves back and frowns down at me. Before I can even get the letter out and unfolded, she exhales rather loudly. A sign that I'm coming to recognize as a precursor to an incoming round of scolding. I lower the letter and look up, waiting patiently. Her dark brows furrow and her mouth tightens into a line.

"What's the problem now?" I ask.

"You're still not sleeping. The bags under your eyes have bags of their own." I touch my face and then quickly remove my hand when her eyes narrow further. "Don't tug at the skin on your face," she chastises. "Wrinkles, my Queen, wrinkles."

"Your Queen is much too busy to sleep," I mumble, feeling a bit like a child when she fusses as she does.

"Regardless," she snaps. "Promise me, you'll find time to get the rest you need." Celine squats until her face is directly in front of mine. "Swear it, or I'll go hunt down Lord Too-Handsome-To-Be-So-Cranky and tell him just how much of a toll all of this is taking on you."

"Solomon knows I'm not sleeping." I deadpan to hide the weird feeling that takes hold of me. "He'll just laugh at you."

"Or he'll lock you in your room for an entire day to make sure you're resting," she counters. I have to admit, it does sound like something he might do.

"Fine." I wave the letter between us as a makeshift white flag of defeat. "I'll find time to rest—*later.*"

Celine frowns, but nods her consent. "I suppose that's the best I can ask for," she murmurs.

"Great," I say. "Now that we've got that out of the way, may I proceed?" Celine waves her hand before turning and striding to the closet. As she opens it and begins rifling through the clothes waiting there, I turn to the envelope in my hand.

The paper is a thick, fine-quality stationary—no doubt from someone within the castle walls. I can't imagine Lord Frederic has sent me anything from Rozentine, and even if he had—the envelope would have arrived with some wrinkles. This one, however, is pristine.

Knots form in the pit of my stomach. Few people would be so confident in sending a visiting royal a letter so early in the morning. Solomon would just show up—as would Argyle. So that leaves the Bartoli Royal Family and … the Rozentine Ambassador. I split the seal, tearing the emblem in two before withdrawing the page and holding it up.

Long, looping script stretches out into only a few short sentences. The letter is clearly written by the hand of someone who's practiced their writing until it was perfected. Meticulous and almost delicate. Relief melts the tension riddling my body as I read the note.

"It's just the Ambassador," I inform her. "He'd like to have tea this morning."

"Lord Byron?" Celine peeks out of the wardrobe and I nod.

"Yes." I set the letter down, drumming my fingers along the edge of the table. "Do you think he wants to discuss Rozentine?" I ask. "He's closer to the Bartoli Royal Family. Perhaps he's managed to convince them."

"You're his Queen, Your Highness," Celine replies, ducking into the wardrobe and finally returning with a set of fabrics in hand. "Whatever you wish to discuss will be the topic of your meeting. I think this will do for the occasion of meeting with him." She holds up a very Rozentine-like gown, stretched down from neck to ankle, but thankfully, the sleeves are transparent. In the Bartoli heat, Rozentine clothing is probably sweltering. Tiny rubies decorate the front bodice and the edges of the neckline.

I consider it. "You don't think that's too much?" I chew at my lip, feeling guilty for even wanting to wear it.

"You're a Queen. Everything you wear is supposed to be too much."

Who made these rules for royalty? I wonder. Why does my Queendom come with the excess of silk and jewels?

Would I be less of a leader if I dressed in something less costly? Would I be less of a Queen?

"Fine, but don't tell Solomon just yet," I say.

Celine frowns and tilts her head at me. "May I ask why?"

I bite down on my lower lip and turn my gaze back to the stationary in my hand. "It's just a feeling," I say, "but I think Lord Byron won't be as open about what he wants with Solo looming over both of us, and I need to know what he truly thinks—not just about the Bartoli's but about me as well."

Celine's face pinches tight and a line forms between her thick, dark brows. Only she doesn't say anything to deter me. Instead, she merely shakes her head and sighs. "If that's what you wish."

I wish for a lot of things, I want to tell her. But all of the things I wish for are difficult to come by. Rebirth. Understanding. Freedom. The only thing I can do now is give my people what they *wish* for: hope and a Queen that will actually rule them fairly with love and sacrifice.

Celine sings softly as she laces me into my dress and slips matching silken slippers onto my feet before expertly tying back half of my hair. She nestles the slender ring of a crown onto my head, frowning slightly. "You'd think your betrothed would have made you something finer."

"Unfortunately, I think my betrothed might like to downplay everything I am. Including my title."

She nods, a few soft waves of her hair falling forward around her face. "One shouldn't say things if they don't have anything nice to say. Right? Then, in this case, perhaps I'll keep my lips sealed tight." Celine offers her arm, and I take it, allowing her to accompany me.

Together, arm in arm, I'm struck with an odd sense of nostalgia. The kind that reminds my heart that I had this whole life wildly different from the one where Solomon and I trek through the woods and hide away on a boat. The gowns, the parties, and the people with their titles belong to a different version of myself. A version I struggle to find even now when faced with much the same. When I return to Rozentine, things will be different. There is no denying it. I am different. I need to make a difference.

The thoughts plague me all the way until we reach the sitting room where Lord Byron has arranged tea. Celine pats my hand once before she knocks as if she's heard the roaring of thoughts rattling against my skull.

Silently, the door opens before Celine even has the chance to lower her arm. It leaves me to wonder if the man was standing on the other side of the door waiting for us.

"Princess Devonry." Byron steps back and bows fully. His attention slides to Celine, who now stands with her hands clasped before her, ready to be useful as her unofficial position would require. He nods in her direction. "Lady Celine."

"Lord Byron, I'm so thankful you requested tea today. Really, I must apologize for not asking to meet with you sooner, myself. I'd planned on it, but with everything that happened in getting here…" I let my words trail off, knowing he'll get my meaning.

Lord Byron adjusts, moving to allow me space to walk around him. "It's no problem, Your Highness," he says with a quiet smile. "I understand it's been quite difficult for you and our Kingdom."

I head for the couch and chairs that circle a small table with the waiting tea kettle and cups.

It's a far more modest room than I expect from the Bartoli royals. This room could even be described as cozy with its warm wood floorboards, the light brown walls, and the bookshelves lining the space. One large window, with curtains opened to let the sun in, makes the room feel much larger than it is, though it couldn't be bigger than my bathing chamber back home. Given more space, it might actually have much likeness to my father's study.

"Yes," I say, responding to Byron's last comment. "It has, and I thank you for your understanding."

"You have dealt with far more than a girl your age should. It was clear to me that you may need time to settle before…" He runs his hand through his graying hair. He appears every inch the perfect nobleman. His suit is pressed and his shirt is buttoned to his throat. Not even a hint of discomfort or worry graces his features.

Smoothing my hands down my dress, I lower onto the couch. Celine is quick to follow but never sits. Instead, she arranges our cups and begins pouring tea while the Ambassador perches himself at the edge of one of the chairs directly across from me. Purple eyes lock on mine.

"I appreciate your patience." I smile. "You must tell me what life is like here, so far away from your home. I'm finding it is much different than I expected, even after all those lessons about this culture."

"Ah." He smiles in return. "They have been most welcoming to me. I don't deserve such kindness but I appreciate it, nonetheless. I can only hope you are also being treated as befitting your crown."

I offer a hum in response. Treated as befitting my crown? Perhaps the Ambassador doesn't know about the Crown Prince's behavior. "Lord Byron," I begin, "as an Ambassador for Rozentine, I feel like we share a kinship. May I speak candidly in your presence?"

"Of course, Princess." His head dips, the light gleaming off the strands of his hair as the baby hairs fall loose around his face. "I am your humble servant."

"Bartoli is nothing like I expected," I tell him.

He chuckles. "Yes, it's quite different from Rozentine, but in a beautiful way. Differences make you love it all the more."

I press my lips together. Maybe the land itself is beautiful, but ever since I arrived within these borders, I've felt nothing but hostility and pressure. As if the eyes of the royal family are haunting me through the hallways. The expectations. The performances. The amount of people I can trust seems smaller and smaller every day.

Byron might be my Ambassador, but his immediate response tells me that he is another stranger in this foreign country, even if his purple eyes are familiar and his countenance reminds me of home.

Celine hands me a teacup and saucer. Steam rises and with it the sweet scent of the herbs. With a measured smile, she hands Lord Byron his tea and lowers herself to the cushion at my side. She's quiet, but her presence is calming.

Another reason I'd wanted to have this meeting without Solo breathing down my neck was to gauge how Lord Byron treated me without my guard. I'm thankful, still, that I'm not alone.

Sucking in a breath, I try to keep the smile plastered on my face. "Yes, it's very pretty," I reply through clenched teeth. "Unfortunately, however, I'm finding my time here difficult. There doesn't seem to be any sense of urgency. It's as if no one cares for Rozentine. I almost wonder if the Bartoli Royal Family wants to continue our alliance." Byron's face reddens at that last comment as he coughs into his teacup, sputtering and choking as he sets it down with a loud clatter.

Calmly, I return my teacup to the table as well. "You've known these royals far longer and more personally than I.

Is there any advice you might be able to dispense to assist your country?"

Byron coughs again and then, with shaking hands, lifts the cup from its saucer once more, bringing the tea to his lips. He sips slowly before pulling away with a sigh. "The Galeanos are often difficult to handle, that much I can certainly agree with you on. The world here runs on their schedules and their schedules alone." Setting his cup down again, Byron takes his time stirring in more sugar.

"I understand that, but I hope you realize time is of the essence here." I hear my voice harden, growing colder in tone. "The longer I remain in Bartoli, the longer Nasir holds dominion over my—our—Kingdom. Lest you not forget that Rozentine is meant to be ruled by the descendants of Aerea, not outsiders."

"You and I are outsiders in their Kingdom," Byron reminds me. I narrow my gaze on him. Yes, it was the right call, I realize suddenly, to not have Solomon here. I fear had he been present for this fiasco, Lord Byron would be hung upside down by his boots over the edge of a balcony right about now. I can't say that the image doesn't appeal to me.

"You know," Byron continues, sniffing and leaning forward, "I *do* think there is something you can do that could assist you in this current predicament. Actually, it's the reason I requested to meet with you in the first place."

It's hard not to scoff at the word or his apathy. *Predicament.* This is more than a predicament. This is an act of war between two countries who were supposedly allies. I took a risk coming here. I put my hope in my betrothed and that hope has borne *nothing*—no help, no salvation, just cold, dead fruit fallen on the ground.

I take another sip of tea, careful to keep my expression neutral, if not bordering on pleasant, when on the inside

I'm an angry riot of a mess. Byron expects me to be the Princess I've always been. Dutiful. Polite. *Ignorant.* The problem with ignorance, however, is that it can never be returned once it's lost.

Playing the part is a struggle now. I've begun to notice my own change so intensely, and I find I don't hate who I'm becoming, even if it means I'm not the Princess—or the Queen—anyone expected. Sometimes, what people need isn't what they expect but something completely different.

"My heart belongs to Rozentine. I am nothing if not a man born and bred by my homeland." He sits a little taller as the words leave his lips, but they ring hollow in my ears as if some intuition inside of me is telling me that they're lies. "My role here, in part, is to act as your advisor while you are on foreign soil. So please understand that when I speak to you in this capacity, I am merely trying to offer the best solutions for our country."

"I don't doubt that," I say, though the wariness in me grows. My father was never without his advisors, and now I find myself alone in the darkest times my country has seen in centuries. I am facing far more than my father ever did, and with it all, I have nothing more than a single guard, a lady, and ... well, I'm not exactly sure what to call Argyle.

"To appease this *unrest...*" I notice he doesn't say Nasir's name. I wonder if he's afraid I might break down in tears if he did. "I must suggest that you hasten your marriage to Prince Enver. The sooner our countries are officially unified, the better. Only then can you fully gain the support of Bartoli to take Rozentine back."

Shock rolls through me so severely that my hands go numb, starting at my fingertips and spreading to my knuckles and wrists. I set my cup down harder than I intend to, a loud *clack* ringing out between us. Long seconds of silence stretch one right after the other. I need them. To *appease* the way my fingers tremble, I interlock them and set my hands in my lap. Even Celine shifts in her seat, uncrossing and recrossing her ankles.

"You think this marriage will solve the problem with Nasir?" I ask. Byron blinks heavily at the mention of the Prince's name. Nevertheless, I will not act as if my monster has no name. "I must say, I am a bit surprised at the suggestion. After all, it was a Galeano that killed my father, your king. And now you are certain that continuing with this marriage to another Galeano might fix this?" I gesture vaguely, trying to keep my rising anger hidden. Anger not just at this idea but at myself. For I thought similarly not long ago.

"Prince Nasir," his throat bobs, "as I've noticed, is not *mentally* well. His actions, while as terrible and truly disgraceful as they were, should not reflect on the rest of his family. Prince Enver wishes for nothing more than for you to be his bride so that his country and ours might find peace once again."

"It is funny then that they sent Nasir in place of his brother, my betrothed, for my coming of age. Did they think so little of me then? I'm curious if the sentiment remains to this day."

His head bobs in agreement. "A decision I'm sure they deeply regret."

"Are you sure, or do you know they regret it?" The words come out more cutting than I'd intended. Celine leans against my side, the warmth of her body a reminder of her support.

A muscle in his jaw ticks. "I misspoke. I know they regret it. Prince Enver has confided in me more than once over this worry."

"He has, has he?" I wonder whose pocket this Ambassador truly sits in. It doesn't feel like mine. He might be here as a representative of my country, however he doesn't appear to have strictly my desires in mind.

"You are giving me much to think about." The corners of my mouth lift into a grin, but I don't feel that spark of a genuine smile.

"This marriage will solve everything, I'm sure of it. It's what your father would have wanted."

My spine stiffens at the mention of my father, as if this man … this practical stranger, would know anything of my father's wants. I'm sure he might not even be able to recall the last time he spoke with or laid eyes on my father. How could he possibly know anything?

Celine makes eye contact with me then. Whatever she sees in my face is enough for her to rise from her seat. "I'm afraid we have another commitment, Lord Byron, so the Princess should be on her way."

"Oh, yes." I play along and stand. Byron is quick to rise and offers another one of his low bows. "Thank you for your knowledge and assistance in this matter. I will be thinking of this conversation and be in touch to let you know how we will move forward."

"Yes, your Highness. Of course," he answers, nothing but manners.

I give him one last look. One that I hope shows him the might of my crown. Then Celine and I disappear from the sitting room and walk together in silence until we have nearly reached my room. The halls remain empty except for a pair of passing guards who walk by stone-faced in the opposite direction.

"What are you thinking?" Celine whispers.

"I'm thinking I wish things were different. Can't you gaze up to the stars and tell me what I should do?"

She laughs at that. "I'm afraid my ability doesn't quite

work like that." She sobers quickly. "However, I can tell you how my gut feels."

"And how is that?" We both pause outside my door. Silence eating away at us.

"I don't trust him."

"Interesting," I say, "I don't either."

16

SOLOMON

The past few days have gone by much the same as every other day spent amongst the Galeano Family. Terribly irritating and painfully slow. Truly, I might rather enjoy being sent off to war again rather than endure another dinner where Prince Enver tries to charm his way into my Princess' heart.

Admittedly, the man had stood a chance. Young and eager to serve her country, Devonry had seen Prince Enver as a solution to our problem. As if her father had been able to see into the future and the Prince was his final parting gift. It is by my own stroke of luck, or by the meddling of the gods themselves, that he'd revealed his true self so quickly and so thoroughly.

Perhaps I should thank the man. The monster inside of me chuckles, wicked and quick like a strike of lightning. The idea of my blade separating his head from his neck strolls through my imagination.

I've bided my time in the shadows, out of sight but never far from the Princess and her daily activities, only to end my days talking Devonry through different skills she'll need. All the while, I remain at odds with myself on when I should and should not touch her. She responds to my nearness, fate tugging her in my direction. How does she not see it yet? How does she not feel this living, breathing bond between us? Only in our dreams does she permit me to be so near. And I—a greedy bastard—take advantage of every moment. Even during waking hours, with Argyle at my side, these dreams consume my thoughts and cannot be shaken.

The halls of the castle are dark except for a few scattered lamps left burning. Two guardsmen pass us with curious eyes, unmotivated as their shifts come to an end. Most have seen me wander the halls early in the morning hours when our dreams have come to an end and my body is ablaze. So they must think very little of us as we make our way to Devonry's chambers. Only that perhaps it is odd how tonight Argyle has joined me.

"Do you think I drink too much, still?" Argyle's question pulls me back to reality. I meet his gaze, finding it sullied with genuine concern. His brows furrow over his mismatched irises.

"In comparison to how I found you, I think you drink very little. Why?" Though our voices remain soft, the sound still carries, bouncing between stone walls.

"No reason." He scratches at the bit of stubble growing along his chin. "Actually, there is very much a reason."

"Celine." I nod. I am no stranger to the ferocity of a woman.

"How did you—" Argyle snorts. "Yes, Celine. That little minx has found every reason to point out my inadequacies. I feel much like a child again. Except now I'm intrigued by the nursemaid scolding me. Violently intrigued."

Pressing my lips together, I try to suppress the urge to

frown or laugh. Honestly, I'm not sure which one might come first. "I don't think most women like to be compared to your nursemaid." He rolls his eyes. "But if you think you drink too much, then drink less. Or drink the same amount. Does it truly matter?"

Devonry's door comes into sight as we turn down another hall. My steps quicken, my strides lengthening as my body screams to be back in her presence. Argyle easily keeps up. The time has finally come to introduce Devonry to this so-called expert on Awakened abilities. My worry eats away at my patience.

"And if your Princess pointed out that you drank too much or that perhaps she thought the trouser-boot combo you fancy looks a little unfashionable, what would you do?"

I glance down at my trousers and boots. "Are you only asking because *you* don't like my outfit?"

"Yes." He wags a finger. "But that is not the point."

We stop just outside her door. The space between my eyes begins to ache as my brows pull together at the direction of this conversation. "You are smitten."

"And you are not?" Argyle lifts his chin.

Pinching the bridge of my nose, I sigh. "Fine. If she thought I drank too much I'd never touch wine again. If she … insisted my clothing was not adequate, then perhaps … perhaps I might be inclined to wear something that she found attractive. But if you ever breathe a word of that to her, I'll gut you myself."

My friend laughs, grabbing my shoulder to hold himself upright. I shrug him off, raising my hand to knock when the door swings open. Devonry's pewter gown is simple enough and without all the extra frills that might make our travels more difficult. The strands of her hair, more strawberry-tinted in the dim firelight, are pulled out of her face, only a few pieces left to frame her face.

"What's so funny?" Her lips twitch, so close to a smile but never truly turning into one.

"What do you think of Solomon's trousers and boots?" Argyle leans against the door frame. The inches between him and Devonry are much less than I'd prefer. Still, the silence that follows his question has me shifting under my Princess' scrutiny.

I stuff my hands into my deep pockets, only succeeding in making myself feel that much more of a fool. My jaw clenches. Part of me waits impatiently for her to laugh at my expense. Instead, her attention travels over my form and then slowly meets my gaze.

"They are quite nice." Devonry blinks, looking between Argyle and me. A flush warms the back of my neck.

"If we are done questioning my fashion sense, might we get on with the evening?"

Argyle only smiles widely at my question, Devonry's gaze still a burning sear on my skin as she nods. Meaning to hurry us along, I lean forward and take the handle of Devonry's door. Her body goes still. The smell of flowers floating amongst saltwater clings to her and I slow further, if only to keep her scent a second longer. My chest brushes her shoulder as the door shuts with a soft click. When I straighten, I can't tell if it's the shadows or if a blush darkens her cheeks.

"Lead the way," Devonry whispers, motioning down the empty hall.

Together we walk the halls leading out of the castle. Silence clings to us, and occasionally, I sense Devonry's eyes wander in my direction. A smirk threatens my lips. When I finally look her way, I catch her staring and lift my brows in question. What is she thinking? Better yet … what is she remembering of our dreams? Her cheeks burn bright again and she glances away.

We do not encounter another guard even when we break free of the suffocating castle and walk out in the dew of the yards. The toes of my boots glisten under the moonlight as the dampness coats them further with each step.

The steady sound of feet meeting the ground in rapid succession, along with the swish of heavy skirts, gathers my attention. I stop, turning back around toward the noise. Argyle and Devonry pause a step later.

Brown skin, dark hair pulled into a tight bun, and bright, eager eyes greet us. Hands fisting in the front of her skirts to keep from tripping, Celine pushes through the doors and launches herself into the yard. Her slippered feet come to a halt but slide through the grass, almost sending her right onto her backside if it wasn't for Argyle who readily steps forward and catches her arm.

Celine yanks herself from his grasp. "You three," she sucks in a ragged breath, "will not leave without me."

"And how do you know we are going anywhere?" Argyles gives Devonry a side-eyed glance. The Princess only shrugs.

"The stars told me." Celine's brows knit together before my very eyes, her face scrunching. The tighter her features become the wider Argyle's smile grows. "The two of you should not be going anywhere alone with the Princess. As if your training sessions out in the courtyard aren't enough fodder for gossip."

"Gossip?" Argyle laughs. "About the three of us? What could they say?" He draws his tongue over his bottom lip, his attention turning toward Devonry appraisingly.

"Don't," I bite out. "Wherever your mind is going right now ... you better find a way to turn it around."

Celine's jaw drops at Argyle's blatant suggestion. I

chance a look at Devonry who snorts a laugh. "If only wishes came true, Argyle."

She could at least pretend to be more offended by what he is suggesting.

"Argyle Alfred Toussaint." Celine fists her hands at her side, her skirts bouncing back to her feet. "Never even suggest such a thing again."

"Oh, it's all in good fun." He pats Devonry's shoulder. "Right, Princess?"

My teeth grind together, a low growl building in my chest. Red pulses in my vision.

Devonry gently pushes his hand away. "You could only dream up something like that. Though perhaps Solomon might take you up on the offer alone." She looks up with large, innocent eyes. The slightest turn at the end of her lips makes it clear she knows exactly what she is playing at.

"Not a chance." I shake my head, swiftly turning back toward the stables. The others follow, Celine catching up to Devonry's side and linking their arms.

"Come now, the lot of you are no fun. And I am a lot of fun. If you know what I mean—"

"We know what you mean. We are just rather uninterested in the offer," Celine interrupts Argyle and both girls turn to each other and snicker.

I have to smile a bit too, because watching Argyle squirm after all the things he puts me through is perhaps my only real entertainment these days. So when he *humphs* and ends up walking at my side, sending sad puppy dog eyes in Celine's direction, I tilt toward him and lower my voice. "Your middle name is Alfred?"

His puppy dog eyes turn to daggers. "It is not, although I refuse to tell that woman my middle name, so she just keeps making up new ones for me. Alfred is possibly the most offensive one so far."

"And you're still interested in pursuing this…?"

"How could I not be?" He smiles once more.

My mind draws back to every moment that Devonry and I have tried to hate each other over the years. Perhaps he is not any different than I.

17

DEVONRY

When Solo reaches for my waist, I balk and take a step back. "I can do it," I insist.

His head tilts to the side, but he doesn't argue with me. Instead, he merely gestures for me to proceed. With a quick inhale, I reach up, latching onto the edge of the horse's saddle and then hook my foot into the stirrup. Bouncing on the ball of the one foot left on the ground, I heft myself up and over the saddle. My stomach slams into the seat and all of the air I held in rushes out.

I wish I'd worn trousers.

I hear Solo's sigh behind me and then a big, firm hand touches the round of my ass and pushes. I yelp, the sound echoing into the night, as I jerk my leg over the other side and sit up.

I whip around to hiss at him. "I said —"

"Scoot forward," he demands, not letting me finish.

I blink in astonishment. Since when has he become this fucking rude? No, that's a ridiculous question. He's always been rude. I'm the one who's an idiot for expecting better. I shuffle forward on my butt, gathering the skirts around and under me to ensure that I'm adequately covered. The cloak I'm wearing thankfully falls long enough to cover the skin bared by the astride seat I've taken.

Without waiting another beat, Solo latches onto the back of the saddle in a far more elegant move, hefts himself up into the seat and takes the reins once more. I narrow my eyes back on him, but he doesn't respond to my attention. Instead, one muscled arm wraps around my middle and lifts me against his chest.

I gasp and scramble to slide my other leg back over the horse's back and finally, my skirts fall into place, rising a little higher on my legs as they're bunched up between my thighs. "There," he says. "Perfect."

"You couldn't have gotten extra horses?" I grumble with irritation.

"We don't want to draw attention," he replies smoothly.

Solid reasoning, I know, but with the heat of Solo's chest pressed into my back, I wonder if that risk was worth it. Solomon's arm remains around my side, keeping me plastered against him as the horse shifts beneath us, stepping forward and backward as if to adjust its new weight. I glance back over Solo's shoulder, finding that Celine and Argyle have finished getting onto their horse as well, and Celine is in much the same position. Her face is pinched as she tries to lean as far forward as she can to stay away from Argyle who, for his part, appears merely amused at her blatant display of hatred.

"Ready?" Solo calls.

"Lead the way," Argyle replies, and together, the four of us head down the pathway toward the same seaside village we had come from merely days ago.

Solomon steers the horse over the rocky cliffside and the scent of salt and water invades my nostrils. I lift my face to the dark skies, turned nearly black now that the sun has long since set. Stars glitter against the backdrop. How the horse and Solo seem to know where they're going, I don't understand. Other than the moon and stars, the path is as dark as a nightmare, crawling with shadows against the ground and visions of emptiness.

The man at my back, however, doesn't even hesitate. Every once in a while, as time passes, I can't help but cast another look back at him. I always find his gaze centered forward, the luminous glow of his red irises brighter as we grow further and further from the fires of the palace. Perhaps his abilities allow him to see in the dark. I realize I've never actually asked him. We don't talk about his abilities.

"Is there something on my face or do you just enjoy admiring the view, Highness?" Solo's voice sounds somewhat amused.

I shake my head. "Your eyes are glowing a little," I tell him.

His frame shifts closer, his rigid abdomen brushing my arm. I wrap them around myself to keep from reaching out. Curiosity holds me bound though. The memory of that one time after we'd escaped the Sunfire Palace and I'd forced him to bathe with me in the forest creek fills my mind. It had been dark then, too, but not so dark that I hadn't seen the way his body was riddled with dips and curves. The outline of muscles had been as clear as day. Now, they're against me and it's an act of futility not to think of them.

"It happens," Solo says quietly.

I blink and find that I've looked away from him. I return my attention to his face. "Does it happen often?"

"You watch me enough, do you not know?" His mouth curves upward. He's teasing me. Bastard. Somehow, I don't mind. Not that I would tell him that, though. I narrow my eyes before veering to the darkness beyond the cliffside.

"I'm just now noticing," I say with a sniff. "I'm not as obsessed with you as you are with me."

"*That's for damn sure.*"

Whipping my head back to him at those words, I glare at him. Solo, however, keeps his face trained upward, and for a moment, I wonder if I imagined them. "Why?" I demand.

As if he's being purposefully dense, Solo slowly tips his face down and those twin pools of blood-red irises meet mine. "My abilities allow all of my senses to be heightened," he says before tapping his temple with a singular finger, indicating his eyes. "This is the result of using them."

"I knew that," I mutter. I just … hadn't realized they could glow with such a low intensity. In the past, when I've seen him use his abilities, they were brighter, stronger. Now, they still glow, but with a dullness that in some ways appears to cut through the darkness like the embers of a fresh fire.

I remain quiet for the rest of the long ride. It feels like more than half of the night has passed by the time we actually reach the seaside village. My ass cramps with soreness as Solomon pulls the horse's reins to the side, directing the creature toward an open stable.

Spotting the half-asleep attendant, I quickly reach back and flick up my hood to cover my appearance. Solomon does the same. As the horse makes its way to the entrance, the man jerks awake and stands abruptly.

"Staying for the night, sir?" he asks.

Solomon merely nods and then offers the man a coin from inside his cloak. The man takes the coin, eyes bulging at the silver glint of it. He quickly gestures inside. "There are two stalls at the back readily available," he says before taking the coin between his teeth and biting down. When the metal doesn't move under the slight pressure, he chuffs with pleasure. "This'll do for the entire night," he says before glancing back to where I suppose Argyle and Celine are taking up the rear. "For two?"

"Yes," Solo's voice comes out gruffer than usual, as if he's attempting to make it even deeper than it naturally is.

"Fine then, sir." The attendant nods and steps out of the way as Solomon leads the horse further back into the stable. A slow glance around the space—at the mostly empty stalls and the dirtied ground—makes me realize just why he was so excited to receive Solo's silver coin. It was likely far more than this place is worth. The fact that Solo hadn't asked for change in return meant the attendant would welcome us and not ask many questions later.

Solo gets off of the horse first, sliding to his feet in a fast, solid movement before reaching up. I don't get a chance to protest as his hands find my waist and lift me from the horse. My teeth sink into my lower lips as I bite down the urge to squeal at the sharp movement. My chest meets Solo's and slowly—so imperceptibly slowly—I slide against him until my own feet find the flooring of the filthy stable.

My heart beats erratically inside my chest. My face burns as I duck and turn away, yanking myself from his grip as subtly as I can manage. I don't think I manage it quite well enough, though, as Solo's attention remains on me as I stride across the stable and recline against a closed stall to wait. More and more, I find myself absorbing every touch between us. My insides hurt and rebel at the resistance, but I can't help it. He can never know the things I've both imagined and dreamed. The ways in which I've found my own senses craving his nearness.

Perhaps, after this night, once we realize my abilities, I'll have more power to hold those back. I fight the idea, but it's not completely insane to consider that I'm only thinking of Solomon in the same ways one might a lover because he's been the one by my side through all of the things that have happened to me. He's the only constant in my life now. The one ray of good in the otherwise cruel world I've been unceremoniously dropped into. I close my eyes and send a silent prayer up to the Gods.

Please, I beg. *Please don't let me ruin this. Please give me the strength to fight. Please…*

"Highness?" I blink and jolt when Celine appears in front of me. "We're ready."

"Oh, right. Thank you." She reaches for me and I allow her to take my hand. Already, Solo and Argyle are waiting at the mouth of the stables, and the two of us hurry to catch up with them, our skirts trudging through the dirt and moldy hay on the ground.

"This way," Argyle calls back. Together, the four of us head down a new path, taking a set of stone stairs down further and further until when we emerge, we're in a wide open space.

Heat presses against my back. Sweat collects at the top of my neck and slides down my spine beneath my cloak and dress. My breathing grows heavier as Argyle and Solo march across the space and into yet another alleyway. Solo pauses and turns back, waiting as Celine and I lag behind. Celine grumbles under her breath, likely unaware of how easily I can hear the way she's cursing Argyle.

I snicker, but she merely retracts her hand and glares ahead. "I'm going to tell him to slow down, Princess," she says, and before I can stop her, she picks up her pace, speeding past the waiting Solomon, her eyes set on the back of Argyle's head.

Solo watches her go with a placid expression and doesn't start walking again until I pass him. "Do you need to rest?" he asks.

I shake my head. "No, we don't have much time to do this," I say. "It took too long to get here and it'll take the same amount of time to get back. If we want to do this without being found out then we need to be back in our beds before sunrise."

The acute feeling of his attention sears into the side of my face, but I refuse to look back. Instead, I put one foot in front of the other and doggedly follow behind Argyle and Celine, hoping that Argyle's contact will be able to help us the way we need.

I'm suddenly doubting myself and every action and decision I've made since that bloody night. I close my eyes and a flash of red and the glint of a metal sword flashes across my mind's eye. I just want this all to be over and I'm willing to do whatever it takes to see it through, even if it means giving myself over to my own abilities; I refuse to let Rozentine be ruled by a traitor and a murderer.

18

DEVONRY

It's another half hour of walking before Argyle finally slows down ahead, and for most of that time, I'd enjoyed Celine's furious face as she beat against him. Her voice hadn't carried so far back to hear what she'd said, but it was clear that Argyle had sped up even more just to try and leave her in his dust. Unfortunately for him, Celine was dogged in her pursuit to chastise him.

By the time we manage to come to a standstill, the four of us finally catching up with each other, his face is drawn and there's a vein bulging in the side of his forehead, pulsating each time he clenches his fist. Solomon glances around where we stand. Sand crunches beneath our boots and ocean waves crash against the shoreline. It's cooler here, so close to the water, and I shiver as a breeze flits by dragging my hood from my head. Though I draw my cloak around me my lowered hood gives me a reprieve as fresh air soaks into my cheeks. I sigh in relief.

"Argyle." Solo's voice deepens. "You said your contact lived here. I see nothing but sand and rocks."

"Just wait." Argyle turns his face out to the sea and

then back. He pivots until the entire front of his body is facing the side of the cliffs—directed away from the port that is but a speck in the distance from where we're standing.

"If you've brought us out here only to—" Celine's tirade gets cut off as, with a groan of exasperation, Argyle grabs her by the front of her cloak and drags her against him. My mouth opens in shock as he yanks her up onto her toes, bends his head, and slams his lips into hers.

Stunned silence echoes across the sandy beach for several beats and then, finally, he pulls back and licks his lips. Celine is utterly frozen. "Finally," Argyle says. "Blessed quiet."

At that, her face turns molten red and I wince, preparing for a shriek to rival that of mimicking birds after a battle. Instead, though, she shakes her head and turns away from him. She stomps in the opposite direction of the shoreline and doesn't stop until she reaches a rock formation where she turns and plops down with her arms crossed. Rage is clear as day on her face. Both Solo and I look at Argyle, who appears much the opposite. In fact, gone is the scowl that he wore, and in its place is a rather pleased grin.

"Argyle," Solo calls. "Time is of the essence. If your friend is not here, we'll have to head back to the—"

He doesn't get to finish his statement as Argyle suddenly whirls around and the sound of churning water reaches my ears. "What…" My question drifts away as the shadowy outline of a small vessel appears out of the fog. A dim light appears at the end of the boat as it sails closer. I take a step forward and nearly slip as the sand slides out from beneath my feet. Thankfully, Solo catches me and rights me just as the small vessel comes alongside the beach's shore. Water splashes violently against the wood, and then a new lamp appears in the darkness from a tender that bobs against the waves, growing closer and closer.

"Your friend … lives on a boat?" I find myself asking as I stand alongside Argyle at the shoreline.

Sand crunches behind us as Celine hurries away from the rocks and pauses at my side. Argyle remains silent with his hands planted on his hips, and as the tender finally hits the shallows and comes to a jolting halt and more splashes sound, I catch sight of a black flag waving further above the original ship. My head snaps to Argyle and when he still doesn't look at me, I turn to Solo.

Anxiety wreaks havoc on my insides. I shift toward him instinctively. "Solo?"

He must hear the nervousness in my tone because he draws nearer and touches my forearm. "Don't worry, nothing will happen to you, Devonry."

Pirates. Argyle's friend is a damned pirate.

When a man appears at the edge of the water, dragging a rope attached to the tender he rode in, Argyle finally moves.

"Yulis," he calls as he strides forward.

The man—Yulis—lifts his head and his haggard face splits into a wide grin. He quickly releases the rope and reaches for Argyle as the two join hands, clasping each other's forearms like long-lost brothers. I bite down on my lower lip as the three of us—Solo, Celine, and I—watch the proceedings. Yulis appears far older than Argyle with graying temples that streak into darker hair. His face is weathered by the sun, stretched taut in places and browned from burns long since past. His slender, yet wiry frame is covered in a dark coat, thin stained tunic, and well-worn brown trousers. Argyle greets him with a bright smile that, for once, doesn't look faked or forced.

"It's been too long," Argyle says, sounding like he means it.

"You've gotten taller, boy," Yulis replies. "When I got your bird, I was surprised that you would be in Bartoli, especially this close to the palace."

"Yes, well, there are circumstances…" Argyle drifts off and turns back to the group of us.

Solo is the first to move, leaving Celine and me as his hand slips off my shoulder. He approaches Argyle and Yulis. "Solo," Argyle says. "This is my old friend Yulis."

"It's a pleasure to meet you, sir," Solo says, holding his hand out. Yulis releases Argyle and takes Solo's hand before peering curiously over his shoulder.

"You as well, young'un," he says. "I see you brought a few pretty birds with you as well."

I stiffen but don't respond to the comment. "Yulis," Argyle's voice turns serious as Solo retracts his hand from the man. "We thank you for coming after you received my message, but we're low on time. If we could join you on your ship, I'll tell you why I needed you to come so quickly."

Yulis eyes Solo and then Celine and me. For a moment, I swear his gaze lingers on me, and on impulse, I lift my hood back into place. Still, his attention seems to bore into me. As if he already knows who I am. My breath catches in my throat. Though the slave traders from Carion City weren't necessarily pirates, this man reminds me of them in many ways. He's rugged, with a smattering of scars that show on his arm and down his neck. It's clear he's been in many fights before and suffered just as many wounds from life.

I bite down on my lip, waiting for him to make his decision, wondering if he'll offer us his wisdom and if it'll be enough. It shouldn't matter to me what his profession is

—*it doesn't*, I tell myself—as long as he can help me do what needs to be done.

"Alright, let's get on then," Yulis finally says. "The boys have been pretty excited to see you again. Let's not keep the lot of them waiting long."

"Dev." Solo turns back and calls for me.

"Are you sure about this?" Celine asks quietly as she follows behind.

"Argyle is Solo's friend," I tell her, "and I trust Solo." With my life … with everything.

I hurry toward Solo and take his hand as he helps me into the tender. When Argyle moves to do the same for Celine, she practically hisses at him and climbs into the small boat herself, seating her body next to mine at the far back with a glare in his direction. Solomon, Argyle, and Yulis each help to push the boat back into the deeper waters before hopping in themselves. Solomon takes a seat across from us as Argyle and Yulis stand on either side, picking up paddles and directing the boat back toward the larger vessel waiting on us.

Fog collects on the surface of the water, drawing my attention for the longest time, and it isn't until we get nearer to the ship, that I turn my gaze upward. Black aged wood and peeling paint greet me as we bump alongside the waiting ship. A rope ladder dangles over the side. Argyle sets down his paddle and reaches for it. As he ascends the ladder, Yulis nods to the rest of us.

"I'll go up next," Solo tells me. "Then you follow. Then Celine."

I nod my understanding and wait as he ascends the ladder. The tender bobs back and forth, smacking against the hull of the bigger ship again and again. It isn't until I see Solo's body disappear over the top that I grab ahold of the rope and follow him. The frayed ties burn against my palms as I urge myself up, pushing my weight against the ship as I hook a foot into one rung and then the next. It sags under my body, but I cling to the sides of the ladder and keep moving, up and up some more as my lungs squeeze and shudder, begging for more air. Sweat slips down the side of my face.

Two strong hands reach over the ledge and in relief, I grab ahold of them. Solo drags me over the edge of the ship's railing and I gasp for breath, bending in half as I hold onto him. There's a call below and then Celine's head pops up. This time, when Argyle goes to her, she actually allows him to help her. Once she's stable on her feet on the deck, an unknown man disappears down the ladder.

"What…" I can't catch my breath.

"Don't worry about it," Solo says calmly, keeping his hands on my back as I straighten. I fumble with the clasp of my cloak, needing it off. Solo's hands stop me. "Not yet," he warns.

"I'm hot," I say, practically begging. I can't deal with this thing for much longer. It's heavy and exhaustion is clinging to my limbs.

Solo's lips twist and as he looks down at me, he grimaces. *Regret? From him? Am I seeing things?* "I know, love," he says, shocking me further with the gentleness in his tone. "But bear with it a bit longer. Wait until we're in the Captain's quarters."

With a groan, I release the clasp. A moment later, Yulis' head appears over the lip of the deck and in the flashing movement of a man used to a physical life, he bounds onto the deck of the ship and shakes out his limbs. "Let's go," he says to our group. "My first mate will take care of the tender."

Solo wraps a solid arm around my back as he leads me after the man. I stumble and lean against him, feeling drained and we haven't even done anything yet. Celine marches ahead of us with her head raised high—if anyone were to guess, they'd likely think she's the royal here. I can't even manage that much right now.

As we walk, several men aboard the ship call out Argyle's name, waving in recognition. Argyle smiles and waves back. It's clear they want to talk more, but Yulis doesn't stop and therefore, neither do we, not until we enter a wide room at the back of the ship beneath the stairs that lead up to the uppermost deck where another man stands at the helm. I stare up at him until we duck into the room and the door closes behind us.

"Can I—" I don't get the question out before Solomon's hands are already working at the clasp of my cloak and he's helping me peel it off. Though not much weight by itself, the second the cloak is removed, I feel lighter. A relieved sigh escapes me and without thinking, I practically sag against Solo's front, pressing my forehead into his sternum.

His body tenses, and when I mean to pull away, the wide breadth of his palm lands on the back of my head. He strokes my skull gently. *Offering me comfort?* If so, it doesn't last long.

"Alright, boy," Yulis says, breaking the silence. "You've requested my presence here. Now tell me what it is that you need."

I look up and step away from Solo. Together, we turn toward Yulis as he takes a seat behind a wide wooden table. There's a map spread out across the surface, kept in place by dual blades jutting up from the edges, embedded in the wood underneath.

Argyle moves to stand before him. "Many years ago, you helped me to Awaken my powers when I needed it," he begins. "I've brought someone who needs your expertise."

"Another Raven?" Yulis shakes his head. "Argyle, you were an exception to my rule. You should know that I don't assist those of noble blood without a price."

"We're willing to pay it," I say quickly.

His gaze turns past Argyle to me. Sharp golden brown eyes meet mine. "I take it you're the Raven," he says.

"No."

"Devonry—"

I shrug off Solomon's grip as he touches my arm and strides toward the table, not stopping until I'm mere feet from the man. "I am no Raven, sir," I explain. "I am Devonry Estrand of the House of Sunfire, Crown Princess and the rightful heir of Rozentine."

My announcement is met with icy stillness. Yulis' eyes never leave my face, as if he's searching for a hint of deception. He won't find it. I straighten my spine and meet his gaze.

"I was told that the Princess had never Awakened," he says.

"That's changed," I answer. "But ... I need more help."

"So, you've Awakened, but you can't completely control your abilities then." He tsks in the back of his throat. "That's much like that boy over there, at least when I first met him—a half Awakened child is dangerous." Hearing someone call Argyle a boy is odd, but Argyle doesn't seem particularly offended. As if he's used to being referred to as such by this man. My curiosity about their relationship, though, isn't important in the face of what this man can do. If he was able to help someone else who was only half Awakened like myself, then that means he can do so now. If I can convince him, that is.

"Will you help me?" I ask.

"Will you pay whatever I demand?" he replies.

"Within my abilities … yes."

Yulis continues to stare at me and I feel like a butterfly pinned beneath glass. His eyes scan me from my face to my hair and down the length of my body. My muscles tighten beneath my dress as his attention falls to my breasts. A low growl rumbles behind me.

"Be respectful," Solo practically snarls. He's quiet. One second, he's somewhere in the room behind me, and the next, he's at my side.

Yulis, for his part, doesn't react. Instead, he shifts his attention to Argyle. "You seem to have found yourself quite a new strain of friends," he comments. "A new master too."

Argyle bows his head slightly. "I am my sole master, sir, as you always taught me. Who I choose to follow and assist is by my decision and mine alone. I owe this man a life debt," he nods to Solo. "And in return, I consider him a friend."

"So, you're saying you've not become an advisor to royalty?" Yulis barks out a laugh as if the idea is ridiculous. His attention switches back to me. "Do you realize who you've come to for help, Your Highness?"

"Solomon trusts Argyle with his life," I say. "And I trust Solomon. Who you are doesn't matter to me, only the skills you have."

His lips stretch wider. "Spoken like a better ruler than most," he replies. *A compliment?* I blink at him in surprise. From the reaction I'd received when I revealed my lineage, I hadn't expected as much.

Yulis blows out a breath and leans back in his chair, dragging a hand down his face. "Forcefully awakening powers too quickly can cause complications," he states. "In some instances, it can even cause death." He lifts his head. "Are you sure you're willing to go that far?"

Solomon tenses at my side. "Yes," I say before he can speak. "I will do whatever is necessary. I have to master my Awakened abilities as fast as possible."

"To take back your kingdom?" he clarifies.

I nod.

He sighs. "I'd heard about the mysterious disappearance of the Crown Princess," he says absently. "There's a bounty out for you, you know."

I frown. "A bounty?"

"Oh yes, it seems the current regent that's taken over in your absence is dead set on finding you and bringing you back. What's curious to me, is why you're here, Princess."

"The current regent?" Flames of hatred and anger sear my insides. "Prince Nasir?"

"That's who I heard was in charge." Yulis nods.

A tidal wave of emotion so intense that it nearly breaks me in half sweeps through me. The air around me crackles. Yulis' eyes widen and he stands abruptly. I can't focus on him though. I'm too concerned with the war happening inside of me. My hands curl into fists at my sides, trembling as I try to repress the emotions that threaten to overwhelm me so completely that I cease to be Devonry and become someone else instead. Someone ruled by rage.

"Stop her!" Yulis barks the command. "Now!"

I don't know what he means, nor do I care. To think that Nasir is being considered as the regent of Rozentine. *My* fucking Kingdom. The place I was born and the homeland of my ancestors, reigned over by a traitor who slaughtered my father. The sound of my own breath is loud in my ears. That, combined with the strange pounding in my skull, fills my head, drowning out the sound of the others' voices. *How dare he ... how fucking dare he!*

A sharp stabbing pain pierces my flesh and I gasp and jerk my head down to see that blood is pooling in my palms; my nails have sunk past my skin, deeper. Red wells up and drips down over my fingers.

"Devonry." I look up at the sound of Solomon's tight voice. He steps in front of me, blocking off the rest of the room and his hands come up to cradle my head. "Look at me," he commands. "Breathe calmly."

I am looking at him. I am breathing. What—my chest collapses and I gasp as a spiral of heat strikes up my back. I bow away from it as I cry out, my choked scream disappearing before it can even manage to come out. All the while, Solo's face remains in front of me. Never moving. With shaking hands, I reach up and latch onto his arms. My nails stab at him as I clutch onto the only stable thing in my vision.

"Breathe," he repeats. "Inhale."

My lips part and I suck down as much air as I can physically handle.

"Exhale," he says.

I do so. He repeats the words, and as he does, my body responds, following his commands like it's the most natural thing in the world. I'm trembling, unable to stop the fine tremors in my body even as I can feel the heat inside of me calmly recede. The fires, once stoked, now dissipate. My anger, though still there, cools considerably. I lean forward, pressing my face into Solomon's chest. The scent of him—like an ocean breeze—invades my nostrils. I drag it in more and more, hoping that it soothes me back into a sense of tranquility.

It doesn't work the way I want it to, but after several long minutes of just breathing him in, I do feel composed enough to lift my gaze.

"What … was that?" I ask, pulling my hands from his arms as I stare at their still-shaking forms.

"That," Yulis states, "was exactly why I said that half Awakened children are dangerous."

I look up and blink when I realize that Yulis is as far from me as physically possible while still remaining in the room. He's standing at the door with his back against the pane and his face drawn tight. Several feet down, Celine also has her spine pressed into the wall, only she doesn't appear to be there of her own volition. Instead, Argyle stands over her, his back to me as his much larger frame swallows most of hers.

"Now, do you understand the need for expediency?" Solo says dryly, glancing back at them.

"Yes." Yulis nods. "We will discuss payment later. For now, I will take you where you need to go to finish Awakening your powers. If—Gods help us—she erupts before then, I fear it'll set this entire ship ablaze."

With that, Yulis rips open the door and storms out into the night. His shouts can be heard as he barks orders to his men to set sail until the door swings shut behind him. I stare after him, stunned by the strangeness that just overcame me and what it could possibly mean.

"Get off me, you brute!" Celine's annoyed grunt breaks the tension in the room and, still in the circle of Solo's arms, I peer over his shoulder to see her shove Argyle away from herself. Her cheeks are flushed and her eyes spark with intense emotion—somehow, I truly don't think it's all irritation.

Argyle coughs as she delivers another rather rough shove right into the center of his abdomen. "Not even a kiss of thanks?" he asks teasingly.

"I had every belief in Her Highness, thank you very much," Celine snaps.

Belief in me? To do what? No … I realize. Not to do something, but to *refrain* from doing something. My gaze finds Solo's face. His expression, though, could have been carved from granite.

"Solo?" That earlier anxiety returns tenfold.

He doesn't look down at me as he yanks me against him, pressing my face forcefully into his chest. "It's alright, Devonry," he says. "Everything will be alright."

Curiously, as I inhale the strikingly clean scent of soap mixed with Solo's natural musk, I find his words comforting. As if they're not just said to offer me solace, but instead, a sharp oath intending to tell me something else. Intending to tell me that he is here with me and he always will be. Protecting me, even from myself.

19
SOLOMON

"**S**olomon?" Waves crash against the hull of the ship as we stand by the railing, watching the Bartoli Empire's coastline. Yulis directs the ship himself now, steering the vessel through the waters alongside the beaches and around a massive cliffside. My gaze scans the coastline, searching for signs that we're being followed. There's nothing.

In my arms, Devonry shifts. The temperature of her body is warmer than normal. Of course it is, I think. After what we just witnessed in the Captain's cabin, no doubt she will struggle to lower her body temperature until the last vestiges of her anger have abated. My hands tighten against her arms. She had nearly seared me with her power. I'd never felt such an all-encompassing fire. It had felt as though I'd flown directly into the sun.

Her eyes had sparked, fires had danced along the ends of her hair, and her skin had glowed. All the while, she didn't even appear as if she was aware of what she was doing. It had frightened Yulis and put Argyle on edge. Out of the corner of my eye, I spot him hovering several feet away near Celine.

"Solomon, look at me." My heart hammers against the inside of my chest and since that moment in the Captain's quarters, I haven't been able to stop touching her. Though I know one slip and she'll burn me, I will happily accept a scar given by her. It had incited something inside of me to feel the way she'd clung to me. Her eyes locked with mine. Her nails had dug into my skin past my clothes. She'd needed me, relied upon me, and refused to release me until she knew it was alright.

Blood hunger pierces my gut and I close my eyes. A sharp punch smacks into the side of my abdomen and I open my eyes and look down. Devonry's pale face is illuminated by the moon above as well as the few lanterns scattered about the ship. After so many weeks of travel on the last ship we were on, a few short days on land hasn't made her forget to balance herself back on the water. The ship beneath us rocks back and forth with the ocean waves and as if she's done it her whole life, Devonry sways with the movement.

"Why aren't you saying anything?" she demands, her lips pursing together in irritation.

"There's nothing to say, Princess," I say, forcing my voice to remain calm.

"Something just happened in there and there's nothing to say about it? What happened? What did I—"

"It's better that you not think about it," I interrupt. "Once we do what Yulis tells us and your powers are Awakened, it shouldn't happen again."

Gods willing, whatever Yulis has planned for us, whatever we need to do to fully Awaken her will be the solution we need. As strong as I am, as many years of practice as I've had to Master my own abilities, I am not of the House of Sunfire. I am not Aerea's descendant. That title can only belong to her, which means that Aerea's ability can only belong to her. When I'd seen it, though, I hadn't realized how strong it would be. How overwhelming.

I had to give it to Yulis; any other man would have fled without a warning or second thought. He'd at least managed to stay as I'd calmed her. How I had, though, I still don't comprehend. The skin over my palms feels rough and tingly, as if still healing from a wound. The Goddess Queen's power was full of flame and rage. As I'd quickly ushered her out not long after Yulis had left, I'd spotted the dark scorch marks against the floor where her feet had been.

"We came here for a reason," Devonry says, her tone tight and clipped. "That's to help me fully Awaken. Don't you think it's counterintuitive to keep secrets?"

Secrets? I've kept so many secrets from her and she still has no idea. Another certainly won't change anything at this point. My vision is hazed over in red. I glance down at her, settling my eyes on her face. Despite her less-than-pleased expression, I can still admire her beauty. The softness of her cheeks. The long lashes that hover around her crystalline eyes. More hunger spikes jab into my abdomen. My fangs ache to descend. Her throat bobs as she swallows and I catch onto that movement. My tongue swells.

"It's not that it's a secret." I force the words out one by one. "It's that knowing does you no good." I rip my gaze from her throat and return it to her eyes. "Please, trust me on this."

Devonry's expression immediately becomes wary. She inhales sharply and pulls from my grasp, turning to walk toward Celine. My hands tighten, but she doesn't stop or turn back. I could keep her by my side. It would be easy enough with my strength, but I don't. I let her go, watching as she storms off, not stopping until she is next to Celine. Thankfully, despite what occurred in the room, Celine acts no different with her. She opens her cloak and offers her the warmth of her body as the two of them peer out across the ocean and Bartoli's cliffside.

Argyle's attention is centered on them as well. Despite the fact that several of Yulis' men have approached and are currently lingering around him to catch up, every so often, his gaze moves to Celine. I get it. If I didn't have years of keeping my emotions and desires under wraps just to remain near Devonry I would have the same expression when I look at the Princess.

The ship turns abruptly, wind changing direction as the front is steered past the cliffside, and just as I'm about to call out to Yulis to demand an explanation, a large opening appears. A slit of a cave. The heat of the open Bartoli sea drops dramatically as the ship enters. In my periphery, Argyle excuses himself from his old friends and comes to my side at the railing.

"We're almost there," he states.

"Where is *there*?"

His face is expressionless, but beyond him, Yulis' is filled with pinched concentration. The waters within the caves are nearly black below and the cave walls themselves are glimmering in some sort of luminescent light that's dull, but thankfully enough for Yulis to steer the vessel. The stone walls are sloping, smooth towards the waters, and growing more jagged the higher up they go. The walls of the cave grow closer and closer to the sides of the ship until I worry we'll collide. Just as I'm sure we're about to, the cave walls drop away and the soft sounds of voices echo up to the top of a massive inner section of the cave. "To the caves that hold Thevaros' tears."

"Thevaros' tears?" I repeat Argyle's words before

glancing at Celine. If she hears him, she doesn't let on. If she feels something from these caves, too, she doesn't react. Then again, from my understanding, she's still a bastard child of the noble house of Starfall. Perhaps her abilities aren't that powerful. "What does this place have to do with Starfall's ancestral God?"

"There is a legend," Argyle replies. "That Thevaros came to the mortal plain in a human body. This is that human body's eternal resting place."

"Then the waters here are what we need?" I cast a glance up to Yulis as he whistles for one of his men to take his place at the helm.

Argyle shakes his head. "Not here, further in, much deeper than these waters."

"This is where you came." It's a statement, not a question, but Argyle nods anyway. This is not his first trip to Bartoli, which explains how he knows so much about their customs. He'd come here before—many years before I'd ever met him, and this man, Yulis, was his teacher.

"Ladies, gents," Yulis calls out, "we'll be taking a tender to the rocks, and once there, we'll disembark."

My attention falls on the man with renewed interest. It is the duty of a guard to see any potential threat to his charge and though I trust Argyle, this man is now suspicious. How does he know so much about Awakened abilities when it appears that he, himself, is not one of us? He's quite informed about Rozentine for a pirate. What else does he know?

As if sensing my internal thoughts, Argyle's hand finds my shoulder. "He's a good man," he says. "He'll want payment for bringing us here, but he wouldn't harm you or the Princess."

"Can his loyalty be bought?" I keep my gaze trained on the man as he moves forward and lifts a rope ladder from one of the barrels scattered about the deck. Together, he and two of his men set about preparing to make land.

"His services," Argyle says, "but never his loyalty."

"Then who is he loyal to?" Unknowns are dangerous.

"Solomon." Argyle rounds me and stands before me, blocking my path and turning my attention to him. "Yulis raised me. He's been around a long time and in his time at sea, he's met many nobles—both Ravens and not. He's a good man. I trust him with my life and I trust him with this group."

I scowl and shake my head. Pressing a hand to his shoulder, I move to stride around him. "Devonry means more than—"

"I trust him with Celine's life." Those words give me pause. My gaze moves back to his face. Argyle drops all pretense, his dual-colored eyes boring into me with a silent plea. "I suspect I'm not the only one who's found himself led by the leash of a woman as of late, my friend. Please, trust me. Yulis is worthy. He will not betray me—us. If you want the Princess to fully Awaken, she needs to enter the caves and do exactly what he tells her to do."

My gaze shifts from him to the railing where Celine and Devonry remain, craning their heads over the side to look down into the bottom of the cave. I watch her, wishing we had another choice, but since we don't, there's only one thing I can provide. Myself. "She won't go alone," I say.

"Solo, this is something she needs to do—"

I glare at him. "She. Won't. Go. Alone." I repeat the words, harder and angrier than before.

Argyle huffs out a breath. "Fuck." He releases me to scrub a hand down his face. "Fine," he snaps. "Have it your way, but just know—I warned you, and so will Yulis."

I nod, and without further response, I move past him to

Devonry and Celine. As soon as Yulis is ready, he gestures for our group to follow him, and follow him, we do—down the ladder and into the smaller boat yet again. Yulis and Argyle maneuver the smaller vessel through much shallower waters. Together we leave the ship behind, anchored in the center of the massive cave. Drifting further into the darkness as we give ourselves over to a place brimming with an energy of the divine.

20

DEVONRY

All is quiet for a short while. There are no animals here in the caves save for what lies beneath the water's surface. Then, as Argyle and Yulis turn down a deeper, darker tunnel, Yulis begins to hum low in his throat.

Pricks of awareness creep along my arms, up my neck, and down my back. For a man who looks as rough as he does, Yulis' voice carries a note of softness. Or perhaps that's simply the echo into the upper chambers of the caves reverberating back at us. Whatever the case, it calls to something inside my breast. It isn't until he parts his lips and begins to recite the first verse that I realize how gentle a deep voice can sound.

.   .   .

Yulis sings a song of a haunting quality, and the air around seems to grow colder. I wish I hadn't left my cloak behind. Celine, whether she realizes the movement or not, shuffles closer and presses her arm against mine as her head turns toward where Yulis stands at the back of the boat.

Across from me, as the darkness encroaches around us, Solomon's eyes grow ever brighter. My lips part and I inhale icy air, filling my lungs to almost bursting. When I release my breath, it comes in a shuddering wave.

Long gone are the betrayers
That brought the man here
And deserted two in their place
Thus what the Great Traveler sought
Was not lost, but found in Her tears

Trust broken. Betrayal. Fear and hope. Yulis' song slips inside of me, bringing forth emotions I've been carrying around for so long and yet have been unwilling to look at. My hands clench into fists against my thighs. I swallow roughly, ripping my attention from Solo's face to stare out over the vast inky shadows around us.

What little there is to see, is illuminated by the lanterns we carry. Rocks jutting up out of cave walls. Long, sharp, and jagged points formed at the top of the cave, hovering above our heads like axes waiting to fall. All it would take is one small quake of the land beneath us for them to fall and crush us. Somehow, though, I find myself unafraid as I stare up at them.

The deeper the vessel goes, the darker it gets, and the more the Awakened feeling stirring inside of my chest that sings back to Yulis' sad song grows restless. I stand abruptly, the boat rocking slightly. My head turns. There's a pull deep within these walls, and like a string tied around my heart, it tugs.

"Your Highness—" Celine reaches for me, anxiety coating her tone. I can hardly hear her call. The rope wrapped around my insides is too loud. It rings with nearness.

Evil rests not in this place, as Deceivers Designed
Behind left, only a gift for the blessed
Bathe yourselves in Her spring divine
Find what you seek before sunrise
Open yourself to what's been repressed

Confused, I look back at Yulis. "*Her* spring?" I repeat. In all the incarnations I've read of Thevaros, he has always come back as male. The song had said that the tears were the Gods', so why would it be the girl's spring?

As if he understands my thoughts, Yulis' lips lift at the corners. "Thevaros would never have cried had he been locked in here alone," he replies. "But the sailors who trapped him, in their fear, sacrificed one of their own. The legend says that she forgave her betrayers before she perished alongside Thevaros' human body. That, more than anything, made Thevaros truly understand that to be human is to be kind, to be forgiving. He cried for her and disintegrated into the springs that rest further into these places because of her. A God does not weep for his own life but for the lives of those he cherishes."

My chest aches at his words. A hand captures mine and I whirl around, jolting when I see that Solo has leaned forward. "Sit down," he urges gently.

"No need," Yulis says, capturing all of our attention once more. "We're here."

The boat jolts as it makes landfall, catapulting my body forward. My feet slip out from beneath me in one fell swoop, and I stumble right into Solo's body. Strong arms band around me, capturing me and lifting me before I can right myself. With his warm chest against mine and his firm hands gripping my arms, my heart tugs for a completely different reason as I turn my gaze up and meet his ruby irises.

"I warned you…" The chastisement comes out of him before I think he can stop it, but he doesn't go further, and, instead, moves his hands down from my arms to my waist. He grips me firmly, albeit gently, and lifts me over the side of the tender and onto a sandbar.

As he releases me, I turn and survey our surroundings. Argyle hops out of the boat and together, he and Solomon jerk it more onto the small beach within the caves. The brown sand is wet and sinks beneath my booted feet as I walk up the small hill. No sooner had I strode away only a few yards from the tender than the sand gave way to a rocky surface.

"Your Highness, please wait!" Celine calls after me, the sound of her voice tight. I turn back to see her struggling to get the mass of her skirts over the edge of the tender. She manages it, but only after Argyle finishes his duties and moves to help her. Sharp irritation fills her face as he places his hands on her body, lifting her about the waist the same as Solo had done for me, and deposits her on land.

"So, that legend you talked about…" I prompt, turning back, "and that song, they tell the story of Thevaros? Of this place?" It had to be. Only one God was ever known as a Great Traveler, and why else would he mention the legend if it didn't have to do with what we came here for?

Yulis remains at the end of the tender, holding up the oar he'd used to steer us here and resting his chin on it as he stares out past me and toward the darkest part of the caves.

"Thevaros landed on this empire long ago, before it was Bartoli, before people had even gathered under rulers. They were simply sailors and fishermen, hunters and gatherers. Thevaros was curious about the human children that inhabited this world. He sought to understand mankind and so he gave himself a human body to do so. But having a human body did not give him the knowledge he wanted. He had to interact and *live* as if he were human."

"What does that mean?" I ask.

"Despite his human body, he maintained the abilities of a God," Yulis replies. "He did not understand that, to mankind, those abilities were frightening. He thought that they would treat him as such since his body was like theirs. He was wrong."

Of course, he was wrong. Humans found comfort in what they knew, while the unknown was always a source of fear.

"Legend claims that Thevaros was told by a group of sailors that a young woman was trapped within these caves and could not find her way out. Thevaros felt deeply saddened by the poor woman's predicament and volunteered himself to find her, since he knew that he would not truly die should anything befall his human body and the same could not be said for the sailors. Once he entered the caves beyond here"—Yulis pauses to gesture behind me— "the sailors rolled rock after rock to block the entrance. Upon sunrise, they knew the waters would come in and drown Thevaros' human body; thus, his abilities would no longer be a threat."

My chest seizes. The trusting God, betrayed by those he wished to help. That was what his song had meant.

"The woman was, in fact, not lost, though. She'd been ostracized by her clan and as such, they'd brought her to the caves and tied her up to be executed by drowning."

"What had she done?" I close my arms around myself as the cave's coldness seeps through me.

Yulis' dark eyes met mine. "She had been born with a deformity," he says. "That is all." Meaning her only sin had been to be born different. I bite down on my lower lip, tasting blood.

Yulis continues his story, though his eyes grow unfocused. "Thevaros could sense the woman's soul deep within these caves and he dove down into the waters to a section only accessible from beneath the sea. He found her and released her from her bindings, but by then it was too late. The two were trapped. Thevaros could have used his powers to free himself, but to do so would have killed the woman—the very reason he'd come. For long hours, they spoke of things and Thevaros admitted that he'd only become human to try and understand them. He asked her why those men would betray him, why they would hurt her simply because of her deformity and she merely told him that it was the human way."

The human way. I shudder at the reminder of how deeply I'd come to know it. Betrayal. Broken trust. A pool of red flashes behind my eyelids. A night stained in blood. A burning deep down grips my throat tight, but I push it down. I cannot lose control here.

"Thevaros didn't understand the woman's calmness in the face of death. Unlike him, she would not have another chance in this realm. Where Gods are reborn, humans ascend. She didn't seem to mind and he asked her why."

I knew the answer before he spoke it.

"'Because you are here with me,'" he said. "But even as she said the words, the woman cried, and when Thevaros demanded to know why, she told him it was because she felt sorry for him. Sorry that she had been used to trap and destroy him, but at the same time she was so happy that she was not alone."

My gaze drifts away from where Yulis stands next to Celine and Argyle on the sandbar to Argyle, himself. His hands remain on her body, something she doesn't seem to notice as they also watch Yulis. Curiously, I tug myself away and turn to look at Solomon.

Unlike everyone else, he's not looking at Yulis at all. He's looking at *me*. A strange sort of tension bubbles up in my stomach, different from the tug at my heart. Fire collects in my lower abdomen before slowly and softly spreading throughout my body, like flames eating away at a dried forest. Try as I might, I cannot turn my eyes away. He holds me captive even as Yulis finishes his story.

"The woman held Thevaros through their final hours and as the water reached up to their faces, he finally seemed to understand what he'd been searching for the whole while." Yulis' voice grows distant in my head the longer my eyes are locked on Solo's. There are various shades of red in his gaze, swirling shadows that dive over one another, each one trying its best to be the brightest even as they darken at the edges. It only serves to make the circle of his eyes stand out more.

"Upon their deaths, Thevaros bestowed the woman who had taught him that the human spirit was a complex creature with a kiss. He, too, cried. His tears mixed with hers as she confessed that she forgave her clan a long time ago. Even amidst kindness, there is cruelty, and even amidst wickedness, there is love. That was Thevaros' lesson."

Kindness and cruelty. Wickedness and love. Two sides of the coin. Both are human.

Solomon blinks and tears his gaze away from mine, releasing me from the strange imprisonment and I gasp for breath. I nearly stumble in my haste to put further distance between us as I step to the side and lean against a large rock. Solo, for his part, moves further away. Perhaps he senses that I need the distance.

Celine is the first to speak now that Yulis' story has ended. "H-how do you know this story? What does the legend mean now?" she asks, her voice shaking.

When I glance her way, I find that she's not pulled herself away from Argyle as I expected. She appears unaware of the way she sways into him—as if she can't help but seek comfort after such a sorrowful tale. As kind as she is, I suspect the story must fill her with a sense of regret. Shame. Remorse. Regret for Thevaros and the poor woman. Shame for the humans who betrayed them both. Remorse for their lost lives.

As for me, those feelings are overshadowed by the amount of rage that lingers at the betrayal of the humans Thevaros trusted. Just as I had trusted Nasir, wanted to be better, wanted to help him … and now, I know nothing but blood and pain. Thanks to him, my future has been changed. My destiny. Unlike the woman from the story, I don't know if I believe that forgiveness is so easy to give. In the face of my own death, I'd wanted nothing more than to tear Nasir limb from limb, and even still, I want him to feel the same agony he's dealt to me.

"All sailors know the tale," Yulis replies, recalling me from my thoughts. "There is a cave, like in the story, accessible only from the sea." He points down the long, dark tunnel. "You must go to it, and dive into the waters. Wash yourself in the pool there. Immersing oneself has proven to help Awaken the full potential of those descended from the Gods."

"It's true," Argyle says. "It worked for me. It will work for you too, Princess."

"Be careful, though," Yulis warns. "The divine spirit of the cave gives life as well as takes it. Staying too long and absorbing too much of it will overwhelm those who are already Awakened." That last part is directed at Solomon who begins walking back toward me.

His footfalls are nearly silent on the sand and remain so when he reaches the rocks. "We appreciate your advice," Solo says. "But still, she will not go alone."

Solomon reaches my side and stops, peering back. Celine frowns and then takes a step forward, away from Argyle. His body tenses, but he lets her go. "You cannot go alone," she says.

I look up at Solomon. "I won't be alone."

"No," she shakes her head. "I mean both of you—you cannot mean to—"

"We have no right to stop them," Argyle interrupts her. "But we will be here upon their return."

I divert my attention to Yulis, whose expression has returned to normal after having taken on the far-off gaze of a man whose mind had traveled far away. "I am merely a guide, Princess," he says. "I do not recommend going with your soldier, but I am not going to stop him."

A chuckle leaves me and with a wiry twist of my lips, I offer him a small smile of understanding. "I don't think anyone could stop him, Yulis, but thank you. Truly." I put a hand over my heart. "Your advice and guidance have brought us here. Whatever happens, please know that none of it was your fault."

Yulis' face goes slack with shock at my words. "Your … Highness…" His words stop abruptly and he turns, his shoulders shaking as he coughs. "Return before sunrise," he says quickly. "Or the water will fill the cave, and like Thevaros—the two of you will be trapped inside."

Solomon nods and as we turn toward the tunnel, Argyle's voice echoes up the cave walls.

"There are plants within the tunnel walls that will illuminate when you get further in," he says. "But take Yulis' words to heart. If you, of all men, are down there for too long, your Awakened abilities may rage out of control." Argyle's focus shifts from Solo to me and back. "If you truly care for her, then do not let your beast get the best of you."

Solomon's expression darkens, but he nods to his friend before turning back around and stomping forward.

Beast? What does that mean? I look up at Solomon with a frown, trailing at his side. Perhaps bringing him along is not such a good idea. "If it's truly that dangerous, I can go alone," I say, only to be cut off as Solo reaches down and grabs ahold of my hand. He weaves his fingers between mine, and without looking at me, Solo brings my hand up to his lips.

His red eyes turn down to meet mine again. Hot breath feathers across my knuckles. A shiver slithers down my spine and an aching hollow opens up inside my chest, almost as if I can sense what he's about to say. "I will either live with you, my Queen, or I will die with you." A crueler oath, there never was.

21

SOLOMON

There is fear to be had in what is unknown. Yulis and his tale of the great god, Thevaros, linger in my mind. How much of what he speaks of is true? How much is fiction meant to scare? There is no way to know.

The rise of the hairs on the back of my neck leads me to wonder if the ghost of Thevaros haunts these caves to this day. Does he watch each heavy step I take with my water-logged boots? Does he see my queen with her gown damp enough to mold to her slender frame as she wades through his tears to his final resting place?

Yulis and his boat wait at our back, docked on the sandbar, much like a mourner comes to sit alongside a grave. At this late hour, the sight of their silhouettes outlined by the light of their lanterns sends a shiver of annoyance through me. This is not the last they'll see of us nor do we require their watchful eyes.

Devonry grimaces. Her hand finds my forearm, gripping me tightly even as the water lessens. Our feet dig into the sodden sands leaving behind deep footprints that threaten to steal her slippers right off her feet.

"Do you need assistance? Shall I carry you?" I ask if only to placate my own need to ensure her wellbeing. The look she gives in answer though suggests she's more keen to murder me and make this my final resting place as well.

Ahead of us, rock looms in large arching formations. Water glistens from every angle of the cave's ceilings, dripping like tears off its edge. Beyond it there is little to see, even with my enhanced eyesight, everything inside fades to black.

Delicate fingers dig into my forearm, the Princess grunts as she yanks her foot from the sinking sand. I wait for a moment, letting her adjust her shoes and garment. Awareness travels up my spine. Even as I close my eyes I can feel her nearness. My skin heats where her hand rests. Each breath she takes fills my own lungs in reflection of the strength of our bond she knows nothing of. So close to what remains of a god, in a place more holy than we've ever encountered, I can't ignore the tug of our souls.

Well, perhaps she knows a little. I think as she moves closer to my side, her hand never straying.

Gentle waves reach us but with only the barest amount of water that trickles through well-worn rivulets. The scent of salt clings to our clothing. Another more earthy scent comes from within the cave, brought to us on a breeze that causes Devonry to shiver.

Crimson coats my vision, making every angle of the cave more precise. The drops of water look more like blood now than tears. I can't allow my mind to stay on that thought for long. Hunger thrums within me. Saliva floods my mouth and my fangs start to push further through my gums.

"I can't see anything," Devonry whispers. The moonlight comes to an abrupt end about two feet into the cave.

She toes at the line where the sand starts to meet more solid larger rocks.

"I'll be your eyes," I answer, opening the map Yulis had sent with us. The paper is wrinkled and worn, the drawn images faded over time. And to think Argyle would have sent her out on her own. I can think of a thousand different ways she might have hurt herself.

Then as if to prove me wrong she lets me go and ventures forward. Her feet navigate the uneven entrance as she holds her hands in front of her feeling along the wall with one, the other stretches into the open air.

I sigh and shake my head before tracing our path on the map and curling it back up. "Do you know where you're going?"

"I thought you were my eyes?" she says, disappearing into the shadows, her tone lightening to further jest. "Hurry now, Solo."

Shoving the map into my waistband, the thick parchment scraping against my skin, I follow. Each step is a carefully calculated movement. The bottoms of my boots squeak as they slide against slick stone. Her thin slippers, though they can't be comfortable, might actually help her stay steady enough. They allow her feet to curl and grip against the odd angles of the ground.

With my abilities, I'm able to see her form, inching forward in the darkness. There is a steady trickle of water somewhere far off that echoes much like the sound of her labored breathing.

"Are you doing alright up there? We've got a ways to go before the cave forks into several paths."

"I'm—" Her silhouette disappears around a bend. "Oh! Solo, come here."

My skin hardens for a moment. A flash of adrenaline coursing through my body as I lose sight of her and she calls to me. I move faster. Paranoia nipping at my heels. Barreling around the corner, I nearly run through Devonry before she stops me with a hand to my chest. Light trickles down from the top of the cave, casting its soft glow over her features.

"This place truly is magical." She smiles up at me, a balm to my wariness.

There is no sky, nor a glimpse of the moon, but there are stars. Brilliant and bright, thousands of clustering dots hold the darkness at bay. Despite the height of the ceilings, could I pluck a star and hand her one? Could we hold a piece of the sky within our palms? I brush a finger over a cavern wall, the creamy green cast of light staining my skin. Devonry takes my hand and smears the color across my fingertips. Her smile widens as the glowing green transfers to her.

The Princess never needed me. She made it this far on her own.

I stare down at her trying to remember exactly why I have it so set in my head that she needs me. At this moment, I'm not sure that she's ever *needed* me. Yet here I was treating her as if she were far more fragile than she is.

"It's lovely," I whisper back, our gazes locked. The stretch of my muscles and the hardening of my skin shift and dissipate along my back in a matter of seconds. I roll my shoulders trying to ignore the sensation and start forward again, offering my hand to help Devonry over a particularly large boulder.

Her hand in mine sends a tingling sensation up my arm. She pulls her attention away from me, glancing at our hands. Does she feel what I feel?

Devonry clears her throat and slides her fingers out of mine. "I, uh, won't lie. I'm quite happy to be out of the castle even if I had to ride on a pirate ship and am cold to the bone." She gestures down at the dress hugging her body.

"You've never been one to stay in one place for long." I nod, trying and failing not to picture her body every time I blink.

"Half the fun of running was making you chase me." Her laugh bounces between the walls but dies too quickly. "Before, I mean."

"And are you still running from me? Or is it no longer fun?" I listen as her steps slow behind me but never stop. "Dev?"

"It isn't a game anymore." Her voice is strong. "I'm not running."

I swipe my hand through the thick of a spider's web, sinking my fangs into my lip to hold back my grin. "That's my Princess."

She lets go of a breath. Quick steps catch her up until she is just behind me once more. Silence keeps us company as we move amongst rocks and shallow puddles. The dim glow of the crystals and algae overhead leads us on until we reach where the path opens to several others. I pull the map back out, matching the openings with the script and drawing in my hands. Devonry stands at my side, staring at the map with an intensity that might suggest she's memorizing it. I only roll it back up and store it away after she gives me a nod.

Light trickles into most of the openings. At least five are easily seen and three I can only really make out with the help of my abilities. Devonry moves past me, heading for the third opening without pause. The deeper into the cavern system we travel the more earthy the air becomes. The salty scent remains though it is much lighter than before, almost an afterthought.

"You know," Devonry begins, speaking over her shoulder. "Bartoli is quite beautiful. Though I struggle to see such beauty within the palace."

I huff a laugh, hating the way my voice turns to venom. "You don't think Prince Enver is beautiful?"

She exhales loudly. Even without her turning around I can picture the look of annoyance on her face. The curl of her lip. The scrunch of her nose. She speaks with a contemplative tenderness. "Do you think they are in on Nasir's betrayal?"

"That was always a risk we were taking coming here." My jaw clenches at the reminder of how fiercely she wanted to run into the arms of her betrothed as if that would make it all better. She was raised for this—to be married off for her country, and I was raised to watch it happen—yet the idea still turns my insides into a fiery pit.

"It could be that I made a mistake, wishing for something that never existed." Devonry steps over the steady trickle that runs down the center of the cavern now. A thin stream of water collecting more condensation and shooting toward our destination. *Thevaro's tears?*

In response, all my joints start to pull, some popping, as my body begs to transition. Persistent hunger nags at the back of my throat. The insistent flair of my abilities demands payment for their use. Usually, I'm able to tame the symptoms to a degree but the power that flows through this place is undeniable. The magic here is thriving. My palm flattens against the wall and I can feel it coursing through this place like blood through veins. Our destination is the heart of it all.

"Is there anyone you trust here?" My voice is rough even to my own ears.

"Celine, Argyle ... *you.*"

"And the Ambassador?"

She hums, her head tilting side to side as she thinks

before she speaks. "He invited me for tea the other morning to offer his *wisdom*." She laughs under her breath. "I'm less than thrilled with his advice. As for his loyalty and my ability to trust in him…" She shrugs. "He could be in the pockets of the Galeanos. I can see his perspective, I suppose; it also used to be mine. But it doesn't sit right with me. I don't know, it feels wrong in my gut." A hand goes to her stomach as though she can feel the sensation now.

"And what was this advice he gave you?" I tongue the back of my fangs trying to will them away.

"To bring the wedding forward. Marry Enver as soon as possible."

All the air in my lungs leaves me. I practically choke on it. "He said that?"

She chuckles. "That was nearly my reaction as well, but he is positive that the marriage will sway the family and encourage them to finally take action."

"They have hardly tolerated our presence from the moment we arrived. Prince Enver possibly being the vilest of them all. That man is a fucking weasel. Couldn't even come for your coming of age which started this mess in the first place. He can't even treat you with the decency you deserve, acting like you're something he's purchased instead of an actual human being." The tips of my fingers burn. My nails extend. "What shit advice, pardon my language."

"As if I've ever cared if you cursed." She shrugs.

"Marrying that creature will only make matters worse if you ask me." Words are spilling from me now. My vision shifts rapidly from the red haze to tunneled and narrowed with focus. "Prince Enver wants a way to control you. To own you. He wants to have the upper hand and he thinks you are owed to him. Your virginity is the prize that only he is deserving of. If that man lays a single hand on you—"

"Solomon." Devonry comes to a stop. Her brows are drawn down and her mouth parted with the slightest hint of a smile. "If I didn't know any better I'd say you're jealous."

Immediately, I close my mouth and press my lips into a tight line. Speaking is not doing me any favors at the moment. The effects of my anger still trickle through me. I've gained at least an inch in height.

"Stop." Devonry laughs louder. "I was only making fun … but you are? Jealous? Aren't you? Solomon Winett."

My fingers find my temples, rubbing circles even if it does little to help. The Princess beams up at me now, a wild and playful grin brightening her face.

"Jealous?" *Always.* "No." I shake my head fighting against my smile. "You simply misunderstand me."

"You don't want me but no one else can have me." She pokes a finger at my chest, still fighting her amusement. Every touch sends a ripple of feeling through my body, causing me to stiffen.

I grab her hand, holding it tightly in mine. "Want is not something I've ever been allowed to have, *Little Princess.*"

Devonry gasps at the sudden contact. Her smile fades but never fully disappears. I can feel her gaze on my face, on my body, and the way it bounces between our touch, my lips, and my own eyes. Fangs fully extended, I try to catch my breath but holding myself back from kissing her now is taking more control than I've ever had to exert before.

"Your eyes." She swallows and slips her hand from mine, leaving my skin ablaze. "Your abilities are … just like Yulis said. Do you feel well?" Her attention lowers to the stretch of my nails now basically claws. I curl my fingers into my palms as best I can.

No.

"I'm fine. We need to keep moving. The spring should be around the next bend." I walk past her, hating myself for every second of it. Devonry stays close, watching me through her delicate lashes.

The trickle of water becomes wider, as does our hollowed passageway. Moisture thickens the air. A fresh wave of warmth and humidity dampens our clothing. We're close. More crystals dot the space above us now. Clusters even gather at the highest peaks of the walls.

Devonry gives me several long glances. Worry gathers in the set of her mouth, the moment of her teasing now past. Still, I push ahead, desperation seeping into my mind. Thoughts of her spin in my head. She needs this. She needs her full ability. My discomfort is nothing.

Ahead of us the path ends, giving way to a small pool. Beyond the water is only more rock. This appears to be the obvious end. Had Yulis not given us direction we'd think we'd come this way for nothing.

Looking from me to the water, Devonry lowers to take her shoes off. I hold out a hand to stop her. "Keep them on. We don't know what's on the other side; you might need them. The dress too. The fabric might be heavy in the water but you're a strong swimmer right?"

"Strong enough." She agrees. We both know that she'd run off a time or two to swim with the commoners. I have vivid memories of having to get my boots more than muddy, dragging her out of the shallows while she splashed me. That was not long after I'd returned. We were practically still children.

"The map can't come with us any further." I can still feel its imprint against my torso even after I pull it free and balance it on the lip of a rock. "We have to trust that what Yulis says is right. We dive."

"We dive. Together." Devonry's words are quiet, even as they resound inside my head as if she's screamed it out to the world.

Inhaling, I hold a hand out to her. Devonry settles her grip against mine, squeezing once before we jump.

22

DEVONRY

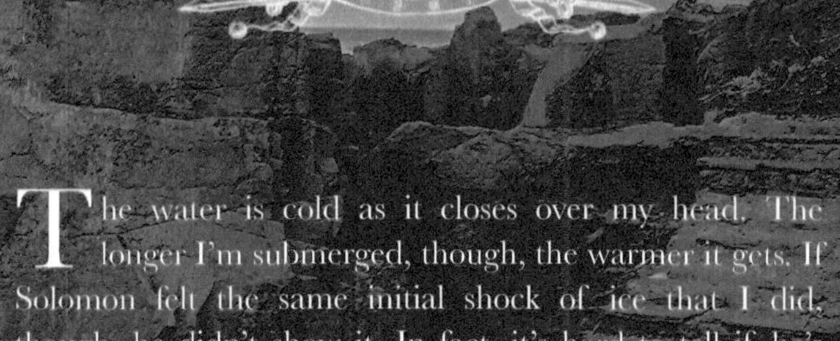

The water is cold as it closes over my head. The longer I'm submerged, though, the warmer it gets. If Solomon felt the same initial shock of ice that I did, though, he didn't show it. In fact, it's hard to tell if he's showing anything at all. Beneath the surface is so dark that I'm not entirely sure how we're meant to find the path to the underwater cave.

Several seconds pass and then, as my eyes adjust to the darkness, I see it. The crystals embedded in the rocky formations under the water's edge glow and illuminate a path. A tug on my hand has me whirling around, the mass of my skirts catching at my legs but then loosening just as quickly. I see Solomon's face illuminated by the crystals' light. He nods to the side and I follow the gesture, spotting a darkened hole several yards away. His hand wraps around my wrist and pulls me along with him.

I clench my jaw to keep from swallowing any water and kick my legs after him. It takes far longer than I anticipate —no doubt due in part to how weighed down we are by my dress skirts. But finally, blessedly, as my throat burns for relief and my lungs threaten to explode, we dive through the hole and find ourselves caught up in a quick current that drags us straight through a shortened underwater tunnel.

Moments later, our heads crest above the surface. My lips part and I gasp for air, sucking down lungfuls of it and coughing and sputtering as I bob up and down in the shallow water. Solomon releases my wrist to wipe the water from my eyes with his massive palm.

"Are you alright?"

Still coughing, I give him a sharp nod. *Just dying,* I think. *Nothing to worry about.* I don't say as much though and from the look he gives me—all brooding and pinched —I'm not entirely sure I have him convinced that I'm fine.

Together, the two of us wade towards what looks like an open ledge. We climb onto the hard surface and I feel as though my body is growing heavier and heavier. To try and relieve some of the weight, I lift my skirts and begin wringing them out. Water drips from the ends.

"Let's hurry." Solomon's words are full of concern and the deep v between his brows hasn't smoothed out. With a sigh, I release my skirts and follow after him.

Panting, sweaty, cold, and shivering, I trudge down the cave, spotting similar crystals in the walls—though much smaller than those I'd seen underwater. The further we walk, the warmer it gets until the chattering of my teeth finally subsides. It's not long until we reach it—the pool of water.

"This is it?" I look to him for confirmation.

"I think we need to dive beneath this one." Solomon's face is turned down to look at the glowing waters. It's frothy at the edges. Lighter in color than the blackened waters we'd had to swim through to get here. It's a minty green color and it smells … sweet. Like rich soil and flowers.

I swallow roughly, closing my palms around my upper arms. All I need to do is submerge myself again. That's what Yulis had said. My heart beats rapidly in my chest. "Princess?"

Forcing my gaze up, I meet the ruby-red irises of Solomon's gaze. He holds out his hand. "It will be alright," he assures me. "I've got you."

I take a deep breath and swallow down the sudden bolt of fear that warns me this might not work. If Solomon is here, then I can at least try, and if it doesn't work … well, we'll cross that bridge when we come to it.

Gingerly, I take Solomon's hand and he guides me from the rocky edge of the damp and empty cave into the waters. I expect it to be as cold as the ocean water, yet as my body is submerged I find the temperature is more comparable to a bath. Warmth chases away the chill and soothes all of my aching muscles.

Fabric floats around me and bubbles chase after me, grazing my body to pop at the surface. Droplets of water bead on my skin and I blink away what drips down my forehead. A moment later, Solomon steps into the pool with me.

"What are you doing?" I demand, breathless as I close my arms around my chest. It hadn't occurred to me before what happens now—my dress is clinging to every crevice of my body and beneath the fabrics, I can feel my nipples harden.

"Wherever you go," he says. "I go." Then he disappears beneath the water.

Not a second later, Solomon emerges before shaking the strands of his soaked hair out of his face. A crimson light pulses through his pupils. The skin on his face looks taut. Dark circles shadow underneath his eyes that I swear weren't there moments before.

"I thought I had to do this on my own," I reply. "Your abilities … if you're here for too long—" Hadn't Yulis said that this place might overwhelm anyone with already Awakened abilities with its divine spirit?

"I will be fine," he insists.

My heart is no longer racing, but full-on sprinting inside my chest. My breaths come faster and faster as he swims nearer, cutting through the water like an agile predator.

"Take a deep breath and we'll swim to the other side." His voice reverberates within the space.

"You don't need to be in here," I remind him.

The look he gives me is silent but powerful. Then he nudges my side. "Move," he orders.

I grumble my acquiescence, but put strength into my legs, kicking through the water to the other side. I really hope this works. It has to. Just on the other side of these waters, beneath the surface and within these walls, lies my salvation. My resolution. My future. My Awakening. A nervous flutter fills my stomach making me feel light despite the heaviness of my dress.

Solomon counts us down, my fingers growing tighter around his. If there is one thing I can be confident of, it is him. So I hold on to him as if my life depends on it, as it so often does, knowing it's not a new burden for him to carry.

"One … two … three…"

I suck air into my lungs, desperate to get my fill before swimming into the unknown, then thrust myself below the surface. My heart thuds loudly in my chest. It's echoing pounds inside my head.

Salt stings my eyes as I force them open. Little light reaches into the water's depths leaving us surrounded by near darkness for several moments. Then, the crystals glow brighter, illuminating the silent undersurface of the pool. My head turns. I never realized how loud the world is until now, where here, under the water, I can hear nothing. It's quiet. Peaceful.

Then the peace is broken when Solomon's hand tugs on me again, reminding me that I can't stay. With every kick, my slippers threaten to pull themselves from my feet. Still, I keep pace with Solomon while he guides us forward. His grip leads me deeper into the warmth, past where I might guess the cavern wall is. The water surrounding us gets warmer, though we pass through several cold spots that send goosebumps over my skin.

My lungs ache for air, the shadows somehow never ending. The water never ending.

Solomon kicks harder, propelling us forward, pulling me along with him far faster than my body might ever be able to move on its own.

Only when I start to wonder if we'll ever find the other side and my body begins to beg for air do we finally see light glimmering overhead. The butterflies that had grown in my stomach burst in a thousand different directions. My limbs tingle all the way to the tips of my fingers and toes.

We break the surface. Liquid gives way to the moisture-coated air I drag into my lungs. The smell of musk and salt is replaced with the earthy scent of dirt. I wipe at my stinging eyes and gasp. Fissures in the rocks overhead send light to fill the cavern so bright that if I didn't know it was the dead of night, I'd assume it was the sun. More of the glowing crystals, perhaps?

The rocky ledges that were behind us have been replaced with softer sands that lead to thick-trunked trees and moss-covered boulders. There is a buzz in the air. A thrumming of life. The soft pitter-patter of movement and, even farther away, a beating of wings.

Everywhere we look there's green, as if the color itself has been seeped into the rock and soil. The fact that this is no ordinary cave—that it's filled with life and warmth and vines and the chirping of bugs—is proof of the gods' hands at work. If there had been any doubt in my mind before that this truly is a place fit for Thevaros it has left me.

I carefully pull my hand from Solomon's and catapult myself towards the end of the pool. My feet find the soft earth and my dress tangles around my legs. I pull at the fabric, unsure what to do with myself now that I'm here.

Solomon trudges a few feet onto the beach before dropping himself onto his backside. With his knees bent, he rests his arms over his legs and drops his face toward the ground. His chest heaves as he takes in air.

"How many people do you think know this exists?" I say as I take in the area around us. Everywhere my eyes venture, nature has captured in its snare. Purple flowers vine up the nearest tree, only a few paces away, and disappear within the green canopy that reaches for the light above.

"Not many, or it wouldn't be as well preserved." He doesn't lift his face to answer but curls himself tighter into the position he's sitting in.

Water drips off my skin, glowing as it reflects the crystals. I watch as it drips from my sleeves and trails along my arm. Every step squeezes liquid from my slippers until I lower to Solomon's side. His red gaze lifts long enough to glance at me before he leans back on his arms and stretches his legs out in front of him. His features remain tight and his muscles tense despite the relaxed posture.

"We made it." I bump into him. Heat burns along my

shoulders and up the back of my neck, followed by the prickle of a shiver forming along my flesh. "Thank you for coming with me. I'm not sure I could do this without you."

"I think you would have done quite well without me, Devonry."

"Oh, yes. I could have done this without you." I chuckle, trying to hide the nervous tingles that encompass my lower stomach. "But it's nice that you're here."

"Are you…" Solomon turns toward me, a grin fighting his lips. The tips of his teeth still manage to poke out. "Are you teasing me?"

"I'm trying to be serious for once." The urge to nudge him with my elbow rises but it's easy to ignore.

"Well, you're welcome," he mumbles, eyes searching me.

His gaze lingers on my skin far longer than it should. I'm acutely aware of every inch of myself. Where the dress molds to my frame and how the material bunches at my knees where my legs bend beside me. My hands fidget in my lap under his scrutiny.

"What am I supposed to do now?" I ask, letting my attention wander to the vines that climb along the rocky walls.

"I suppose you are to bathe in it. As Yulis said." He wipes the back of his palm across his forehead, slicking away beads of water and sweat. Only then do I notice how warm it is here. Not so hot as to be uncomfortable, however there is a slight sheen of perspiration slicking my body already.

"Naked?"

"Do you typically bathe in your clothes?" He tips his head and raises his brows.

The heat that was formerly on my shoulders and neck makes its way up to my cheeks and ears. "That does make sense, I suppose." Scraping my teeth over my bottom lip, I stand and pull at the laces of my dress. "Look away," I whisper, catching Solomon's eye.

He hums a laugh but tips his chin up and closes his eyes. "It's funny how we still play at decency, isn't it?"

"I am not playing at *anything*, Solo." I bite the words out.

Material falls to my feet as I shrug out of the last of it. Air touches every bit of my bare skin leaving me vulnerable. I hurry to pull my slippers off, ready to submerge myself so my body will be hidden. Casting one last look at him, I confirm his eyes are still shut and hurry into the water.

Water licks over me. Ripples cast themselves in large, repeating circles in the pool around me. I stop only when I can remain flat-footed and the water still covers my chest.

I turn and meet his gaze. The collision of his crimson irises against mine leaves my mouth dry. Solomon's foot twitches against the sand. Even at our distance, I swear his body trembles. He tears his eyes away, baring his teeth, and then as if he's resigned himself to something, he returns to me.

He stares, unashamed at being caught. I search myself for feelings of guilt, shame, embarrassment, or anger but find myself only curious. Curious what attention from Solomon might truly be like. Not the angry back and forth we play at. Not even the same attention he gives me when we are civil and practicing with my abilities. No, I want to know what it's like to receive Solomon's attention as if I was some other woman. How might he treat me if he *wanted* me? How might I touch him if I admitted my want for him?

He clears his throat and rolls his shoulders before placing his hands in his lap. "Do you not find it odd that we pretend as if we have not slept in the same bed? As if we have not bathed in the same rivers? As if I haven't already seen every crevice of your body?"

My insides clench at the reminder. Memories of stripping my clothing off as fiercely and as quickly as I could manage while emotion overtook me play inside my head. I remember the way Solomon had balked at me as if the sight of me might be the most terrible thing he'd ever seen. But then he'd removed his clothes. And I'd remember just what a man is supposed to look like. Every part of his form had glistened in the sun, showing off his hard-earned muscle and the scars of war.

Sighing, I cup water in my palm and splash it over my shoulders before scrubbing my palm against my skin. "Being a royal—a Queen—is hard." As if that statement clears everything up. Yet it remains true. My life is for my kingdom, which as I've been told for years also includes who I should and should not care for in such a way. So I'll pretend, as I have for so long, that I've behaved as a Queen should.

Again, I wait for that wave of emotion to hit me and remind me that I've broken all these unspoken rules. The feelings never come.

Perhaps I am sick of pretending as well. Because whatever game we are playing at … well, I like playing it with Solomon. A little too much.

"It's hard being a Queen's guardsman." Solomon nods along. He clasps and unclasps his hands in front of him, blinking down at his lap.

I tilt my head back and massage my scalp. Prickles of sensation dance along my skin. When I right myself, I watch as the water that dances over my flesh glows. I splash my face, the same iridescent drops clinging to my lashes.

My breath quickens as do my movements. I can't help

but touch every inch of myself, fascinated as light sprouts and fades against me. *It's working.*

Every part of me is weightless, like I might rise from this pool, sprout wings, and fly away. Heat collects in my palms, burning at my fingertips. Warmth races up my spine and over my scalp.

Please. Please. Please. I plead with the gods.

Aerea. My goddess. Warmth spreads throughout my limbs, invades my veins, and rises to the surface of my flesh. For a moment, I feel her. Perhaps even for a slight second, I am her. All powerful. Made of fire. Made of life.

With my next breath, I can taste the lingering salt of the air, the crispness of the leaves, the sweetness of every bloom, and the musk of the earth. I can see bugs scurry over tree roots and can make out the definition of each leaf on every plant. The world seems infinitely large but also incredibly small, for only in this breath, in this place, am I a goddess. The sound of foliage rustled by small animals and the pitter-patter of their feet meets my ears. Even the soft wash of water that meets the sand is loud and noticeable. More so than those things, there is the rush of shallow breaths in and out of lungs. Not my own.

My attention lands on Solomon. Still sitting on the small rocky edge, he moves his head slowly from side to side. His eyes are closed and his hands dig into the soil and rocks. Sweat drips from the tip of his nose.

"I think this is it," I call out to him.

"Hmm?" He blinks several times, his eyes a beam of red.

"I think this may actually be working." Hope blossoms in my chest. "I feel … divine. Should I dress and we get going?"

"Yes, of course. I'll look away." His words are rushed before he stands and moves toward the brush.

I cut through the water, my movements swift and sharp. As I rise from the pool, my body feels impossibly strong as though I might find a reason to lift many things or sprint to the next city at speeds I've only seen Solomon capable of. I am Awakened.

Despite my dress being soaked earlier, it only feels damp when I pull it back on. I blink away the last droplets of water from my lashes in surprise. How long had I been in there? Minutes, I'd thought. I glance at Solo as I tie my stays and shove my feet back into the slippers. He paces the tree line, his back still turned. Running my hands over my skirt, I make my way toward him.

Worry seeps into the back of my mind. We've stayed too long. Time ticked away unnoticed.

"Should we head back?" I ask when I'm only a step away from him and he still hasn't turned my direction. "Solo?"

He spins on his heel. His features twitch for a moment, nostrils flaring, eyes wide, glowing. A beat passes and then another as he breathes deeply, his focus centered squarely on me before finally settling. Now that I'm so close to him, it's easy to see the changes in him. The texture of his skin has grown rough, tight. The tips of his fangs which had once been barely visible, are more prevalent.

He takes a step back. "I didn't hear you."

I frown up at him. He always hears me. His senses are the sharpest I've ever known. I'm not sure if I should ask, as he seems uncomfortable, but something is definitely wrong. "Should we head back?" I prompt, motioning for the water. Yulis' warning rings in my head. Are Solomon's abilities being affected? If so, then the price of his presence is being paid, which means I have to get him out of here.

"Yes."

I hold my hand out. He stares at my palm.

"*Devonry…*" Pain lances through the way he says my name. Fear strikes my heart. Something is most certainly wrong.

"It's okay, Solomon." I speak gently. "Let's go back."

His exhale is long and drawn out, but he pulls his hands free from his pockets and places his hand in mine, engulfing my fingers. The points of his nails graze along my skin but never scratch or pierce.

We move in silence back into the pool. I count down our breaths and into the depths we dive. Solomon propels us forward with every stroke of his arms and kick of his legs. It's easier for me to keep up with him now, I notice. He guides me more than pulls me.

Hand in hand, we go through the darkness until the soft glow of crystals tells us we've made it to the other side. Harder we swim, searching for the surface and only finding more water.

My fingers tighten against his. Worry drives me faster, only for my free hand to reach out and touch the glowing crystals. Fully submerged. I search and search in the dark, led only by those bioluminescent rocks. My eyes never find it, and I realize why.

The underwater pathway is closed. There is no getting back. We're too late.

23

SOLOMON

When it becomes clear that the path back to the surface is gone—the hollow tunnel filled with never-ending darkness and water—Devonry and I return to the cave of Thevaros' tears. As we crawl onto the rocky surface next to the waters, I breathe heavily through my nose. Everything hurts—like a fire has crawled up from my belly into my throat.

Devonry coughs and sputters, "Damn it!"

I would laugh if I had the energy. The sight of my precious little Princess cursing because of this, because of me. It's quite an amusement. Unfortunately, I'm too concerned with how my abilities will now affect not just me, but hers as well if she's forced to stay with me for too long. Will we drown down here? I glance back at the waters. Yulis' story had gotten something wrong—or perhaps thousands of years have been long enough for this place to form—but it doesn't appear as if the water will rise to swallow us whole. Small blessing though it is, I'm grateful.

The salvation of air in my lungs does not quell the

thrashing thoughts within me. She is Awakened but at what cost? Yulis warned that the water would come and it has. More of my skin hardens along my arms and torso. My eyesight narrows on Devonry as she swims for the water's edge then quietly sets herself down in the sand.

"Damn it all," I mutter to myself, before following and lowering stiffly to her side. We shouldn't have come. We could have found another way. Now there is no way to escape and nowhere for her to hide from the monster I'm becoming.

Hunger like I've never known before eats at my insides. A gnarled creature forms in my gut and shreds through my organs. Sweat collects at my brow and as subtly as I can manage, I turn and wipe it away.

"Are you okay?" Devonry's quiet voice fills the cave and its tunnel.

I ignore her question, fearing that if I try to answer it now, I'll show her just how not okay I am. I was the one who insisted on coming. I knew the potential consequences. My nails lengthen as that violent creature stabs at me again, making my fangs throb. There's no fighting the red haze that fills my vision. So, I close my eyes and rest my head back against the mossy rock behind me.

The damp scent of soil invades. Argyle had said he'd been here before. He, too, swore that we would drown if we stayed well past sunrise. What then, is this place? It feels more like a forest than an underwater cave. It's warm. Too warm.

My skin stretches across my muscles as something within reaches for the surface and moves against the underside of my flesh. Sharp whips of pain slash me. I turn on my side, away from the burn of Devonry's gaze. She hasn't spoken again since I refused to answer her question.

With my eyes shut, all I can do is focus on the war that rages within. Desire. Need. Thirst. A hiss slides from between my teeth, whistling into the air as the creature shifts under my flesh again. My abdomen clenches from the discomfort.

I feel heated, as if I'm being lit on fire. Bile threatens to burn through my throat. I begin to count my breaths one by one for something to keep me focused. When she's asleep, I'll move further away. If need be, I'll gnaw off my own fucking legs so that I can't attack her.

As time passes, the crystals on the walls seem to dim—almost as if they're mimicking the rise and fall of the sun outside. That would make sense, if not for the fact that it is because the sun has risen that we're now trapped here. Perhaps the crystals' divinity means something else. Whatever the case, the darker it gets, the more aware I am of the body of the Princess so close to me.

Beware the beast. Argyle was right. I should have known better, but what other choice was there? I could not let Devonry come to this place alone. I could not let her be trapped alone.

"Solomon, this is ridiculous. I can tell you're in pain. What's wrong? Is it your abilities?" The soft, cool touch of her hand against my forehead has my eyes popping open. Despite how much I crave her skin on mine, I snarl at her and jerk away.

I jolt to my feet, staggering to the other side of the cave. "Go to sleep," I command. "Do not think of me." My words are low, my voice more animal than human. It's too close.

Please, I beg silently. *Please don't let me do anything to harm her.*

Still, the growing nearness of the Blood Madness rides me like a steed into battle.

"I can't sleep knowing that you're in pain." Devonry's words are angry, concerned. "Why won't you let me help you? You're burning up. Perhaps I should get some of the water—"

"No!" I bark. That damned spring is the cause of this. Any more of it and I fear I won't be able to resist my urges.

Wrapping my arms around my body, I slam my spine into the rocky wall. The crystals along the sides and ceiling of the cave flicker with light before dimming further. Blood drips from my biceps where I cling to my arms, forcing myself to remain where I am. To not go to her. To not take the delicate flesh of her throat between my fangs and drink as I sink my cock into her body.

"Solomon, stop!" Devonry snaps, standing up from the ground. "Let me help you!"

She takes a single step forward. "Stay away!" The command is harsh, but her face merely hardens and she stomps forward, batting away my words as if they're not the last ditch effort of mine to keep her safe.

If she touches me again, I swear…

Devonry stops just feet from where I stand. With a groan, I bend over, sinking my knees into the floor of the cave. Plants growing through the cracks and over the surface soften my fall.

"Solo?"

My throat is dry, scraped raw of any further words. I hunger for her. Bleed for her. Want and need her. Why can she not understand that I am also a danger to her too?

My vision grows murky. Shadows and spots of light dance around my head. Never before have I begged for anything save for Devonry's safety—now, I beg for it again. The Gods, if they're even listening, turn a blind eye to my plea. Cruel bastards.

"This is your abilities, isn't it?" Devonry presses again. I sense, more than see her go to her knees alongside me.

Her soft, floral scent—like roses in bathwater—clings to my nostrils. It filters past the wet, damp mud and soil around us. I want more. I want to taste her. Another groan floods out of my lips as I turn my claws inward and stab at my abdomen to keep myself from taking advantage of her nearness.

She needs to go away.

She needs to flee, but the words won't come out.

All these years—training, fighting, protecting, denying myself what I want most in this world—all for her, and now, they will perish in the most callous of ways. I can picture it already. Her soft pale flesh beneath my palm, gripping her neck, feeling the beat of her heart, her blood rushing through her veins.

Thump. Thump. Thump.

The pulse of it sounds in my head. Monster. Evil. Vile creature. I am all of those and worse. Because, despite all I have done for Devonry, deep down, these desires are not brought about by the Blood Madness. They have always been there. Repressed. Unattainable.

Once more, her soft hand touches me. The coolness of it reaches beneath the clothes that linger on my flesh. I capture her hand and bring it to my lips. *More.* The beast inside is demanding. It seeks her out, scents her flesh.

"Tell me what to do," Devonry's tone turns pleading. "I'm scared, Solo. Please…"

"Shhhh." My gruff voice comes out deeper than ever before. Now that her skin is on mine, there is no stopping.

I pull her forward, stretching out my legs as I lift her and deposit her against my thighs, her legs on either side of my lap. Her breath hitches. Gods, how I wish I could see her more clearly, but with the blood pulsating through

my veins and the murky black and white sight of my abilities, it's nearly impossible. Between us, my cock strains
against my trousers. In one final effort to keep that piece of
me separate—at least here in a world not full of our
dreams—I push her slightly back. But I can't release her,
not the way I should.

Is there truly any more use in fighting off these urges? I wonder.
Have I merely been fighting a losing battle?

She was never meant to be yours, Solomon. King Vernon's
words of warning from so long ago penetrate my delirium.

He was wrong. She was always meant to be mine.
Devonry was born as the other half of my soul. Her gasp
as my clawed hands find her waist echoes into the cavern.
She begins to speak, her voice rising and falling with
nervousness as her hands touch me, roving all over as if she
is seeking the thing that's ripping me apart, not knowing
that it's inside.

"Let me help you," she whispers again, her hands
pulling at my shirt. It comes off quickly and easily and I
rest back against the wall as her cold skin begins to heat up.

"You always help me…" I mutter absently as she tries
to work her way down to my pants, only to have me
capture her hands and bring them back to my chest.

"W-What?" Her confusion is palpable, but my attention is fixated on her arousal. It permeates the air around
us. My sweet little Princess is wet for me. My torn stomach
rumbles even as the flesh knits itself back together. Her
blood and her honey. Both belong on my tongue.

"Solomon," she blows out a breath as she says my
name, "I don't know if you've forgotten, but up until a few
weeks ago … we were at each other's throats constantly." I
feel more than see it as her head dips, coming closer. It's
not close enough for me to capture her lips, not by sensation alone. "You said you didn't hate me, but … we cannot

erase the years of dissent between us as easily as that. You've never considered me helpful before, and it's my fault you're—"

"*No.*" Her fault? Never. If anyone is to blame, it's myself. "I didn't see Nasir's betrayal coming," I confess. "I am a failure to you."

Soft fingers brush the sweat-dampened strands of my hair back. "No one saw it coming," she whispers back to me. "I was closest to him, and I still … sometimes I still can't believe what happened."

The longer she speaks, the less pain seems to invade me, as if her voice is distracting me from the spiral of agony in my body. So, unthinkingly, I clutch her closer. "Please…" I beg. "Keep talking."

"Why?" she asks.

"It hurts less when you do," I admit.

"W-what do I talk about?"

"Anything." I twist my face side to side, feeling the warmth of her skin now as it rises in temperature. "Talk about anything, my Goddess, but please talk to me. I cannot bear this agony without it."

She stiffens in my hold, but in the next breath, she relaxes and even bends her head to mine. "Do you remember when we were kids?" she asks, and thankfully, she doesn't wait for a response. "The first time I met you, I thought you had the most gorgeous eyes I'd ever seen. It was like staring at the sun through red stained glass." Her voice is quiet, calm. Soothing.

"I know you've always been Awakened," she says. "It's rare to be born completely Awakened and even my mother was impressed by your abilities." There's a brief, hazy memory of the Saintess Queen. I'd not known her long before she passed, but I recall a kind face and a voice not unlike Devonry's.

"I pitied you…" Devonry's admission shocks me and I finally force my head up to look at her. Her eyes are glazed over as she cups my cheek. The beat of her heart picks up speed as I breathe in her scent, filling my lungs with it.

"Pitied me?"

"Everyone acted as if you were already a soldier," she says. "You were so mature." Her fingers play along my jawline, so light I can hardly feel it. I close my eyes once more and press my face into her palm, needing more of her touch.

"You were a child."

"Everyone was a child once." No longer, though. In fact, my desires are very much those of an adult. My cock throbs.

"Not you," she denies. "You were never treated as a child. You were always expected to put me before you."

I shake my head, pressing my brow to her sternum. "I didn't do it because I was expected to," I tell her honestly. "I did it because…"

My words halt in my throat. There is still a possibility, I realize, that even with her Awakening complete she won't recall. She won't understand my ties to her. Would it be cruel of me to bind her with the truth now?

"Solo?" She tries to lift my face again. I resist. The hunger is abating, now, but only because she is near. I know the moment she releases me, it will come roaring back. It will consume the last vestiges of my sanity and then I will cease to be Solomon Winett and I will become a beast merely wearing a human's skin.

"I need blood," I say abruptly.

"Blood?" she repeats. "Is this about the consequences?" She tugs at my chin, and I recline away from her. My thighs tense beneath hers. The heat of her pussy is right there, so very close. The vibration of her lifeblood taunts me, flooding my senses.

"Every ability has a downside." I remind her of our conversation all those nights ago on the balcony. "I need blood, or I'll lose control of it." A weakness I hate to admit, but one that's now necessary to warn her. "I'll hold it back, but … I fear I won't be able to leave with you when the sun sets once more. When that comes, you'll need to —"

"What about mine?"

The world stutters to a halt. All sounds—the water, the whistle of air, the breath in my lungs—freeze. "What?"

"Why would I leave you?" Devonry demands, her brow pinching into an angry frown. "If you need blood…" She shifts and reaches for the ties of her chemise, loosening them as she does. The fabric around her front sags slightly. She tips her head, offering me a sight I'd never thought I'd see so long as I lived. "Drink, Solo," she says. "We're leaving this cave together."

The beast inside me awakens and my voice dips lower than ever before. "*What if I want more?*"

"What?" Her tone is breathless and I bite down hard, grinding my teeth.

"Taking a person's blood can be a sexual exchange." *Can be*, my mind repeats. It isn't always necessary, but with her … I cannot imagine sinking my fangs into her throat and being able to resist the urge to take her in other ways.

A moment passes, then another and another, until the silence screams through my head. "Forget it," I snap. "Like I said, you need to stop this. If I attack you, then you should—"

"What, run?" she snaps, sounding irritated.

"Fuck." A groan rumbles up my chest as pain spreads through my limbs. "Yes, you should run."

"It's okay, Solo. I'm willing to give you what you need." She inhales sharply, the sound echoing softly back to me. "Even if that means…" Her hesitation is clear. Gods, why did we linger too long? Why hadn't I paid more attention? It's all my fault that she is trapped here with me. "Virtue means nothing if you can't keep me safe, Solomon," she says. "So, even if it's something sexual, I can handle it."

"*No.*" My fangs punch out of my gums, releasing from their confines despite the word that barrels past my lips. She has no clue what she's offering me. I cannot. One taste would not be enough and as hungry as I am—as much as this thirst is riding me—I fear that I wouldn't be able to stop.

"I'm not asking, Solo," Devonry says, her hands on my body—too hot, too close, too much. "Drink from me."

"I … can't." My body swells despite my words, muscles clenching as they lengthen and grow. The scent of her grows stronger. The soft brush of her skin on mine is burning away at what little resistance is left within me. The beast of my Awakening is rising to the surface now whether I want him to or not.

The sounds of nature return. Water bubbles, rising from the depths, streams of it filtering over rock. My head pounds. My parched throat burns. She doesn't know what she's offering. She can't know.

"Solomon." Devonry's voice is breathy but firm. "I'm offering you my blood of my own will. Please. Drink."

My lashes flutter. And as if the crystals can sense my impending defeat, they go completely dark—casting the two of us into pitch black.

I feel drunk with her scent, her warmth, her words. I reach for her, the tightly leashed control I've managed to maintain for two decades erased as if it had never existed the moment her words leave her lips.

Before I can stop myself, before I even truly realize my actions, I've closed my arms around her and spun the both of us. Her back lands against the soft stone and dirt beneath us.

Dream or not. Reality or falsity. The Gods have answered my prayer. I only hope they can answer my next one.

Please, *save her from me.*

Because I won't.

24
DEVONRY

There is no fire, but there is warmth—a heat so wicked that it threatens to burn me down to my very core. It sends sweat down my spine, and at the same time, it calls to me like an old friend. Like a memory ... one I should know but can't recall. It escapes me, slipping from between my fingers like smoke.

Fingertips trace the shape of my face, making my whole body jerk in surprise. Through the shadows, I sense him. His breath is hot and damp in my face. I can taste his need. His torment. It's violent, like the man himself.

Solomon's nails, usually filed down, are sharp and vicious. His true Awakening has peaked. The monster within is as close to the surface as I've ever felt it, leaving him balancing on the thin line of control. Something hot and hard presses insistently against my inner thighs. That warmth from earlier steals up and over my face as my own response softens my insides. My teeth rake against my lower lip as I try to catch my breath.

The Gods are cruel creatures.

Of all the men they could bring so low, why did it have to be him?

And why—oh why—do I have to *care?*

Solomon tries to be gentle, but it's almost as if he can't help himself. His grip is punishingly tight, so much so that he threatens to break me into a million pieces. I almost hope he does. Then I would be freed from these emotions, these physical reactions to him. He turns his hand until just the tip of his sharpened claw touches my jawline.

"So soft," he mutters. "You're always soft, and you smell like the realm of the Gods. You smell like divinity itself." The sound of his raspy voice, heavy with lust and something deeper ... darker, makes me shiver in his arms.

As if to prove his point, he leans closer, skimming his nose over my throat in a way that makes my heart jump straight to a gallop inside my veins. He inhales deeply, a harsh groan rumbling up his naked chest as it presses against my front. I close my eyes, squeezing them shut against the never-ending darkness surrounding us.

I've seen Solomon naked before but never this *intimately.* Even then, he wasn't the massive creature that now cradles me in his arms. The stone walls surrounding us invade us with their frosty coldness, but here, in the space where his skin brushes mine, it's like being licked by fire. The sounds of bugs chirping, the feel of soil under our bodies, and hard rock at our backs and sides sweeps all around us. None of it is enough of a distraction for what lies before me, for the man—the monster that lies before me. I didn't know how a woman should feel when a man presses between her legs.

A part of me hates that he's the one to introduce me to the sensation.

In days past ... weeks, months? ... I would not be doing this. A Princess' virtue is a bargaining tool. It is proof of sacrifice. Whereas other women are allowed to take lovers at their discretion, a Princess—a future Queen—is held to a much higher standard.

Nonetheless, what use is virtue to a Kingdomless Princess? What use is it when there is no one to follow, no one to rule, no one to protect?

My heart pounds inside of my chest, a wild, untamed thing. My lashes are wet with unshed tears and so much emotion, it clogs inside my throat. I've known Solomon since we were children—angry, resentful, bitter children who took out our frustrations on each other.

He's not my friend. I *hate* him. Or so I thought…

"Are you frightened?"

His question has me arching my head back to look down into his darkened face. Shadows dance around his features. The cavern echoes back his words to me, but I don't know how to answer. *Am I frightened?* It would be wrong to say I'm not at least a little scared of him. He's so … big. His muscles are swollen with power, bulging his arms to the size of small tree trunks as they wrap around me, keeping me securely locked against his chest. His Awakened form is almost that of a monstrous creature with only a hint of the human man left behind.

I should fear him, I think, yet somehow … I can't bring myself to. Of all the men in the world, Solomon is the one I can trust. The only one that I know with a certainty that is centuries old and soul-deep would never harm me. My earlier hatred—childish and comfortable as it was—is gone.

I shake my head. "No." My voice bounces off the walls, the unsteady sound a reflection of how on edge I feel. I may not be frightened by Solomon, but I am afraid of what continuing with this will mean for us.

Some people believe there is room for an untold

amount of emotion in the human body, but I disagree. There is only so much hatred one can harbor before it taints one's soul. The part that hates the man currently lying over me, pressing his lips to my skin, and circling his hips between my thighs has dampened.

A gasp escapes me and I arch my head back as fire sparks down my spine and spreads throughout my body. It's not right. It's not fair. Solomon is … he left. He walked away when we were children, after making me care, after befriending me, and when he came back, he was different. Battle changed him. It changed *us* so wholly that I thought there was no coming back.

Maybe at one point, he was my enemy, but now … he's my savior. And right now, he *needs* me to be *his* savior.

"Solo."

His head jerks at the sound of my voice and his lips pull away from a sweeping kiss in the crook of my neck. As they do, I can feel the sharp pinpricks of his elongated teeth. I tremble at the reminder of the cost of his abilities. With shaking hands, I reach between us and the front of my dress loosens over my breasts. His hands clamp on either side of my hips as he holds himself above me.

Only the barest shape of him is visible in the darkness, but still, I can see the way his chest pumps with effort. His shoulders are wide and strong. His arms encase me, making me feel tiny against the wide expanse of his chest. Sweat slicks our skin, making every movement of bare flesh against flesh smooth. I wonder if he's blushing. Solomon isn't the type, but the bare skin against mine feels hot enough. Perhaps that's just the power of his Awakened abilities—the connection of his bloodline to the Gods as a nobleman of Rozentine. Whatever it is, it feels divine.

"Highness…"

I shake my head. "No, don't call me that." Not here. Never here.

A pause and then, "Devonry?"

If it weren't for Solo, I'd be dead, or worse—locked up in the Sunfire Palace as a puppet Queen trapped by the man who stole everything from me. My home. My life. My family. My *trust.*

All around us, I hear nothing but the sounds of eerie nature. The open cave makes it all echo inside my head. The slow drips of water sliding over stone. Fish splashing in nearby pools of water. And outside, the wind blowing and rustling the leaves clinging to trees.

I tilt my head to the side, offering my throat to him. "Take what you need," I tell him.

Claws contract and release at my sides, those sharp nails of his threatening to dig past my clothing and right into my skin. Long moments pass and my embarrassment and reserve are shaken. I glance back at him, trying to see his expression, no matter how futile it is.

"Solomon?" My voice echoes off the stone walls, unsure. It takes a moment but when he finally responds, it sends all the blood inside my body rushing to my face, as well as … other places.

"I should not want you as I do, Devonry," he says, his voice quiet and gripped in dark desire.

"I-it's not your fault," I tell him, reaching up. My hand slides over the side of his face, feeling how hard his skin has gotten. It's like cold marble against my palm, but as I move upward into the silky strands of his hair, I realize that hasn't changed at all. The inky black locks of Solomon's hair slide through my fingers like the finest of fabrics. I shiver as I stare at where I expect my hand to be in the darkness, and when I turn my face back to his, I realize there's a new light.

A red light.

Solomon's eyes are glowing, the crimson of his eyes illuminating as they shine down on me, and for the briefest moment, I can see his expression. My breath catches in my chest. His lips are twisted back in a horrifying grimace and the sharp pointed tips of his canines poke through. *His fangs.* Straight, white, and sharp at the ends, they peek out over his lower lip, stabbing into the soft flesh there as he unintentionally bares them. Solomon looks like he's in agonizing pain. The bloody glow of his eyes is slanted down on me through the slits his lids create. He looks like he wants to both consume me and rip himself away at the same time. It's a war within him—the desire to have me and release me.

I can't let him. Aerea warned me—the Goddess said that there would come a day when I might need to make a choice. I thought it was my first kill, but maybe it's this. Maybe this is the true sacrifice.

Solomon wants me, that much is clear from the hard length of his shaft straining against his trousers and the perspiration that glitters across his skin. The tawny darkness of his flesh calls to me. I inhale sharply, my mind fogging over with uncertainty. A wave of enigmatic emotion that I can't quite express or understand swarms me. I want to help him. I want to ease the pain he's feeling, but I don't know how, beyond giving into what he's currently doing.

I blink back tears as I set my hands to his skin, feeling the heat radiate along my arms and through my own body. Solomon might look like a monster now, as he battles his own inner demons, but he has never been more beautiful to me.

Virtue be damned; I will always be the true Queen of Rozentine—with or without it. And if it takes the loss of my virtue to help Solomon remain sane as his power reaches new heights, then so be it.

Without giving him more time to agonize over it, I circle my hand to the back of Solomon's head and arch up against him. The front of my dress falls down and the sleeves catch along my arms for a brief moment. I'm messing this up. I'm supposed to be seducing him, making sure he takes my blood and … everything else.

He saved me from a fate worse than death, now it's my turn to save him from himself, from insanity.

"I could hurt you." He sounds angry, and I know a part of that anger is directed at me for not doing what I was told originally. For not running when this first started.

"I don't care," I reply. "You need this, and…" Hated, though it may be, I reveal the truth. "I need *you*."

The sleeves of my gown fall further, exposing more of my upper body as I brush against his chest. The gown's neckline gapes down past the tips of my nipples as they scrape into the hair-roughened surface of Solomon's pecs. Feeling the pricks of his hair against my smooth skin makes me shiver. His muscles tighten, forming like hard rocks beneath his flesh. My nerves tense with anticipation. My thighs tremble beneath him as I press my lips to his unyielding mouth.

"Please." I whisper the word even as I tremble with humiliation. I've never begged or pleaded before. It feels wrong. Especially when I'm doing this to try and save him. I need him to be saved, though. It's a selfish desire, I admit. I cannot imagine a world in which he doesn't exist. I cannot lose him now and most certainly not to his own Bloodlust and powers.

Come on, Solo … I mentally urge him. *Help me. Please.*

Either he hears my internal plea, or he finally gives up on restraint—whatever the case, in the next instant, I hear the low growl of his assent and his mouth opens under mine. A gasp escapes me as he shoves his tongue between my lips, diving deep and stealing away my thoughts as his clawed hands find themselves on my hips.

He yanks me forward and suddenly I'm sitting astride him—that hard length of him from earlier rubbing up and down against the sensitive place between my thighs. I gasp again, but no air infiltrates my lungs. It's all been sucked away, leaving no room between us.

Sparks dance between the spaces of my fingers as I clench my hand in his hair and relish in the kiss. I've been kissed before—small pecks here and there. Stolen. Hidden in nooks and crannies of the palace before my betrothal by curious and hopeful noblemen. But this is something completely different. It's different even than all of those dream kisses. I didn't realize it then, but those were a watered-down version of what I feel now.

Against Solomon's enhanced form, my body is small. My hands aren't even half the size of his and the breadth of his shoulders encompasses me as his tongue tangles with mine. I'm surrounded by him—by the wild nature of his scent, like fire and wet soil. He invades my every pore, driving out all thought.

Never in a million lifetimes would I have predicted this is where we'd end up, but now I can't deny that this was always where we were meant to be. When he pulls back, the rhythm of his breathing against my face lulls me into a sense of satisfaction. It tells me I'm not the only one suffering here.

"Devonry." His voice is rough and dark, filled to the brim with torn desire. The sound of fabric tearing makes me jump as I realize his claws have sunk past the folds of my dress and ripped through the sides. Cool air brushes across my hips. Solo doesn't seem to be aware of it, but he pushes my dress up my legs and thighs. "I'm sorry."

Sorry? Why is he sorry? My addled brain is too consumed by him to understand. Too fallen in lust to realize the changes happening. Solomon rears back and just before he strikes, I see it—the face he makes.

Eyes red and full of something more than human, his canines lengthening even more than I thought possible. I don't hesitate. I turn my cheek and arch my back, ignoring the embarrassment of my bare breasts brushing against his chest once more. I offer my neck and he takes it. Fangs sink deep as he draws my blood inside of him.

Perhaps … I think as my eyes slide shut and those little sparks I felt on my skin earlier sink inside of me, warming me from the inside out. *Perhaps, the Gods are not as cruel as I thought* … Because in all of my days, I never thought that giving in to the man I've hated for years could feel so fucking good.

25
DEVONRY

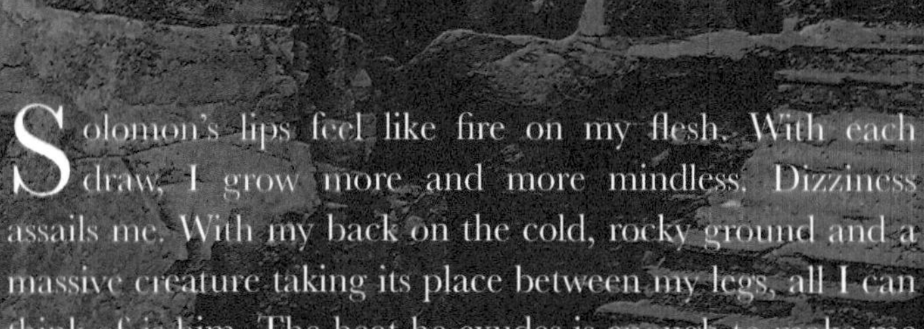

Solomon's lips feel like fire on my flesh. With each draw, I grow more and more mindless. Dizziness assails me. With my back on the cold, rocky ground and a massive creature taking its place between my legs, all I can think of is him. The heat he exudes is enough to make me forget all else. Until he pulls away.

Solomon's outline is bigger than ever before. His pupils are pinpricks in the sea of his blood-red gaze. His body remains tense, suspended above me as if he's warring with himself inside. *Of course he is*, I think to myself. Solomon is, above all, an honorable warrior. He wouldn't ever take something from me like this unless I truly pressured him into it. Even if this is what he needs.

Even if I can't see his face as clearly as I want to, I know as well as I know him that his features are likely etched with guilt. Reaching up, I cup my hand to his cheek and he turns his face into my palm, nuzzling the skin there. His lips are wet and his tongue comes out, swiping over them and my skin. The sensation sends shuddering waves of fire through my skin and down into my bloodstream. It's not even purposeful, I know. His seduction is natural. He doesn't mean to, but he's pulling me in the same way the ocean waves move back and forth in an age-old rhythm that can never be stopped.

"Solo…" My voice is hoarse, quickly disappearing in the near dark of the cave. My heart races against my breast. "You need more."

"Devonry…" The deep, brassy baritone of Solomon's groan echoes around us. He sounds more and more like an animal. My insides tighten. "You smell so fucking good."

His head dips and, once more, I feel the pressure of his lips on my flesh. My hand falls from his face and I arch up as he opens his mouth and his tongue touches my throat again, right where he bit me the first time. Instead of sinking his fangs back into my flesh, though, he teases me as he licks a path over the rapidly thudding beat of my heart and then down. He nibbles along my collarbone. My hands find his hair, sinking into the silky, slightly wet strands and gripping tight. I need something to hold onto, something to ground me.

As he descends further, I feel myself rising to meet the press of his lips and tongue and teeth. My back bows upward as he cups one breast in his hand, squeezing the sensitive flesh just tight enough that I'm made all too aware of his strength over me. I'm panting, dragging in lungfuls of air that don't seem to be doing anything for the fast-retreating sanity left in my own mind.

It's not enough. "*Solomon*." His name is both a plea and a warning on my tongue.

"Do you want something, love?" Solo asks, his heated breath brushing over one erect nipple.

A second whimper escapes me and I can't help but press my thighs together, rubbing as some spark of sensuality blooms inside of me. A low growl rumbles from him, the sound reverberating from his chest to mine and then I feel his hand disappear from my breast and instead, meet the skin of my legs. I gasp as my legs are suddenly yanked open and Solo drapes them over his thighs. He freezes with one hand on my ankle and the other on my hip bone where he's shoved my skirts up even further.

"*Fuck.*" Air brushes over the place between my legs and I realize with hot embarrassment that I'm not just wet, I'm fucking soaked. More and more of that strange wet juice oozes out of me and I shiver, trying to press my legs back together even though he's now holding them open with his body.

"Tell me you want this, Devonry," Solo commands. "If you do not, this is your last chance to refuse me. I can't…" Solomon's voice is gruff, damn near swallowed by the thundering of my own heartbeat. "I can't hold off for much longer."

This is him holding off? I feel as if I'm on the verge of a mental breakdown where my body is not my own and he is still holding back. I shake my head. "No, I do," I say quickly. "My answer is yes, Solo. You need this."

His grip tightens and I wince. He doesn't seem to notice. "I didn't ask if *I* needed this," he hisses back at me. "I asked if you wanted it—I will not take you if this is something you do not want, regardless of what it will do to me."

I grit my teeth and arch up, reaching for his neck. I hang suspended for a moment, viscerally aware that my breasts are bare, and despite how dark it is for me, I have no doubts that Solomon can see everything. He wants me to admit something that I've been taught is shameful. Wanting this—sex—is different from the necessity of it. I'm frightened of more than the change that will come afterward.

These last few weeks—months—have changed me. So much so that even in this moment, alone with Solomon, ready to give up the last of my innocence feels like no sacrifice at all. If he needs to fuck me to maintain his sanity, then yes, I want it. I need him and I want him to be happy, sane, and whole.

This time, I press my lips to his. Sharp canines bump against my teeth and as if he can't help himself, Solo kisses me back. His tongue duels with mine, chasing and retreating like we're two sides of a grand battle and yet neither of us truly wants to win.

"Yes," I whisper as I break the kiss. "Yes, I want this."

Seconds arch into minutes. Finally, Solomon speaks. "Then, by the Gods, I'll fucking have you, Devonry."

My back hits the ground once more and Solo descends over me. The heat of his breath drifts over my breast a split second before fire races up my spine and his lips and tongue make contact. Solo drags one nipple into his mouth and sucks. A shocked cry leaves my lips and my legs tighten around him. His hands move up to my waist, holding me still as the torture begins.

Wickedly hot fire sears into my flesh as he nibbles at the hardened tip of my breast and then moves to the other, cupping them with his big hands. The second he leaves the first nipple, though, cool air washes over it—forcing the peak to tighten even further. A hunger like I've never known rumbles in my stomach, pulling against my insides.

Each bite of his teeth as he rolls my nipple inside of his mouth makes me arch my back against the stone, pressing up into him and seeking something new. Desperation has me yanking at his hair, pulling the strands as I drag him up, and when his head pops away from my breasts I dive for his lips. I kiss him with all of the combined anger and desire that swarms within me.

More, I need more.

A low chuckle breaks our mouths apart and it takes me a moment to realize that it came from him. "You shall have it, Princess," Solomon replies.

Had I said that out loud? I don't have a chance to wonder for long as Solomon carefully pulls my hands from his head, gentling me with kisses to my temple and cheek and jawline as I whimper and try to pull him back.

"Trust me, Devonry," he beseeches.

"I need…" I don't know what I need, but I know if I hold onto him perhaps I'll find the answer.

"I know what you need, love," he replies, sinking further and moving away from me.

Panic sets in and I'm grasping at strands in the dark, thankful that I can still at least feel him against my thighs and legs. "S-Solo?" I call out as confusion spills into my mind. How can what I need be him moving away from me? No, I need the exact opposite. I don't know why, but I have the sense that I need something more—something exactly like what I've had in my dreams. I need him inside of me.

Solomon presses my legs open further, spreading them impossibly wide. I know that were it lighter in here, my embarrassment would make me cover myself and shy away from his touch. I can't. Not now. Thumbs press against the sensitive inner flesh of my thighs, his claws scraping slightly and making me shiver.

"Beautiful…" The word is so quiet, it's lower than a whisper and I almost miss it.

"What—" I begin to ask, only to be cut off as I feel Solomon's hot breath against the place between my legs. The place that's coated in wetness. I gasp and tremble as I feel him grow nearer.

"So damn beautiful," he says again.

Anxiety crawls up my throat accompanied by another emotion I can't name. It's a greedy emotion, one full of avarice and yearning. It isn't until I feel the wet brush of a tongue up my slit, my pussy, that I realize what it is.

Arousal.

"Ah!" I cry out, and as if he were waiting for it, Solomon dives down and suckles against my weeping slit as if he's a starving man. His tongue prods against the nub at the top, my clit, swiping alongside it and causing more tendrils of fire to spread throughout my lips.

I'm a panting, sweating mess. My hands find the back of his head and I press him down harder, needing more of this sensation spilling into my veins. I'm afraid that if he doesn't continue, something terrible will happen to all this energy building inside me.

Solomon, for his part, doesn't seem to mind my pressure. In fact, he obliges me with no resistance. His tongue continues to flick against my nub, back and forth, until my lower back locks up, and only then does he delve down even more. He licks up the juices leaking from my body. His hands clamp against my thighs and drag them around his neck as he drags his tongue into my pussy—and finally, blessedly, he strokes it inside.

My thighs contract and release as I feel the dark strands of his damp hair drag against my skin. I'm shaking, crying, and unable to control myself as another gush of wetness leaves me. Solomon seals his mouth over me and gulps it down. He growls, a sound of approval, as his claws dig into my legs.

"Solo!" I scream his name as I come undone, feeling my body ascend from itself. Tears linger on my lashes for a split moment before falling down the sides of my face.

All the while, Solomon sends me higher and higher. He eats at me like a madman, crazed with lust. His tongue thrusts in and out before retracting and reaching for my clit once more. One hand removes itself from my leg and then I feel the telltale sensation of a thumb pressing down over the little button.

I thrash against him. "No, no nonono," I beg. I can't do it again. It's too much. My body shakes against him as I press on the top of his head, trying to push him away. Solomon's strength, however, is no match for mine—even Awakened as I am.

I try again. "Please, it's…" It hurts. My stomach muscles cramp, but Solomon ignores me and he presses against my clit regardless, strumming it as he licks against more juices slipping from my pussy.

"You taste divine, Princess," he whispers against my secret flesh. "Give me more … quench my thirst."

A sob breaks free as my body can't seem to help but follow his command. I seize once more, the world around us vanishing in an instant as the sounds disappear and nothing is left save for the sensation coursing through me. His heat. His torment. My heart gallops inside of my chest, running so far and fast that I fear it will burst forth and leave me.

For several moments, I remain suspended in that world of white consciousness. When I finally do drift back to reality, it's to find Solomon lifting me away from the rocky floor. He reclines back against the wall and brings me with him, depositing me onto his lap. The sweet, wet scent of moss and water invades.

I collapse against his chest, breathing harshly as I try to make sense of what I just experienced. Solomon's hands begin to move—sliding between us as he grips the closure of his trousers and practically rips it open as he frees himself. I sit back and look down. My lips part in shock.

I'd known … I mean I'd felt the long thickness of him

beneath his trousers, but now with Solomon's cock standing before my eyes, a new feeling of unease enters me. It's so big I'm not sure if it will fit. I chance a peek at his face and blink in astonishment.

His eyes are glowing, brighter than before, and his upper lip is pulled back as his fangs have fully descended. Solomon fists himself with one clawed hand before reaching for me with the other. He grabs me around my throat and drags me closer until the head of his cock is pressed against my lower belly.

"Devonry…"

I know what he's going to do before he does it, and I know I have to stop him. "I'm not going to say no," I tell him quickly. "It's too late to back out now."

He bares his teeth at me and my words, his glowing blood-red gaze descending to where he has his fingers clasped around my neck. Hunger rumbles in his throat, a low growl emitting from him.

"It is your first time," he says. "It will hurt."

"I don't care," I tell him and find that I actually mean the words. It truly doesn't matter to me if it hurts or not. The fact stands, it's him. It's Solomon. My friend turned enemy now turned … I don't know what we are if not lovers after this.

Gently, as slowly as I can to show him my intention, I let my hand drift down to meet his. Solomon's body tightens as I clasp my much smaller fist around his as it tugs against his shaft.

"I want you to feel pleasure too," I say quietly.

His head dips down, chin meeting his chest as his eyes slide shut—cutting off the glow. "You have no idea the pleasure you've already brought me, Princess," he mutters.

Funny, I think. I used to hate how condescending his calling me 'Princess' sounded. Now, though, it feels like an intimate endearment. Something private between the two of us. Even if the word isn't, his tone of voice as he says it is.

I nuzzle my face against his temple. "Please, Solo," I plead quietly. "Please take me … I need you."

Shoulders tense, cock throbbing against our combined fingers, Solomon raises his head once more and opens his eyes. "If you need me, my Queen," he whispers. "Then I am yours."

26

SOLOMON

Her scent is intoxicating.

Stars brighter than any I'd ever seen in my life, from the relative safety of the Sunfire Palace to the bitter and cruel battlefields, dance behind my eyelids. I am quickly fading, and in my place rises my inner beast.

Despite her claims that she isn't afraid, I can taste her fear in the air and the beast inside of me luxuriates in it. It does not matter to him what she feels so long as she is near and so long as she is ours.

The sensation of her clenching around my tongue as she came lingers in the back of my mind. The memory of her scent, soft and sweet, like rich, divine fruit is delicious. Knowing that I held her between my palms, in my grasp, and that she had consented to be there is a heady drug that consumes me, driving me to the brink and beyond. My monster growls for more. Her wetness as it had slipped over my tongue and down my throat had been delicious. My craving for more is overshadowed only by the desire to have her seated upon my cock. The cock currently clasped between our hands.

Devonry's chest rises and falls with the rapid pulse of her breaths. Soft blonde lashes flutter as she peers into my face, hesitant yet determined. Carefully—so as not to cut her with my claws—I remove my hand from my cock and hook them behind her ass, dragging her forward until the softness of her pussy lips meets the underside of my shaft.

A gasp escapes her. "Solo…" Eyes hooded with desire, Devonry's hands find my shoulders. She hasn't bothered to cover herself—too absorbed in the things I'm doing to her to notice that she's practically stripped bare before me. Me —her once enemy.

Her breasts are tipped in light, rosy areolas, her nipples hardened and jutting outward as she scrapes across the bare flesh of my chest. She's still wet, the scent of her tantalizing, cloying, and sweet as it permeates the air around us. I want to bury my face back into her pussy and drown in it. For once, I don't want to do what is right. I want to take what I want.

I want to rip her open and fill her so full of me that she'll forget there was ever a time that we were not connected.

"Solomon, how much longer are you going to make me wait, I—"

I don't allow her to finish her sentence. Instead, I release her throat and lift her with my clawed hands. Canting her hips in the right way, I position the head of my cock at her entrance before dropping her onto my lap, letting gravity do the work for me. She sinks onto my cock with a slowness that speaks of her virginity. A groan rumbles up my throat. Vile, painful tightness clenches around the head of my shaft. Devonry's head falls back as she cries out at the sudden intrusion.

"Ah!" She squirms upon me, her thighs trembling with

effort and when her head drops back to mine, I see the tears glistening in her eyes.

It's too late now, though. There's no backing out. She's right there, so close. Almost … *mine*. A snarl erupts from the beast within as I sink my claws into her hair and rip her head back. She cries out again as I bring her body closer. She shudders as my cock invades her and that shuddering turns to soft, pleading moans as I nudge her throat with my fangs once more. I scrape them up her neck, letting her feel their sharpness without piercing her skin again. Not yet.

The first time had been out of sheer need. Hunger. Now that the initial Blood Madness has abated, I want her out of her mind with desire before I bite her again.

I tilt my hips and she slides down another inch, flinching in my grasp. Clenching my teeth and pulling away from her throat lest I bite into her too soon, I grasp at her hip with my free hand and stare into her eyes.

"Breathe," I command her.

"Please," she beseeches me with both her words and her watery gaze. "Solo, kiss me."

Never before has there been an order from a royal that I have been so unable to resist. If a kiss is what she craves, then a kiss she will have. As I slam my mouth to hers, taking her lips with a fervor that I've known for years and have never had the opportunity to express, I force her down onto my cock, breaking through the barrier of her virginity.

Devonry's scream is swallowed by my tongue and lips. Her insides clamp down upon my shaft with the strength of a vise. It takes all of the willpower I possess not to completely lose myself and thrust her upon the ground and rut into her. Instead, I maintain the kiss, gentling my hand in her hair and directing her as I please. Tears slide between us, over her cheeks, and into our mouths. I taste them and though it makes me a vile bastard, they taste as sweet as her pretty cunt. So much so that I crave more of them.

Hunger gnaws at my gut, demanding I thrust my cock into her pussy and take her the way beasts are meant to. I combat the urge. Knowing that this is likely causing her immense pain, I allow her to remain seated for as long as it takes. So long that it feels as if I will simply combust without any friction or movement at all.

As many times as I've tried, no other woman has felt the way she does. As I am inside of her, she, too, is inside of me. She permeates the very air I breathe. Takes me over as if I am little more than a slave to her whims and I have no desire to refuse her.

"Shhhh." I break away from the kiss and hush her gently. It's meant to be reassuring, but I can tell that it isn't. Her tears have abated but there's still a flush to her cheeks that speaks of how uncomfortable she is. I'd hoped that by allowing her to come before I entered her, she would feel less pain, but I know that I am larger than most men. More so in the state that I'm in.

Still, there's a piece of me that clings to her as satisfaction rolls through me. No one else has had her. Not Nasir. Not that damned Prince Enver. I, alone, have taken the Princess' virginity. Stolen, though it is, by my own circumstances, pride fills me.

"It … hurts," she whimpers as her hands arch up to my shoulders. She wraps herself around me, her skin sticking to mine as sweat beads pop up between us. "Is this how it usually is?"

"I'll make it better," I assure her, sounding further and further from human as I've ever been. Still, the beast is slowly acclimating to my control. He is satisfied to be inside her … for now. Then, simply because I cannot bear her pain for long, I reach between us and lightly press my thumb against her clit. She jumps in my arms and a soft moan spills from her lips. Pressing harder, I circle the sensitive little nub over and over, clenching my teeth as the rushing of her blood fills my ears.

Now that my cock has taken her, my fangs are throbbing even harder for their turn. Her insides relax. The muscles of her cunt squeeze me in rapid bursts as she begins to squirm once more upon my lap.

"Solo … is this it? This can't be it, is it?" Devonry peels herself back from my chest and looks me in the eye. Her cheeks are blotchy with her recent tears and as rosy as her hardened nipples. My fangs dig into my lower lip.

"No," I tell her. "This isn't it. I am waiting for your comfort."

Her brows scrunch together, forming a confused v between them. "Waiting?" She shifts against my lap, her pussy rising slightly with the movement and then descending the scant inch she'd pulled free. Her lips part in shock and a moan is ripped from her throat. "Oh, Gods…" Her jugular bobs as she swallows. "That felt…"

I know. I know exactly what she felt and if she's comfortable enough now that it doesn't hurt, then it's time. I leave her clit and grip her wrists. Carefully placing her palms upon my shoulders, I reach for her waist and meet her gaze.

"Hold on," I order. "Don't let go for any reason."

Her breath hitches. "Are you going to feed from me?" she asks.

My tongue touches the backside of one fang. There's no doubt in me now. "Yes," I answer her. "I am."

With that, I lift her and then thrust back into the tight

cavern of her no longer virgin cunt. Devonry cries out, her head falling back. My forehead throbs where I feel horns pushing against the underside of my flesh.

Not yet, I silently urge myself. The beast doesn't need to be released. I can maintain this. With Devonry, I can hold it back. I must.

"Solo!" The sear of Devonry's nails digging into my shoulders is like fire licking against my skin.

I lift her up and thrust into her once more, forcing my shaft to penetrate the tight vise of her pussy again and again as she cries out and latches onto me. With her head still craned back, the spark of instinct takes over. My gaze locks onto the rapid pulse of her blood under her flesh and without any more thought, I strike.

My fangs sink into her as my cock delves into her insides. She clenches around me when my teeth clamp onto her neck. Blessed lifeblood flows over my tongue and my cock pulsates within her. The sheer pleasure of her blood filling my mouth nearly sends me over the edge of release. It is by the slenderest of threads that I manage to resist the urge.

A beast may linger within me, but a beast I am not. She will come again, shuddering around my cock and under my fangs. I will make sure of it.

I gulp down several mouthfuls of her blood. It slips easily past my tongue toward my throat, draining into my stomach with the smoothness of liquid sugar. It's tangy, the crimson liquid. Spicy and hot. She tastes of fire and ash and it's addicting. I swallow more as the echo of her moans reverberates around the cave, spiraling off the walls and returning to where the two of us sit, our bodies combined so completely that it's hard to feel where I end and she begins.

Dizziness assails me. I pull back from her throat and

open my eyes to see twin holes where my fangs have pierced as they leak with more blood. I lick the trails and seal a kiss over each one before they slowly finally cease to bleed. Now that she's Awakened, her healing abilities will only grow stronger.

My cock throbs against her inner walls and I reach down to thumb her clit once more, finding that my claws have retracted. The pressure at my forehead has disappeared as well.

I love her implicitly. Hunger for her pleasure like a starving man. She knows not how I would slay the world if she would only ask it of me. All it would take is one small command from her and I would end the Bartoli Royal Family—become her assassin and puppet.

I thrust into her again, my cock deeper in her than it has ever been before. I lift her and let her fall, over and over as her moans grow louder, deeper, more needy. Years. I've waited so many years for this exact act and now that it's here, it's so much more than I ever anticipated.

The sweat makes the short, choppy strands of her strawberry-colored hair cling to her forehead and temples. Her flushed face is tight with expectation, her lips parted and pale at the corners. Her skin feels blazing hot to the touch. I commit the sight and feel of her to my memory. Her round blue eyes are sparkling with hazel flecks. Her blushing cheeks. The way her body seems to gyrate against me without her even being aware.

My hips stutter and stop as my release quickly crashes over me, but her body doesn't. Panting, I grit my teeth as Devonry takes over where I stop. She raises her feet against the stone and falls upon my shaft, pushing down into my lap as she chases her own release. Even if she's new to the sensations, her body knows the path to our destination.

She moves in the way people have for eons. Up and down, over and back, she fucks herself onto my cock with fury and need. Choked, begging sounds erupting from between her lips. I doubt she even notices her own actions.

Gathering her close, I slide a hand into her hair, feeling the soft strands and inhaling her scent once more, until it's the only thing that fills my lungs. My desire for her cannot be stopped by mere physicality. My love. My dedication. My obsession.

My vision switches into one of Bloodlust—even though my gut is full of her blood. The thought of Devonry doing this with someone else, with another man, is so sudden and repulsive that it makes my body react with instinctive cruelty.

I yank her down, fucking into the tight recesses of her body as she screams and then I flick my fingers over her clit. Her eyes are squeezed tightly shut and that just won't do.

"Devonry," I call out to her, "look at me. Look at who's fucking you."

Pale lashes lift and her glittering blue-hazel eyes meet my furious stare. "Say it," I growl as I flick her clit again, bringing her ever closer to a shuddering release.

Her body tightens all over and her back bows. Her lips part on a shout.

I force her back down, thrusting all the way to the base of my cock and holding her there even as she squirms and resists, needing more friction if she's to come.

"Please…" Her sweet pleas are music to my ears, but they're not enough.

"Look down," I demand. "See how perfectly we fit together.

Grasping ahold of her, I raise her up and let her fall

back down until her pussy is entirely against my groin. Her head tips forward, shadows dancing between us as she follows my order and glances at the place where we're joined together.

Her inner muscles quiver at the sight. I press my lips to her ear, wrapping a hand around the back of her neck. "Who's fucking you, Princess?" I breathe against her, soaking in the way she shivers at my words. "Who's cock are you taking into your sweet pussy?"

Panting breaths slip between us. A beat passes and then another and another. Finally, she lifts her head and her eyes meet mine. I blink as a golden hue swallows her irises, her Awakened power shining through.

"Y-you," she stutters out her answer. "You are. Your cock is … taking my pussy."

"Say my name." I need to hear it on her lips. My finger rubs incessantly against her clit. So close, I'm almost there. I rock my hips into her, withdrawing and fucking back into her with shallow thrusts that are like flames licking along my cock.

"*Solomon!*"

That's all it takes. That one sharp cry from her and it's over. I thrust up into her and hold her tight as I come. As I do, I feel her muscles contract and release against my shaft. Her entire body goes rigid for a brief moment and her lips part on a garbled shriek as release takes her over.

White slams into my bloody vision. Everything around me, except the feeling of her against me, disappears.

Mine. This soft, female body that resides over me—the soul that matches my own—is mine.

My eyes flutter shut and I wrap myself around her, holding tight as everything else fades away. Nothing matters save for her, save for us, save for what she does to me. Deep down, there's a strange sensation of tugging. My heart follows the movement and a deep, masculine voice, very much like my own, speaks.

Now, you know, he says. *She was always meant to be yours.*

27

DEVONRY

I wake with a soreness between my legs that I'm not accustomed to. A moment later, all of the memories of how that soreness got there slams into my mind and I feel my cheeks heat.

Sitting up, I gingerly take stock of where I am. Gone is the man who'd been beneath me when I'd collapsed against him after what felt like the longest and most pleasurable intoxicating sensations I've ever had. Instead, I'm left alone, though cleaner than I remember and redressed. Had Solomon wiped me down and adjusted my clothes? It's the only explanation.

Carefully dragging myself to my feet, I peer around the cave wondering where in the Gods' realm he'd disappeared to. My thighs tighten with the aches that are new to me, yet I manage to still keep standing with a hand on the moss-covered cave wall. After a few more moments of maintaining my balance, I feel stronger and leverage away from it. I stride over to the water's edge and glance into it, searching beneath the surface for a sign of Solomon's dark hair.

There's nothing, but strangely still, is the fact that the once cool cave has now grown warmer. Sweat clings to the back of my neck and it has nothing to do with the actions of earlier.

"Solo?" I call out, keeping my voice even so as not to sound too panicked.

Silence meets my light call and nervousness creeps up my throat. Not a minute later, though, I hear the telltale sounds of footsteps echoing through the cave. I turn toward it and spot a figure in the darkness—illuminated by the pinpoints of light along the walls and ceiling—coming toward me.

"Solo." Relief hits me and I step forward. Solomon doesn't say a word until he comes fully into view, stopping a few feet away and just out of arm's reach. "Where were you?"

He gestures behind him. "There's another opening," he says. "I found it as you slept—after some thought, I realized it didn't make sense for there to be so much life down here if it was sealed off from the rest of the world and the only opening was underwater."

"Is that why it's so warm?" I ask, crossing my arms over my chest.

His eyes descend, moving over my front and I bite down on my tongue to keep from saying anything as the memories of him kissing, licking, and suckling at my breasts invade my mind. When his gaze moves back to mine, it's with an expression I can't quite figure out.

"Yes," Solo replies. "It appears that, since the time Argyle was last here, something wore away at the rock formation on the outside of this cave. There's a hole several paces down."

A sigh of relief leaves my lips and I stumble forward.

"That means we can get out." My excitement is uncontainable.

Solo's gaze follows me, intense and unsettling. Unable to meet his eyes, I direct myself from where he'd come and start moving. If I stop to think about what happened between us then I'm not sure what will happen. He's not talking about it, though, so that makes me think perhaps I shouldn't either.

As I start to head down the same path he'd come from, Solomon's shadow falls in line behind me. "I thought this cave was originally small," I say as we walk.

"So did I," he admits, his tone far more human than it had been amidst our … well, when he'd fucked me. "It was only once I'd gained some semblance of my mind back that I realized how strange it was that there's so much moss growing when it needs soil and soil comes from above. Then there were the sounds of insects crawling about."

I shudder at those words. I'd been trying not to think of the insects.

"The cave appears small from where we were at the pool, but…" Solomon steps ahead of me—his broad back blocking out some of the light coming from the walls. "Around the bend here—there's a small passage."

Both of us stop at what appears to be a slit in the wall. I glance at him before looking back to the jagged opening. "You've already followed it out?" I ask.

He nods. "It's safe, Princess. It's narrow and damp, but it opens up above the rocks after a certain point, and you'll be able to smell the sea."

Despite his words, I still hesitate. Staying here isn't an option, but as I look at him, I wonder if … the moment we leave this place, will all memory of what happened here disappear? Will the two of us go back to being who we were before?

A hollowness creeps into my chest, an ache I've never felt before—even before my mother's death and then my father's. It feels as if there's a piece missing in my heart, something close, only not quite whole.

"Princess?" Solomon's warm palm lands on my lower back. His touch ignites a flame inside of me. Slowly, I turn back and tip my head up, staring at him.

He frowns at me as his brows draw together in two lines of confusion. The piece clicks into place. How long, I wonder, has he been wearing his mask? How did I not see it before?

Solomon moves closer and dips his head. Both of his hands come up and he cups my face, twisting my head first one way and then the other before urging my chin up. His expression tightens as he stares at the place on my throat where he bit me. If I'm honest, it is a bit sore, but nothing worse than that. In fact, I distinctly recall that when he'd bitten me, the first *and* second time, I'd felt more sensation in my body than ever before. It'd been like riding a wave of euphoric pleasure. Of course, that means nothing in the face of his own guilt.

"I'm sorry," he murmurs.

I smile as I feel his thumbs rub up and down my throat soothingly and shake my head before lowering it and meeting his eyes. "I'm not," I tell him. "I'm not sorry at all." Not for what he thinks.

If there's anything I should be sorry about, it's how long it took me to realize the truth. Why he's been next to me all this time, and what hardships he must have had to face. I don't quite understand it, but I know—deep down in the marrow of my bones—that Solomon Winett is far more than a guard.

He is the noblest of warriors. The kindest of barbarians. The deadliest of foes. And the most loyal of allies.

"I'm fine." My words come out choked, and in an effort to not be overcome by my emotions, I divert my gaze from his and pull away. "Let's go. I'm sure the others are waiting for us."

I feel Solomon's gaze on my back, boring into me as I slip into the crack and begin to inch my way forward. Jagged rocks clip my sides and dig into my back and front. I don't know how he managed to get through this as large as he is, but I can sense him just a few steps behind me, following me into the dark. I have the strangest inkling, too, that this isn't the first time, nor will it be the last. For some reason, I think if I asked him to dive into a volcano and burn to ash for me, he would.

It's a heady and dangerous thing—to have that much power over someone. He doesn't know, can't know, that I fear he might have that same exact power over me.

Seconds stretch into long minutes and the two of us continue creeping through the narrow passage where it seems as if something split the rock apart. It doesn't feel like two different formations colliding, but that a sharp blade had been thrust through a singular stone, allowing the warmth from the outside to enter as well as the air and insects. All of the plant life and the strangest sensation of not being in a cave but a rather rocky forest makes sense now.

The further we go, the tighter the already too-narrow channel gets. So much so that once we reach a point, there's no way I can turn my head back.

"Solo?" I call out, unable to look at him. Anxiety tinges my tone.

"It's alright," he urges. "Keep going. Almost there."

"Are you sure?" I demand. What if he's wrong? What if there's no end to this? What if we reach it and it's just a plain wall and then we're stuck and die like this, inches away from each other but all alone?

"Don't panic," Solo says, his voice soothing as if he can sense the quickly rising tide of my emotions. Fear squeezes my throat and I stop to take a breath, sucking it in and pausing when something lands on the top of my forehead.

I blink my eyes open, seeing very little in the dark, but when the wet droplet on my forehead slides down and then over my cheek, I flick my tongue out and taste salt. Salt … sea. I start to move faster. Solomon follows behind, gaining on me if the rising heat is anything to go by.

A light winks into existence. "I think I see the exit!" I cry in excitement.

Panting and exhausted, sore and weary, I don't care that the rocks are ripping at my clothes, tearing at the fabric. All I care about is freedom. Almost … almost there.

I don't realize how close we are though, because as the light grows brighter and my movements faster, the rocks sharper, I stumble out of the crevice in the stone and nearly go head-first over a cliff. My startled shriek is abruptly cut off as a hard hand grips ahold of the back of my gown and drags me back. I stumble and fall into Solomon's chest as he rips himself free of the stone as well.

Together, the two of us go down in a heap. I'm cut and bruised. He's bleeding along his face where a stone that jutted out from the wall of the tunnel must have sliced him. But we're alive and we're out. Late morning sun greets us. I can't help but laugh. Mere months ago, I never would have thought it possible.

Me—the proud Crown Princess of Rozentine—and Solomon Winett, Warrior and bodyguard. In a foreign land, holding onto each other for dear life after what was likely the most startling of nights. I close my eyes and tip my face to meet the warm sun. My insides tremble with what feels like relief. The sun sinks into me, past my flesh, and into my soul. It revives me.

Solomon's hands on my upper arms are gentle, and after a beat, he adjusts himself and then gets to his feet, reaching down to help me as well. I take his hand and rise to my feet before I look over where we managed to come out. It's a narrow ledge, no more than a few feet deep and wide on either side. I peer over the cliff, seeing crashing waves that spray salt water up the side of the rocky formation.

"Do you think we need to climb down?" I ask hesitantly.

Solomon points up. "It'd be easier and faster to go up," he says. I follow the direction of his finger and realize that he's right, there's a much larger cliff above us. It likely connects with the mainland.

"How do we meet the others?" I ask.

Solomon's face pinches tight as he considers it. Then he shakes his head and gets down on one knee. "One thing at a time," he says. Let's get up to a bigger cliff first and see if we can survey the rest of the area."

I nod. "Okay."

Solo clasps his hands together and I step into his intertwined fingers, tightening my hold on his shoulder and reaching out with my free hand. He waits below as I dig my fingers into the wall of the cliff and slowly, but surely, make my way up. The few times I miss a foothold and slip, I hear him curse and look back to see him with his arms outstretched, preparing to catch me.

It isn't that far though, only about ten feet. So, once I manage to crawl over the lip, I look back to find him bending at his knees and leaping up to capture the top of the cliff's edge that I just had to climb to. Instead of climbing himself, he merely jumped. Height is an advantage that I don't have—not over him.

I sigh even as I stand and look out over the ocean. In the distance, I spot a familiar ship. "Solo!" I yell. "I think that's them!" I start waving frantically. "Do you think they can see us?"

Solomon gets to his feet alongside me and peers out at the ship, narrowing his eyes. They glow briefly and then go dull once more. "Yes, it's them, but no I don't think they can see us."

Slowly, I lower my arms back to my side. "So, what does that mean?" My chest tightens. I clench my fists into my soiled and damp skirts. "We're not stuck here, are we?"

"No." Solomon turns to me and grasps me by my shoulders. "Do you remember our training?" he asks suddenly.

I frown and rear back from him. "Yes, but what does that have to do with—"

Solomon doesn't let me finish. He quickly turns me to the front of the cliff and moves behind me. "Lift your arms," he commands. I do as he says, trembling as I feel his nearness so close. Memories of the night before—or rather this early morning—flash through my mind. I still can't get the feeling of his hands on me, of his lips touching indecent places, or of his cock…

With a shocked gasp at the direction of my own thoughts, I flex my fingers out. Heat pours through me. "Yes," Solo says, his breath whispering over my ear. "Now, unleash a fire into the ocean. It'll catch their attention and bring them to us."

The heat fans outward, past my limbs and into my fingertips, burning hotter and hotter until it erupts before me. A flame brighter than any I've had before. It shoots from my palms and fingers right over the edge of the cliff

—flying several feet over the ocean before it dives downward.

Solomon straightens and I look back to see his eyes glowing once more as he stares, with purpose, at the ship hovering in the waves. His lips curl into a smile. "They saw it."

"They did?" I turn back to see a flag being yanked up —the center mast. "They're coming?"

He nods, eyes scanning the horizon. His brows are lowered as he stares over the cliff's edge and towards the bobbing waves. The corners of his mouth are turned down despite his next words. "They are."

A burst of relief fills me and, without thinking, I throw my arms around him. Solomon stiffens for a brief moment before returning my embrace. So caught up in the knowledge that we're going to be saved, it takes another second for reality to hit me.

Yulis, Argyle, and Celine are on their way. We're going back to the Bartoli Palace, and even if my Awakening is complete … we still have the matter of taking back Rozentine to deal with. Prince Enver. Nasir. None of this is over.

I pull away from Solomon and look up into his eyes. Even without the glow of his ability, the red hue remains. I can't forget what happened, but … I also can't acknowledge it either. It was for survival. Solomon says nothing, but I watch as a guarded look descends over his expression, cloaking his emotions as he always has.

Somehow, it hurts even more than ever before and I feel powerless to do anything about it.

28

DEVONRY

The sun casts its warmth across my face. The day has begun and it has left us all behind, leaving us scrambling to catch up. Life in the castle will have already started with plenty of time to notice our absence. I squint up at the sun even as I descend the rope ladder. Splinters from the rough fibers dig into my palms, and the planks of wood hold my weight but wobble with my nervous steps.

Yulis watches over the railing, his mouth puckered and hands gripping the railing tightly as though I may set his ship ablaze at any given moment. I want to smile at him, to thank him for his help, and to relieve his worry, though I doubt it would do much good. The low pull of his thick brows says enough about his distaste for nobles, much less royalty. Though we are only a few minutes from the shore, it doesn't seem quick enough to get us away from his boat and crew.

Large hands grip my waist, offering me assistance on the final step. I flinch at the soreness of the bruises hiding beneath my dress. Solomon holds me steady for another moment as our little boat rocks and I find my balance. His hands have been my undoing. The slightest touch and my body shivers with the memory of his hardened skin and the feel of it moving against mine, the ache of his claws piercing through fabric to prod at my flesh.

The bottom of Celine's skirts come into view as she lowers onto the first rung. I shake away my dirty thoughts, silent as I move away from Solo's touch.

"Do you think they've noticed my absence?" I ask, lowering onto a plank meant for sitting.

"Unless Prince Enver has gone out of his way to knock on your door," Solomon pins me with a look of playful annoyance. "Then we can just pretend it's as if you were unwell and bedbound."

"Oh good," I mumble, a flush hot on my cheeks as he holds my stare. It's too easy to remember his lips, teeth, tongue … *oh gods*.

The boat teeters on the waters again and Celine drops the last bit. Hands on her hips, she shakes her head. "I'm so glad to be off this ship."

"Seasick?" Solomon asks, offering his arm for her to hold as she walks a pace to her own seat.

Argyle skips several rungs, sliding down the ladder with a loose grip on its edges. How he manages to do so without burning up his hands is beyond me, but then again he grew up in this environment.

Celine glares in his direction. "I'm sick of something alright."

I laugh gently as does Solo, who makes his way back to my side and sits. Argyle mirrors him, though Celine leans into her side of the boat to avoid their bodies brushing. Solomon's arm rests against mine and I care not for putting distance between us. It's … nice.

The first mate settles in his own seat and takes to rowing. Silence falls over our group as we watch the ship sail farther away while the shoreline grows closer. Winds tousle my hair, surely a tangled mess after last night, yet I can't help but soak in these last few minutes of freedom. Inhaling, I try to memorize the way the coastline smells. I take in every bit of the gorgeous Bartoli landscape. The cliffs with their dark overhangs, the sea crashing against them, and the tan sand.

The walk from the beach back to the stabled horses is a breathless jaunt as we all hurry to make up for all our lost time. None of us speak as we get into the saddles and the men dig their heels into the horses' sides. I let myself relax against Solomon's body. In turn, he rests his cheek against the top of my head for a moment. It's easy to pretend that we're just two people, not a Queen and her guard. I can relish in the softness of his hold around me, contrasting with the desperate, rough way he'd touched me hours ago. My heartbeat doubles in my chest, my imagination keen to take the idea and run away with it. I should steer my thoughts clear of that particular activity. *Should.*

Behind us, Celine and Argyle speak in quiet but harsh tones. The bickering between them easily reminds me of those old married couples who can get away with saying exactly what is on their mind and still know their partner loves them deeply. In other ways, they remind me of Solomon and me. Anger and hate is easily the quickest layer of defense when you need to guard your heart.

Is that what I've been doing all these years? Guarding my heart? It had felt as though, when he'd returned and looked at me as if I was the scum of the earth, part of it had broken. Perhaps I've been holding him at arm's length ever since. I don't want to do that anymore. Not even a bit.

Since leaving the Sunfire Palace, being with Solomon —no matter how long it took for me to admit it—has felt right. Holding him in that cavern while he needed me and

I had needed him felt and still feels as though it was a dream. Something my mind is begging for.

My fingers brush over the small scabs on my throat. Two pinpricks where his fangs had sunken into my neck, where he had fed from me. The marks feel small, hardly noticeable, and likely to be gone before the next morning.

Solomon strokes his thumb over the wrinkled bit of my skirt over my thigh. He holds the reins but his arms are relaxed in front of us. We keep the horses at a strict pace without galloping like madmen toward the castle.

Something turns sour in the pit of my stomach as soon as the grounds come into view. We'd succeeded in what we'd left to do, although now more than ever I dread being back here with the Galeanos. More fake smiles will be had. More dealings with Prince Enver and his blatant disregard for what should be a thriving betrothal for a thriving alliance.

These royals won't be dealing with the same woman who'd come to plead for assistance anymore. I've returned Awakened, and I cannot allow myself to be bound to the standards for which they'd like me to live. Now, it is my turn to make the rules.

A few stable hands linger around the yards busy with chores. Several look up from their work but say nothing as we return and hand over the reins. With a bow, they take the horses away for care.

"We need to get you back to your room before anyone else sees you." Celine looks me over with a frown, shouldering past Solomon and Argyle. She plucks a leaf from my hair and runs her hand down my sleeve to knock away dirt.

"Take good care of her today," Solo says to Celine. "Make sure she rests."

"I'm fine." I wave a hand at him in dismissal and hook my arm into Celine's. "Don't you worry about me."

"I believe it is in my job description to always be worrying about you." He attempts to smirk but his face quickly falls serious as he turns back to Celine and repeats, "Make sure she rests."

"What do you want me to do? Chain her to her bed?" Celine chuckles and Solo's eyes flare crimson. "Have you met her? She'll do as she pleases, but I promise to enthusiastically suggest it."

"That's enough of that," I half whisper, half hiss. The burn of hunger in Solomon's gaze at Celine's jest sends bolts of my own desire straight to my core. I turn and pull Celine away toward the castle, worried my thoughts are displayed so clearly on my face. With a smile, I look back over my shoulder to give Solo one last glance. His arms are crossed over his chest and his gaze is locked on me. The corner of his mouth quirks up, one hand lifting from his bicep to give me a small wave. My stomach does a flip. Turning away from him is suddenly harder than I'd anticipated.

Celine and I move in unison, quick and quiet to return to my rooms with little notice. The halls are as they usually are. There is no flurry of movement as they search the grounds for the missing Rozentine Queen. We pass only a few servants busy with work and a couple of guards leisurely strolling the corridors.

The world remains as it always was before me, I suppose. It comes as almost a comfort to know that I am not needed here, that one less country needs me at their beck and call. Rozentine is enough responsibility, and I never gave much thought to the needs of Bartoli anyway.

Making the last turn, the sound of knuckles rapping against the large wooden doors echoes down to us.

Malcolm, dressed head to toe in his white and gold, knocks at my door then stops when he sees us heading in his direction. He bows low with a strained smile that falls away when he straightens and takes in my appearance.

"Your Highness," Malcolm says. "I've been looking for you."

Celine's hand tightens against my arm. It takes all of me not to try and tame the wrinkles of my dress or straighten the layers that appear thrown on haphazardly.

"I'm so sorry. We should have mentioned it to someone. We snuck away so I might be able to ride horseback for a while. I'm afraid I may have let myself have a little too much fun," I answer.

That certainly is one way of putting it.

"Oh." He clasps his hands behind him. "Well, I hope you enjoyed our horses. We take pride in their care. The finest in all of Bartoli."

"Yes, they are lovely, but never mind that, what is it that you need me for?"

"The Royal Family has decided to grant you an audience to discuss your request."

The breath is stolen from my lungs with his words. Two emotions rise and war against each other with the notion. *Finally*. This is what I've been waiting for, fighting for, since I arrived. I was on the verge of giving up on the Galeanos, but this … this is a glimmer of hope for my kingdom.

But…

I am a promise to Bartoli. Between our kingdoms. Yet, last night I gave a part of myself away. It's hard for me to feel guilt over it, not truly, but the part of me wonders if I've failed my kingdom.

"How lovely!" Celine interjects when I do not speak. "Let us get her changed into attire fit for the Royal Family and we will be there."

"Wonderful." Malcolm gives another bow. "I will let them know and return to escort you."

"Thank you," I manage as he strolls back down the hall.

Celine opens the door and ushers me inside. "So much for all that rest you were about to get. Let's get you out of this gown."

"I'll need a new pair of slippers as well," I mumble. Celine makes quick work of the stays and nudges fabric off my shoulders, carefully guiding it down my body. I step out of the dress standing in only my shift.

"Yes." She disappears to retrieve a new dress while I kick out of my slippers. A thin layer of sand outlines where my slipper had been. I do my best to wipe it away. Small bits of sand are still stuck between my toes when she returns. If only we had time for a real bath.

Celine drapes a gold dress over the back of a chair and steps up to me. She finds the hem of my shift and pulls it over my head in one swift movement. She gasps. "For the love of Thevaros, what happened to you in that cave?" She reaches out a shaky hand finding bruises on my hips where Solomon's fingers had dug into me. It hadn't hurt at that moment.

"I'm okay." I scoop up her hand and hold it in mine. "Promise."

"But…" Celine draws the word out, waiting for my explanation with the light tap of her foot.

"Are you familiar with the costs of being part of the House of Blood?"

She blinks rapidly. "Devonry."

"Yes?" I squirm and reach for the fresh shift she'd brought over. Once it's over my head, she leans in and inspects my neck.

"Oh, good gods! I thought that was a bug bite. I didn't

think it was an actual *grown man* bite." She runs a hand down her face, perhaps trying to wipe away what appears to be an ever-growing smile.

"The bruises are healing rather quickly though. Probably thanks to being Awakened," I mutter, repeatedly running my hands down the shift. "And nothing is visible, so there shouldn't be any questions."

Celine shakes herself from her stupor and gathers the rest of my gown, helping me into it. "You gave your permission for this?" I nod. "You know … I've also heard that the act of feeding can be very *sensual*." She draws the last word out and her eyes widen with suggestion staying on my face even as she tightens the laces of my dress. "Hmm?"

I let out the last of the breath caught in my lungs, trying to stifle the start of a laugh. "You've heard or are speaking from experience?"

She snorts and ignores the question altogether. "Should I have any concerns about this affecting your arrangements here?"

Should she be? Possible. Shouldn't I be? Certainly, yes. Still, I can't seem to feel more than the ounce of guilt I have for not feeling all that guilty in the first place. If Prince Enver had been the man I'd hoped for … if the Galeanos had been kind or shown me the respect our alliance is deserving of…

"I'm not sure," I finally answer.

Celine chews her lip as she runs a brush through my hair and braids the front half away from my face. "Was he kind to you? How are you feeling today? Was he *good?*"

"Celine!" I gape at her shameless line of questioning. "Solomon is always kind. He isn't always nice." I laugh. "I feel mostly normal. And he was good." *So good. Maybe too good. I'll never be able to get it out of my head good.* My face burns hotter.

"I had to ask!" She chuckles, wiping down my face and arms to remove the last of the dirt. "We will not fret about this any longer, then." She turns away, returning with a bit of powder to dust over the tiniest bit of scab remaining on my neck. "Whatever you do, whatever you need, my Queen, know that I will be here supporting you." She squeezes my shoulders before turning me toward the door. With one last comforting smile, she opens the door and follows me out into the hall.

Malcolm stands a few feet away, staring attentively at a gold and white Bartoli banner hanging from the wall. He turns, eyes scanning over me, then gives another bow. "You look lovely. Shall we?" He offers his arm.

The mixture of emotions inside of me turns over again and again until I'm certain my insides are a knotted mess. This could be it. This could be the help we've needed, the reason we've traveled this far.

Unless I've ruined it.

Is there any way for the Bartoli Royals to truly know what I'd been up to at the odd hours of the night and into the morning? Can they see the loss of my virginity as clearly as I feel the steadfast change in myself? Do they notice the thrumming of power now lurking so freely and fully within me?

There is no denying it. Last night changed me.

I'm fully Awakened now. Aerea's gifts—her power— are mine as it was always meant to be. Kings may forge wars, but Queens turn pain into prosperity, into power. All that I was before Nasir's betrayal—the naive, silly little princess—is no more. I, Devonry Estrand, am the rightful heir of Rozentine, and I decide for myself what is proper and what is not.

It's so simple; I feel like a fool for not seeing it for so long. The weight of expectations and traditions were a burden I never needed. Solomon is what I needed. He is who I've always needed. His loyalty and care. I don't regret what I did. What I gave to him was of my own choice and he's more deserving than any Prince I might barter an alliance with. There is no pretending I don't care for Solomon any longer. How can I act as if I have not longed for it, in my dreams and my imagination?

The hallways pass in a blur, Malcolm quiet at my side and Celine trailing behind. Only when the throne room doors come into view do my thoughts return from their haze.

Arms clasped behind his back, Solomon turns in my direction. The dirt-smudged clothing from last night is gone, replaced with a fresh new uniform of black on black. Leather straps and silver buckles hold his sword and a row of daggers around his hips.

My steps slow. What air I'd been breathing before doesn't seem relatively as easy to take in. It's too thick. Too hot.

Solomon's features remain blank but he tilts his head in question. When I finally inhale properly, the corner of his lips twitch upward. "Malcolm. I'd be happy to escort the Princess inside."

"That won't be necessary," Malcolm says. "The Galeanos have requested her presence and her presence alone."

"I am her guard." He steps forward and Malcolm tenses.

I pat the man's arm and carefully step away. "It's alright, Solomon. I can go in on my own." Solo stares at me. Quite possibly staring through me. A flush of warmth works its way over my face.

He concedes, giving me a low bow before stepping aside. "I'll be right here should you need me."

That alone is enough to give me the confidence to face these royals. I steel my spine and face the doors. Malcolm shuffles past, grabs the handles, and swings them wide. Upon their thrones, the King, Queen, and my betrothed look down at me.

29

DEVONRY

Enver's lips stretch into a thin, self-satisfied smile. Whatever they're about to ask of me, I know it does not bode well. I remain silent and poised, though, as I wait. The discomfort I'm forced to deal with as I stand before them, a royal in my own right, slowly festers in my chest. Anger. Frustration. Betrayal. These are all emotions that this family has made me feel. Still, I wait.

I wait and I wait until finally, they deign to break the silence.

"Princess," Queen Helena is the first to speak, "thank you for coming."

I tip my chin back and look up at her where she sits on the dais. "You summoned me," I say.

"Yes, we have," she agrees before nodding to her husband. "We've been deliberating on your predicament as of late. We appreciate your patience as it is quite a delicate matter."

Slices of fury infiltrate my veins. When I smile back at her, I grit my teeth. "Yes," I reply through clenched canines. "The matter of your second son, Prince Nasir, assassinating the King of an allied country and staging a coup is quite a *delicate* matter."

"We wish to help you," Prince Enver says.

My attention turns to him. "I'm glad to hear that—" I begin, only to be cut off as he continues speaking, talking over me as if I hadn't spoken at all.

"Upon the fulfillment of our marriage contract, Bartoli swears an oath to send soldiers to Rozentine to retrieve Nasir and bring him back to our lands to stand trial."

My heartbeat races against the inside of my breast. I stare at him, unblinking. "Excuse me?"

Enver rises from his seat and moves to the edge of the dais before descending. "It's true that the Bartoli Royal Family is responsible for not watching over Nasir close enough to realize his plans," Enver says. "For that, you have our sincerest regret."

"Your regret…" He draws closer and it takes every ounce of willpower that I possess not to back away. "Nasir broke our alliance," I say. "He slaughtered my father, King Vernon, in cold blood. He attempted to kidnap and hold me prisoner, and all you feel is *regret*?"

Enver's expression doesn't change. For all his words might say, his face remains placid and unchanged. Lip service, that's all this is.

"We will, of course, help our allied Kingdom of Rozentine," Enver says. "Once we're married, we will have no other recourse but to take back what belongs to us."

"Belongs to *you*?" I parrot back.

"*Us.*" He repeats the word as if it holds meaning. The true meaning is clear. Enver takes a step toward me, coming nearer as he continues talking. "This is a good thing, Devonry," he insists. "Once we're married—officially—our soldiers will be your soldiers."

"And my Kingdom will become yours," I state.

His smile spreads. "Yes, you understand."

"The original marriage agreement stated that though I would reside in Bartoli, I would have full control of Rozentine. I am their Divine Queen, after all. You and your family have no right to rule it."

But perhaps ruling is not what he's after. Rozentine is known for far more than being a monarchy. It is home to some of the strongest noble lineages in the world. The power they have, the industry of our cities, and the people of the land that my family has governed for ages. There is more to a country than its leader.

Enver reaches for my hands. I don't think. I simply step away from him and glare. He pauses, his brows creasing as he stares back at me. Is he confused? Why? Anyone would be upset at this news. Their agreement to help my Kingdom is wholly reliant on a marriage I no longer wish for. Perhaps, before … I might have been convinced that this was the only way and I had at least hoped—no, I'd naively thought that the Bartoli's would be honorable in this matter.

"What happens if I refuse?" I demand.

Behind Enver, a low scoff of insult sounds. I divert my gaze up to see King Florian's eyes centered squarely on me. All this time, he has let his wife and son do the talking. They are not the rulers here. He is.

I circle Enver and move toward him, pausing several feet back from the dais as I bow lightly. "Your Majesty," I state. "From one monarch to another, do you not think that this is a misguided attempt at making things right? As it stands, the Bartoli Empire can be held responsible for the assassination of King Vernon."

The word 'war' lingers upon my tongue, but I hesitate to say it. Once it's out in the world, there is no taking it back. Threat or not. A war would devastate them as well as me. My people do not need blood and battle. They need peace and safety. Safety I thought I could get from my allies, but apparently all I get is an ultimatum.

"You are a smart girl, Princess," King Florian states. *Girl.* As if I am not a woman. As if I have not been crowned the rightful heir of Rozentine. "These are our terms. They are no different from what we previously agreed upon."

"That was before your son's betrayal," I snap, raising my head.

Out of the corner of my eye, I spot a few guards leaning away from their posts against the walls. King Florian must also see them, for he lifts his hand, stopping their movement with a flick of his fingers.

"The wedding will take place in three days," he announces. "Once you and Enver are married, we shall send troops as promised."

"And what if Enver and I are not to be married?" I demand, pressing.

"Then there will be no troops, Princess." No troops. No attempt at saving a Kingdom his son had taken and ruined.

Anger like poison seeps into my veins. "I see." Those are the only words I can muster. The only ones that don't have the vilest of curses attached to them.

"Devonry—"

"Thank you for the audience, Your Highnesses," I say, cutting Enver off. Even as I feel him come up to my side, I ignore his presence. "You've given me quite a lot to consider."

"What's there to consider?" Queen Helena muses. "We will begin the wedding preparations immediately and in just over three days, you will return to Rozentine with your husband at your side to reclaim your throne." She turns to the King and flutters her lashes. "A magnanimous offer, my King, if I do say so."

He harrumphs but is obviously pleased by her praise. I have nothing more to say—or rather, I fear that if I linger in this room amongst these royals, I will say something that will do more than damage my own reputation; it may wreck any chance of help I might be considering from them. I bow once more, and when King Florian waves his hand at me dismissively, I turn and stride past Enver toward the same double doors I came in.

I don't quite make it there before the soft yet quick footsteps of Prince Enver catch up with me. "Devonry," he calls. "Devonry, wait!" I draw to a halt as his hands land on my arm and pull me to stop at the doors.

We're far enough down the throne hall to be unheard by others, but still, he looks around and then gingerly urges me over to a secondary hallway alongside the throne room. I don't say a word as he tugs me with him, yanking me with a tight grip that doesn't seem to be aware of the breach in royal etiquette. Then again, I can't say that I'm surprised. Even if he knows it, Enver strikes me as the type of Royal to pick and choose which times to use it. He drags me to a set of glass doors and out onto a balcony. I yank away from his touch. Once we're alone and the doors are closed, he blows out a breath and turns to face me.

"You must understand that this is best for both of our countries," he says.

"Is it?" I challenge. "Or is this another way for your family to maintain its control?" My resistance to my fury is fading fast.

"You will still rule Rozentine," he insists.

"Will Nasir be punished for his actions?"

Enver's face twists into a grimace of annoyance. "What?"

I step closer to him, close enough that I can smell the faint hint of sweat and something spicy—like incense. "I want your brother punished for what he did to my father," I tell him.

"H-he'll be put on trial, of course," Enver says.

"No." I shake my head. "That's not good enough. I want assurance that Prince Nasir will meet a satisfactory punishment befitting his betrayal."

Enver's back straightens and his lips turn down. "All trials held in Bartoli are fair and just."

I tilt my head to the side, observing him more closely. His face is smooth. No shadows beneath his eyes. His hair glistens with cleanliness and his shoulders remain back and proud. The sight of him fills me with outrage. Fair? Just? No. What has happened to Rozentine is a violation, something he doesn't seem to understand. It doesn't appear as if he even cares, and that is truly what fans the flames of my anger.

Hardship. Adversity. Pain. Loss. I wonder if he's ever experienced any of those things.

"Is there a reason you won't give me a straight answer?" I ask.

The breath he blows out is exaggerated. "I don't know what you want from me," he snaps.

"I want Nasir executed," I snap. As the words leave my lips, I realize just how true they are. Oh, how my mother would burn with disappointment. A failure of a pacifist, I might be. But a failure of a Queen is not something I will accept. If that means taking another life then so be it. "I want Prince Nasir dead for what he did to me and my Kingdom."

Enver's mouth falls open. He stumbles back a step, reaching out for the balcony's railing as he gapes at me.

"You cannot be serious," he says, shaking his head. "Royals are rarely executed."

I know that fact, and it is why I have no doubt that the worst punishment they would give him is to be locked away for the rest of his life, but I can't be satisfied with that. Knowing that he's out there, alive, makes my blood turn to rot in my body.

"If you can swear to me that Nasir will be executed for his crimes, then I will consider the ultimatum your family bestowed upon me."

Enver shakes his head and scoffs, his mouth twisting into a cruel sneer. "It's not an ultimatum, Devonry, it's—"

"Yes or no," I cut him off. "Will Nasir be executed for his crimes?"

He stares at me for a long moment. Finally, when he speaks, he turns his head away from me. "You're nothing like I expected," he says.

"Funny," I reply. "You're everything I expected." Weak. Unwilling to answer the simplest of questions. So full of his own self-image he doesn't realize that a Queen in desperation for her people is far more deadly than anything he's ever known.

I turn and stride for the balcony doors and as I slip back into the corridor, he doesn't try to stop me. Of course not. That would mean he had to give me a solid answer. As he never has before—not through letters or appearances in my life—it doesn't surprise me that he remains silent even now, with his brother's life hanging in the balance.

Passivity is the cruelest inaction.

30
SOLOMON

"How sad for you," Argyle coos as he lays down his cards. "You really are quite shit at this."

The thing is, I am not so terrible at cards. Honestly, I should be able to beat Argyle, especially because he's been sipping rum for over an hour now. I gather the deck with a sigh.

My mind is still in the moment when Devonry emerged from the throne room. Her cheeks were red with anger. I swore even her hair had darkened several shades. A curse was already waiting on her lips as the doors shut behind her. I'd have been at her side in only a few steps, but she only shook her head at me.

"Would you like to speak of it?" I'd asked, desperately trying to hold onto my calm. What had they said to her? What had they asked?

"Later." She'd responded through gritted teeth. She needed space and time and certainly, I could give her that.

Yet the day is slipping away. The sun is now nothing but a sliver of rays staining the horizon orange and purple.

Later may have come and passed but I dare not intrude on her. Not yet, at least.

Argyle tips the last of the bottle into his glass. The honey-colored liquid comes close to splashing over the rim as he swirls the drink. Its strong syrup scent perfumes the air between us.

My glass remains half full, the drink unable to soothe the rising anguish inside of me. I push it further away with the back of my hand before shuffling our cards and dealing again.

"Are you letting me win?" Argyle squints in my direction while I lay my first card down.

"Do I ever *let* you win?"

He rubs a hand over his jaw. "You have a point. So, why am I all of a sudden beating you at every hand? It's not even fun anymore."

A knock sounds at the door. I stiffen.

Please let it be Devonry.

Argyle's eyes narrow. "Are you going to answer that?" Another minor knock as if the person on the other side is rethinking being here.

"Get out," I tell Argyle, standing and making my way to the door.

"What? Me?" He holds a hand to his chest.

"Yes." Turning the chilled brass knob, I pull the heavy door open. Still in the same dress I'd seen her in earlier, Devonry turns in my direction. She'd been looking down the hall, one foot in front of her as though she was thinking of walking away. "Argyle was just leaving," I say by way of greeting.

"Was I now?" He finally drops his hand on the small table we'd been playing at and rises. Giving the Princess a less-than-enthusiastic smile, he swipes his drink up and finally emerges into the hallway. "You should know, Princess, I was winning." He gives a bow and saunters off.

"I didn't mean to interrupt." Devonry's attention keeps drifting one way and then the next. "Can I come in?"

I open the door further allowing her room to enter. She walks into my chambers in much the same way she always has, with an air of confidence only royalty can pull off. Here and now, it may appear as if nothing between us has changed. Devonry could turn around and insult me at any moment and I'd poke back with the same broiling anger I've always held. Yet she remains silent, looking over the game that had been played and the now empty bottle of rum.

"If you're thirsty, I could call for something," I ask, unsure of where to put myself so I remain standing at the door.

"No." She stops her perusal. "I don't want anyone knowing I'm here."

"Right." My teeth sink into my lip as I bite down. "Do you, ah, want to talk about what happened in the throne room now?"

Her skirts twist around her legs with the momentum of her spin as she turns toward me. Gold rims her blue-gray eyes. At my sides, my fingers twitch with the need to touch her skin to ensure she's well and that the meeting with the Galeanos didn't harm her.

"They are pushing for the marriage as Lord Byron was."

One sentence. One commitment we'd both known was coming. It shouldn't be a surprise, but I still feel a wave of shock pass through my system. Had I fooled myself into thinking that last night might really make our realities any different? Certainly, I'd hoped.

"Once we are wed they will send soldiers into Rozentine to collect Nasir. They've agreed to have him stand trial. Not that it is enough for what he has done." Disgust sours her features. Her mouth curls down as slight wrinkles appear between her eyebrows. "If there is no wedding, there will be no assistance in breaking Nasir's stronghold."

"And?" I force myself to stay still.

"And?" Devonry flops down on the chair Argyle had been in only a few moments ago. With a groan, she tilts her head up and stares at the ceiling.

"What do you want to do?"

Every part of me screams her name. My mind is a frantic chatter of *'mine, mine, mine.'* She isn't mine though. As much as I want to claim her and keep her. Devonry belongs to our kingdom. And maybe more so, Devonry belongs to herself.

Still, my soul begs for hers. There is no fiber of my being that might somehow survive not having her after everything we've been through. I know the tenderness of her touch. My body has tasted of her want. She has been mine, and I need her … I *need* her. Forever, I need her.

"Solomon." She closes her eyes.

Part of my heart might already be shattering. This is where she tells me to stay away from her. The bit where she says she and that damn prince were always meant to be. Outwardly I'm a stone statue, unable to move even the slightest. Internally … I'm a fucking disaster.

"I don't want to pretend," she says, her voice hardly above a whisper. "What we did together … we can't act as if it didn't happen."

The truth. I've ruined her. All the blood drains from my face.

Holy Levim.

Guilt rises like bile. "Devonry," I plead, "I never meant—"

"You don't understand." A coy grin plays on her lips. "What happened between us, in front of the gods, nature, and the power that makes up our entire beings, was beautiful. I regret *nothing* we did. Not a thing." I take a slow breath in. "Do you hear me, Solomon Winett?"

She crosses one leg over the other waiting for my response. All I can do is stare. I'd spent the day replaying every fucking second of being in that cave with her, over and over again. I've reveled in the joy and freedom that I'd always been denied. Then I'd spent hours nearly sick with guilt, the commands to which I'd sworn myself to repeating inside my head.

Our proximity to one another has been and will continue to be important. One's soulmate always amplifies the power of the other. Together our abilities will be at their peak—which makes for a better guardsman and a better queen. By the King's own command, we were never supposed to be *together*.

"I have no intentions of marrying Enver. How can I be a part of the family that is responsible for my father's death? Still, the Galeanos have set the date. They want us to wed in three days," she continues.

The hold that had kept me in place finally releases. I take a step forward, and another until I find myself lowering into the seat across from her. Devonry clasps her hands in front of her on the table, watching me earnestly.

"You do not wish to marry the Prince?"

Say it. I need to hear it again.

"I will not be marrying into the Galeano family. No." The Princess holds my gaze, daring me to suggest otherwise.

Relief, as cold as ice, surges through my veins. There is no mistaking her words now. Devonry, *my* Queen, will not be marrying that scum, Prince Enver.

A hint of mischief passes over her features and for a breath she is the girl she was before her father's death. She's rebellious and excited. It only lasts for a short time though. The weight of everything that has come to pass quickly settles back down on her shoulders.

"Then we must leave. We cannot stay," I say with certainty. Now that the Bartoli royals have her, I cannot imagine they will let her go easily. Not with Rozentine in their reach. Still, we must try.

"I don't think Prince Enver, much less his parents, will allow it. You weren't there to see the look in their eyes … the greedy glint and assured confidence that they'll be getting exactly what they want." She spreads her palms flat against the table. "I wonder how much of this they'd planned together. Or if Nasir just simply gave them this … *gift.*"

Nothing about this situation could even be comparable to a gift. Devonry lost her father and her kingdom in one single swoop. I'll not let her lose her chance to make her own choice too. Even if it may be selfish on my part.

"Don't worry about the Galeanos. If you wish to go, I will not let them keep you." The words come out as a possessive declaration, the beast under my flesh stirring.

"You'll keep me then?" she asks, a brow raised and a coy smile lifting the corners of her mouth.

My face warms. "I'll do more than keep you, should you allow it."

"I just might," she whispers, touching a hand to her smirking mouth.

Does she remember the taste of our kiss?

I clear my throat and close my eyes in an attempt to

beat back the onslaught of images that my mind conjures. Her soft flesh under my body, her hair fanning out against the stone, and the twist of her expression as she came on my cock.

"We can leave much as we did yesterday, at the changing of shifts. There are servants that Argyle is friendly with and I'm sure a coin in their pocket may help give us more time if they were to spread word that you are ill in your room. We'll find a ship. We'll sail for home." I take her hand, pulling it away from her mouth. "We are going to figure this out."

She turns her hand over and interlocks our fingers. And fuck, my thoughts get away from me. For once, we are not at war with each other; she is not running. It isn't because I'm losing control and I need her help. Devonry grasps my hand of her own free will and with the special care one might offer their lover. My heart takes off at a speed it's not known before.

How easy would it be to lay her across this table? Here there would be no darkness to hide what we might do to and for each other. I might kiss every angle of her body and claim it as my own. There would be no tender flesh safe from the wicked mark of my fangs. Nothing to stop me from sinking into that perfect fucking pussy. Together we would come, again and again and again until we were too spent to stand. Too spent to talk. Even then I may not stop.

She squeezes my hand. "Once they realize we're gone, don't you think they'll bar all the ships from leaving port? And a few coins in the pockets of the help is risky when their loyalties and livelihoods depend upon this family."

She's right.

"You said you are to be wed in three days?" Her head bobs in agreement. "That's not a lot of time to work with but it's enough. Let me talk with Argyle. He'll send a bird to Yulis for his immediate return, and we can travel home upon his ship."

"So we leave in secret?" Her face is lit with a new hope, one I hope doesn't burn out.

"Yes."

"What of the Ambassador?"

Lord Byron. The man has been somewhat of a puzzle to me since I first met him. He moves like the shadows around the castle and any conversation I've tried to hold with him has conveniently come to an end before he can say all too much. Is he worth trusting?

"I'll admit he is quite a mystery to me. I cannot say one way or another if telling him is in our best interests. Though I do err on the side of caution."

Devonry lowers her head to our entangled hands and presses her forehead against them. "He has done his part to advise me. Even if I disagree, I think our sudden disappearance might be disrespectful and jeopardize his life here." The words are mumbled against the table. When she sits back up, her forehead is pink where skin met skin. I lose a fight to the smile that forms. "I think we should tell him."

"I can go." I agree, though she quickly shakes her head.

"No, I'll find a way to tell him. It should be my responsibility." In one fluid movement, her hand leaves mine and she stands, eyes lingering on the room around me. "Let me know when we hear word from Yulis."

"Of course." I nod, also rising.

"Alright." She looks through her lashes up at me, hands wringing in front of her. My chest warms as her attention bounces from mine to my lips, and chest, then back up.

"Alright," I repeat absently, inching nearer until her scent burns at my nose.

"I really should be leaving now, I think…" Her teeth worry over her lip. "So it doesn't look … suspicious."

Nothing about the way she says that sounds the least bit convincing. "I'll walk you back to your room."

"Oh, that's not necessary. It's not far." Her exhale is loud, the fidgeting of her fingers becoming more apparent as she lets her hands go, puts them behind her back, and then at her sides to fist the material of her gown.

Am I making her nervous?

"I know." I can't help but smile.

"Alright," she repeats.

"Alright."

At the door, I offer her my arm. The soft touch of her hand as she balances it carefully on my arm, is enough to make my body rigid with want. I swallow past the lump in my throat and the demanding sensation to seal her away in my room for the evening before heading for her room.

Everywhere her body brushes mine brings my skin to life, tingling reminders of what she is to me, of what we've done together. These halls could be brimming with people and I would care not. Even as we both remain overwhelmingly aware that this arm-in-arm walk is one that does not happen often, especially within palace walls. My place as her guardsmen is a few steps behind her, rarely in front of her, and even more rare at her side.

We reach her room, neither of us letting go of the other. Silence cradles us in the hall. With care, I take her hand from my arm and run my fingers over her calloused palms. "I have spent many years thinking about what it might be like to touch you in such a way."

"Have I … does it meet your expectations?" Her

breath is shallow. The curve of her breasts rising against her dress to reveal the slightest bit of cleavage.

Recklessly, I let myself bring a finger to her collarbone. I trace a line across her chest, up the vein in her neck, and cup her cheek. Devonry leans into my palm, her eyes glued to my face.

"You've exceeded every single one of my expectations."

Somehow, the space between us has disappeared. So now every inhale and exhale she makes I can feel against me. My fingertips tease at her hairline and the silk feeling of the strands. Her lips, so perfect and full, are near enough I could taste her if only I dared…

Her mouth parts, for air or to speak, I'm not sure because in the next moment, my lips are pressed to hers. My queen yields to the kiss, like oil melted in the heat of the sun. What I give, she takes and gives back tenfold. She's sweet on my tongue and fire in my veins.

Devonry relaxes into my arms, her fingers digging into my shirt and holding me in place. As if I would ever voluntarily end this moment—

Her door swings open, revealing the blur of dark hair. "Oh my," Celine sucks in a sharp breath. "I am so sorry."

My mind screams in protest as the Princess takes a step away from me, leaving my arms empty. Her eyes are wide, cheeks pink, and lips swollen with our kiss. "Thank you for walking me back," Devonry says, twisting to look up and down the hall before she rushes past Celine and into her room.

"I—ah, have a good night, Solo," Celine whispers, her gaze never meeting mine as she hesitates but ultimately closes the door.

Once again, I've found myself with a wall between me and what I want. I still feel her kiss on my lips. The shape of her slender frame in my arms is burned into my very being. The scent of her lust is the perfume that holds to my clothing.

Yet here I am.

Alone.

Wishing. Wanting. Waiting.

31

DEVONRY

For most of my life, I'd attempted to be the perfect daughter. The perfect Crown Princess. The perfect Royal. Maybe perfection was difficult to strive for, but I'd been taught that was what I needed to do. Sometimes I failed. Sometimes I didn't agree, but ultimately, I understood that my life was never truly my own. I understood that my life would be ruled by my blood, that my destiny was to be less than human and more of a figure beyond reproach.

Now, I realize that there is nothing truly perfect in this world. Royals are as corrupt as the average man or woman. It doesn't matter in which status a person is born. They are either, at their core, good or evil. Either wicked and greedy or careful and forgiving. Somehow, that, too, feels like a lie I've been fed.

If, at our core, we are either one or the other, then does my deeply rooted hatred for Nasir and my desire to see him executed for his crimes against me and my people mean I'm a bad person? Or does it mean that people can change? That they can be so altered by their circumstances that they cease to be who they were before? If so, what does that mean for my betrayer? Was he always cruel? Or did that come about because of some misguided love for me?

All of these thoughts permeate my mind, sinking deeper and deeper until they drift into my dreams. Dreams that turn quickly into dark swamps of sorrow and pain. Screams drift back to me as I walk down a path by feel alone. They echo in my head, crying out for help. Some of the voices are recognizable. Most of all, Jacin's.

My feet move faster and faster until I'm stumbling through branches and brush, over thorns and hot coals. Smoke slithers up from the ground, turning corporeal as it clutches onto me, tugging at my limbs and clothes— holding me back as I force myself to keep going.

Fabric rips and flesh rends. Blood leaks down my legs and arms. A thorn cuts across my cheek as I struggle through the fog. "Jacin?" I cry out. "I hear you! I'm coming!"

Silence greets my words and, suddenly, all of the screaming stops. As if the dream itself had been waiting for me to speak. The strands of smoke drift away from me and I come to a standstill, turning as I sense someone behind me. I've become so accustomed to the darkness surrounding me that when I spot the bright light shining from the woman who appears at the mouth of my path, I flinch and lift my hand to cover my eyes.

"Daughter of mine, come here." I blink and slowly, my palm lowers.

"Mom?" I pivot toward her and leave the darkness behind. My feet continue to bleed, leaving wet red spots behind as I walk toward the woman in the light, but as I reach her, I realize I was wrong. The woman standing there isn't my mother.

I pause as she reaches her hand out to me. "Take my hand."

I don't want to. My chest shakes. My eyes burn with unshed tears. I'm frightened, I realize. Though I haven't said anything, she offers me a smile and continues to hold out her hand. Her face is smooth and unblemished by time. Her eyes are large and round and golden. Her hair is a brilliant red at the roots, falling in heavy waves down her face and over her shoulders until it reaches the ends, where the red morphs slowly into a pinkish hue and then white.

"You may stay here if you wish," she says after a moment. "But then you won't learn the truth."

"The truth?" I repeat her words. Turmoil keeps me stationary and I'm both unable to turn back or take her hand. But I can't stay like this forever. I need to make a choice.

"Yes," the woman says. "If you want to know, then you'll have to come with me."

"What about Jacin?" I look over my shoulder, stopping as her fingers latch onto my face and turn me back to her.

"That's not Jacin," she tells me. "That's the darkness trying to lure you inside."

Her palm drifts down my throat, moving to my arm, and then further until she winds her fingers through my own. "Now, come…"

A refusal sticks to my tongue as she pulls me along. My feet move on their own, following the strange woman out of the dark, and once I'm entirely ensconced in the light that surrounds her, I look down and find that all of my cuts and wounds have miraculously disappeared.

The sweet scent of nature tickles my nose. "What…" I tilt my head upward. "What is this place?"

The woman leads me further onto a wide-open plain. Grass tickles my feet, the blades sweeping across the tops of my toes playfully … as if they're alive and sentient. *That's not possible,* I think. *Is it?*

"This is your past, daughter mine, and your future." When she speaks, it sounds as if the wind is curling around her words, absorbing them and bringing them to me. It is as if the entire world surrounding her is so fond of her creation and presence that it does all in its power to aid her in anything she wishes. Be that speaking … and a frightful thought occurs, but also if she were to wish for my death.

The woman chuckles and turns back to me, her lips curving into a gentle, amused smile. "I don't wish for the death of myself, so why would I wish for yours?" she asks.

I blink and heat steals across my face. "Did you read my thoughts?" I ask.

Full, pink lips purse. "I didn't read them so much as you sent them to me."

"I…" I didn't mean to do that. I didn't even know I could.

"Well, I suppose you can't," she says. "Not with others anyway, but the relationship between you and I is different."

"It's different?" I repeat. "How?"

"Because we are one."

That makes no sense. She's standing right before me, as clear as day. I can see that we have two separate bodies. There's no—

"Hold up your hand," she commands, stopping abruptly and lifting hers as well as she interrupts my wayward thoughts.

Hesitation holds me spellbound in captivity. I don't want to and yet curiosity demands I try. The woman smiles knowingly. "Curiosity is a damnable thing, isn't it?" She shakes her head. "Now, hold up your hand, child. This is not a test and it will not hurt. I merely wish to prove it to you."

As if to, once again, aid her in her desires, I feel a sudden rush of air at my back. I stumble forward, nearly colliding with the woman before me. My hand lifts on instinct and as our fingers touch, the shock of something otherworldly slams into me. From every angle, the presence of this place becomes my awareness. From the grass beneath my feet to the wind surrounding me, to the light brush of sunlight upon the top of my head. I feel it all. More than feel it, it resides inside of me, filling me to almost bursting. There is so much life in the world, it's a wonder I have not sensed it before. How had my senses become numb to it? How had I never noticed it?

"You feel what I feel when we touch because you are who I am, Devonry, and I am who you are."

My lips part, but no words escape. The meaning behind her statement is confusing, like a massive fog has descended upon my mind, and as I wade through it to find the understanding, it grows thicker and thicker.

The woman smiles again. This time, though, the curves of her lips tremble ever so slightly. As if she's saddened by my response. She lowers her hand and takes a step back. "It's alright," she says. "You're not ready. Close, but … not yet."

"Wait!" I call out for her as she turns away, but she doesn't answer. Instead, she continues walking—gliding, really—across the plain toward a very large oak tree. I trail her, picking up speed. How can a woman so slight and small seem to run without doing more than walking? Perhaps the ground is moving for her. Whatever the case, she arrives first and when I finally get to her side, I'm panting.

The wide trunk of the oak tree is thick and dark in

color. Sweating slightly, I look up into its gnarled branches that span outward. Shade covers the two of us as the woman turns and rests her back against the tree's thickest part. She sighs before sinking down. Just before her butt reaches the ground, however, a root shoots up from beneath the ground and curves into place, providing a thick seat for her.

I stand back and stare. Just as before, the tree appears to be easing her path. As if it's curling itself around the woman to provide a secure resting place, a chair for her to remain. Almost as if the tree, itself, wishes to wind around her and hug her to its breast.

I shake my head. Strange. This dream is so very strange.

"Come." The woman pats a place on the root at her side. "Sit with me. We must talk."

Left with little recourse, I join the woman on the root, sitting at her side gingerly—half afraid the tree will find it offensive that I've sat next to its master. Nothing happens, though.

"Why am I here?" I finally ask, turning to the woman. I need answers and this time, I'm not going away until I get them.

"Because the time is coming fast, darling," she replies. "And I'm afraid that, in this life, destiny has been set awry.'"

"Destiny?" Does she mean my destiny?

"Yes." When she answers, I'm not sure if she's confirming or answering my unspoken question. She turns her face up to the sky and for a moment, I'm given the opportunity to truly look at her.

So few people have the same smoothness of skin that she does. It makes it difficult to discern her age. She could be nineteen, or she could be fifty. Her hair falls in curling waves over her shoulders and down her back. The red and white blend seamlessly. Her lashes are long and dark, arching out over her cheekbones and throwing shadows down her face when a ray of sun peeps through the leaves and branches overhead, stabbing right into her face. Instead of getting irritated or flinching, she merely smiles, closes her eyes and tips her head back further to allow the sunlight to caress her flesh. Like a considerate human allowing a gentle pet to nudge them insistently.

"There is a story you must hear," she says. "It is ancient —as old as time itself—or rather, older probably. It was so long ago that I've forgotten what came first."

"What came first?"

"Yes," she chuckles. "Time or love."

"That's obvious," I say. "Time must have come first. If not for time, there would be no one to love."

"You think so?" The amusement in her tone might have sounded condescending coming from another, but something tells me that this woman has never felt condescension toward anyone or anything a day in her life. "How do you know that time did not blossom because of a great love? That a love so massive and widespread did not, one day, explode and create the world you now know?" Before I can answer, she continues. "No, there is no telling. Not anymore. When you've lived as long as I have, the older the memories are, the more faded they become. That is why I had to be reborn. It was why *you* were born."

"Why I was born?" I feel like a parrot, repeating everything she says like this, but it's not making sense.

She reaches over and lays her fingers on mine where they rest on the root of the tree. Once again, I'm assailed by the *awareness* of everything. It is as if she is transferring her sight into me. All at once, it is the *knowing* that makes it too much. I've seen it all before, felt it—one at a time—but when you are so vastly conscious of every thing and creature, living and not, it is overwhelming. Like trying to suck in air through the smallest hole.

"Love was born here," the woman says. With her free hand, she gestures to the area surrounding us. Beyond it, still sits the darkness, but it never encroaches. Almost as if this place is protected—or it is simply too scared to step into the light. I get that. The light is blinding when you've been in the dark for so long.

"This is the birthplace of my soul," she continues, "and my heart's mate."

"Who is your heart's mate?" I ask, my curiosity not yet abated. It only grows the longer I remain at her side. Despite the difficulty I'm having breathing, I find I want to know more. I want to know everything.

Her soft lips twist upward and I suspect it's the thought of her soulmate that causes the action. "He is blood and victory," she states. "He is the strength and hope that lights the path of life. He is the opposite of my being and yet, the completeness every creature seeks."

I stare at her for a moment more. Odd, so very odd, are her words. They speak reverently and yet, she never says a name. "Devonry, my heart's mate is—" She stops, turning to me in shock as her lips part and form into the perfect 'o.'

"Oh dear," she says. "We're out of time. I didn't think —" Her brows crease down and suddenly, I'm shoved off the root. "Wake up!" she yells. "You have to wake up!"

"Wait, what?" Startled, my back lands on the ground. *Hard.*

There is no grass. Instead, rocks dig into my spine and the tree above us grows larger, its branches extending outward, turning blackened at the base and white as ash at the tops.

"You have to wake up!" the woman screams. "Before it's too late."

"Before what is…" My bewilderment evaporates into horror as the woman's face melts down and her body lengthens. Even as her voice rings in my head, crying out for me to wake up, the form she takes morphs into something else. Something fearsome.

A giant snake raises its head, a forked tongue flicking out to taste the air around us as it slithers closer to me. "No!" I scream, scrambling on my hands and butt. "No!" Again, the woman screams and her words echo through my head.

Wake up.

32
DEVONRY

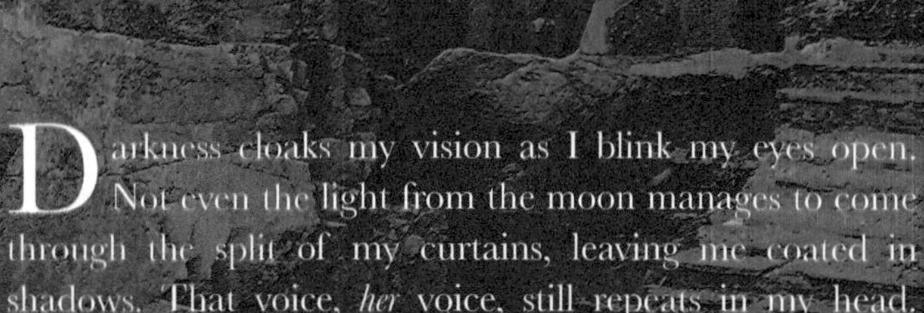

Darkness cloaks my vision as I blink my eyes open. Not even the light from the moon manages to come through the split of my curtains, leaving me coated in shadows. That voice, *her* voice, still repeats in my head. Sweat dampens my skin, my clothes clinging to my shivering form.

The hair along my arms rises. Fear catches and holds my breath hostage.

Wrong. Something is wrong.

My mattress shifts. Weight separate from my own moves from the foot of my bed and creeps along my legs. Something darker takes form. Large and long but without the shape of limbs or the stature of a human *something* hovers over me.

I blink again, trying to understand and hold the scream already building in my chest. A dream? A nightmare? No. My fingers curl into the bedding. Whatever this is, it's real. My heart pounds in my chest at the realization.

Still, the shadow doesn't come into focus. Instead, it sways. Something brushes my calf through the blankets. A firm but boneless curling and writhing against my leg. The figure pulls back.

Move. Aerea's voice screams.

Ripping the blankets from my leg, I twist away, rolling from my bed and onto the floor. The sheets try to cling to my body as I flee and tangle between my legs. My bare feet smack against the tile in rapid succession and I stumble to a stop to shake off the last of the bedding. My headboard rattles against the wall with a bang, the shadow now where I had once been. Heat burns at my palms, my vision brightening to a pearlescent gold. Fire dances at my fingertips, illuminating the twisting, vial creature coiling in my bed.

Two thin vertical pupils surrounded by deep violet irises watch me. A snake, as thick as a man and as long as two, opens its mouth to reveal its fangs with a hiss. Each tooth is as long as my hand and comes to a deadly point at the end.

Horror floods me. This *thing* would have consumed me whole had I not awoken.

The snake's tongue flicks at the air, its body coiling once more. Muscles ripple beneath thick, shining scales. I let flames circle in my palm and hurl a ball of fire before it can lunge. My bedding takes to the flames, the monster darting off the mattress in one smooth movement. There one moment and gone the next.

"Celine!" I shout, the taste of smoke blooming off the blankets thick on my tongue. "Celine!"

Firelight brightens my room, chasing away what darkness the creature tries to lurk in. I cough into my sleeve, backing into the wall and keeping my attention on the form that climbs over itself in the opposite corner.

Celine bursts through the door with a ferocity that rattles the walls. In turn, the snake straightens and bares its fangs. She comes to an abrupt stop before jerking herself into the door. Her hand comes to clutch her dress, wrinkling the white of her nightgown. "By the gods!"

"Get Solomon!" I scream, tossing another ball of flames toward the snake as it inches in her direction. My rug takes to the fire next, creating a distinct line between us.

Hurry. Please hurry, I plead with the gods.

The monster rises to the height of one man, the rest of its body resting in messy circles below it. Its head dips and bobs as it tests the rising flame. Purple lights the wide shifting eyes. A powerful glow. A magical glow.

Not possible.

Yet, if I've learned anything … more is possible than I ever thought could be. This being is Awakened. The power of our gods flows through its veins.

More smoke billows up to my ceiling, forcing me to keep my sleeve over my nose and mouth. My eyes sting from the smoke until they start to water. Still, I dance with the snake, staying as far from it as I can. Though now I wonder if it's truly a snake at all. An assassin with an Awakened form? Someone with noble blood? *No. No…*

The warmth from the fire quickly fills the room. A new sheen of perspiration soaks me thoroughly. I edge toward the door and the fresh air that waits on the other side. Shouting erupts in the halls, but before I can make it to the doorway. The snake lurches over the rug. Its long-scaled body slides against the tile. A quiver runs like a wave along its tail shaking off any fire that tries to cling on.

The sharp edges of its fangs glitter in my golden vision only for the briefest of moments before I'm darting away. My abilities don't feel as though they are enough. Not in the face of this Awakened beast that shakes off my flames as though they're only a mild inconvenience.

Tucked away next to the mirror, my bow waits. I swear

I hear the snake's teeth clacking as its jaw opens and closes in behind me. The air is heavy with the scent of burning fabrics. It threatens to choke me with every breath I take. Still, the beating of my heart can be felt throughout my body and heard within my ears.

When my fingertips meet the smooth wood of the bow, I'm reminded of the girl I was before. The girl who could only run from her problems. The one who needed protecting.

I'm not running now.

I move with the ease of muscle memory. Nocking the arrow, taking aim, and settling my erratic breathing even as the snake slithers toward me in a smooth side-to-side motion. I pull my arm back, the ghost of my lessons guiding me, perhaps even the very power of Aerea herself. I let go.

The arrow slices through the air. It hums as it carves a path through smoke and flame, sliding along the snake's face. The monster shakes as a line of blood wells, hissing in what I assume is pain.

A body fills the doorframe. Red eyes glow like a beacon of death into the heat of my room. Solomon. Argyle at his heels.

As if following the direction of my eyes, or perhaps as if he can even sense the Awakened beast that lives in Solomon, the snake's head turns toward the door. It tilts its head, its tail twitching.

Solomon pulls his sword free from the sheath. The last of the dying flames reflects off its surface. Only then do I finally lower my bow.

"Fuck, that's a big snake." Argyle's jaw drops open.

"It's about to be a dead snake," Solomon growls.

The animal recoils. Does it know? Can it understand us?

Before Solomon can drive his sword into the snake's belly, it shoots past me, knocking my curtains from the wall and nearly taking them with it as it dives out the window. Smoke follows the gust of air from its movements, making it more transparent and easier to see the blackening of the walls, ceiling, and bed frame.

"Follow it." Solomon gives Argyle the one command, and Argyle's gone, running through the halls and on his way out of the castle.

The feral glint in his eyes and the way he stalks through my room, checking for anything else that might be lurking, is all too familiar. My stomach turns, acid burning at the back of my throat. This man, this beast, my guardsman … is all too similar to the boy who saved me from my first assassin. From his frantic movements around my room to the gentle way he takes me into his arms, he's a long-lost version of himself. Maybe the version that's always been there but was hidden by the scars of war.

When Solomon holds me and I shake as the adrenaline leaves my body, it's like we are kids again. For a second it's as if he never went to war at all.

33
SOLOMON

The trembles of her body slow with every minute that passes. Ruffled strands of her hair catch along the shadow of a beard I'd not had time to shave this morning. The scent of smoke still permeates the air and perfumes her hair. Her palms skim my sides, her fingers still warm from the fire she'd conjured.

"Are you hurt?" I demand more than ask, pulling her away only to inspect her body. Sweat has made her sleeping dress hug her curves, creating places where the gown is sheer.

"I—uh, I think I'm fine. I might have stubbed my toe, but that's all." Devonry traces her torso eyeing for injuries. We both exhale when neither of us finds anything of concern.

Celine paces the room, stopping only to pull aside the curtains to look out the window. She squints into the distance. Dark strands of hair have fallen out of her braid, framing her troubled features. "What was *that*?"

"A snake, I think," Devonry whispers, taking a few steps to run her fingers over her ruined bedding.

With the toe of my boot, I scuff against the last of the already dying embers. Her flames had scorched several things but ultimately dyed out before utterly ruining her room. A small grace, I suppose. My eyes find her, constantly drifting up and over her to confirm she's fine. She's safe. Alive.

My own body still feels the effects of the power thrumming through me. Celine's startled voice broke through my sleep and pulled me from my bed before I even registered I was moving. I'd slipped into my boots, thrown a shirt on, and grabbed my sword belt. Awakened power hurtled me through the halls and right to my Queens open door. It was quieter than I'd expected it to be. I didn't rush in to find a screaming, terrified little girl, but a woman with a bow strung up in her hands, fighting back.

I'd seen her before; I'd seen the wicked creature before her. Scales shone from the firelight, its long body writhing with an unearthly ease. Fangs and all, the creature had shown me its face. I'd felt no fear, only blistering anger. However, something had flashed through the snake's eyes. Something intelligent that recognized that it had just lost this fight. I could only hope now that Argyle finds it and puts it down.

"Do you think that was purposeful?" Devonry finally yanked up her sheets, revealing the mattress, somehow untouched beneath.

"Is it common here that large snakes find their way into the castle? I've never heard such things." Celine pulls herself away from the window and makes herself busy with pulling the chard bits of fabric from the bed.

"This was no accident," I growl. When something of this size that's as deadly as that snake had been, makes its way into the room of royalty … it's never a coincidence.

Devonry's face pales. "Did you see its face? Those *eyes?*"

"Awakened eyes." I nod even as Celine's breath hitches at the words.

"Awakened? You think that thing has a master?" Celine drifts by, pulling fresh bedding from a chest next to the wardrobe. Her eyes are glassy, distant but not seeing into the future, more lost in the past than anything.

What good is a future seer if she didn't see this coming? I keep my bitter thoughts to myself. However, I can't hide my scowl.

"Purple eyes." I make a point to test her bed's sturdiness, the structure still intact somehow. With the fresh bedding, one might never have thought it'd been in flames only minutes ago. Well, unless they looked at the scorched ceilings and the blackened rug at the foot of the bed. "Out of curiosity, have you spoken to the Ambassador about our plans?"

"I did. As we'd decided, I sent him a note to let him know that I will not be wedding Enver."

My hand rests against the hilt of my sword. The leather of the belt feels odd against the softer material of the pants I'd gone to bed in. I can't help but tap my still-lengthened nails against the metal.

"You don't think?" Celine says, after a glance at Devonry whose focus has drifted to the burnt rug.

"Purple eyes," I repeat. "Awakened. All too similar to that of the House Daemonium."

"But that makes no sense," Devonry says, a tearful sheen in her eyes. My heart drops to my stomach. "Why? Why would a Rozentine House betray me?"

"Maybe those are thoughts for tomorrow when you've gotten some rest." Celine steps to Devonry's side. I watch as she embraces her Princess with the concern of a dear friend. "Let me take your ruined bedding and the rug out with me, and if you leave your window cracked, you might rid the room of the last of the smoky scent." Her attention falls on me. "I will leave her in your care, Solomon."

"Thank you, Celine," I answer quietly.

Reluctantly, Celine pulls away from Devonry. She takes a single deep breath before steeling her spine and gathering the bedding and rug. With one last look about the room, Celine sighs and closes the door behind her.

"How am I going to sleep after that?" Devonry lowers herself to the edge of her bed.

"I'll be near. I swear it."

The gold around her eyes is still vibrant, her abilities still simmering under the surface. She slouches, looking as worn out as I'm sure she feels. "Please stay."

"Just outside your door." I nod, already accepting that no further sleep can be afforded me.

"No." She shakes her head, the length of her hair brushing against her shoulders with the motion. "Stay in here, with me."

I swallow. She doesn't know what she is asking. Since coming back from the waters of Thevaros my body craves hers in such a way that is nearly soul-crushing. I've had a taste of her. I need more.

And under the nose of the Bartoli Royals? They know not of our plans to leave. However, Enver has suspected my feelings. But staying in her room ... a blessing ... a curse.

"I'll take the chair." I concede. In no world could I be far from her tonight. I might as well accept that being in her room is the best option for her safety.

"Solo." She pins me with a look that screams '*are you really that dense?*'

Maybe I am. Perhaps I should be for both of our sakes. Someone has to be thinking about her reputation.

"Devonry." I take a step toward one of the sitting chairs. Where the rug had been is now only a black scorch mark on the tile floor.

"Come lay with me…"

A smirk pulls at my lips. "I remember not long ago you were unwilling to sleep in the same bed. I remember you cowering behind the safety of a pillow. Sound familiar?"

Her eyes narrow to two thin slits. "If I recall, Lord Solomon Winett of the House of Blood does not care much for pillows."

"Not when they are between us."

Devonry presses her lips together but is unable to hide the way they start to curl at the corners. "So that settles it then? You'll come to lay by me?" She pats the bed.

I chuckle. "The floor will be just fine for me. I'll be right there." She follows the point of my finger to the space between her bed and the still-open window.

"You are ridiculous." She huffs. "If you sleep on the floor, then I will also sleep on the floor."

"I'm the one being ridiculous?" I snort.

"Yes."

"Well, I suppose you leave me no choice."

She grins, though it doesn't quite reach her eyes. With a few steps in her direction, I'm at the bed. She scoots herself back, watching as I kick off my boots. Her eyes follow my hands as they go to my sword belt and I remove it with a single hand then hook it around the bedpost.

The fresh bedding is as smooth as silk and feather-soft, truly fit for a Queen. My room has never been filled with such luxuries, although they've been offered before. I pull the blanket back, letting her slip beneath it before I find my way to her side.

We lay together, staring up. If we don't think about it, the soot almost appears as if it's the night sky peering in at us. Specs of the stone poke through like the dotting of stars. Only her elbow brushes my arm. That alone is enough for my body to react, blood rushing to places it shouldn't in moments like this. My wicked, sinful body.

"Goodnight," she whispers.

"Goodnight."

A breeze rattles the open window. The smoky smell is nearly forgotten even though the snake remains painfully prominent. I'll close the window once she's asleep, but for now, I can't fathom the idea of her having to breathe in any more of the fumes still lingering.

She closes her eyes, yet her body remains tense. I lay there, gaze moving constantly as I listen for any and all sounds. All I can hear is Devonry's breath. After several all too-long minutes, she sighs and rolls to her side. My weight on her mattress pulls her to me.

Devonry's body molds to mine. Her back settles against my chest, and the tips of her toes—surprisingly cold—brush against my pant legs before finding their way to my skin.

Her flesh against mine ignites something dangerous in me. The monster moves within me, more in control than I've ever been. Devonry is under me in mere seconds, her torso framed by my arms.

Her breath hitches, eyes snapping open. The fear she'd had before is gone, replaced with this half-hooded look of want. And that's all it takes.

I press my mouth to hers, wishing away all the horrors that plague her. Her lips part. Devonry kisses me back as though I'm the only thing that might soothe the worry riddling her body. She drinks me in as I do her.

Until we are lost to the world, and all that exists is us.

34
DEVONRY

Solo's kiss is hauntingly familiar. It melts any hint of resistance within me in a single instant. Arching my arms up around him, I part my lips and kiss him back. His tongue tangles with my own, but his eyes remain open all the while staring back at me.

A million times, I've seen those eyes. I've anticipated them. Hated them. Rejected them. Now, I can't turn away from them. They pull me deep and drown me in bloody waters. His skin is hot beneath my touch. His hair is like the softest of a bird's feathers. His body hovers over mine, pushing me down into this very mattress I'd been attacked in.

Slower, his kiss turns softer than before and as he pulls his mouth from mine, I moan helplessly. He hushes me with light and gentle touches. His hands brushing over my skin as his head descends down. Solo kisses my jawline and then the sensitive place behind my ear. A gasp rattles inside my chest and then he kisses my rapidly beating pulse where it flutters at my throat.

We are treading dangerous waters, I know, but the ship

has set sail and there's no turning back now. There is nothing more that he could take from me that I wouldn't give him willingly. Two fingers press into my sternum and I suck in a breath, glancing down. Solomon meets my gaze once more and then carefully, with excruciating slowness, he drags them between my breasts and over the soft curve of my belly.

My breath hitches. "Solomon…"

His fingers pause. "The way you say my name…" His chest rumbles. "I thought that you'd say it with a hint of hatred forever. I didn't know how beautiful it would sound like this."

"Like what?" I chance the question, both curious and unnerved by the strange sensations rolling through me. A need—wild and untamed—threatens to consume me.

"Like you love me."

Love? Solomon? I press my lips together to keep them from trembling. My hands fall away from him and land on the mattress. *Can I ever feel love? Is it something I'm allowed?* Shame invades, encompassing the arousal that he created within me.

"If you're going to do this," I say quietly, turning my gaze to the front of his trousers, "then don't speak of love. That's not what this is."

It can't be.

He stiffens and I can sense his hurt. Not my intention but necessary, nonetheless. Rozentine is still in danger. My life hangs in the balance. There's no room for love between us. No space for it in my life. Not when I know that I may have to sacrifice everything for Rozentine. If I do love him then that will only ensure he will become one of those sacrifices.

"You're still my guard, Solomon," I state, feeling the words burn over my tongue. "Remember that. I can't …

deny that I want you—that I liked what we did in that cave and I crave more, but there's nothing else I can give you. If you can't accept that, then perhaps we should stop this here."

I squeeze my eyes shut and half expect him to pull away from me completely. Withdrawing affection would make sense, after all. I just told him he can't expect anything beyond this—a physical relationship as well as that of a Queen and her warrior. A beat passes. Then another and another. My breath sears the inside of my throat as I wait for his decision. The weight of my words lingers between us like a cruel blade swaying back and forth. One wrong move and it'll slice us through.

"So, this is it, then." His fingers retract from my body, but he remains over me. I open my eyes and peer up at him, but Solomon is no longer looking at me. Instead, his head is dipped down, chin to chest. He breathes slowly, deeply. "If protecting your body … and pleasuring it is all I can have, then that's enough. I'll make it enough."

I frown and push my elbows back into the bed. Before I can open my lips though, Solomon reaches down and grips the bottom of my nightgown. "Wait! What are you—"

My words are swallowed by a gasp. He yanks my gown up and over my head, divesting me of the last barrier I have. Now, nothing is separating us but hair and his trousers. My breasts rise and fall as I realize that this is his decision. He won't stop. A part of me is pleased, while another—deeper part—aches.

Heavy, scarred palms land on my thighs and push them apart. Warm air blows over my sensitive flesh. Just like before—in the cave—Solomon moves back on his knees, bending down toward my pussy.

"Wait!" I say again, pushing against the top of his head

to stop him. "W-why do you have to do that? Can't you just … put it in?"

Solomon tips his head back up. His eyes pierce me clean through, nearly stopping my heart and my breaths with the intensity inside of them. With deliberate movements, Solomon captures one of my hands and drags it down to his lap. I jump as he forces my fingers to clasp onto the thick, hard length of him inside the leg of his trousers.

"Do you not remember how I took you, Princess?"

Heat steals over my face, flushing up my cheeks and down toward my breasts. I bite down on my lower lip and nod in jerky movements. "You said, after the first time, it wouldn't hurt like that again."

"*Feel me.*" My stomach contracts as his hand on top of mine urges me to close my fingers around his length. A shiver moves through me. When that doesn't seem to be enough for me to understand his meaning, he growls and pulls away. He releases me just long enough to unbutton the front placket and free himself.

Long and hard, Solomon's cock bobs into view, rising from a thick, dark thatch of hair that matches the same color on his head. His skin is so much darker than mine. Even marred by various scars, he's beautiful.

"Now." Solomon recaptures my hand and places it back upon his shaft. I try to close my fingers around him, but they don't reach. My lashes flutter as I glance up from his cock to his face. "Feel me," he repeats. "Look at my cock and tell me what you see."

"It's … heavy," I say. "And thick." I stroke a finger down the length of him counting down from tip to base. One … Two … Three … Four … Five … Six … I get halfway before he stops me with a groan.

"What else?"

"You're quite … big?" I guess since I'm not entirely sure. After all, his cock is the first I've ever seen outside of paintings and sculptures, and he is certainly far larger than any of those.

"*Yes*," he hisses. "My cock is big enough to rip you open if I'm not careful. That's why I must do this. That's why I must prepare you."

I blink up at him. "Do you … lick every woman you bed the way you do me?" It's a cruel question. One I don't know if I even want the answer to.

And as if he knows that, Solo doesn't answer. Instead, he raises his palm and pushes me back on the bed. My spine hits the cushions. Solomon's gaze moves over me, slow and sensual. I have the distinct feeling that he's committing this to memory, that he's trying to trace each and every part of this moment. I bite down on my lip again so hard this time, that I taste blood. His nostrils flare and his hand snaps up, grabbing ahold of my face.

"Don't," he warns with a growl.

My lips part, but it's too late. More blood flows over my tongue at the tear in my lip. He snarls and dives down. His mouth slams into mine with all the self-contained fury I saw in his gaze. He seals his lips over the tear and licks across the open wound. My stomach clenches and that sensation travels downward. Deeper and deeper, filling me from within until it spills between my legs as arousal resurfaces.

When Solomon pulls away from the bloodied kiss, the rawness of his expression almost frightens me. His eyes are glowing a deep crimson red. His brows are lowered. His canines aren't fully descended, but they are far more prevalent than when he's calm.

Arms hook beneath my thighs and I muffle a scream as I'm suddenly yanked down all the way to the edge of the bed. I try to sit up as my ass hits the lip and Solomon stands up. One of his hands presses me back and then, with those ruby eyes still on me, he slowly gets to his knees and hooks each of my legs over his shoulders.

Confusion, fear, and need war within me. In the end, though, need wins out. I recline back as he moves closer and the heat of his breath drifts over my pussy. My body cramps with hunger and the desire to feel him again. When his lips touch my clit, I nearly levitate off the bed. Only by the strength of his grip do I remain where I am.

Solomon's hand lands flat on my belly and holds me in place as his lips move over my pussy. He licks up first one side of my opening and then down the other. A strand of dark, inky black hair falls over his forehead. I pant, my chest rising and falling with rapid movements. Moonlight pours through the window and glistens on the floor and bed.

Shoving one knuckle into my mouth, I bite down as I repress the moans that threaten to leave me. Glowing red eyes stare up at me as Solomon eats at my delicate flesh. My throat closes as I meet his gaze. I'm locked within it, unable to drag myself away, afraid that even if I wanted to, he would capture me and pull me back into his snare.

Awareness prickles at my skin, all along my arms and down my thighs to my toes. I try sitting up again and between my legs, the reverberation of Solomon's responding growl nearly makes me gasp as it slides from him and into me.

"S-Solo?" I blink down at him, reaching for him. My hand grazes the top of his forehead, pushing the flopping locks of his black hair back. He growls again and I wince as the sound deepens. He's almost animalistic.

Despite my obvious uncertainty, his mouth never leaves me. In fact, in reaction to my attempt to sit up and speak, he seems to grow even more determined. His tongue delves into my opening and thrusts into me and on his next growl, the sound makes my clit vibrate.

I cry out, unable to stop myself as my back arches. My hand locks onto him, gripping his head. Solomon's hand on my belly turns soothing. Long, rough, masculine fingers brush my skin gently. I whimper and he rumbles in pleasure. *At the sound?*

My eyes slide shut as Solomon's fingers drift lower and lower. "My Queen..." The words are breathed over wet flesh and it takes a moment for me to realize that Solomon is actually calling for me.

Forcing my head up, I open my eyes and look down at him. Solo moves back and pierces me with his stare as he very deliberately brings his fingers to my pussy and then, slowly, pushes them inside. They're thick, though not as thick as his cock had been. Still, I react—gritting my teeth as they stretch me open.

"Do you know how beautiful you are?" he asks.

I swallow the thickness in my throat and part my lips to respond. Words escape me though. Like fluttering little butterflies, they quickly move out of my reach as he pulls his hand back and thrusts his fingers back into me, curling them up against my inner walls.

"Ah!" I cry out, arching against the movement as my body bows into and away from him simultaneously. My lower half can't seem to stop clamping down as he moves back into me. My hands slap the edge of the bed and my nails dig into the cushion of it.

"There you are, my Queen," Solomon breathes. "So beautiful ... I just want to consume you."

Those words sink into me and although I feel as if all of the air has been dragged out of my chest and refuses to return, I force myself to straighten. "Solomon..." I reach for him. My hands cup his face, fingers trailing down over the proud aristocratic bridge of his nose to his full lips. They part and he nips at one fingertip, the red of his gaze brightening slightly.

He wants to consume me. The thought is so ridiculous. Doesn't he realize I'm already consumed by him? We're two opposing sides of an ancient fairytale. The Queen and the Beast. He's got me ensnared in his jaws and I don't want to escape.

Bending, I place my forehead against his. Our breaths mingle together. His thumb circles my clit, sending lightning blades cutting through my insides. My body trembles, held under his masterful touch. I'm on the edge of being broken and if I come away from this with a few new scars, I think that would be fine. Those scars would remind me of him. So there's no way I'd hate them.

"Take me," I whisper. "Please ... Solo, I can't take it anymore. Please, I want ... I need it."

His fingers withdraw from my pussy and the emptiness leaves me feeling hollow. I don't care that I'm begging for something so improper. I'll get on my knees if it gets me what I want, what I need from him.

"*Fuck.*" The sharp curse that leaves him has me craning my neck as I look down at him. When he meets my gaze, he looks almost angry. "You really know how to drive me insane, don't you?"

My lips twitch. "You've told me I'm good at it," I reply. Beat after beat passes and my wet insides leak down my inner thighs. Still cupping his face, I look directly at him and ask, "Am I ready enough for what you're going to do to me?"

Fangs flash as he bares them at me. Then, without warning, his hands reach under my thighs and scoop me up off of the bed. "I fucking hope so," he mutters.

My spine hits one of the bed posts and I gasp as I'm nearly folded in half. My legs dangle over his arms and I'm held up by little more than the wooden post at my back and Solomon's chest. "Put it in," he commands, and it's one I can't refuse.

Quickly releasing his face, I reach down and palm him. His cock juts out, thick and tall. My head spins as he leverages me up and positions the head at my opening. With little else to hold onto, I wrap my arms around his neck and suck in a breath as he slowly eases me down.

Heavy breathing and aroused growls filter through my ears. Sweat drips down our skin, making us stick to each other. I don't mind it, though. I like sticking to him. The heat of his body combined with my own makes me feel that hollow feeling disappear—the jagged piece of myself that's been missing for so long fits perfectly when he bottoms out inside of me.

"By the Gods..." he whispers harshly. "You're so fucking tight, Devonry."

"Maybe you're just too fucking big," I whimper. Despite my words, though, I like it. He fills all of the places inside of me I never knew needed filling. Pleasure swarms through me, lighting me up like the cause of a flame.

The thick hard rod that is Solomon's cock withdraws from my pussy and thrusts back inside in a singular movement. I cry out again and bury my face against his throat as he fucks me. Over and over again, he takes me as I begged him to. My sex clenches around him and he groans, the sound like music to my ears.

All the fear and anxiety from earlier evaporates and fades away. I pull away because I can't take another moment without his mouth on mine as he takes me the only way a man should ever take a woman—with fierce need.

"*Solo*." That one word escapes my lips before his crash down on me. It's as if he can sense just what I need, anticipate everything my body craves. We are two halves of a single whole. He devours me like a monster and even if it means I'll forever be contained within the belly of the beast, I let him.

Rough fingers dig into my thighs and hoist me higher before dropping me down over his cock. Again and again, he thrusts into me. Sparks dance behind my eyes. His teeth clank against mine with the fast, coarse onslaught. He drives me into the post at my back, harder with each penetration. Wave after wave of euphoria reaches out to me, fingers capturing me and dragging me into a world of white and sensation.

My head arches back and I fear that I won't be able to stop myself from slamming it onto the post. Then, suddenly, the post is gone from my spine. There's nothing but air and growling for a few seconds before I find myself back on the bed and a massive man crawling between my legs.

"You wanted to take me, my Queen," Solomon practically snarls. "Then take me now, take my cock and come."

He thrusts back into me and a scream echoes up my throat, halting abruptly as he clamps a hand over my lips. Eyes watering, body seizing, I look up at the face that appears over mine. Strong jawline, ruby irises, elongated fangs sharper than before—Solomon looks like he's barely holding back his Awakened form as he drives himself into me. His cock pummels my insides and the frenzy he's created morphs into something gentle and thrilling.

As I drift down from the elated high, Solomon grunts and stills inside of me like he had before. A warm rush fills me as he unleashes his own pleasure. Without thinking, one of my own hands drifts down to my belly. Fingers lightly grazing the skin above my belly button, I look up into Solomon's red gaze.

The moment between us passes too quickly and when he pulls out, I feel more desolate than ever before. I tighten my thighs and bring them up to my chest. He stands and stares at me before turning his back on me.

"I'll get a cloth to clean you." I don't answer him. Instead, I tuck my head against my knees and feel something in my chest breaking. Perhaps it's my heart.

Before and now again, we didn't use any sort of protection. I knew—from the gossiping of court ladies—that there were skins men used to cover their cocks to prevent unwanted pregnancies. But … Solomon had never used such a thing with me and I didn't want him to.

A child, though, in our circumstances wouldn't be a good thing. I am going to refuse Enver and leave for Rozentine, but still … my life is constantly at risk. Still, as I wait for Solomon to return, I picture what it would feel like. For my stomach to grow and swell. For a little boy with bright red eyes the same color as his father's to look up at me.

I fall asleep like that, leaning against the bed with my legs to my chest and my arms wrapped around them. When Solomon comes back, cleaning me up before moving me beneath the sheets, I hardly rouse.

Why is it … that the sweetest of dreams are always the most unattainable?

I am nothing more than a rotten beast. I know the dangers of releasing myself inside of her, yet I could not stop myself. No, more than that, I hadn't *wanted* to stop myself. A primal urge had taken over and demanded that I spill my seed within her and, even now, as I enter her chambers once more, carrying with me a bowl of warm water and a cloth meant for washing, I cannot find it in me to feel regret.

Devonry lays, curled into the bed in much the same state I'd left her. Only now, she's slightly curled on her side with her face tucked against the sheets and pillows. Gently, I set the bowl and cloth down on the stand alongside her bed and adjust her body. She stirs only mildly, groaning as I lift her into my arms and carefully draw the covers back to put her in place.

Once done, I clean her using the items I had brought with me. Washing her body as I drag the water-soaked cloth up and down her limbs, pausing when I reach the alcove of her sweet pussy. Gritting my fangs, I drag the cloth through her soaked folds and rinse away the lingering effects of my insolence. Wishing that I was, instead, pushing the rest up inside of her so that it might take root.

Devious are the emotions that war within me. To claim or not to claim. In the end, she is not mine to claim. She never was. King Vernon's words still reside within me, scolding me for my actions. Before, in the cave, I used the excuse of the divine power to justify what I'd done. Now, though, there is no justification. Only lust and greed.

Once I'm finished wiping her down, I redress Devonry in a new nightgown stolen from the wardrobe. The material is soft and nearly transparent. Lifting her body into place as I thread her arms and head through the holes is an effort in restraint. Every flash of her naked body makes my cock harden all over again. The apparent exhaustion on her face as she barely even rouses from her sleep keeps me in check.

She nearly died tonight, and all because I'd been complacent in thinking she was safe within these walls. My eyes alight on her face as I take a seat alongside the bed and watch her lashes flutter against her cheeks. My fingers itch to stroke the smooth flesh. I curl them into fists, stabbing at my palms with my short, blunt nails.

Minutes stretch into hours. She continues to sleep as I watch her, unable to tear my eyes away. I find myself hungry for each breath she takes, for every small minute detail of her face. The barely there smattering of light freckles—one on the underside of her jaw, another alongside her ear, a few speckled on her arms and shoulder. I wish to kiss each of them, to open my mouth and tongue the salty skin of her body and descend further until the ripe taste of her coats my teeth.

I am nothing but a ragged animal, leashed by this sometimes fragile and sometimes fierce woman. I am possessed by her. Eternally owned. These chains that bind me are of my own doing. My actions, now, have taken on a life of their own. Justifications aside, the longer I remain near her, the more I will come to crave her. There will come a time, I fear, that I won't be able to let her go. Even if it's for the good of her Kingdom, even if sacrifices must be made, the thought of her within someone else's arms...

My claws arch out, and the once blunt nails turn sharper. Blood coats my palm. I release my fists and bring my palm to my lips, licking away the crimson liquid as I watch her face. My cock throbs against the inside of my trousers and a part of me wishes to reach inside and palm my hungry shaft as I watch her sleep.

My eyes feast upon her. So unaware. So beautiful. So unknowing of how beloved she is to me. Deep in my soul, I know it wouldn't take much to convince her to love me. She is reliant upon my strength. After its first bloodied taste, she is afraid of betrayal. She knows that I would never act against her. Yet, as much as the hatred in my body burns against Nasir, I can also understand.

To cherish and want her and be rejected is vile. It's painful. For years, as I stood by her side, as her attendant and guard, I'd wanted little more than to chain her up, steal her away, and keep her for only myself.

Had I done so, her smile would have faded. Her lashing tongue would have dried up. Her spirit would have broken. And it is her spirit that I love. Her soul. The outward body may be stunning, but inside resides the truth of my devotion.

So lost in my reverence of Devonry, I almost miss the rising of the morning sun within the window. Steps sound in the hallway, and soon the door creeps open with a light knock. Celine appears, her dark curling hair pulled back into a tight braid that draws her features into a severe look. I stand. Now that she is not alone, I can drag myself from her bedside and try to maintain some of my sanity.

"Lord Solomon?" Celine approaches, lowering her voice as she cuts a look toward the slumbering Princess.

"Help her get ready when she wakes," I tell her.

"Nothing else happened?" she asks, worry coating her tone as she bites down on her lower lip.

"I was with her all night," I assure the woman. "I doubt anything will happen so soon after last night's attack. Not when whoever orchestrated it must know how on guard we are now."

Celine bobs her head in a firm nod and then moves to Devonry's bedside. I don't stick around to see her wake the Princess. I fear now that if I look at her, sleep still in her gaze, as she rouses from the bed I took her in … I might demand Celine's absence and take her again.

As I step out into the hall, a familiar figure pushes away from the wall opposite the doors. Argyle gives me one look and nods his head to the side. Like me, he appears to have not slept at all. Dark shadows sink into the skin beneath his eyes and his jaw is covered in morning stubble.

"Did you find the snake?"

Argyle's lips twist into a scowl and he shakes his head. An unspoken curse lingers on my tongue. "I don't think it was a regular snake, do you?" he asks.

"It's suspicious," I reply. "It was clearly released into her room with a purpose."

"What's the plan then?" he asks once we're out of earshot of the Princess or Celine—should they leave the chambers in search of us.

"We leave," I say. "It's no longer an option but a must."

Argyle nods. "Yulis would be willing to take us back to Rozentine—for a fee, of course."

"Payment will be discussed later, but as long as he's trustworthy, we will accept his aid," I reply.

"I figured you would say that," Argyle says. "So, I sent a bird messenger to him last night immediately after the attack."

"And?"

He sighs. "The earliest he'll be able to return is tomorrow morning."

A curse rises from the depths of my throat. Another day stuck in this Bartoli den of vipers. But I trust that Argyle's words are true. He isn't the type to delay a matter so important. Another day it is, then.

"What do you want to do until then?" Argyle asks.

I want to slaughter the entire Bartoli Royal Family for their attempts to intimidate and extort Devonry, but that would cause a whole different scale of issues to face. Over lashing back at the Bartoli's, I know what Devonry's choice would be. Rozentine is too important to her, and until such a time that Rozentine becomes her grave, I will have to follow her wishes.

"We will wait." I grit the words out against my better judgment. "Once Yulis is close, we will meet him at the beaches as before and we will leave. It's better to keep this secret. We don't want to let on that we're planning to flee, or else they may attempt to restrain our movements."

"That's a good plan," Argyle replies. "And I agree. Something tells me if they think the Princess will truly refuse or run from their demands, then their *hospitality* will change drastically." His eyes glitter at the term ' hospitali-ty.' Both of us are well aware of the stipulations of that hospitality. Then again, he's always seemed to have a deeper understanding of the Bartoli culture than anyone from Rozentine I've known.

"Argyle." His head lifts sharply as I speak his name. I

level a look at him. "I appreciate all that you've done for me and the Princess these last few months. Your insight has been more than beneficial. But I can't help but ask, is there more I should be aware of?"

He inhales sharply. "You're asking if there's a connection between the Galeanos and me?"

I nod. That is precisely what I'm asking.

My friend remains quiet for a long time. Nothing except our breathing and the slow, continued rise of the sun in the background filling the space between us. When he speaks, it's with a throaty voice. "There is," he admits, "but I cannot say what just yet. All I can tell you is that it will not affect my loyalty to you, old friend."

Dual-colored irises meet mine. The dark brown and crystal blue of each beseeching me for trust. I blow out a long breath, closing my eyes as a dull throb begins to thread itself around my head. "Okay," I say. "I can't say that I won't ask again, but if it has no immediate effect on the Princess, then you may keep your secrets, Argyle."

"Thank y—"

"For now," I snap, interrupting his response. I open my eyes and meet his. "You will need to tell me at some point; this is not an open-ended bargain. Make no mistake. Should your secrets place Devonry in harm's way, no matter our friendship, I will not hesitate to cut you down."

His lips part. Perhaps in shock. He shouldn't be. My loyalty is first and foremost to her. Then the country she rules. Then my loyal allies. After a moment passes, Argyle nods his understanding.

"Still, I thank you, Solo," he says. "I know it is difficult to accept no answers from me for the time being."

I turn my head from him and scan up the empty corridor. The pillars and walls feel tighter than before. More suppressing. "Yes, well, there are other things to focus on.

What more do you know of the attack? Did you find anything else out?"

"I don't believe the snake was sent to kill Her Highness," Argyle replies.

"No?" I look back at him. "Then why? Merely to wound?"

"Yes." He nods. "I think the Bartolis are already suspicious that she wishes to leave. She didn't exactly respond well to their prerequisite for aid, being that she would honor the marriage contract."

"If that's true, then you could be right. Killing her wouldn't get them what they want, however wounding her would keep her here. If they do mean to kill her, they likely wish to do so either after she's been married to Prince Enver or produced an heir for both bloodlines." The thought of that Prince setting his hands on what belongs to me—body and soul—boils through my blood. I barely repress the urge to snarl as the words escape my lips.

"We will ensure that never happens," Argyle states.

Yes, we will. Devonry is not a tool to be used as they think she is.

"I think it's best if we don't mention the attack," Argyle continues. "Even if it was their doing, they would use it as an excuse to increase security surrounding her, which would make sneaking out later to meet Yulis difficult."

"You're right," I agree. "It would be wise to keep what happened last night to ourselves. We'll have Devonry confine herself to her room—say she isn't feeling well."

Argyle nods. "And then once morning comes and we've received notice that Yulis is approaching, we'll escape."

Even as the plan falls into place, my stomach rolls with awareness of danger. This place is no longer a safe haven but a lair of deceit. Each shadow is a new enemy. All with their sights set upon my Princess.

36

DEVONRY

Yet another knock sounds at my door. I groan into my pillows and shove my face further into the smooth surface of the cover to muffle the noise. Celine is already rising from her seat next to the bed, setting down her embroidery with a heavy sigh.

We both know what comes next and who waits at the other side of that door. They'd been persistent throughout the day, knocking every couple of hours to see if I'd suddenly become well for company. Lord Byron and Prince Enver speak in soft but demanding tones when Celine opens the door. Neither my own Ambassador nor the Prince is much in the face of a determined lady such as Celine.

She waits until the door clicks shut behind her and the sound of the men's stomping feet is fading down the hall to return to her seat. Her features are taut, her knuckles white as she grips the front of her gown when she walks.

"The Prince?" I ask, daring to lift my head.

"It would seem he's never heard the word 'no' before." She offers a sanguine smile before dropping into the chair.

"What is this, the sixth attempt?" I stretch, my muscles protesting and joints popping with the motion. Every part of me feels like I've been wrung out like an old rag. The bend of my fingers reminds me of the fire I'd brought so readily to my palms. It conjures other memories too. The feel of Solomon's skin. His fingers intertwined with mine. The soft, silky strands of his hair.

"Pfft," Celine blows at the bits of hair surrounding her face. "By my count, this is their seventh attempt. At least he is pretending to care."

I snort and sit up. My stomach down to my very core aches with a clear reminder of the last couple of days. Heat floods my face at the thought even as I keep my lips pressed together. Guilt gnaws at the back of my mind. Of all people, Celine isn't someone I need to keep secrets from. She already knows of my experience in the cave … but admitting that I've allowed it to continue … that I want it to…

I can't force the words to form on my lips.

Pulling the blankets from my lap, I push myself to stand. Pink and orange streak across the sky and count down the last of the day. A tremble passes through me as a breeze rattles the fresh curtains that have been hung.

Somewhere out there lives that thing. That beast who'd snuck into my bedchambers. I close my eyes and I can still feel the presence of it. The sensation of being watched has yet to leave me. But when I open my eyes, it's only Celine there, with her nimble fingers forcing the needle through her fabric again and again.

I've dozed on and off throughout the day, worn from the use of my abilities and from *other* activities. Now, I couldn't sleep if I tried. The sun may be disappearing but I'm finally ready to start my day.

"Are you ready to dress?" Celine asks without looking up.

"Let me just freshen up, and I'll dress myself," I respond with a light pat on her shoulder.

"Are you quite sure, Princess?"

I nod. *What if Solomon has left his mark on me? What if there are bruises that I can't pretend somehow came from the snake?*

My friend doesn't question me further as I drift to the bathing chamber. I splash cold water on my face before letting the material of my nightgown fall from my body as I stand before the mirror. There are no bruises. No bite marks in the process of healing. Nothing. The only reminder of what I'd done with Solomon last night is the persistent soreness between my legs. The woman who stares back at me is not the same as the one I'd seen in mirrors at the Sunfire Palace. Before everything.

Where before I was slender with the gentle curves of womanhood, I've become harder—stronger. Muscles define my arms, legs, and the lean smoothness of my stomach. Calluses scar my once soft hands. My hair is shorter, darker even. What once had been purely white, blonde now looks almost orange as I turn in the light. I smile at myself, proud of who I am becoming and possibly even afraid of her too. A few lines appear around my eyes, and for a moment I see my father's face on mine. I'd always been told I looked similarly to my mother, but there is no denying the attributes of the once great king.

It is him who I think of as I dress. Slipping into fitted trousers, a shirt that molds to my skin, and leather boots. There will be no fine gowns as we disappear into the night.

When I emerge from the bathing chamber, I go still as I watch a dark figure slipping over the balcony's ledge. Another follows quickly behind. My heart hammers inside my chest until a pair of glowing red eyes finds mine. Every ounce of air that had been seized in my chest escapes me in one quick exhale.

"Did we startle you?" Argyle asks, pushing the doors wide and striding into the room. His eyes scan the space before falling on Celine who rises from her seat.

"I might be on edge after yesterday," I admit, looking down at my feet.

Solomon leans against the door frame, still cast in shadows. "Did she rest?" he asks Celine.

"Between the Prince and the Ambassador showing up every hour on the hour, yes." Celine strides to my side, offering me her back. "Would you care to undo my laces?"

"If you need help undressing, I would be more than happy to volunteer." Argyle bounces on his toes like an eager child.

I loosen her laces, not needing to see her face to know she's scowling. When the layers of her dress fall away, there isn't skin or shift below but an outfit much the same as mine, one meant for moving, riding, and running. She must have been warm in all her layers, although I never once heard her complain.

"There are guardsmen at the end of the halls, watching your door. Extra precautions set by the Prince for your protection. Yet somehow, his men didn't notice when a snake had slithered across his grounds and into your room." Solo rolls his eyes. "How do the two of you feel about heights?"

Celine audibly swallows. But I'm no stranger to it. Not after everything Solomon and I have been through. Even before that, I'd never been a stranger to sneaking out the window. That silly, reckless, but hopeful girl is long gone but even those rash choices I'd made have helped me now.

"I think Prince Enver suspects *something*. Paranoia runs deep within the Galeano Family." Argyle walks a few paces, pressing his ear to my door before he shrugs. "By the time he realizes we're nothing but specs on the horizon, it will be far too late for him to stop us."

"Time is not on our side though." Solomon straightens and finally steps into the room. "We should go and quickly."

"We can carry you down." Argyle waves us forward. The men lead us out onto the balcony and I chance a look over the edge. This distance isn't like jumping out of a tree and one wrong move could make for a very long fall. Perhaps it isn't far enough to kill a person but it might be hard to run from the Bartoli Castle with two broken legs.

So when Solomon offers his back, I clasp my hands around his shoulders and cling to him. I breathe him in, noticing the way his hands curl around my thighs. Celine huffs but ultimately is hefted up onto Argyle's back as well. She closes her eyes tightly as they near the edge and buries her face in his neck. I catch his snicker as it's caught in the wind.

I don't close my eyes though. Not for a single second. If anything, I watch too closely, examining the way Solomon's fingers find every lip and edge of stone as we descend the castle wall. The moon rises, casting our shadows in blurring shapes before us. Every breath Solomon takes I can feel against my body. The shift of his muscles sends a beckoning want directly between my legs. Try as I might to ignore the feeling it remains.

"Are you frightened, my Queen?" Solomon whispers as we near the grass below.

"No."

"Then why are you gripping me so tightly? If you squeeze me any tighter, you'll be cutting off my airflow." He chuckles.

I force my body to relax, whispering my apologies into his ear.

The moment his feet hit the ground, I drop from his back with more grace than Celine as she flings herself away from Argyle. Her wide, watchful eyes scan me from head to toe, no doubt looking for some sort of injury or sign of distress. I smile back at her and her shoulders lower from her ears when she gives me a small smile back.

"Argyle, the horses." Solo tilts his head in the direction of the stables. Argyle winks his one ocean-colored eye at Celine before he disappears into the night.

"I am so glad to be back on solid ground," Celine says in a hushed tone as she falls to my side.

"You weren't much for the ship either. Is there much you do like?" With his fingers resting on the hilt of his sword, Solomon's glowing eyes take in our surroundings. A heartbeat passes before he gestures for us to follow him.

"Stability," she mutters.

Solo huffs a quiet laugh. "Argyle will meet us at the servants' entrance."

The three of us move like ghosts, not daring to make a sound as we slink through the darkened corners of the courtyard. Solomon slows us when guards pass, hiding us in shadows until they can no longer be heard. The gates are visible at the end of the dirt road that leads away from the castle. Our steps become eager and swift as we hurry to them.

A pounding sound starts, quite softly at first but growing rapidly louder. The gallop of horses. Everything squeezes inside my chest. Sweat slickens my spine.

Argyle rounds the castle mounted on his horse. Weapons are strapped to his body and the horses themselves. The horses leap over shrubs charging in our direction. Argyle looks over his shoulder, his body riddled with tension.

"Fuck." Solomon hisses, his hands finding my waist. In seconds the horses are upon us and my body is being lifted off the ground. I reach for the horn of the saddle and drag my leg over with the momentum of Solomon's strength. Before my rear meets the seat, his body is behind me, cradling me in his warmth.

With one hand, Argyle pulls Celine into the seat with him. The color of her face lessens with worry as she, too, casts a look behind us. I do not want to look. I do not want to know. I only want to be gone. But moving as recklessly as we are is far more dangerous, and remaining ignorant is not a luxury I can afford any longer.

"What is happening? Rushing will call attention to us. It will get us caught," I call into the wind that threatens to pull us from the back of our steed.

A long echoing blast of a horn sounds from the castle. The sound cuts through the night and bites at our heels. My body turns hot and then cold before I can register the light suddenly flooding the courtyard. Lanterns are being lit at every corner. The castle itself burns brighter, waking up from its slumber.

"It's too late for that now," Solomon calls just as the shouts of the guard rise up all around us.

37
SOLOMON

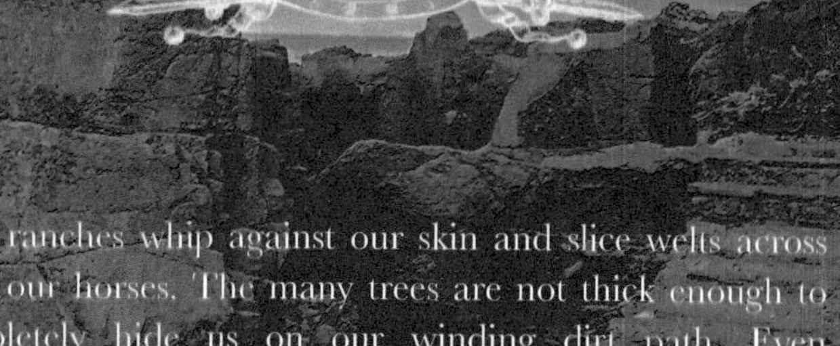

ranches whip against our skin and slice welts across our horses. The many trees are not thick enough to completely hide us on our winding dirt path. Even Devonry catches the darkened silhouettes of men far too close for my liking when she peers through their spindly forms. A startled gasp parts her lips.

Light from the moon shines down on us like a beacon. It illuminates the fear on all of our faces and shows us the path that leads away from the Bartoli Castle. The moon is friend and foe all in one.

Voices call out behind us, guardsmen giving instructions. Every shout creates tension between my shoulders and awareness prickling down my spine. The thundering of their horses resounds so loudly through the woods that it feels as though they surround us. I suppose it's possible that they do.

Devonry clings to the saddle, her golden eyes like twin stars guiding me through this night. I will not fail her. I cannot fail her. I refuse. She is my motivation. Devonry is my heart and without her, I cannot possibly live.

Celine's cry sends a flock of birds into flight as an arrow cuts over Argyle's shoulder before burying itself in the nearest tree. Argyle pulls her closer, tucking her against his body with grim determination. His heels dig into the horse's side, lurching them forward until we are side by side again.

Faster. Move faster, I silently will our horses and send a prayer to the gods.

A shadow passes overhead. Then, once more, in another arching circle. With dark feathers and glowing red eyes, a bird screeches. It swoops lower, cawing with the same ferocity over and over like a warning bell.

"The bird is from Yulis," Argyle shouts. "He must be near the beach waiting for us." He casts a weary glance behind him. "They'll expect us to head there. What are we going to do now?"

Where do we go when the enemy waits in every direction?

"Can you send him a message back?" Devonry startles at the boom of my voice by her ear. The leather covering the horn of the saddle darkens from the heat of her palms circling it. It's a good sign though, that she hasn't actually set anything to flame.

"I can do that." Argyle clicks his tongue twice before shoving two fingers into his mouth and whistling. Overhead the bird dives in one last circle before dodging tree branches and landing on Argyle's outstretched arm.

"Tell him what's happened. Warn him not to dock and to stay far from the beach."

"Take the reins." Argyle pushes the leather off into Celine's hands. Their bodies rock together with the gallops of their horse. She nods, holding firm despite her trembling hands. He hisses through his teeth, fumbling with the small paper and coal tied to the bird's slender leg.

Together, Devonry and I duck down in unison to avoid a low-hanging branch. Her body melds to mine, our breaths in sync as if for a moment we've become one. She turns to look behind us; the noise of the guards is no closer but certainly no farther, either.

"Don't," I bite out as she arches to try and peer over my height. "Don't look back."

"How can we lose them?" Her face is upturned, her features bright from the glow of the moon above and the otherworldly brilliance of her eyes.

There is no answer to her question. Or maybe there are too many answers to her question. If we could move faster, or perhaps if we knew we could outfight them, there might be a chance. Scenario after scenario comes and goes in my mind's eye. Each one is more dangerous than the last, all of them only possible if everything happens with stark perfection.

I hone my hearing, breathing in the warm, damp air as we near the sea. There are so many men following us. More than even I can count. How many more are separated from that group coming for us from another direction? The Galeanos didn't just send their measly night guardsmen after us. No, what's behind us is an army. It does say something that he didn't underestimate us.

"Go!" Argyle shouts, thrusting the bird into the air. Another arrow flies by, aimed at the bird who expertly dodges it and heads into the sky like a shooting star.

Pain slices across my bicep. Air passes through the break of fabric now flapping in the breeze from the swift cut of an arrow. *Too close. That was too close.*

My Queen stiffens in my arms. "Are you hit?" Devonry moves in the seat, her eyes searching, anger and fear mixing dangerously in that gaze.

"I'm fine." Just a scratch, shallow and already healing. But if it had been her … if they dared to hurt her…

Fresh fury floods my veins. The forest turns to the deepest shades of crimson all around us as Bloodlust builds. Everything comes to a clear focus until I can make out the veins on the leaves and every rock and a dirt-covered pebble that lays before us on the path. The rise and fall of Devonry's breaths as she brushes against me has me kicking my heels into the horse's sides once more.

She growls through her teeth, the fresh scent of burnt leather overpowering the scent of salt and earth. Within the halo of my hold, she arches and twists, pulling her leg over the saddle.

"What in the name of Levim are you doing?" I growl against the wind. Another arrow darts between our charging horses and Argyle curses. We're running out of woods, losing what little cover we have.

If Devonry hears me, she makes no indication of it. She turns entirely in my arms, reaching behind me.

The pounding of hoofs grows louder. With it, the rise of my worry and the build of my powers. My muscles burn as they stretch. The familiar ache as my skin hardens and my teeth elongate. "Devonry!" I shout and she doesn't even blink.

The fullness of her Awakened abilities is focused, her attention honed in on the men behind us. This is not a woman on this horse with me. This is a goddess. And she moves with the steady grace of one, her arms lifting as she rises with a bow in hand. Nothing and no one has ever been so fucking beautiful.

"Devonry." Her name passes through the clench of my jaw and the grind of my teeth as worry tortures my mind while pride grows in my chest.

She pulls an arm back, notching her arrow in place.

Her breath slows, even and calm, despite being in this impossible situation. The vibration of the bow string hums. An arrow lost on the wind.

A blood-curdling cry follows. Death comes. It rings in my ears. No one is safe.

38
SOLOMON

Only when I hear the heavy *thunk* of a man's body toppling from a horse's back do I finally allow myself my next breath. Devonry already has another arrow strung and the heat of her flame draws forth a new sheen of perspiration over my brow. The shouting behind us grows more frantic at the sight of her fire-tipped arrows.

Another arrow thrown. Another body drops. She is strength and violence. A Queen of fury and passion. She is a goddess wrought of fire and life and I am blood and victory at her back.

I throw an arm around her body, holding her tightly as the horse leans into another turn of the trail. Her skin burns white hot under her clothing, only bearable to touch with this small sliver of protection between us. Fire is drawn to her palms as easily as beckoning a lover. The same look of steely determination I've witnessed during training pulls at her face. Only now she draws from our connection unaware of the tug of our abilities.

The tug of her magic sends a prickling awareness

through my limbs. I can sense the depths of her abilities, swift and strong like a current coursing through her.

Men roar in surprise as their clothing catches and Devonry's arrows sink into their flesh. The daughter of the famous Saintess stands on top a horse, a warrior in her own right. What once her mother had forbidden, she is now perfecting. For when a kingdom is ripped from its rightful Queen, the Queen fights back. And my Queen … she'll burn them all to the fucking ground.

The cropping of trees surrounding us thins further, giving way to valleys. From here the path to the beach is visible and certainly a promise of our own demise. So we turn to the rising hills and the steep incline of the cliffs. Drifting from the path, our horses gallop over wetter lands with their tall, weedy grasses pulled at odd angles from the winds drifting from the sea.

"They're slowing, I think," Devonry shouts, already reaching for her next arrow.

"Stop shooting at them." I hold her body tighter as she stretches for her quiver.

"They shot us first!"

"It's easier to ride without you shooting those arrows." I glance up and she scowls past me at the men. "They aren't aiming for you. I'm the target. You're worth more to them alive." She lowers her bow but clings to it even as she drops back into the saddle. "Let's not forget that I am the wicked creature who keeps stealing you away from the handsome Prince. Any arrow they cast is meant for my own thieving heart."

She leans into me, her flesh still fevered and her eyes golden flecked. "If you're the one stealing me away, then I'm the jewel who leapt into your greedy hands."

Oh, how far we've fallen.

Those words play over in my head as we push our

horses with relentless demand. Our bodies rock together in time with the steady pounding of hooves. The space between us and the Bartoli men grows only for the distance with the edge of the cliffs to quickly disappear. There is nowhere left to go, nowhere to run. So only when we are upon the last of the land do we drop from our mounts.

Argyle pulls Celine down with him, his hands never leaving her, even when he stands as her human shield. His throat bobs as he looks down into the waves that thrash against the large rocky cove below. The sea is darker than the night sky tonight, nearly black. Water builds into large angry waves that churn with the promise of death. "Should we climb down?"

"Down the side of a cliff?" Devonry asks, pushing her hair away from her wind-kissed cheeks. Her brows furrow as she considers the notion, walking so close to the edge that I take an involuntary step forward.

"There isn't time for that." My knuckles turn white as I grip the hilt of my sword. Not even the Blood General has the might to bring down an entire army and only a fool might think he could.

Soldiers are quickly approaching, leaving behind the trees as we had. Only the length of the valley separates us. It's not enough. Perhaps I am not enough.

We cannot outrun them. It would be impossible to outfight them. Then what options remain? Our surrender? That might only end with my body swinging from the end of a noose.

"Look!" Celine cries out, pointing out into the waters. All of us follow the point of her finger to the sails filled with wind that carry the pirate captain to our aid. Yulis' ship is an angel bobbing against the sea. Whether it's the angel of death or one of mercy is still to be determined.

The sight does nothing to ease the torment inside of

me. She is not safe yet. Danger still lurks at the hands of those gaining on us with every minute we remain here. Within me, the monster still croons for spilled blood not certain that it's enough.

I suck in a ragged breath, looking toward Argyle. He meets my attention. Acceptance shines there and he nods in understanding. We move as one back to the horses, wordlessly pulling free the last of the swords and daggers strapped to them.

"You mean to fight them." Celine gasps, scurrying after us. "You are outnumbered at least twenty to one."

"I've always been fond of bets where I am the least likely to win. The richer the reward." Argyle smiles, but I can see the sorrow behind his gaze, the worry as it settles into his bones. "Take this." He thrust a harness and dagger at Celine. "Buckle it beneath your skirts. Worse comes to worse, tell them you were taken against your will and use the dagger if they dare to touch you."

"Argyle this is madness! This isn't a game to be won! There is no bet! And if you die right now I will never forgive you!"

"Is this your way of saying you've grown fond of me?" He leans down and presses a kiss to her forehead.

Celine reels back, clutching the dagger. "You're an idiot."

"Never claimed to be anything more." With that, he turns back to me as I slap at the horses' hinds and send them running across the tall grasses. "Together we live. Together we die. But I'm taking as many of these bastards with me as I can." He bares his teeth. "May the gods feast on their souls."

The calm of battle soothes the fraying of my nerves. Bloodlust claims a fraction of my mind knowing there are throats ready to be ripped away from their bodies. At my side, Devonry stands motionless. Her eyes drift slowly side to side as though she's looking for an exit. The heaviness of her thoughts shows as she throws the quiver over her shoulder and grips her bow with renewed conviction.

"I won't go back to him," she whispers.

She'd rather die here than be his bride. Nausea teases my stomach at the very thought.

Seconds tick by, dragged forth by time as though it cares not for the people standing at a cliff edge wishing for only a moment longer. The earth quakes with the vibrations of so many men on horseback, closing the little space between us. It rattles my bones.

Two horses emerge at the front of the group. Prince Enver rides on a horse so massive it looks more beast than tamed animal. The armor strapped to his body reflects the fullness of the moon and the brilliant glow of stars. At his side, glowing purple eyes are locked to where we stand. Our Ambassador, no less a traitor.

I care not for them. Nor for what they may want to do with me when they get here. If I have to lie, bleed, or slaughter for my Queen's safety though, I will.

Ripping my sword from the hilt, I look to Devonry. "I devote my soul to your rule. I dedicate my blood to your reign and will follow you into the void forevermore."

39

SOLOMON

The nearer they ride the clearer everything becomes. With his eyes glazed over in a purple sheen stare at my Queen never once flickering to meet my own gaze, I see him. Our *Ambassador*, Lord Byron. I see through him and the perfect poise of his exterior.

We shouldn't have trusted a man so far removed from the Court of Rozentine for so many years. It's clear his loyalty no longer lies with us, but that is not the betrayal that grips my heart in a shuddering grasp. A line of puckering pink skin runs across his cheeks and cuts through his beard to end somewhere behind his ear.

Lord Byron has done more than sell himself to the Bartoli Royals. He's attacked my Queen. The worst of all sins. There is no doubt in my mind that the wicked snake with the same eyes of the House of Daemonium is truly this man. Devonry's arrow grazed her mark, cutting one clean streak across his face. Now he's here with the injury to prove it.

What bravery he must have for showing his face in front of me with such definitive proof.

When the Ambassador's attention finally shifts to me, he smiles. He fucking smiles. As if this is a game and one that he thinks he's won. But the game isn't over yet because I'm not done playing.

The soldiers stop no more than a few yards away. Prince Enver and Lord Byron lower themselves from the backs of their horse, walking with cruel certainty to stand before our small group of runaways.

"I shouldn't be surprised," Prince Enver snarls. He slides a hand through his sweat-slicked hair and shares a glare between Devonry and me. Neither of us moves under his scrutiny but heat comes off of Devonry in thick, angry waves that I swear echo through our bond. Her anger is mine. It is shared and it is dangerous. "I thought I warned you away," he continues before spitting at my feet and raising his arms at his sides with a laugh. "And now you've got nowhere to run."

A few soldiers chuckle in response. All the Prince's theatrics do is force more of my abilities to surge through me, the pulse of his blood through his veins flashes in vision. I snap my fangs in eager reply. Yet, he is not where my true anger lies. What else could we expect from foreign royals? From the family whose son was so evil as to deceive my Queen with his friendship?

No, it's Lord Byron whom Devonry expected something from. The crown's coin has supported him in all his luxuries here across the sea. King Vernon had trusted him... she'd wanted so desperately to trust him too. In return, he'd thrown her to the wolves as soon as he was able.

"Return the Princess," the Ambassador steps forward.

As he moves, so do I. I take my own step in his direction and level my sword between us, the tip pointed at his throat. He only watches the blade with clear disdain.

"For her, you'll need to get through me. And how I wish you would try." My fangs are far past being hidden, my body stretched, and my skin hardened like stone. His own flesh ripples to reveal the dark scales of his serpent, there one moment and gone the next. "You have betrayed your country, broken a sacred vow between yourself, our Queen, and our gods."

Byron strokes a hand over his beard and clicks his tongue. He wears no armor like the Prince but his clothes are as fine as any other day in court as though he'd never bothered to dress for the night. "What I did, what I *do*," he says quietly, "is merely what is right for us all. The Bartoli's are meant to be your shield. They are Gods chosen to protect our House of Sunfire. Our Goddess. Our Queen."

Fresh warmth coats my back. Devonry steps to my side, her hands still clutching the bow and arrow loosely nocked. I shift to put myself between them because *I* am her shield. I protect our House of Sunfire. *My* goddess. *My* Queen.

"Let me pass." Her voice demands attention, her words a command.

"Devonry," I warn, but she only looks at me with the ferocity of her position. Every fiber of my being screams to hold steady, and when I give her space the motion feels stiff and wrong.

"It is not their choice to return me or decide where I will be taken. It is not your choice either." She holds her bow tighter, stretching the skin tight over the back of her hands. "I will not return to the Bartoli Castle. Let us go."

"Unfortunately, this is not up to you." Enver eyes the sword I still have pointed at Byron's throat. "I so hate to be the bearer of bad news, my dearest, but you have a wedding to show up for."

"You are bound by contract. Your father signed your hand over to the Bartolis," Byron confirms and I lean forward until the blade grazes his skin. The wind carries with it the scent of the sea and my Queen breathes it in for a moment before squaring her shoulders. "I won't hand my Kingdom over to the Bartoli Empire. Nasir's assassination of King Vernon calls for war and an end to whatever agreement had been held between our countries."

"That is not true—" Enver starts.

"I came here in good faith." Her voice rises, her fury glowing on her skin. "I fled my home in hopes that my betrothed might find it in him to come to our rescue, but all you and your family have done is disrespect us. You laugh away your brother's misdeeds and play me as though I'm only a pawn to you. I am no pawn. I am the Queen of Rozentine and I will not see my country fall to your selfish agenda."

Enver's eyes flare. "We wish for nothing but peace and prosperity between our countries."

"I beg of you, my Princess, listen to him," Byron whispers, earning him a few drops of blood that trail down the column of his throat.

"Shut up!" I hiss, watching as the blood runs down his skin, the reminder of my hunger leaving me in a growl.

Several soldiers have their own weapons pulled free though none of them dare to move forward and be the first to understand exactly how I earned my title as the Blood General.

Muscles in Prince Enver's jaw flex. He only watches Devonry, though, with a similar hunger in his eyes. The look of a man with what he wants so clearly within his grasp. His attention trails over her and the tight fit of the riding outfit that shows off the perfect shape of her body.

"It does not have to come to this," Enver says. "My love, come with me and I can make all things right."

Liar. The monster in me screams. It stirs at the sight of him extending his hand toward Devonry. *Mine*.

Devonry only looks at his palm, her lips curling into a sneer. "And what might you do if I refuse you?"

"Don't," he counters.

Her voice raises again. "What might you do, Prince Enver? Try to hurt me? My friends? Kill me? Hold us captive until I cave to your demands?" She pauses to allow him to answer, but he only holds her gaze and keeps his hand suspended between them. "What will you do?!"

Enver shifts closer to her. In turn, I swing my sword from the Ambassador to the Prince. Several men step forward, met by Argyle and even the might of Celine who wastes no time ripping her dagger from under her skirts. Argyle looks down at her with a mixture of awe and frustration.

"This is ridiculous." The Prince finally drops his hand. "I am a *Prince*. You are a *Princess*."

"Queen," Devonry and I say in unison. My heart swells with pride.

"Not yet crowned," Enver points out.

Though my attention stays with the Prince, in my peripheral vision the Ambassador takes calculated steps. Every small movement puts distance between my sword and his heart. He moves with purpose, aiming himself so that he'll find himself behind Devonry.

"Upon my father's death, I became the rightful ruler of the country that your brother is holding hostage," Devonry corrects.

"You cannot be recognized without ceremony, and what further strength you can provide your great country with our alliance and me at your side." What little patience Enver shows is quickly dissolving the longer they speak. His cheeks burn red as his anger begins to show through the calm exterior he presents.

Byron takes another step. Too close. He's fucking too close to her.

No.

A roar echoes inside my thoughts. Then it's echoing through the valley, over the cliffs, and across the sea as it rips from that terrible dark place within me.

He won't touch her.

He won't breathe the same damn air as her.

Much less live to see another blessed day.

If ever I was sane, I know nothing of it now. The monster within me lunges to the forefront of my consciousness, the rawness of my true being coming into complete accordance with the snapping of teeth and the rush of my body colliding with his. Breath leaves us both as we slam together.

Fangs sinking into flesh, I suck one long draw of blood into my mouth. My brain never even registers the suddenness of my movements. Byron screams, his hands clawing at my face, nails breaking against my thickened skin. His shouts as I pull away, ripping skin, muscle, and tendon alike. The Ambassador's lifeless body falls limply to the ground. I don't watch it fall the way the soldiers around us do, however. I can sense their horror as more than one takes a definitive step away. Cowards.

Facing the Prince, I reveal my blood-covered fangs. A trail of crimson runs like a river down my chin and drips onto my shirt. My vision pulses. The cast of my red-hued gaze narrows on Enver whose jaw has gone slack. "Touch my Queen and you will die."

40

DEVONRY

Touch my Queen and you will die.

Those words echo through my mind as Solomon's form stands before me, facing off against a literal army with our backs against the cliff's edge. The air that brushes over the tips of my fingers is blistering as if the rising heat that lifts from the ground is being sucked into my hands all at once. As the sun sheds its light across the Bartoli lands, I feel it beat down on the top of my head, further warming me. My heart pounds, racing faster and faster as flames lick against the inside of my flesh. The sand dunes in the distance glisten beyond the spindly forest that juts upward from the coastline behind Prince Enver.

His eyes meet mine beyond Solomon's wide shoulders and he beseeches me, holding out a pleading palm. "Please, Devonry," he calls. "Stop this. Come back to me to Bartoli. You know it is the only way."

The only way? No. Only the easiest path is closed to me. The destiny the woman in my dreams—Aerea—talked about has been cut off. If I want to get it back, then the path of resistance is the only way.

I shake my head, turning my cheek against Enver's plea. "No," I say. "I am not a Bartoli bride. I am Devonry Aerea Estand, daughter divine of the Goddess Aerea, Crown Princess, Queen of Rozentine. You are not my only hope or my only path, Prince Enver."

The snapping black flag of Yulis' ship in the near distance, bobbing against the waves, draws my eye. A weighty feeling settles in the pit of my stomach. We are now faced with not one but two paths. Go forward into Enver's arms and let ourselves be captured, let myself be forced into an arranged marriage with the brother of my enemy—the family of my ex-friend and ally. There is always the chance that we could escape later. That even if I can't be free—perhaps Solo, Argyle, and Celine could be. Or … I could take a chance. My heart flutters at the second thought.

Trust … I will catch you, my Goddess, the wind whispers. Trust is a hard thing to find when you've lost it. Right now, though, as the wind curls around me, soothes the heat upon my skin with its gentle breeze, I find I am incapable of refusing the universe's offer.

I step forward, latching onto Solo's arm. He jerks his head back for a moment, eyes glowing an angry crimson. When he attempts to brush me off, likely thinking that I am trying to stop him because I am giving in, I hold on tighter.

"Solo." He meets my gaze. "We need to go."

"There is nowhere for you to go!" Enver yells.

I tug and Solomon takes a step back, hesitantly following my silent demands. A low growl erupts from his throat as the sound of metal scraping reaches our ears. I look up to see that Enver's soldiers have unsheathed their swords and are beginning to approach.

When Solomon stops, I yank harder. "No," I whisper-hiss to him. "Follow me. Don't concern yourself with them."

Turmoil cascades over his expression, tightening his jawline as he grits his teeth so hard that I worry he'll shatter them. I continue to pull him back and as if sensing my plan, Argyle grabs ahold of Celine and drags her along with him until the four of us feel the edge of the cliff at the backs of our heels. Celine whimpers and clings to Argyle's arm as he wraps himself around her.

"Shhh, it's alright," Argyle soothes. "It will be alright, trust in the Princess."

I pause. *Trust.* How funny is it that Argyle is the one who makes me realize the truth about trust? It goes both ways. Not only have I had to trust in others, but they must also trust in me. Not just Solo and Celine and Argyle, but the whole of Rozentine has placed their trust in me. I can't let them down. Not now and certainly not here—thousands of miles from my home and my people.

"What are you planning?" Solo demands, his voice low and rough with the beast of his Awakened form rising to the surface as the danger around us grows that much greater.

I take a breath. "Argyle…"

"Please tell me you're not going to make a liar of me, Princess," Argyle replies sharply.

Before I can respond, Enver calls out over the heads of his approaching soldiers—their stomping footsteps kicking up dust in a cloud around their legs. "Don't do anything stupid, Devonry!"

I laugh. Stupid was coming here. Stupid was trusting the wrong people. Stupid was ever thinking I should have left my country and relied upon someone else for support. "The only stupid thing I've done," I call back, "is expect honor from the family that slaughtered my father."

"We—"

I don't let him finish. "Grab onto me!" I scream.

Argyle jolts forward, one arm wrapped securely around Celine as he does. With my grip on Solo and Argyle's on me, I no longer think about it. I take the final flying leap—dragging the rest of them over with me as the cliff disappears from our feet.

Celine's scream of terror echoes in my ears, but I force my panic to the back of my mind as wind pushes up from the sea and rocks jutting out from the waters below. My back burns and the skin over my spine stretches. Pain shoots through my limbs and I tighten my hold on both Argyle and Solo. Our limbs link together, hands clutching my forearms as their weight drags them down faster than my own body.

My teeth clank into each other as fire spirals through me, burning into my flesh and bones. With a scream of pure agony, I feel the burst of wind at my back and then the lick of flames. I open my eyes and catch a glimpse of the bright red flame-coated wings that lift out of my back. I focus my energy on them, watching and feeling as they stretch and move up and down—carrying us away from the menacing spikes of rocks below.

Sweat drips from my forehead, soaking down my face. My bones feel as if they're being stretched beyond capacity. They burn and ache. The fire, itself, doesn't feel hot—but the agony of trying to control wings that weren't there minutes before extends my stamina too thin.

Barely a few yards away from the edge—just out of the reaching threat of Enver and his soldiers—the wings evaporate and we plummet straight down into the ocean below. Celine's cry and Argyle's grunt reach my ears. I feel Argyle's hand release me, most likely in an effort to hold onto Celine. Solo's arms come around me.

"I've got you," I hear. My vision winks out, blackening at the edges before swarming inward.

Solo's body is so warm that when the water closes over my head, the rest of the world feels like ice. Arrows coated in frost stab at me from every angle. I open my mouth to a scream, but nothing comes out. Instead, water comes rushing in, choking me as bubbles of air rise from the depths of my lungs. Solo grips me tight enough to crack bones as I feel his legs beneath us kick for the surface.

Further and further I grow from the world of the conscious, but by some force will, I manage to keep myself awake long enough for our heads to breach the surface.

"Devonry!" he screams my name, shaking me as much as he can.

I cough and sputter, water spewing from my lips as I try to breathe and open my eyes. The sky is a pinpoint above me, surrounded by darkness, but still there. Thank the Gods. My breaths come raggedly, broken. Solo's hand drifts down my back, meeting flesh and I glance back to find that the fabric over my spine has been burned away, the edges blackened as it leaves a massive hole right where my wings had been.

Wings, I realize with more awareness. *Wings of Flame like Aerea herself.* Tears burn the backs of my eyes. A whimper leaves my lips.

"Devonry, what's wrong? Are you wounded?" Solo tries to capture my face in one of his hands as he holds us steady above water.

I can't tell if the wetness on my face is from the spray of the sea or my own tears. Whatever it is, though, I can't respond to Solo's questions. All I can do is groan as I sink closer to him, pressing my face into his chest. It's all too much to keep my eyes open.

"Devonry? Devonry!" Solo's cries grow louder and

more panicked. Guilt eats away at my insides, but try as I might, I can't reassure him.

Fear grips me tight as I feel Solo begin to power through the water. I don't know where he's going or what his plan is until I hear the cries of others—familiar voices. They aren't enough to rouse me completely, but I do manage to crack open my eyelids as the sight of Yulis' ship wades toward us. We must have landed far closer than I realize for Solo to swim here so fast.

I want to ask where Argyle and Celine are, if they made it, but I can't. My voice is swallowed by the threat of unconsciousness that assails me.

"It's alright, it's going to be alright." Solo's voice is tight, but he continues to repeat himself. "Just stay with me," he begs. "Stay with me, Devonry. Please don't…"

He doesn't finish that last statement, or maybe he does. I'm not sure. If he did, then I simply didn't hear it. Because as the water drags against the remaining fabric of my clothes and my body is lifted into a tender boat, the world spins and that darkness that's been creeping in at the edges of my vision since we leapt off of the cliff finally stretches it's thick black arms over me and takes over, drifting me into a sickly sweet oblivion.

EPILOGUE

DEVONRY

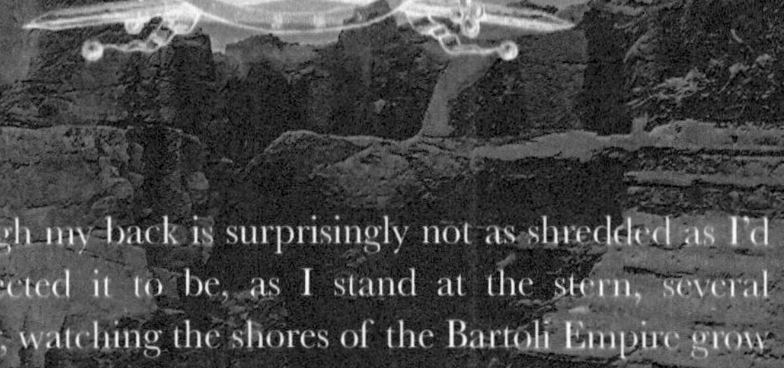

Though my back is surprisingly not as shredded as I'd expected it to be, as I stand at the stern, several hours later, watching the shores of the Bartoli Empire grow further and further away—it still stings and burns. I'm not so naive anymore to think that this is the last we'll see of Enver. No, they'll come for me and Rozentine. That much is clear.

Air that tastes of the sea and salt splashes up against the hull of Yulis' great ship—*The Wicked Rogue*, I've learned it's called. A pirate ship sanctioned by no country or kingdom. Yet, a pirate ship that has saved me *twice* now.

I close my eyes and inhale deeply. At my side, Celine edges closer, the heat of her body reassuring as much as it is comforting. *She'd make a wonderful mother and nursemaid*, I think to myself. But I need neither now. What I need most are allies, soldiers, and confidants. People who can help me take back my kingdom by whatever means necessary.

"Your Highness, I've brought you some tea." Celine's quiet voice forces me to open my eyes and turn to meet her gaze. She holds a chipped white teacup in her grasp and carefully offers it to me.

I chuckle as I take it. I don't know why it's so funny, but even in my exhaustion, the stained and chipped outside of this glass reminds me of my current position. Once, long ago, it might have been a perfectly fine cup. Now, though, it's broken, wounded, cracked. Just like me. Yet still, it's able to hold liquid. It's still able to perform its duties.

As if she can sense my thoughts, Celine tilts her head as I lift the cup to my lips and slowly sip the hot liquid. "You know," she begins, "I've heard that in distant countries, the act of throwing away broken and chipped tea sets is seen as offensive. Instead, they take them and fill the cracks and broken holes with liquid gold, letting it harden to replace what the cup has lost, often making the sets even more beautiful than they were initially."

I pause, the cup still held to my lips. Slowly, I lower it again and look at her. "What an interesting tradition," I muse aloud.

Beyond the shimmering sea, the sun is beginning to set over the horizon. The giant, bulbous, glowing ball of fire appears larger than ever as it sinks below the surface of the ocean. I should be grateful to be safe, to be alive—grateful that Celine and Solomon and Argyle are as well. Yet, I find gratitude difficult. I find it … not abhorrent but infuriating.

I am anything but grateful for the pain I've had to endure. Be it fate or be it something else, Nasir has hindered my ascension to the Rozentine throne, and all for some misguided love. Without thinking, I pivot my head and find myself peering curiously over Celine's shoulder at where Argyle and Solomon stand together with Yulis, talking in low voices. Solo catches my attention, lifting his head and tilting it my way.

Does he know, I wonder, *what I'm thinking?* Something tells me that even if he did know the inner darkness that seems to now permeate my mind, he wouldn't judge me for it. If anyone could understand the change I'm going through, perhaps it's him.

"I don't know what the future holds," I confess to Celine as the ship rocks back and forth with the waves. "But I do know that it's time to stop running away from my problems and seek help outside of Rozentine."

Rough but feminine hands reach for mine. I blink and look down as Celine's fingers grip one of my hands and pull it away from the teacup. Her fingers are slender but marred by small cuts that are ages old, reminding me that despite the way she acts, she was raised outside of a noble house.

"It's alright to be frightened by the thought of the future, Your Highness," she whispers.

"It's not the future that frightens me."

Her brow puckers.

I look down at the tea, noting the thin, black squiggles at the bottom of the cup. "It's myself," I tell her. "I'm frightened by what I will become in order to get my Kingdom back."

I've already killed someone, and I find so little remorse in that action. He'd been a bad person. A slave merchant, someone who stole the lives of others and profited off of them. Still, I'd been taught that all lives mattered. Every soul held potential. Why then ... did I feel so much ease continuing my life after stealing one away? If my mother could see me now, she would be horrified.

Celine's fingers on mine turn hard. She grips me tight and pulls my hand to her chest. "You have survived these fires," she says. "And you will survive far greater ones in the future."

I release a breath and set the teacup on the edge of the

railing. Unwilling to offend or hurt her feelings, but unable to bear her kind touch, I gently pull my hand from hers. "I am the fire," I tell her. "Whether I am purifying or destructive has yet to be seen."

Celine closes her eyes at those words, and when next she opens them, a dim glow begins to illuminate from within her irises. My breath catches as the hairs along my arm stand on end. The silvery hue comes from somewhere within her—her own Awakened ability being pushed to the forefront the way it did when we first met.

"Time is not your ending." As she speaks, her words sound overwritten by a different tone of voice, something more profound. "There cannot be light without darkness nor darkness without sunfire. You fear what you do not know, not what you expect. No evil will consume you, only your own shadow. Take the heart of your soul and trust in him."

Confusion swirls within me as she blinks and the illuminated glow of her gaze disappears. Celine shakes her head as if the power left her feeling dizzy but then refocuses on me. "You're not alone," she says, this time sounding much more like herself.

Inhaling, I turn my gaze past her once more to find Solo still staring at me. Whereas I was meant to watch the sunset, it feels as if he cannot leave me alone. The memories of our bodies intertwined have yet to leave my mind.

Take the heart of my soul ... and trust in him. Those had been her words. Not her. Not me. *Him.*

It's clear who *he* is. Solomon. The heart of my soul. The reincarnation of Levim. Aerea's soulmate. *My* soulmate. If he knows or not ... no, I don't want to know if he does. It will be something we can face after everything is over.

I turn back to the stern and lift the cup from the railing, curling my free hand over the wood and digging my nails into the scarred surface to try and ground myself. "Nasir will die," I say quietly. "Regardless of if my mother wanted it or not, I can't let what happened to Rozentine go."

"If that is your will," Celine replies. "Then we will help you."

"I think it's time," I say, "for the House of Raven to be brought into the light. No more hiding. No more shame for circumstances beyond their control. I'm changing and so will Rozentine."

Celine nods her agreement and as she is so damn good at, instead of leaving me be, she steps closer to my side and stares out over the sea along with me. The last of the sun's rays disappear, but her presence reminds me of her words —that I am not alone.

I won't have to face this battle by myself. But Nasir … Nasir will. For, in death, there will be no one with him. In death, he will be the same as any other man. Alone.

THANK YOU FOR READING!

Thank you so much for reading Dawn of Fate and Valor. We hope you enjoyed the continuation of Solo and Devonry's story.

If you liked this book, please don't forget to leave a review here.

If you'd like to know how the story ends, you can now pre order the final installment here.

ABOUT LUCINDA DARK

Lucinda Dark, also known as USA Today Bestselling Author, Lucy Smoke, for her contemporary novels, has a master's degree in English and is a self-proclaimed creative chihuahua. She enjoys feeding her wanderlust, cover addiction, as well as her face. When she's not on a never-ending quest to find the perfect milkshake, she lives and works in the southern United States with her beloved fur-baby, Hiro, and her family and friends.

Want to be kept up to date? Think about joining the author's group or signing up for their newsletter below.

Facebook Group (Reader Mafia)
Newsletter (www.lucysmoke.com)

ALSO BY LUCINDA DARK

Fantasy Series:

Awakened Fates Series
Crown of Blood and Glass
Dawn of Fate and Valor
Wings of Sunfire and Darkness

Twisted Fae Series (completed)
Court of Crimson
Court of Frost
Court of Midnight

Barbie: The Vampire Hunter Series (completed)
Rest in Pieces
Dead Girl Walking
Ashes to Ashes

Dark Maji Series (completed)
Fortune Favors the Cruel
Blessed Be the Wicked
Twisted is the Crown
For King and Corruption
Long Live the Soulless

Sky Cities Series (Dystopian)
Heart of Tartarus

Shadow of Deception

Sword of Damage

Dogs of War (Coming Soon)

Contemporary Series:

Gods of Hazelwood: Icarus Duet

Burn With Me

Fall With Me

Sick Boys Series (completed)

Forbidden Deviant Games (prequel)

Pretty Little Savage

Stone Cold Queen

Natural Born Killers

Wicked Dark Heathens

Bloody Cruel Psycho

Bloody Cruel Monster

Vengeful Rotten Casualties

Sinister Arrangment Duet (completed)

Wicked Angel

Cruel Master

Iris Boys Series (completed)

Now or Never

Power & Choice

Leap of Faith

Cross my Heart

Forever & Always

Iris Boys Series Boxset

The *Break* Series (completed)

Break Volume 1

Break Volume 2

Break Series Collection

Contemporary Standalones:

Poisoned Paradise

Expressionate

Wild Hearts

ABOUT REBECCA GREY

Rebecca Grey leads a busy life. Somewhere between raising two kids and daydreaming about being a reality television star, she writes. As a reader she enjoys books filled with arrogant boys—who she would never waste her time on in real life—and large fantasy or paranormal novels. Much of her love for these things is reflected in her books.

Learn more at Rebecca's website below!

www.rebeccagreyauthor.com

ALSO BY REBECCA GREY

The Cursed Fae King

The Crowned Fae Queen

<u>The Twisted Crown Series</u>

The Shadow Fae

The Iron Fae

The Lost Fae